W9-BNC-294

Dragons and demons, warlocks and magical quests—and other realms both fearsome and fabulous.

There are wonders within such as you have never dared to dream . . .

Year's
Best
Fantasy
4

Edited by David G. Hartwell

Edited by David G. Hartwell
and Kathryn Cramer

ATTENTION: ORGANIZATIONS AND CORPORATIONS
Most Eos paperbacks are available at special quantity discounts
for bulk purchases for sales promotions, premiums, or fund-
raising. For information, please call or write:

**Special Markets Department, HarperCollins Publishers Inc.,
10 East 53rd Street, New York, N.Y. 10022–5299.
Telephone: (212) 207–7528.   Fax: (212) 207–7222.**

YEAR'S BEST FANTASY

❧ 4 ❧

EDITED BY DAVID G. HARTWELL
AND KATHRYN CRAMER

An Imprint of HarperCollinsPublishers

This is a collection of fiction. Names, characters, places, and incidents are products of the authors' imagination or are used fictitiously and are not to be construed as real. Any resemblance to actual events, locales, organizations, or persons, living or dead, is entirely coincidental.

EOS
An Imprint of HarperCollins*Publishers*
10 East 53rd Street
New York, New York 10022-5299

Copyright © 2004 by David G. Hartwell and Kathryn Cramer
ISBN: 0-06-052182-1
www.eosbooks.com

All rights reserved. No part of this book may be used or reproduced in any manner whatsoever without written permission, except in the case of brief quotations embodied in critical articles and reviews. For information address Eos, an imprint of HarperCollins Publishers.

First Eos paperback printing: July 2004

HarperCollins® and Eos® are trademarks of HarperCollins Publishers Inc.

Printed in the U. S. A.

10 9 8 7 6 5 4 3 2 1

If you purchased this book without a cover, you should be aware that this book is stolen property. It was reported as "unsold and destroyed" to the publisher, and neither the author nor the publisher has received any payment for this "stripped book."

Contents

Acknowledgments

We would like to acknowledge the help of Russell and Jenny Blackford, Jonathan Strahan, BestSF.com, and Locus, in surveying the stories for this year's volume. And, for at least the first half of 2003, Tangentonline.com.

Introduction

~◦~❦~◦~

Welcome to the fourth volume of the *Year's Best Fantasy*, representing the best of 2003. Like the earlier volumes in this series, this book provides some insight into the current fantasy field: who is writing some of the best short fiction published as fantasy, and where. But it is fundamentally a collection of excellent stories for your reading pleasure. We follow one general principle for selection: this book is full of fantasy—every story in the book is clearly that and not primarily something else. We (Kathryn Cramer and David G. Hartwell) edit the *Year's Best Science Fiction* in paperback from Eos as a companion volume to this one—look for it if you enjoy short science fiction too.

In this book, and this anthology series, we will use the broadest definition of fantasy (to include wonder stories, adventure fantasy, supernatural fantasy, satirical and humorous fantasy). We believe that the best-written fantasy can stand up in the long run by any useful literary standard in comparison to fiction published out of category or genre, and furthermore, that out of respect for the genre at its best we ought to stand by genre fantasy and promote it in this book. Also, we believe that writers publishing their work specifically as fantasy are up to this task, so we set out to find these stories, and we looked for them in the genre anthologies, magazines, and small press pamphlets.

This was another notable year for short fiction anthologies, as well as for the magazines both large and small. The last sf and fantasy magazines that are widely distributed are *Analog, Asimov's, F&SF,* and *Realms of Fantasy.* And the electronic publishers kept publishing, sometimes fiction of high quality, in spite of the fact that none of them broke even or made money at it. We are grateful for the hard work and editorial acumen of the better electronic fiction sites, such as SciFiction, Strange Horizons, and Infinite Matrix, and hope they survive.

The small presses remained a vigorous presence this year. We have a strong short fiction field today because the small presses and semiprofessional magazines (such as *Talebones, Weird Tales* and *Interzone*) are printing and circulating a majority of the high-quality short stories published in fantasy, science fiction, and horror. The U.S. is the only English-language country that still has any professional, large circulation magazines, though Canada, Australia, and the UK have several excellent magazines. The semi-prozines of our field mirror the "little magazines" of the mainstream in function, holding to professional editorial standards and publishing the next generation of writers, along with some of the present masters. We encourage you to subscribe to a few of your choice. You will find the names of many of the prominent ones in our story notes.

In February of 2004, as we write, professional fantasy and science fiction publishing as we have always known it is still concentrated in nine mass market and hardcover publishing lines (Ace, Bantam, Baen, DAW, Del Rey, Eos, Roc, Tor, and Warner), and those lines are publishing fewer titles in paperback. But they do publish a significant number of hardcovers and trade paperbacks, and all the established name writers, at least, appear in hardcover first. The Print-on-Demand field is beginning to sort itself out, and Wildside Press (and its many imprints) is clearly the umbrella for many of the better publications, including original novels and story collections.

This was another very strong year for original anthologies. Among the very best were *The Dark,* edited by Ellen Datlow; *McSweeney's Thrilling Tales,* edited by Michael Chabon; *The Dragon Quintet,* edited by Marvin Kaye;

Gathering the Bones, edited by Dennis Etchison, Ramsey Campbell, and Dack Dann; *Swan Sister,* edited by Ellen Datlow and Terri Windling; *Firebird,* edited by Sharyn November; and *The Silver Gryphon,* edited by Gary Turner and Marty Halpern. One continuing trend, evident in, for instance, *Polyphony #2,* edited by Deborah Layne, and *Open Space,* edited by Claude Lalumiere, was toward non-genre, genre-bending, or slipstream fantastic fiction. There were a number of good original anthologies and little magazines devoted to stories located outside familiar genre boundaries, yet more related to genre than to ordinary contemporary fiction—and marketed to a genre readership.

We repeat, for readers new to this series, our usual disclaimer: this selection of fantasy stories represents the best that was published during the year 2003. We try to represent the varieties of tones and voices and attitudes that keep the genre vigorous and responsive to the changing realities out of which it emerges. This is a book about what's going on now in fantasy. The stories that follow show, and the story notes point out, the strengths of the evolving genre in the year 2003.

David G. Hartwell & Kathryn Cramer
Pleasantville, NY

King Dragon

Michael Swanwick

Michael Swanwick [www.michaelswanwick.com] lives in Philadelphia, Pennsylvania. His novels include the Nebula Award winner, Stations of the Tide *(1991),* The Iron Dragon's Daughter *(1993) and* Jack Faust *(1997), and* Bones of the Earth *(2002). Swanwick is also the author of two influential critical essays, one on SF, "User's Guide to the Postmoderns" (1985), and one on fantasy, "In The Tradition . . ." (1994). But in between the novels, he writes short stories, and his tales have dominated the short fiction Hugo Award nominations in recent years. His stories have been collected principally in* Gravity's Angels *(1991),* A Geography of Unknown Lands *(1997),* Moon Dogs *(2000),* Tales of Old Earth *(2000), and as a pamphlet,* Puck Aleshire's Abecedary *(2000), and a collection of short-shorts,* Cigar-Box Faust and Other Miniatures *(2003).*

"King Dragon" appeared in an original anthology published by the Science Fiction Book Club, The Dragon Quintet, *edited by Marvin Kaye. It appears to be set in the same fantasy world as* The Iron Dragon's Daughter. *It is in any case an example of what Swanwick in his essay "In the Tradition . . ." calls hard fantasy, not like the fantasy worlds of other writers but dark, technological, and brutal. It is interesting to contrast it to Pat Murphy's fine and very different dragon story later in this book.*

The dragons came at dawn, flying low and in formation, their jets so thunderous they shook the ground like the great throbbing heartbeat of the world. The village elders ran outside, half unbuttoned, waving their staffs in circles and shouting words of power. *Vanish*, they cried to the land, and *sleep* to the skies, though had the dragons' half-elven pilots cared they could have easily seen through such flimsy spells of concealment. But the pilots' thoughts were turned toward the West, where Avalon's industrial strength was based, and where its armies were rumored to be massing.

Will's aunt made a blind grab for him, but he ducked under her arm and ran out into the dirt street. The gun emplacements to the south were speaking now, in booming shouts that filled the sky with bursts of pink smoke and flak.

Half the children in the village were out in the streets, hopping up and down in glee, the winged ones buzzing about in small, excited circles. Then the yage-witch came hobbling out from her barrel and, demonstrating a strength Will had never suspected her of having, swept her arms wide and then slammed together her hoary old hands with a *boom!* that drove the children, all against their will, back into their huts.

All save Will. He had been performing that act which rendered one immune from child-magic every night for three weeks now. Fleeing from the village, he felt the enchantment like a polite hand placed on his shoulder. One weak tug, and then it was gone.

He ran, swift as the wind, up Grannystone Hill. His great-great-great-grandmother lived there still, alone at its tip, as a grey standing stone. She never said anything. But sometimes, though one never saw her move, she went down to the river at night to drink. Coming back from a night-time fishing trip in his wee coracle, Will would find her standing motionless there and greet her respectfully. If the catch was good, he would gut an eel or a small trout, and smear the blood over her feet. It was the sort of small courtesy elderly relatives appreciated.

"Will, you young fool, turn back!" a cobbley cried from the inside of a junk refrigerator in the garbage dump at the edge of the village. "It's not safe up there!"

But Will didn't want to be safe. He shook his head, long blond hair flying behind him, and put every ounce of his strength into his running. He wanted to see dragons. Dragons! Creatures of almost unimaginable power and magic. He wanted to experience the glory of their flight. He wanted to get as close to them as he could. It was a kind of mania. It was a kind of need.

It was not far to the hill, nor a long way to its bald and grassy summit. Will ran with a wildness he could not understand, lungs pounding and the wind of his own speed whistling in his ears.

And then he was atop the hill, breathing hard, with one hand on his grandmother stone.

The dragons were still flying overhead in waves. The roar of their jets was astounding. Will lifted his face into the heat of their passage, and felt the wash of their malice and hatred as well. It was like a dark wine that sickened the stomach and made the head throb with pain and bewilderment and wonder. It repulsed him and made him want more.

The last flight of dragons scorched over, twisting his head and spinning his body around, so he could keep on watching them, flying low over farms and fields and the Old Forest that stretched all the way to the horizon and beyond. There was a faint brimstone stench of burnt fuel in the air. Will felt his heart grow so large it seemed impossible his chest could contain it, so large that it threatened to encompass the hill, farms, forest, dragons, and all the world beyond.

Something hideous and black leaped up from the distant forest and into the air, flashing toward the final dragon.

Will's eyes felt a painful wrenching *wrongness*, and then a stone hand came down over them.

"*Don't look,*" said an old and calm and stony voice. "*To look upon a basilisk is no way for a child of mine to die.*"

"Grandmother?" Will asked.

"*Yes?*"

"If I promise to keep my eyes closed, will you tell me what's happening?"

There was a brief silence. Then: "*Very well. The dragon has turned. He is fleeing.*"

"Dragons don't flee," Will said scornfully. "Not from anything." Forgetting his promise, he tried to pry the hand from his eyes. But of course it was useless, for his fingers were mere flesh.

"*This one does. And he is wise to do so. His fate has come for him. Out from the halls of coral it has come, and down to the halls of granite will it take him. Even now his pilot is singing his death-song.*"

She fell silent again, while the distant roar of the dragon rose and fell in pitch. Will could tell that momentous things were happening, but the sound gave him not the least clue as to their nature. At last he said, "Grandmother? Now?"

"*He is clever, this one. He fights very well. He is elusive. But he cannot escape a basilisk. Already the creature knows the first two syllables of his true name. At this very moment it is speaking to his heart, and telling it to stop beating.*"

The roar of the dragon grew louder again, and then louder still. From the way it kept on growing, Will was certain the great creature was coming straight toward him. Mingled with its roar was a noise that was like a cross between a scarecrow screaming and the sound of teeth scraping on slate.

"*Now they are almost touching. The basilisk reaches for its prey . . .*"

There was a deafening explosion directly overhead. For an astonishing instant, Will felt certain he was going to die. Then his grandmother threw her stone cloak over him and, clutching him to her warm breast, knelt down low to the sheltering earth.

When he awoke, it was dark and he lay alone on the cold hillside. Painfully, he stood. A somber orange-and-red sunset limned the western horizon, where the dragons had disappeared. There was no sign of the War anywhere.

"Grandmother?" Will stumbled to the top of the hill, cursing the stones that hindered him. He ached in every joint. There was a constant ringing in his ears, like factory bells tolling the end of a shift. "Grandmother!"

There was no answer.

The hilltop was empty.

But scattered down the hillside, from its top down to where he had awakened, was a stream of broken stones. He had hurried past them without looking on his way up. Now he saw that their exterior surfaces were the familiar and comfortable gray of his stone-mother, and that the freshly exposed interior surfaces were slick with blood.

One by one, Will carried the stones back to the top of the hill, back to the spot where his great-great-great-grandmother had preferred to stand and watch over the village. It took hours. He piled them one on top of another, and though it felt like more work than he had ever done in his life, when he was finished, the cairn did not rise even so high as his waist. It seemed impossible that this could be all that remained of she who had protected the village for so many generations.

By the time he was done, the stars were bright and heartless in a black, moonless sky. A night-wind ruffled his shirt and made him shiver, and with sudden clarity he wondered at last why he was alone. Where was his aunt? Where were the other villagers?

Belatedly remembering his basic spell-craft, he yanked out his rune-bag from a hip pocket, and spilled its contents into his hand. A crumpled blue-jay's feather, a shard of mirror, two acorns, and a pebble with one side blank and the other marked with an X. He kept the mirror-shard and poured the rest back into the bag. Then he invoked the secret name of the *lux aeterna*, inviting a tiny fraction of its radiance to enter the mundane world.

A gentle foxfire spread itself through the mirror. Holding it at arm's length so he could see his face reflected therein, he asked the oracle glass, "Why did my village not come for me?"

The mirror-boy's mouth moved. "They came." His skin was pallid, like a corpse's.

"Then why didn't they bring me home?" And why did *he* have to build his stone-grandam's cairn and not they? He did not ask that question, but he felt it to the core of his being.

"They didn't find you."

The oracle-glass was maddeningly literal, capable only of answering the question one asked, rather than that which one wanted answered. But Will persisted. "Why didn't they find me?"

"You weren't here."

"Where was I? Where was my Granny?"

"You were nowhere."

"How could we be nowhere?"

Tonelessly, the mirror said, "The basilisk's explosion warped the world and the mesh of time in which it is caught. The sarsen-lady and you were thrown forward, halfway through the day."

It was as clear an explanation as Will was going to get. He muttered a word of unbinding, releasing the invigorating light back to whence it came. Then, fearful that the blood on his hands and clothes would draw night-gaunts, he hurried homeward.

When he got to the village, he discovered that a search party was still scouring the darkness, looking for him. Those who remained had hoisted a straw man upside-down atop a tall pole at the center of the village square, and set it ablaze against the chance he was still alive, to draw him home.

And so it had.

* * *

Two days after those events, a crippled dragon crawled out of the Old Forest and into the village. Slowly he pulled himself into the center square. Then he collapsed. He was wingless and there were gaping holes in his fuselage, but still the stench of power clung to him, and a miasma of hatred. A trickle of oil seeped from a gash in his belly and made a spreading stain on the cobbles beneath him.

Will was among those who crowded out to behold this prodigy. The others whispered hurtful remarks among themselves about its ugliness. And truly it was built of cold, black iron, and scorched even darker by the basilisk's explosion, with jagged stumps of metal where its wings had been and ruptured plates here and there along its flanks. But Will could see that, even half-destroyed, the dragon was a beautiful creature. It was built with dwarven skill to high-elven design—how could it *not* be beautiful? It was, he felt certain, that same dragon which he had almost-seen shot down by the basilisk.

Knowing this gave him a strange sense of shameful complicity, as if he were in some way responsible for the dragon's coming to the village.

For a long time no one spoke. Then an engine hummed to life somewhere deep within the dragon's chest, rose in pitch to a clattering whine, and fell again into silence. The dragon slowly opened one eye.

"Bring me your truth-teller," he rumbled.

The truth-teller was a fruit-woman named Bessie Applemere. She was young and yet, out of respect for her office, everybody called her by the honorific Hag. She came, clad in the robes and wide hat of her calling, breasts bare as was traditional, and stood before the mighty engine of war. "Father of Lies." She bowed respectfully.

"I am crippled, and all my missiles are spent," the dragon said. "But still am I dangerous."

Hag Applemere nodded. "It is the truth."

"My tanks are yet half-filled with jet fuel. It would be the easiest thing in the world for me to set them off with an electrical spark. And were I to do so, your village and all who live within it would cease to be. Therefore, since power engenders power, I am now your liege and king."

"It is the truth."

A murmur went up from the assembled villagers.

"However, my reign will be brief. By Samhain, the Armies of the Mighty will be here, and they shall take me back to the great forges of the East to be rebuilt."

"You believe it so."

The dragon's second eye opened. Both focused steadily on the truth-teller. "You do not please me, Hag. I may someday soon find it necessary to break open your body and eat your beating heart."

Hag Applemere nodded. "It is the truth."

Unexpectedly, the dragon laughed. It was cruel and sardonic laughter, as the mirth of such creatures always was, but it was laughter nonetheless. Many of the villagers covered their ears against it. The smaller children burst into tears. "You amuse me," he said. "All of you amuse me. We begin my reign on a gladsome note."

The truth-teller bowed. Watching, Will thought he detected a great sadness in her eyes. But she said nothing.

"Let your lady-mayor come forth, that she might give me obeisance."

Auld Black Agnes shuffled from the crowd. She was scrawny and thrawn and bent almost double from the weight of her responsibilities. They hung in a black leather bag around her neck. From that bag, she brought forth a flat stone from the first hearth of the village, and laid it down before the dragon. Kneeling, she placed her left hand, splayed, upon it.

Then she took out a small silver sickle.

"Your blood and ours. Thy fate and mine. Our joy and your wickedness. Let all be as one." Her voice rose in a warbling keen:

"Black spirits and white, red spirits and grey,

Mingle, mingle, mingle, you that mingle may."

Her right hand trembled with palsy as it raised the sickle up above her left. But her slanting motion downward was swift and sudden. Blood spurted, and her little finger went flying.

She made one small, sharp cry, like a sea-bird's, and no more.

"I am satisfied," the dragon said. Then, without transition: "My pilot is dead and he begins to rot." A hatch hissed open in his side. "Drag him forth."

"Do you wish him buried?" a kobold asked hesitantly.

"Bury him, burn him, cut him up for bait—what do I care? When he was alive, I needed him in order to fly. But he's dead now, and of no use to me."

"Kneel."

Will knelt in the dust beside the dragon. He'd been standing in line for hours, and there were villagers who would be standing in that same line hours from now, waiting to be processed. They went in fearful, and they came out dazed. When a lily-maid stepped down from the dragon, and somebody shouted a question at her, she simply shook her tear-streaked face, and fled. None would speak of what happened within.

The hatch opened.

"Enter."

He did. The hatch closed behind him.

At first he could see nothing. Then small, faint lights swam out of the darkness. Bits of green and white stabilized, became instrument lights, pale luminescent flecks on dials. One groping hand touched leather. It was the pilot's couch. He could smell, faintly, the taint of corruption on it.

"Sit."

Clumsily, he climbed into the seat. The leather creaked under him. His arms naturally lay along the arms of the couch. He might have been made for it. There were handgrips. At the dragon's direction, he closed his hands about them and turned them as far as they would go. A quarter-turn, perhaps.

From beneath, needles slid into his wrists. They stung like blazes, and Will jerked involuntarily. But when he tried, he discovered that he could not let go of the grips. His fingers would no longer obey him.

"Boy," the dragon said suddenly, "what is your true name?"

Will trembled. "I don't have one."

Immediately, he sensed that this was not the right answer. There was a silence. Then the dragon said dispassionately, "I can make you suffer."

"Sir, I am certain you can."

"Then tell me your true name."

His wrists were cold—cold as ice. The sensation that spread up his forearms to his elbows was not numbness, for they ached terribly. It felt as if they were packed in snow. "I don't *know* it!" Will cried in an anguish. "I don't know, I was never told, I don't think I have one!"

Small lights gleamed on the instrument panel, like forest eyes at night.

"Interesting." For the first time, the dragon's voice displayed a faint tinge of emotion. "What family is yours? Tell me everything about them."

Will had no family other than his aunt. His parents had died on the very first day of the War. Theirs was the ill fortune of being in Brocielande Station when the dragons came and dropped golden fire on the rail yards. So Will had been shipped off to the hills to live with his aunt. Everyone agreed he would be safest there. That was several years ago, and there were times now when he could not remember his parents at all. Soon he would have only the memory of remembering.

As for his aunt, Blind Enna was little more to him than a set of rules to be contravened and chores to be evaded. She was a pious old creature, forever killing small animals in honor of the Nameless Ones and burying their corpses under the floor or nailing them above doors or windows. In consequence of which, a faint perpetual stink of conformity and rotting mouse hung about the hut. She mumbled to herself constantly and on those rare occasions when she got drunk—two or three times a year—would run out naked into the night and, mounting a cow backwards, lash its sides bloody with a hickory switch so that it ran wildly uphill and down until finally she tumbled off and fell asleep. At dawn Will would come with a blanket and lead her home. But they were never exactly close.

All this he told in stumbling, awkward words. The dragon listened without comment.

The cold had risen up to Will's armpits by now. He shuddered as it touched his shoulders. "Please . . ." he said. "Lord Dragon . . . your ice has reached my chest. If it touches my heart, I fear that I'll die."

"Hmmm? Ah! I was lost in thought." The needles withdrew from Will's arms. They were still numb and lifeless, but at least the cold had stopped its spread. He could feel a tingle of pins and needles in the center of his fingertips, and so knew that sensation would eventually return.

The door hissed open. "You may leave now."

He stumbled out into the light.

An apprehension hung over the village for the first week or so. But as the dragon remained quiescent and no further alarming events occurred, the timeless patterns of village life more or less resumed. Yet all the windows opening upon the center square remained perpetually shuttered and nobody willingly passed through it anymore, so that it was as if a stern silence had come to dwell within their midst.

Then one day Will and Puck Berrysnatcher were out in the woods, checking their snares for rabbits and camelopards (it had been generations since a pard was caught in Avalon but they still hoped), when the Scissors-Grinder came puffing down the trail. He lugged something bright and gleaming within his two arms.

"Hey, bandy-man!" Will cried. He had just finished tying his rabbits' legs together so he could sling them over his shoulder. "Ho, big-belly! What hast thou?"

"Don't know. Fell from the sky."

"Did *not!*" Puck scoffed. The two boys danced about the fat cobber, grabbing at the golden thing. It was shaped something like a crown and something like a bird-cage. The metal of its ribs and bands was smooth and lustrous. Black runes adorned its sides. They had never seen its like. "I bet it's a roc's egg—or a phoenix's!"

And simultaneously Will asked, "Where are you taking it?"

"To the smithy. Perchance the hammermen can beat it down into something useful." The Scissors-Grinder swatted at Puck with one hand, almost losing his hold on the object. "Perchance they'll pay me a penny or three for it."

Daisy Jenny popped up out of the flowers in the field by the edge of the garbage dump and, seeing the golden thing, ran toward it, pigtails flying, singing, "Gimme-gimme-gimme!" Two hummingirls and one chimney-bounder came swooping down out of nowhere. And the Cauldron Boy dropped an armful of scavenged scrap metal with a crash and came running up as well. So that by the time the Meadows Trail became Mud Street, the Scissors-Grinder was red-faced and cursing, and knee-deep in children.

"Will, you useless creature!"

Turning, Will saw his aunt, Blind Enna, tapping toward him. She had a peeled willow branch in each hand, like long white antennae, that felt the ground before her as she came. The face beneath her bonnet was grim. He knew this mood, and knew better than to try to evade her when she was in it. "Auntie . . ." he said.

"Don't you Auntie me, you slugabed! There's toads to be buried and stoops to be washed. Why are you never around when it's time for chores?"

She put an arm through his and began dragging him homeward, still feeling ahead of herself with her wands.

Meanwhile, the Scissors-Grinder was so distracted by the children that he let his feet carry him the way they habitually went—through Center Square, rather than around it. For the first time since the coming of the dragon, laughter and children's voices spilled into that silent space. Will stared yearningly over his shoulder after his dwindling friends.

The dragon opened an eye to discover the cause of so much noise. He reared up his head in alarm. In a voice of power he commanded, "Drop that!"

Startled, the Scissors-Grinder obeyed.

The device exploded.

Magic in the imagination is a wondrous thing, but magic in practice is terrible beyond imagining. An unending instant's dazzlement and confusion left Will lying on his back in the street. His ears rang horribly, and he felt strangely numb. There were legs everywhere—people running. And somebody was hitting him with a stick. No, with two sticks.

He sat up, and the end of a stick almost got him in the eye. He grabbed hold of it with both hands and yanked at it angrily. "Auntie!" he yelled. Blind Enna went on waving the other stick around, and tugging at the one he had captured, trying to get it back. "Auntie, stop that!" But of course she couldn't hear him; he could barely hear himself through the ringing in his ears.

He got to his feet and put both arms around his aunt. She struggled against him, and Will was astonished to find that she was no taller than he. When had *that* happened? She had been twice his height when first he came to her. "Auntie Enna!" he shouted into her ear. "It's me, Will, I'm right here."

"Will." Her eyes filled with tears. "You shiftless, worthless thing. Where are you when there are chores to be done?"

Over her shoulder, he saw how the square was streaked with black and streaked with red. There were things that looked like they might be bodies. He blinked. The square was filled with villagers, leaning over them. Doing things. Some had their heads thrown back, as if they were wailing. But of course he couldn't hear them, not over the ringing noise.

"I caught two rabbits, Enna," he told his aunt, shouting so he could be heard. He still had them, slung over his shoulder. He couldn't imagine why. "We can have them for supper."

"That's good," she said. "I'll cut them up for stew, while you wash the stoops."

* * *

Blind Enna found her refuge in work. She mopped the ceiling and scoured the floor. She had Will polish every piece of silver in the house. Then all the furniture had to be taken apart, and cleaned, and put back together again. The rugs had to be boiled. The little filigreed case containing her heart had to be taken out of the cupboard where she normally kept it and hidden in the very back of the closet.

The list of chores that had to be done was endless. She worked herself, and Will as well, all the way to dusk. Sometimes he cried at the thought of his friends who had died, and Blind Enna hobbled over and hit him to make him stop. Then, when he did stop, he felt nothing. He felt nothing, and he felt like a monster for feeling nothing. Thinking of it made him begin to cry again, so he wrapped his arms tight around his face to muffle the sounds, so his aunt would not hear and hit him again.

It was hard to say which—the feeling or the not—made him more miserable.

The very next day, the summoning bell was rung in the town square and, willing or no, all the villagers once again assembled before their king dragon. "Oh, ye foolish creatures!" the dragon said. "Six children have died and old *Tanarahumra*—he whom you called the Scissors-Grinder—as well, because you have no self-discipline."

Hag Applemere bowed her head sadly. "It is the truth."

"You try my patience," the dragon said. "Worse, you drain my batteries. My reserves grow low, and I can only partially recharge them each day. Yet I see now that I dare not be King Log. You must be governed. Therefore, I require a speaker. Somebody slight of body, to live within me and carry my commands to the outside."

Auld Black Agnes shuffled forward. "That would be me," she said wearily. "I know my duty."

"No!" the dragon said scornfully. "You aged crones are

too cunning by half. I'll choose somebody else from this crowd. Someone simple . . . a child."

Not me, Will thought wildly. *Anybody else but me.*

"Him," the dragon said.

So it was that Will came to live within the dragon king. All that day and late into the night he worked drawing up plans on sheets of parchment, at his lord's careful instructions, for devices very much like stationary bicycles that could be used to recharge the dragon's batteries. In the morning, he went to the blacksmith's forge at the edge of town to command that six of the things be immediately built. Then he went to Auld Black Agnes to tell her that all day and every day six villagers, elected by lot or rotation or however else she chose, were to sit upon the devices pedaling, pedaling, all the way without cease from dawn to sundown, when Will would drag the batteries back inside.

Hurrying through the village with his messages—there were easily a dozen packets of orders, warnings, and advices that first day—Will experienced a strange sense of unreality. Lack of sleep made everything seem impossibly vivid. The green moss on the skulls stuck in the crotches of forked sticks lining the first half-mile of the River Road, the salamanders languidly copulating in the coals of the smithy forge, even the stillness of the carnivorous plants in his auntie's garden as they waited for an unwary frog to hop within striking distance . . . such homely sights were transformed. Everything was new and strange to him.

By noon, all the dragon's errands were run, so Will went out in search of friends. The square was empty, of course, and silent. But when he wandered out into the lesser streets, his shadow short beneath him, they were empty as well. It was eerie. Then he heard the high sound of a girlish voice and followed it around a corner.

There was a little girl playing at jump-rope and chanting:

"Here-am-I-and
All-a-lone;
What's-my-name?
It's-Jum-ping—"

"Joan!" Will cried, feeling an unexpected relief at the sight of her.

Jumping Joan stopped. In motion, she had a certain kinetic presence. Still, she was hardly there at all. A hundred slim braids exploded from her small, dark head. Her arms and legs were thin as reeds. The only things of any size at all about her were her luminous brown eyes. "I was up to a million!" she said angrily. "Now I'll have to start all over again."

"When you start again, count your first jump as a million-and-one."

"It doesn't work that way and you know it! What do you want?"

"Where is everybody?"

"Some of them are fishing and some are hunting. Others are at work in the fields. The hammermen, the tinker, and the Sullen Man are building bicycles-that-don't-move to place in Tyrant Square. The potter and her 'prentices are digging clay from the riverbank. The healing-women are in the smoke-hutch at the edge of the woods with Puck Berrysnatcher.'"

"Then that last is where I'll go. My thanks, wee-thing."

Jumping Joan, however, made no answer. She was already skipping rope again, and counting "A-hundred-thousand-one, a-hundred-thousand-two . . ."

The smoke-hutch was an unpainted shack built so deep in the reeds that whenever it rained it was in danger of sinking down into the muck and never being seen again. Hornets lazily swam to and from a nest beneath its eaves. The door creaked noisily as Will opened it.

As one, the women looked up sharply. Puck Berrysnatcher's body was a pale white blur on the shadowy ground before them. The women's eyes were green and unblinking, like those of jungle animals. They glared at him wordlessly. "I w-wanted to see what you were d-doing," he stammered.

"We are inducing catatonia," one of them said. "Hush now. Watch and learn."

The healing-women were smoking cigars over Puck. They filled their mouths with smoke and then, leaning close, let it pour down over his naked, broken body. By slow degrees the hut filled with bluish smoke, turning the healing-women to ghosts and Puck himself into an indistinct smear on the dirt floor. He sobbed and murmured in pain at first, but by slow degrees his cries grew quieter, and then silent. At last his body shuddered and stiffened, and he ceased breathing.

The healing-women daubed Puck's chest with ocher, and then packed his mouth, nostrils, and anus with a mixture of aloe and white clay. They wrapped his body with a long white strip of linen.

Finally they buried him deep in the black marsh mud by the edge of Hagmere Pond.

When the last shovelful of earth had been tamped down, the women turned as one and silently made their ways home, along five separate paths. Will's stomach rumbled, and he realized he hadn't eaten yet that day. There was a cherry tree not far away whose fruit was freshly come to ripeness, and a pigeon pie that he knew of which would not be well-guarded.

Swift as a thief, he sped into town.

He expected the dragon to be furious with him when he finally returned to it just before sundown, for staying away as long as he could. But when he sat down in the leather couch and the needles slid into his wrists, the dragon's voice was a murmur, almost a purr. "How fearful you are! You tremble. Do not be afraid, small one. I shall protect and cherish you. And you, in turn, shall be my eyes and ears, eh? Yes, you will. Now, let us see what you learned today."

"I—"

"Shussssh," the dragon breathed. "Not a word. I need not your interpretation, but direct access to your memories.

Try to relax. This will hurt you, the first time, but with practice it will grow easier. In time, perhaps, you will learn to enjoy it."

Something cold and wet and slippery slid into Will's mind. A coppery foulness filled his mouth. A repulsive stench rose up in his nostrils. Reflexively, he retched and struggled.

"Don't resist. This will go easier if you open yourself to me."

More of that black and oily sensation poured into Will, and more. Coil upon coil, it thrust its way inside him. His body felt distant, like a thing that no longer belonged to him. He could hear it making choking noises.

"Take it all."

It hurt. It hurt more than the worst headache Will had ever had. He thought he heard his skull cracking from the pressure, and still the intrusive presence pushed into him, its pulsing mass permeating his thoughts, his senses, his memories. Swelling them. Engorging them. And then, just as he was certain his head must explode from the pressure, it was done.

The dragon was within him.

Squeezing shut his eyes, Will saw, in the dazzling, pain-laced darkness, the dragon king as he existed in the spirit world: Sinuous, veined with light, humming with power. Here, in the realm of ideal forms, he was not a broken, crippled *thing*, but a sleek being with the beauty of an animal and the perfection of a machine.

"Am I not beautiful?" the dragon asked. "Am I not a delight to behold?"

Will gagged with pain and disgust. And yet—might the Seven forgive him for thinking this!—it was true.

Every morning at dawn Will dragged out batteries weighing almost as much as himself into Tyrant Square for the villagers to recharge—one at first, then more as the remaining six standing bicycles were built. One of the women would be waiting to give him breakfast. As the dragon's agent, he was entitled to go into any hut and feed himself from what he found there, but the dragon deemed this method more dignified. The rest of the day he spent wandering through the village and, increasingly, the woods and fields around the village, observing. At first he did not know what he was looking for. But by comparing the orders he transmitted with what he had seen the previous day, he slowly came to realize that he was scouting out the village's defensive position, discovering its weaknesses, and looking for ways to alleviate them.

The village was, Will saw, simply not defensible from any serious military force. But it could be made more obscure. Thorn-hedges were planted, and poison oak. Footpaths were eradicated. A clearwater pond was breached and drained, lest it be identified as a resource for advancing armies. When the weekly truck came up the River Road with mail and cartons of supplies for the store, Will was loitering nearby, to ensure that nothing unusual caught the driver's eye. When the bee-warden declared a surplus that might be sold down-river for silver, Will relayed the dragon's instructions that half the overage be destroyed, lest the village get a reputation for prosperity.

At dimity, as the sunlight leached from the sky, Will would feel a familiar aching in his wrists and a troubling sense of need, and return to the dragon's cabin to lie in painful communion with him and share what he had seen.

Evenings varied. Sometimes he was too sick from the dragon's entry into him to do anything. Other times, he spent hours scrubbing and cleaning the dragon's interior. Mostly, though, he simply sat in the pilot's couch, listening while the dragon talked in a soft, almost inaudible rumble. Those were, in their way, the worst times of all.

"You don't have cancer," the dragon murmured. It was dark outside, or so Will believed. The hatch was kept closed tight and there were no windows. The only light came from the instruments on the control panel. "No bleeding from the rectum, no loss of energy. Eh, boy?"

"No, dread lord."

"It seems I chose better than I suspected. You have mortal blood in you, sure as moonlight. Your mother was no better than she ought to be."

"Sir?" he said uncomprehendingly.

"I said your mother was a *whore!* Are you feeble-minded? Your mother was a whore, your father a cuckold, you a bastard, grass green, mountains stony, and water wet."

"My mother was a good woman!" Ordinarily, he didn't talk back. But this time the words just slipped out.

"Good women sleep with men other than their husbands all the time, and for more reasons than there are men. Didn't anybody tell you that?" He could hear a note of satisfaction in the dragon's voice. "She could have been bored, or reckless, or blackmailed. She might have wanted money, or adventure, or revenge upon your father. Perchance she bet her virtue upon the turn of a card. Maybe she was overcome by the desire to roll in the gutter and befoul herself. She may even have fallen in love. Unlikelier things have happened."

"I won't listen to this!"

"You have no choice," the dragon said complacently. "The door is locked and you cannot escape. Moreover I am larger and more powerful than you. This is the *Lex Mundi*, from which there is no appeal."

"You lie! You lie! You lie!"

"Believe what you will. But, however got, your mortal blood is your good fortune. Lived you not in the asshole of beyond, but in a more civilized setting, you would surely be conscripted for a pilot. All pilots are half-mortal, you know, for only mortal blood can withstand the taint of cold iron. You would live like a prince, and be trained as a warrior. You would be the death of thousands." The dragon's voice sank musingly. "How shall I mark this discovery? Shall I . . . ? Oho! Yes. I will make you my lieutenant."

"How does that differ from what I am now?"

"Do not despise titles. If nothing else, it will impress your friends."

Will had no friends, and the dragon knew it. Not anymore. All folk avoided him when they could, and were stiff-faced and wary in his presence when they could not. The children fleered and jeered and called him names. Sometimes they flung stones at him or pottery shards or—once—even a cow-pat, dry on the outside but soft and gooey within. Not often, however, for when they did, he would catch them and thrash them for it. This always seemed to catch the little ones by surprise.

The world of children was much simpler than the one he inhabited.

When Little Red Margotty struck him with the cow-pat, he caught her by the ear and marched her to her mother's hut. "See what your brat has done to me!" he cried in indignation, holding his jerkin away from him.

Big Red Margotty turned from the worktable, where she had been canning toads. She stared at him stonily, and yet he thought a glint resided in her eye of suppressed laughter. Then, coldly, she said. "Take it off and I shall wash it for you."

Her expression when she said this was so disdainful that Will felt an impulse to peel off his trousers as well, throw them in her face for her insolence, and command her to wash them for a penance. But with the thought came also an awareness of Big Red Margotty's firm, pink flesh, of her ample breasts and womanly haunches. He felt his lesser self swelling to fill out his trousers and make them bulge.

This too Big Red Margotty saw, and the look of casual scorn she gave him then made Will burn with humiliation. Worse, all the while her mother washed his jerkin, Little Red Margotty danced around Will at a distance, holding up her skirt and waggling her bare bottom at him, making a mock of his discomfort.

On the way out the door, his damp jerkin draped over one arm, he stopped and said, "Make for me a sark of white damask, with upon its breast a shield: Argent, dragon rouge rampant above a village sable. Bring it to me by dawn-light tomorrow."

Outraged, Big Red Margotty said: "The cheek! You have no right to demand any such thing!"

"I am the dragon's lieutenant, and that is right enough for anything."

He left, knowing that the red bitch would perforce be up all night sewing for him. He was glad for every miserable hour she would suffer.

Three weeks having passed since Puck's burial, the healing-women decided it was time at last to dig him up. They said nothing when Will declared that he would attend—none of the adults said anything to him unless they had no choice—but, tagging along after them, he knew for a fact that he was unwelcome.

Puck's body, when they dug it up, looked like nothing so much as an enormous black root, twisted and formless. Chanting all the while, the women unwrapped the linen swaddling and washed him down with cow's urine. They dug out the life-clay that clogged his openings. They placed the finger-bone of a bat beneath his tongue. An egg was broken by his nose and the white slurped down by one medicine woman and the yellow by another.

Finally, they injected him with 5 cc. of dextroamphetamine sulfate.

Puck's eyes flew open. His skin had been baked black as silt by his long immersion in the soil, and his hair bleached white. His eyes were a vivid and startling leaf-green. In all respects but one, his body was as perfect as ever it had been. But that one exception made the women sigh unhappily for his sake.

One leg was missing, from above the knee down.

"The Earth has taken her tithe," one old woman observed sagely.

"There was not enough left of the leg to save," said another.

"It's a pity," said a third.

They all withdrew from the hut, leaving Will and Puck alone together.

For a long time Puck did nothing but stare wonderingly at his stump of a leg. He sat up and ran careful hands over its surface, as if to prove to himself that the missing flesh was not still there and somehow charmed invisible. Then he stared at Will's clean white shirt, and at the dragon arms upon his chest. At last, his unblinking gaze rose to meet Will's eyes.

"*You* did this!"

"No!" It was an unfair accusation. The land-mine had nothing to do with the dragon. The Scissors-Grinder would have found it and brought it into the village in any case. The two facts were connected only by the War, and the War was not Will's fault. He took his friend's hand in his own. "*Tchortyrion . . .*" he said in a low voice, careful that no unseen person might overhear.

Puck batted his hand away. "That's not my true name anymore! I have walked in darkness and my spirit has returned from the halls of granite with a new name—one that not even the dragon knows!"

"The dragon will learn it soon enough," Will said sadly.

"You wish!"

"Puck . . ."

"My old use-name is dead as well," said he who had been Puck Berrysnatcher. Unsteadily pulling himself erect, he wrapped the blanket upon which he had been laid about his thin shoulders. "You may call me No-name, for no name of mine shall ever pass your lips again."

Awkwardly, No-name hopped to the doorway. He steadied himself with a hand upon the jamb, then launched himself out into the wide world.

"Please! Listen to me!" Will cried after him.

Wordlessly, No-name raised one hand, middle finger extended.

Red anger welled up inside Will. "Asshole!" he shouted after his former friend. "Stump-leggity hopper! Johnny-three-limbs!"

He had not cried since that night the dragon first entered him. Now he cried again.

In mid-summer an army recruiter roared into town with a bright green-and-yellow drum lashed to the motorcycle behind him. He wore a smart red uniform with two rows of brass buttons, and he'd come all the way from Brocielande, looking for likely lads to enlist in the service of Avalon. With a screech and a cloud of dust, he pulled up in front of the Scrannel Dogge, heeled down the kickstand, and went inside to rent the common room for the space of the afternoon.

Outside again, he donned his drum harness, attached the drum, and sprinkled a handful of gold coins on its head. *Boom-Boom-de-Boom!* The drumsticks came down like thunder. *Rap-Tap-a-Rap!* The gold coins leaped and danced, like raindrops on a hot griddle. By this time, there was a crowd standing outside the Scrannel Dogge.

The recruiter laughed. "Sergeant Bombast is my name!" *Boom! Doom! Boom!* "Finding heroes is my game!" He struck the sticks together overhead. *Click! Snick! Click!* Then he thrust them in his belt, unharnessed the great drum, and set it down beside him. The gold coins caught the sun and dazzled every eye with avarice. "I'm here to offer certain brave lads the very best career a man ever had. The chance to learn a skill, to become a warrior . . . and get paid damn well for it, too. Look at me!" He clapped his hands upon his ample girth. "Do I look underfed?"

The crowd laughed. Laughing with them, Sergeant Bombast waded into their number, wandering first this way, then that, addressing first this one, then another. "No, I do not. For the very good reason that the Army feeds me well. It feeds me, and clothes me, and all but wipes me arse when I asks it to. And am I grateful? Am I grateful? I am *not*. No, sirs and maidens, so far from grateful am I that I require that the Army pay me for the privilege! And how much, do you ask? How much am I paid? Keeping in mind that my shoes, my food, my breeches, my snot-rag—" he pulled a lace handkerchief from one sleeve and waved it daintily in the air—"are all free as the air we breathe and the dirt we rub in our hair at Candlemas eve. How much am I *paid?*" His seemingly random wander had brought him back to the drum again. Now his fist came down on the drum, making it shout and the gold leap up into the air with wonder. "Forty-three copper pennies a month!"

The crowd gasped.

"Payable quarterly in good honest gold! As you see here! *Or* silver, for them as worships the horned matron." He chucked old Lady Favor-Me-Not under the chin, making her blush and simper. "But that's not all—no, not the half of it! I see you've noticed these coins here. Noticed? Pshaw! You've noticed that I *meant* you to notice these coins! And why not? Each one of these little beauties weighs a full Trojan ounce! Each one is of the good red gold, laboriously mined by kobolds in the griffin-haunted Mountains of the Moon. How could you not notice them? How could you not wonder what I meant to do with them? Did I bring them here simply to scoop them up again, when my piece were done, and pour them back into my pockets?

"Not a bit of it! It is my dearest hope that I leave this village penniless. I *intend* to leave this village penniless! Listen careful now, for this is the crux of the matter. This here gold's meant for bonuses. Yes! *Recruitment* bonuses! In just a minute I'm going to stop talking. I'll reckon you're glad to hear that!" He waited for the laugh. "Yes, believe it or not, Sergeant Bombast is going to shut up and walk inside this fine establishment, where I've arranged for exclusive use of the common room, and something more as well. Now, what I want to do is to talk—just talk, mind you!— with lads who are strong enough and old enough to become soldiers. How old is that? Old enough to get your girlfriend in trouble!" Laughter again. "But not too old, neither. How old is that? Old enough that your girlfriend's jumped you over the broom, and you've come to think of it as a good bit of luck!

"So I'm a talkative man, and I want some lads to talk *with*. And if you'll do it, if you're neither too young nor too old and are willing to simply hear me out, with absolutely no strings attached . . ." He paused. "Well, fair's fair and the beer's on me. Drink as much as you like, and I'll pay the tab." He started to turn away, then swung back, scratching his head and looking puzzled. "Damn me, if there isn't something I've forgot."

"The gold!" squeaked a young dinter.

"The gold! Yes, yes, I'd forget me own head if it weren't nailed on. As I've said, the gold's for bonuses. Right into your hand it goes, the instant you've signed the papers to become a soldier. And how much? One gold coin? Two?" He grinned wolfishly. "Doesn't nobody want to guess? No? Well, hold onto your pizzles . . . I'm offering *ten gold coins* to the boy who signs up today! And ten more apiece for as many of his friends as wants to go with him!"

To cheers, he retreated into the tavern.

The dragon, who had foreseen his coming from afar, had said, "Now do we repay our people for their subservience. This fellow is a great danger to us all. He must be caught unawares."

"Why not placate him with smiles?" Will had asked. "Hear him out, feed him well, and send him on his way. That seems to me the path of least strife."

"He will win recruits—never doubt it. Such men have tongues of honey, and glamour-stones of great potency."

"So?"

"The War goes ill for Avalon. Not one of three recruited today is like to ever return."

"I don't care. On their heads be the consequences."

"You're learning. Here, then, is our true concern: The first recruit who is administered the Oath of Fealty will tell his superior officers about my presence here. He will betray us all, with never a thought for the welfare of the village, his family, or friends. Such is the puissance of the Army's sorcerers."

So Will and the dragon had conferred, and made plans.

Now the time to put those plans into action was come.

The Scrannel Dogge was bursting with potential recruits. The beer flowed freely, and the tobacco as well. Every tavern pipe was in use, and Sergeant Bombast had sent out for more. Within the fog of tobacco smoke, young men laughed and joked and hooted when the recruiter caught the eye of that lad he deemed most apt to sign, smiled, and crooked a beckoning finger. So Will saw from the doorway.

He let the door slam behind him.

All eyes reflexively turned his way. A complete and utter silence overcame the room.

Then, as he walked forward, there was a scraping of chairs and putting down of mugs. Somebody slipped out the kitchen door, and another after him. Wordlessly, a knot of three lads in green shirts left by the main door. The bodies eddied and flowed. By the time Will reached the recruiter's table, there was nobody in the room but the two of them.

"I'll be buggered," Sergeant Bombast said wonderingly, "if I've ever seen the like."

"It's my fault," Will said. He felt flustered and embarrassed, but luckily those qualities fit perfectly the part he had to play.

"Well, I can *see* that! I can see that, and yet shave a goat and marry me off to it if I know what it means. Sit down, boy, sit! Is there a curse on you? The evil eye? Transmissible elf-pox?"

"No, it's not that. It's . . . well, I'm half-mortal."

A long silence.

"Seriously?"

"Aye. There is iron in my blood. 'Tis why I have no true name. Why, also, I am shunned by all." He sounded patently false to himself, and yet he could tell from the man's face that the recruiter believed his every word. "There is no place in this village for me anymore."

The recruiter pointed to a rounded black rock that lay atop a stack of indenture parchments. "This is a name-stone. Not much to look at, is it?"

"No, sir."

"But its mate, which I hold under my tongue, is." He took out a small, lozenge-shaped stone and held it up to be admired. It glistered in the light, blood-crimson yet black in its heart. He placed it back in his mouth. "Now, if you were to lay your hand upon the name-stone on the table, your true name would go straight to the one in my mouth, and so to my brain. It's how we enforce the contracts our recruits sign."

"I understand." Will calmly placed his hand upon the

black name-stone. He watched the recruiter's face, as nothing happened. There were ways to hide a true name, of course. But they were not likely to be found in a remote river-village in the wilds of the Debatable Hills. Passing the stone's test was proof of nothing. But it was extremely suggestive.

Sergeant Bombast sucked in his breath slowly. Then he opened up the small lockbox on the table before him, and said, "D'ye see this gold, boy?"

"Yes."

"There's eighty ounces of the good red here—none of your white gold nor electrum neither!—closer to you than your one hand is to the other. Yet the bonus you'd get would be worth a dozen of what I have here. *If*, that is, your claim is true. Can you prove it?"

"Yes, sir. I can."

"Now, explain this to me again," Sergeant Bombast said. "You live in a house of *iron?*" They were outside now, walking through the silent village. The recruiter had left his drum behind, but had slipped the name-stone into a pocket and strapped the lockbox to his belt.

"It's where I sleep at night. That should prove my case, shouldn't it? It should prove that I'm . . . what I say I am."

So saying, Will walked the recruiter into Tyrant Square. It was a sunny, cloudless day, and the square smelled of dust and cinnamon, with just a bitter under-taste of leaked hydraulic fluid and cold iron. It was noon.

When he saw the dragon, Sergeant Bombast's face fell.

"Oh, fuck," he said.

As if that were the signal, Will threw his arms around the man, while doors flew open and hidden ambushers poured into the square, waving rakes, brooms, and hoes. An old hen-wife struck the recruiter across the back of his head with her distaff. He went limp and heavy in Will's arms. Perforce, Will let him fall.

Then the women were all over the fallen soldier, stabbing, clubbing, kicking and cursing. Their passion was beyond all bounds, for these were the mothers of those he had tried to recruit. They had all of them fallen in with the orders the dragon had given with a readier will than they had ever displayed before for any of his purposes. Now they were making sure the fallen recruiter would never rise again to deprive them of their sons.

Wordlessly, they did their work and then, wordlessly, they left.

"Drown his motorcycle in the river," the dragon commanded afterwards. "Smash his drum and burn it, lest it bear witness against us. Bury his body in the midden-heap. There must be no evidence that ever he came here. Did you recover his lockbox?"

"No. It wasn't with his body. One of the women must have stolen it."

The dragon chuckled. "Peasants! Still, it works out well. The coins are well-buried already under basement flagstones, and will stay so indefinitely. And when an investigator comes through looking for a lost recruiter, he'll be met by a universal ignorance, canny lies, and a cleverly planted series of misleading evidence. Out of avarice, they'll serve our cause better than ever we could order it ourselves."

A full moon sat high in the sky, enthroned within the constellation of the Mad Dog and presiding over one of the hottest nights of the summer when the dragon abruptly announced, "There is a resistance."

"Sir?" Will stood in the open doorway, lethargically watching the sweat fall, drop by drop from his bowed head. He would have welcomed a breeze, but at this time of year when those who had built well enough slept naked on their rooftops and those who had not burrowed into the mud of the riverbed, there were no night-breezes cunning enough to thread the maze of huts and so make their way to the square.

"Rebels against my rule. Insurrectionists. Mad, suicidal fools."

A single drop fell. Will jerked his head to move his moon-shadow aside, and saw a large black circle appear in the dirt. "Who?"

"The greenshirties."

"They're just kids," Will said scornfully.

"Do not despise them because they are young. The young make excellent soldiers and better martyrs. They are easily dominated, quickly trained, and as ruthless as you command them to be. They kill without regret, and they go to their deaths readily, because they do not truly understand that death is permanent."

"You give them too much credit. They do no more than sign horns at me, glare, and spit upon my shadow. Everybody does that."

"They are still building up their numbers and their courage. Yet their leader, the No-name one, is shrewd and capable. It worries me that he has made himself invisible to your eye, and thus to mine. Walking about the village, you have oft enough come upon a nest in the fields where he slept, or scented the distinctive tang of his scat. Yet when was the last time you saw him in person?"

"I haven't even seen these nests nor smelt the dung you speak of."

"You've seen and smelled, but not been aware of it. Meanwhile, No-name skillfully eludes your sight. He has made himself a ghost."

"The more ghostly the better. I don't care if I never see him again."

"You will see him again. Remember, when you do, that I warned you so."

The dragon's prophecy came true not a week later. Will was walking his errands and admiring, as he so often did these days, how ugly the village had become in his eyes. Half the huts were wattle-and-daub—little more than sticks and dried mud. Those which had honest planks were left un-painted and grey, to keep down the yearly assessment when the teind-inspector came through from the central government. Pigs wandered the streets, and the occasional scavenger bear as well, looking moth-eaten and shabby. Nothing was clean, nothing was new, nothing was ever mended.

Such were the thoughts he was thinking when somebody thrust a gunnysack over his head, while somebody else punched him in the stomach, and a third person swept his feet out from under him.

It was like a conjuring trick. One moment he was walking down a noisy street, with children playing in the dust and artisans striding by to their workshops and goodwives leaning from windows to gossip or sitting in doorways shucking peas, and the next he was being carried swiftly away, in darkness, by eight strong hands.

He struggled, but could not break free. His cries, muffled by the sack, were ignored. If anybody heard him—and there had been many about on the street a moment before—nobody came to his aid.

After what seemed an enormously long time, he was dumped on the ground. Angrily, he struggled out of the gunnysack. He was lying on the stony and slightly damp floor of the old gravel pit, south of the village. One crumbling wall was overgrown with flowering vines. He could hear birdsong upon birdsong. Standing, he flung the gunnysack to the ground and confronted his kidnappers.

There were twelve of them and they all wore green shirts. He knew them all, of course, just as he knew everyone else in the village. But, more, they had all been his friends, at one time or another. Were he free of the dragon's bondage, doubtless he would be one of their number. Now, though, he was filled with scorn for them, for he knew exactly how the dragon would deal with them, were they to harm his lieutenant. He would accept them into his body, one at a time, to corrupt their minds and fill their bodies with cancers. He would tell the first in excruciating detail exactly how he was going to die, stage by stage, and he would make sure the eleven others watched as it happened. Death after death, the survivors would watch and anticipate. Last of all would be their leader, No-name.

Will understood how the dragon thought.

"Turn away," he said. "This will not do you nor your cause any good whatsoever."

Two of the greenshirties took him by the arms. They thrust him before No-name. His former friend leaned on a crutch of ash-wood. His face was tense with hatred and his eyes did not blink.

"It is good of you to be so concerned for our *cause*," No-name said. "But you do not understand our *cause*, do you? Our *cause* is simply this."

He raised a hand, and brought it down fast, across Will's face. Something sharp cut a long scratch across his forehead and down one cheek.

"*Llandrysos*, I command you to die!" No-name cried. The greenshirties holding Will's arms released them. He staggered back a step. A trickle of something warm went tickling down his face. He touched his hand to it. Blood.

No-name stared at him. In his outstretched hand was an elf-shot, one of those small stone arrowheads found everywhere in the fields after a hard rain. Will did not know if they had been made by ancient civilizations or grew from pebbles by spontaneous generation. Nor had he known, before now, that to scratch somebody with one while crying out his true name would cause that person to die. But the stench of ozone that accompanied death-magic hung in the air, lifting the small hairs on the back of his neck and tickling his nose with its eldritch force, and the knowledge of what had almost happened was inescapable.

The look of absolute astonishment on No-name's face curdled and became rage. He dashed the elf-shot to the ground. "You were *never* my friend!" he cried in a fury. "The night when we exchanged true names and mingled blood, you lied! You were as false then as you are now!"

It was true. Will remembered that long-ago time when he and Puck had rowed their coracles to a distant river-island, and there caught fish which they grilled over coals and a turtle from which they made a soup prepared in its own shell. It had been Puck's idea to swear eternal friendship and Will, desperate for a name-friend and knowing Puck would not believe he had none, had invented a true name for himself. He was careful to let his friend reveal first, and so knew to shiver and roll up his eyes when he spoke the name. But he had felt a terrible guilt then for his deceit, and every time since when he thought of that night.

Even now.

Standing on his one good leg, No-name tossed his crutch upward and seized it near the tip. Then he swung it around and smashed Will in the face.

Will fell.

The greenshirties were all over him then, kicking and hitting him.

Briefly, it came to Will that, if he were included among their number, there were thirteen present and engaged upon a single action. We are a coven, he thought, and I the random sacrifice, who is worshiped with kicks and blows. Then there was nothing but his suffering and the rage that rose up within him, so strong that though it could not weaken the pain, yet it drowned out the fear he should have felt on realizing that he was going to die. He knew only pain and a kind of wonder: a vast, world-encompassing astonishment that so profound a thing as death could happen to *him*, accompanied by a lesser wonder that No-name and his merry thugs had the toughness to take his punishment all the way to death's portal, and that vital step beyond. They were only boys, after all. Where had they learned such discipline?

"I think he's dead," said a voice. He thought it was No-name's, but he couldn't be sure. His ears rang, and the voice was so very, very far away.

One last booted foot connected with already-broken ribs. He gasped, and spasmed. It seemed unfair that he could suffer pain on top of pain like this.

"That is our message to your master dragon," said the distant voice. "If you live, take it to him."

Then silence. Eventually, Will forced himself to open one eye—the other was swollen shut—and saw that he was alone again. It was a gorgeous day, sunny without being at all hot. Birds sang all about him. A sweet breeze ruffled his hair.

He picked himself up, bleeding and weeping with rage, and stumbled back to the dragon.

Because the dragon would not trust any of the healing-women inside him, Will's injuries were treated by a fluffer, who came inside the dragon to suck the injuries from Will's body and accept them as her own. He tried to stop her as soon as he had the strength to do so, but the dragon over-ruled him. It shamed and sickened him to see how painfully the girl hobbled outside again.

"Tell me who did this," the dragon whispered, "and we shall have revenge."

"No."

There was a long hiss, as a steam valve somewhere deep in the thorax vented pressure. "You toy with me."

Will turned his face to the wall. "It's my problem and not yours."

"You *are* my problem."

There was a constant low-grade mumble and grumble of machines that faded to nothing when one stopped paying attention to it. Some part of it was the ventilation system, for the air never quite went stale, though it often had a flat under-taste. The rest was surely reflexive—meant to keep the dragon alive. Listening to those mechanical voices, fad-ing deeper and deeper within the tyrant's corpus, Will had a vision of an interior that never came to an end, all the night contained within that lightless iron body, expanding in-ward in an inversion of the natural order, stars twinkling in the vasty reaches of distant condensers and fuel-handling systems and somewhere a crescent moon, perhaps, caught in his gear train. "I won't argue," Will said. "And I will never tell you anything."

"You will."

"*No!*"

The dragon fell silent. The leather of the pilot's couch gleamed weakly in the soft light. Will's wrists ached.

* * *

The outcome was never in doubt. Try though he might, Will could not resist the call of the leather couch, of the grips that filled his hand, of the needles that slid into his wrists. The dragon entered him, and had from him all the information he desired, and this time he did not leave.

Will walked through the village streets, leaving footprints of flame behind him. He was filled with wrath and the dragon. "*Come out!*" he roared. "Bring out your greenshirties, every one of them, or I shall come after them, street by street and house by house." He put a hand on the nearest door, and wrenched it from its hinges. Broken fragments of boards fell flaming to the ground. "Spillikin cowers herewithin. Don't make me come in after him!"

Shadowy hands flung Spillikin face-first into the dirt at Will's feet.

Spillikin was a harmless albino stick-figure of a marsh-walker who screamed when Will closed a cauterizing hand about his arm to haul him to his feet.

"Follow me," Will/the dragon said coldly.

So great was Will's twin-spirited fury that none could stand up to him. He burned hot as a bronze idol, and the heat went before him in a great wave, withering plants, charring housefronts, and setting hair ablaze when somebody did not flee from him quickly enough. "*I am wrath!*" he screamed. "*I am blood-vengeance! I am justice! Feed me or suffer!*"

The greenshirties were, of course, brought out.

No-name was, of course, not among their number.

The greenshirties were lined up before the dragon in Tyrant Square. They knelt in the dirt before him, heads down. Only two were so unwary as to be caught in their green shirts. The others were bare-chested or in mufti. All were terrified, and one of them had pissed himself. Their families and neighbors had followed after them and now filled the square with their wails of lament. Will quelled them with a look.

"Your king knows your true names," he said sternly to the greenshirties, "and can kill you at a word."

"It is true," said Hag Applemere. Her face was stony and

impassive. Yet Will knew that one of the greenshirties was her brother.

"More, he can make you suffer such dementia as would make you believe yourselves in Hell, and suffering its torments forever."

"It is true," the hag said.

"Yet he disdains to bend the full weight of his wrath upon you. You are no threat to him. He scorns you as creatures of little or no import."

"It is true."

"One only does he desire vengeance upon. Your leader—he who calls himself No-name. This being so, your most merciful lord has made this offer: Stand." They obeyed, and he gestured toward a burning brand. "Bring No-name to me while this fire yet burns, and you shall all go free. Fail, and you will suffer such torments as the ingenuity of a dragon can devise."

"It is true."

Somebody—not one of the greenshirties—was sobbing softly and steadily. Will ignored it. There was more Dragon within him than Self. It was a strange feeling, not being in control. He liked it. It was like being a small coracle carried helplessly along by a raging current. The river of emotion had its own logic; it knew where it was going. "Go!" he cried. "Now!"

The greenshirties scattered like pigeons.

Not half an hour later, No-name was brought, beaten and struggling, into the square. His former disciples had tied his hands behind his back, and gagged him with a red bandanna. He had been beaten—not so badly as Will had been, but well and thoroughly.

Will walked up and down before him. Those leaf-green eyes glared up out of that siltblack face with a pure and holy hatred. There could be no reasoning with this boy, nor any taming of him. He was a primal force, an anti-Will, the spirit of vengeance made flesh and given a single unswerving purpose.

Behind No-name stood the village elders in a straight, unmoving line. The Sullen Man moved his mouth slowly, like an ancient tortoise having a particularly deep thought. But he did not speak. Nor did Auld Black Agnes, nor the yage-witch whose use-name no living being knew, nor Lady Nightlady, nor Spadefoot, nor Annie Hop-the-Frog, nor Daddy Finger-bones, nor any of the others. There were mutters and whispers among the villagers, assembled into a loose throng behind them, but nothing coherent. Nothing that could be heard or punished. Now and again, the buzzing of wings rose up over the murmurs and died down again like a cicada on a still summer day, but no one lifted up from the ground.

Back and forth Will stalked, restless as a leopard in a cage, while the dragon within him brooded over possible punishments. A whipping would only strengthen No-name in his hatred and resolve. Amputation was no answer—he had lost one limb already, and was still a dangerous and unswerving enemy. There was no gaol in all the village that could hope to hold him forever, save for the dragon himself, and the dragon did not wish to accept so capricious an imp into his own body.

Death seemed the only answer.

But what sort of death? Strangulation was too quick. Fire was good, but Tyrant Square was surrounded by thatch-roofed huts. A drowning would have to be carried out at the river, out of sight of the dragon himself, and he wanted the manna of punishment inextricably linked in his subjects' minds to his own physical self. He could have a wine-barrel brought in and filled with water, but then the victim's struggles would have a comic element to them. Also, as a form of strangulation, it was still too quick.

Unhurriedly, the dragon considered. Then he brought Will to a stop before the crouching No-name. He raised up Will's head, and let a little of the dragon-light shine out through Will's eyes.

"Crucify him."

To Will's horror, the villagers obeyed.

It took hours. But shortly before dawn, the child who had once been Puck Berrysnatcher, who had been Will's best friend and had died and been reborn as Will's Nemesis, breathed his last. His body went limp as he surrendered his name to his revered ancestress, Mother Night, and the exhausted villagers could finally turn away and go home and sleep.

Later, after he had departed Will's body at last, the dragon said, "You have done well."

Will lay motionless on the pilot's couch and said nothing.

"I shall reward you."

"No, lord," Will said. "You have done too much already."

"Haummn. Do you know the first sign that a toady has come to accept the rightness of his lickspittle station?"

"No, sir."

"It is insolence. For which reason, you will not be punished but rather, as I said, rewarded. You have grown somewhat in my service. Your tastes have matured. You want something better than your hand. You shall have it. Go into any woman's house and tell her what she must do. You have my permission."

"This is a gift I do not desire."

"Says you! Big Red Margotty has three holes. She will refuse none of them to you. Enter them in whatever order you wish. Do what you like with her tits. Tell her to look glad when she sees you. Tell her to wag her tail and bark like a dog. As long as she has a daughter, she has no choice but to obey. Much the same goes for any of my beloved subjects, of whatever gender or age."

"They hate you," Will said.

"And thou as well, my love and my delight. And thou as well."

"But you with reason."

A long silence. Then, "I know your mind as you do not. I know what things you wish to do with Red Margotty and what things you wish to do *to* her. I tell you, there are cruelties within you greater than anything I know. It is the birthright of flesh."

"You lie!"

"Do I? Tell me something, dearest victim. When you told

the elders to crucify No-name, the command came from me, with my breath and in my voice. But the form . . . did not the *choice* of the punishment come from you?"

Will had been lying listlessly on the couch staring up at the featureless metal ceiling. Now he sat upright, his face white with shock. All in a single movement he stood, and turned toward the door.

Which seeing, the dragon sneered, "Do you think to leave me? Do you honestly think you *can*? Then try!" The dragon slammed his door open. The cool and pitiless light of earliest morning flooded the cabin. A fresh breeze swept in, carrying with it scents from the fields and woods. It made Will painfully aware of how his own sour stench permeated the dragon's interior. "You need me more than I ever needed you—I have seen to that! You cannot run away, and if you could, your hunger would bring you back, wrists foremost. You *desire* me. You are empty without me. Go! Try to run! See where it gets you."

Will trembled.

He bolted out the door and ran.

The first sunset away from the dragon, Will threw up violently as the sun went down, and then suffered spasms of diarrhea. Cramping, and aching and foul, he hid in the depths of the Old Forest all through the night, sometimes howling and sometimes rolling about the forest floor in pain. A thousand times he thought he must return. A thousand times he told himself: Not yet. Just a little longer and you can surrender. But not yet.

The craving came in waves. When it abated, Will would think: If I can hold out for one day, the second will be easier, and the third easier yet. Then the sick yearning would return, a black need in the tissues of his flesh and an aching in his bones, and he would think again: Not yet. Hold off for just a few more minutes. Then you can give up. Soon. Just a little longer.

By morning, the worst of it was over. He washed his clothes in a stream, and hung them up to dry in the wan predawn light. To keep himself warm, he marched back and forth singing the *Chansons Amoreuses de Merlin Syl-*

vanus, as many of its five hundred verses as he could remember. Finally, when the clothes were only slightly damp, he sought out a great climbing oak he knew of old, and from a hollow withdrew a length of stolen clothesline. Climbing as close to the tippy-top of the great tree as he dared, he lashed himself to its bole. There, lightly rocked by a gentle wind, he slept at last.

Three days later, Hag Applemere came to see him in his place of hiding. The truth-teller bowed before him. "Lord Dragon bids you return to him," she said formally.

Will did not ask the revered hag how she had found him. Wise-women had their skills; nor did they explain themselves. "I'll come when I'm ready," he said. "My task here is not yet completed." He was busily sewing together leaves of oak, yew, ash, and alder, using a needle laboriously crafted from a thorn, and short threads made from grasses he had pulled apart by hand. It was no easy work.

Hag Applemere frowned. "You place us all in certain danger."

"He will not destroy himself over me alone. Particularly when he is sure that I must inevitably return to him."

"It is true."

Will laughed mirthlessly. "You need not ply your trade here, hallowed lady. Speak to me as you would to any other. I am no longer of the dragon's party." Looking at her, he saw for the first time that she was not so many years older than himself. In a time of peace, he might even have grown fast enough to someday, in two years or five, claim her for his own, by the ancient rites of the greensward and the midnight sun. Only months ago, young as he was, he would have found this an unsettling thought. But now his thinking had been driven to such extremes that it bothered him not.

"Will," she said then, cautiously, "whatever are you up to?"

He held up the garment, complete at last, for her to admire. "I have become a greenshirtie." All the time he had sewn, he was bare chested, for he had torn up his dragon sark and used it for tinder as he needed fire. Now he donned its leafy replacement.

Clad in his fragile new finery, Will looked the truth-teller straight in the eye.

"You *can* lie," he said.

Bessie looked stricken. "Once," she said, and reflexively covered her womb with both hands. "And the price is high, terribly high."

He stood. "Then it must be paid. Let us find a shovel now. It is time for a bit of graverobbery."

It was evening when Will returned at last to the dragon. Tyrant Square had been ringed about with barbed wire, and a loudspeaker had been set upon a pole with wires leading back into his iron hulk, so that he could speak and be heard in the absence of his lieutenant.

"Go first," Will said to Hag Applemere, "that he may be reassured I mean him no harm."

Breasts bare, clad in the robes and wide hat of her profession, Bessie Applemere passed through a barbed-wire gate (a grimpkin guard opened it before her and closed it after her) and entered the square. "Son of Cruelty." She bowed deeply before the dragon.

Will stood hunched in the shadows, head down, with his hands in his pockets. Tonelessly, he said, "I have been broken to your will, great one. I will be your stump-cow, if that is what you want. I beg you. Make me grovel. Make me crawl. Only let me back in."

Hag Applemere spread her arms and bowed again. "It is true."

"You may approach." The dragon's voice sounded staticky and yet triumphant over the loudspeaker.

The sour-faced old grimpkin opened the gate for him, as it had earlier been opened for the hag. Slowly, like a maltreated dog returning to the only hand that had ever fed him, Will crossed the square. He paused before the loudspeaker, briefly touched its pole with one trembling hand, and then shoved that hand back into his pocket. "You have won. Well and truly, have you won."

It appalled him how easily the words came, and how natural they sounded coming from his mouth. He could feel the desire to surrender to the tyrant, accept what punishments he would impose, and sink gratefully back into his bondage. A little voice within cried: *So easy! So easy!* And so it would be, perilously easy indeed. The realization that a part of him devoutly wished for it made Will burn with humiliation.

The dragon slowly forced one eye half-open. "So, boy . . ." Was it his imagination, or was the dragon's voice less forceful than it had been three days ago? "You have learned what need feels like. You suffer from your desires, even as I do. I . . . I . . . am weakened, admittedly, but I am not all so weak as *that!* You thought to prove that I needed you—you have proved the reverse. Though I have neither wings nor missiles and my electrical reserves are low, though I cannot fire my jets without destroying the village and myself as well, yet am I of the mighty, for I have neither pity nor remorse. Thought you I craved a mere boy? Thought you to make me dance attendance on a soft, un-muscled half-mortal mongrel fey? Pfaugh! I do not need you. Never think that I . . . that I *need* you!"

"Let me in," Will whimpered. "I will do whatever you say."

"You . . . you understand that you must be punished for your disobedience?"

"Yes," Will said. "Punish me, please. Abase and degrade me, I beg you."

"As you wish," the dragon's cockpit door hissed open, "so it shall be."

Will took one halting step forward, and then two. Then he began to run, straight at the open hatchway. Straight at it—and then to one side.

He found himself standing before the featureless iron of the dragon's side. Quickly, from one pocket he withdrew Sergeant Bombast's soulstone. Its small blood-red mate was already in his mouth. There was still grave-dirt on the one, and a strange taste to the other, but he did not care. He touched the soulstone to the iron plate, and the dragon's true name flowed effortlessly into his mind.

Simultaneously, he took the elf-shot from his other pocket. Then, with all his strength, he drew the elf-shot down the dragon's iron flank, making a long, bright scratch in the rust.

"What are you doing?" the dragon cried in alarm. "Stop that! The hatch is open, the couch awaits!" His voice dropped seductively. "The needles yearn for your wrists. Even as I yearn for—"

"Baalthazar, of the line of Baalmoloch, of the line of Baalshabat," Will shouted, "I command thee to *die!*"

And that was that.

All in an instant and with no fuss whatever, the dragon king was dead. All his might and malice was become nothing more than inert metal, that might be cut up and carted away to be sold to the scrap-foundries that served their larger brothers with ingots to be re-forged for the War.

Will hit the side of the dragon with all the might of his fist, to show his disdain. Then he spat as hard and fierce as ever he could, and watched the saliva slide slowly down the black metal. Finally, he unbuttoned his trousers and pissed upon his erstwhile oppressor.

So it was that he finally accepted that the tyrant was well and truly dead.

Bessie Applemere—hag no more—stood silent and bereft on the square behind him. Wordlessly, she mourned her sterile womb and sightless eyes. To her, Will went. He took her hand, and led her back to her hut. He opened the door for her. Her sat her down upon her bed. "Do you need anything?" he asked. "Water? Some food?"

She shook her head. "Just go. Leave me to lament our victory in solitude."

He left, quietly closing the door behind him. There was no place to go now but home. It took him a moment to remember where that was.

"I've come back," Will said.

Blind Enna looked stricken. Her face turned slowly toward him, those vacant eyes filled with shadow, that ancient mouth open and despairing. Like a sleep-walker, she stood and stumbled forward and then, when her groping fingers tapped against his chest, she threw her arms around him and burst into tears. "Thank the Seven! Oh, thank the

Seven! The blessed, blessed, merciful Seven!" she sobbed over and over again, and Will realized for the first time that, in her own inarticulate way, his aunt genuinely and truly loved him.

And so, for a season, life in the village returned to normal. In the autumn the Armies of the Mighty came through the land, torching the crops and leveling the buildings. Terror went before them and the villagers were forced to flee, first into the Old Forest, and then to refugee camps across the border. Finally, they were loaded into cattle cars and taken away to far Babylonia in Faerie Minor, where the streets are bricked of gold and the ziggurats touch the sky, and there Will found a stranger destiny than any he might previously have dreamed.

But that is another story, for another day.

The Big Green Grin

Gahan Wilson

Gahan Wilson lives in Sag Harbor, New York. He is the finest living cartoonist of the weird and macabre. His cartoons appear regularly in Playboy *and in* The New Yorker, *and many other publications. They have been gathered in twenty or more collections. He is one of the best reviewers of fantasy and horror, with a regular column in* Realms of Fantasy. *He is an excellent writer of stories. His novels include* Eddy Deco's Last Caper *and* Everybody's Favorite Duck, *and his short fiction is collected in* The Cleft and Other Odd Tales.*

This story appeared in Gathering the Bones, *edited by Dennis Etchison, Ramsey Campbell, and Jack Dann, an ambitious anthology of original horrific and fantastic stories from Australian, UK, and U.S. writers, tales of terror from three continents. Quite an impressive book, we think. "The Big Green Grin" is a cleanly and simply-told story of a curious little boy who discovers a big green mouth opening in the ground in a vacant lot near his home. It occurs to him to do something horrible. Much of the story is told from the point of view of an amoral grackle. This is fantasy of a high order of intensity.*

The green grin began at one edge of the vacant lot behind a flattened plastic garbage can which had been mauled the previous winter during a sloppy snow removal, then swept through many yards of tousled weeds and scraggly grass grown tall and thick through a hot, humid summer and finally terminated at the lot's other edge amid the roots of a young oak which was the only tree present.

A glistening grackle perched on one of the oak's scrawny branches and blinked thoughtfully as it slowly turned its small, shiny head in order to follow the grin's vast curve. The bird had only noticed the line of the grin cutting through the uneven earth a few wing beats or so ago as it was flying over the lot but would probably have paid it no further attention if the grin had not chosen that very moment to lick the edges of its lips with a broad sweep of the tip of its pointy green tongue.

The tongue's tip was rather small relative to the size of the grin but, in regard to the objects in the very pleasant little neighborhood surrounding the lot, it was alarmingly large. It was, to give just one example, every bit as big as a gleaming red family car proudly parked in front of the small apartment building located directly across the street from the lot.

Intrigued, the grackle had allowed his neat little body to drop gracefully down towards the young oak until he was near enough to grip one of its scraggly branches and then he settled himself and his feathers comfortably upon it so that he could study the grin leisurely and in more detail.

Of course this will not surprise anyone who knows anything about grackles, as they are famous for their lively curiosity and well known to be enthusiastic students of any objects or events which are odd or incongruous.

They also enjoy investigating things which glisten and

the tongue, being dripping wet with thick saliva made of green sap, had definitely and very satisfactorily glistened!

After a minute or two of observing the grin do nothing but remain in place, the grackle bent his head to the left to pinch an itchy spot on the upper curve of his wing between the two points of his sharp beak and his bright little eyes caught a movement in a window of the apartment building before which the red family car the size of the tip of the grin's tongue was parked.

A very young blond boy was peering out of the window with the palms of his hands and the tip of his nose pressed against its pane and since his eyes were wide and he wore an amazed expression the grackle was certain that, like himself, he too had seen the big green grin lick its lips with its huge, glistening tongue.

The grackle left off his wing-pinching since the itch had gone away and—with the wonderful detail and clarity which only a bird's marvelous eyes can provide—enjoyed watching a wide variety of expressions cross the young boy's face.

First his look of astonishment faded down into one of intense interest, then that was replaced by a deeply thoughtful sort of frown and following that there came a sly and foxy smile tinged with guilty delight which pleased the grackle very much because it was an almost sure and certain sign that the boy had thought of doing something which would be very interesting to watch!

When the boy left the window with an air of excitement and determination the grackle let his gaze drop to the door of the apartment building and after he had watched it patiently for only a little while he saw it open and the little boy emerge from it just as the bird had expected he would.

But now the boy was no longer alone, now he held the tiny hand of a pretty little girl a year or two younger than himself who resembled him in so many ways that the grackle had no doubt whatsoever that she was the boy's little sister.

The girl was smiling and looking excitedly around herself as she clutched the boy's hand. It was obvious this was a rare treat for her and she was clearly delighted and proud to be out and about in the company of her older brother.

Meanwhile—though the boy was trying his best to conceal it as much as possible—the grackle could easily see vestiges of the sinister and promising smile he had observed before flickering through the boy's bland look of innocence. With great anticipation he watched the boy and girl leave the sidewalk in front of the apartment, cross the road and then enter into the wild late summer foliage of the vacant lot.

The girl hesitated momentarily after wading a step or two into the thick grass and tangled weeds growing up in great profusion from the lumpy earth and asked her brother—she called him "Charlie"—if they really had to walk through this messy place but then he teased her and she pulled herself together and shrugged and marched on gamely.

They had advanced fairly deeply into the lot's miniature jungle when she stopped and bent down to pick up an old discarded doll. Half of its hair was missing and its polka-dot dress was ragged but it still had a sweet, if slightly cracked, expression so she pressed it to her breast and kept it even though her brother scoffed.

The grackle was interested to observe that her big brother was carefully leading her in the direction of the very center of the grin just as the bird had hoped he would. Once again he peered back and forth over the length of the grin. Had he just now detected a faint anticipatory stirring of its lips? He flapped up to a higher branch of the little oak so that he would get the best view possible in case what he eagerly anticipated actually happened next.

Now the brother began to exclaim loudly and point in front of them as if he had just spotted something really interesting and, just as he had planned, that caused the little girl to excitedly move ahead of him in order to see what he had seen. Meanwhile, in a sneaky sort of way, the boy moved directly behind her.

The grackle curled his tongue within his beak and squawked softly to himself as he shifted on the branch of the tree and watched with fierce concentration. The little girl was steadily coming nearer and nearer to the curving center of the big green grin with her big brother moving softly along behind her, carefully keeping just a step to her rear all the way.

Then the bird clutched the branch hard enough for his claws to dig through its bark when he saw her suddenly come to a halt actually standing on the lower edge of the grin with the toes of her best new shoes resting on its vast lower lip.

She knew at once it was something very strange and awful. Her bud of a mouth dropped open and her blue eyes bulged a little in their sockets as she stared down at the thin dark slit spread before her feet and stretching in a smooth and sinister curve far away to her left and right and then out of sight into the thick, sweet-smelling late summer greenness.

The grackle chattered faintly and stirred his dark wings when he saw the big brother slowly and carefully raise his hands up before his chest with both palms pointing towards his sister's back.

Then, with a gruesome unexpectedness, the long lips before the little girl parted with a great sucking and smacking noise to reveal the two long rows of enormous thorns which were the green grin's teeth!

She screamed and dropped her doll and it tumbled down, turning over and over through the air with its tattered, polka-dot shreds trailing pathetically behind until, with an awful accuracy, the vegetable teeth closed just at the right instant for two opposing thorns to pierce the pink plastic torso of the doll with a sharp, startling crack.

The little girl cried out again but this time softly and with concern as she bent down and reached her arms out towards the ruined toy.

Then, just as she bent, as if in some highly complicated, synchronized dance, her brother shoved the palms of his hands forcefully out before him into what had now suddenly become empty space and found himself falling forward and then down and then felt himself landing heavily atop the doll and sprawling upon the locked green teeth which were now all there was between him and the dark, waiting mouth of the grin beneath!

With his hands clawed he stretched his arms forward as far as he could, trying to grab hold of the tangle of weed and grass growing out from the green grin's upper lip but it receded from him as the mouth opened and the teeth once more pulled apart. He felt the doll drop down from under him and shuddered as he saw it vanish into the blackness of the now exposed abyss.

He flipped himself sideways, grabbing the lower teeth and trying to push himself back to safety but they were horribly slippery and terror beat in his chest and raced through his body as he felt his own weight begin inexorably to pull him either into the darkness below or place him properly for the green grin's next ferocious bite!

Suddenly he felt a frantic grabbing at the back of his shirt and after that a determined tugging which was small and did not have all that much force but which was just enough to counterbalance his downward slide and give him the leverage to scramble frantically up the repellent sliminess of the teeth to the green lip behind them and then onto the blessed ordinary earth of the vacant lot!

He looked up at the tear-streaked face of his sister as she helped him struggle to his feet and then the two of them, each leaning on the other, made their way unevenly through the tugging grass and clutching brambles and entangling vines to the smoothness of the road and the surety of the concrete sidewalk and eventually to the smooth, silken safety of the carpet on the floor of their apartment living room.

But the boy would never be able to leave his guilt behind, nor the horror at what he had almost done, nor his gratitude at what she had done and, because of that, his sister would never again be unloved nor unprotected.

To the great disappointment of the grackle!

The Book of Martha

Octavia E. Butler

Octavia E. Butler lives in Seattle, Washington. After years of struggle—culminating in the early 1980s with two exceptional novels, Kindred *and* Wild Seed, *and then award nominations for two fine short stories—her career began to peak. In 1995 she was awarded a McArthur Grant, a large cash prize often called the "genius grant," which brought her to worldwide notice. She also entered a new, strong phase of her career.* Parable of the Sower *and its sequel,* Parable of the Talents, *have strong religious themes. She said in a* Locus *interview, "It seems that religion has kept us focused and helped us to do any number of very difficult things, from building pyramids and cathedrals to holding together countries, in some instances. I'm not saying it's a force for good—it's just a force. So why not use it to get ourselves to the stars?"*

"The Book of Martha" appeared at SciFiction electronically, and this is perhaps its first appearance in print. It is an abstract supernatural dialogue between Martha, a writer, and God. A cross between a biblical fable and a conte philosophique, it's a story about magical power. "That's what I want to write about," she said in that same Locus *interview, "when you are aware of what it means to be an adult and what choices you have to make, the fact that maybe you're afraid, but you still have to act."*

"It's difficult, isn't it?" God said with a weary smile. "You're truly free for the first time. What could be more difficult than that?"

Martha Bes looked around at the endless grayness that was, along with God, all that she could see. In fear and confusion, she covered her broad black face with her hands. "If only I could wake up," she whispered.

God kept silent but was so palpably, disturbingly present that even in the silence Martha felt rebuked. "Where is this?" she asked, not really wanting to know, not wanting to be dead when she was only forty-three. "Where am I?"

"Here with me," God said.

"Really here?" she asked. "Not at home in bed dreaming? Not locked up in a mental institution? Not . . . not lying dead in a morgue?"

"Here," God said softly. "With me."

After a moment, Martha was able to take her hands from her face and look again at the grayness around her and at God. "This can't be heaven," she said. "There's nothing here, no one here but you."

"Is that all you see?" God asked.

This confused her even more. "Don't you know what I see?" she demanded and then quickly softened her voice. "Don't you know everything?"

God smiled. "No, I outgrew that trick long ago. You can't imagine how boring it was."

This struck Martha as such a human thing to say that her fear diminished a little—although she was still impossibly confused. She had, she remembered, been sitting at her computer, wrapping up one more day's work on her fifth novel. The writing had been going well for a change, and she'd been enjoying it. For hours, she'd been spilling her new story onto paper in that sweet frenzy of creation that she lived for. Finally, she had stopped, turned the computer off, and realized that she felt stiff. Her back hurt. She was hungry and thirsty, and it was almost five A.M. She had worked through the night. Amused in spite of her various aches and pains, she got up and went to the kitchen to find something to eat.

And then she was *here*, confused and scared. The comfort of her small, disorderly house was gone, and she was standing before this amazing figure who had convinced her at once that he was God—or someone so powerful that he might as well be God. He had work for her to do, he said— work that would mean a great deal to her and to the rest of humankind.

If she had been a little less frightened, she might have laughed. Beyond comic books and bad movies, who said things like that?

"Why," she dared to ask, "do you look like a twice-life-sized, bearded white man?" In fact, seated as he was on his huge thronelike chair, he looked, she thought, like a living version of Michelangelo's *Moses*, a sculpture that she remembered seeing pictured in her college art-history textbook about twenty years before. Except that God was more fully dressed than Michelangelo's *Moses*, wearing, from neck to ankles, the kind of long, white robe that she had so often seen in paintings of Christ.

"You see what your life has prepared you to see," God said.

"I want to see what's really here!"

"Do you? What you see is up to you, Martha. Everything is up to you."

She sighed. "Do you mind if I sit down?"

And she was sitting. She did not sit down, but simply found herself sitting in a comfortable armchair that had surely not been there a moment before. Another trick, she thought resentfully—like the grayness, like the giant on his throne, like her own sudden appearance here. Everything was just one more effort to amaze and frighten her. And, of course, it was working. She was amazed and badly frightened. Worse, she disliked the giant for manipulating her, and this frightened her even more. Surely he could read her mind. Surely he would punish . . .

She made herself speak through her fear. "You said you had work for me." She paused, licked her lips, tried to steady her voice. "What do you want me to do?"

He didn't answer at once. He looked at her with what she read as amusement—looked at her long enough to make her even more uncomfortable.

"What do you want me to do?" she repeated, her voice stronger this time.

"I have a great deal of work for you," he said at last. "As I tell you about it, I want you to keep three people in mind: Jonah, Job, and Noah. Remember them. Be guided by their stories."

"All right," she said because he had stopped speaking, and it seemed that she should say something. "All right."

When she was a girl, she had gone to church and to Sunday School, to Bible class and to vacation Bible school. Her mother, only a girl herself, hadn't known much about being a mother, but she had wanted her child to be "good," and to her, "good" meant "religious." As a result, Martha knew very well what the Bible said about Jonah, Job, and Noah. She had come to regard their stories as parables rather than literal truths, but she remembered them. God had ordered Jonah to go to the city of Nineveh and to tell the people there to mend their ways. Frightened, Jonah had tried to run away from the work and from God, but God had caused him to be shipwrecked, swallowed by a great fish, and given to know that he could not escape.

Job had been the tormented pawn who lost his property, his children, and his health, in a bet between God and Satan. And when Job proved faithful in spite of all that God had permitted Satan to do to him, God rewarded Job with even greater wealth, new children, and restored health.

As for Noah, of course, God ordered him to build an ark and save his family and a lot of animals because God had decided to flood the world and kill everyone and everything else.

Why was she to remember these three Biblical figures in

particular? What had they to do with her—especially Job and all his agony?

"This is what you're to do," God said. "You will help humankind to survive its greedy, murderous, wasteful adolescence. Help it to find less destructive, more peaceful, sustainable ways to live."

Martha stared at him. After a while, she said feebly, ". . . what?"

"If you don't help them, they will be destroyed."

"You're going to destroy them . . . again?" she whispered.

"Of course not," God said, sounding annoyed. "They're well on the way to destroying billions of themselves by greatly changing the ability of the earth to sustain them. That's why they need help. That's why you will help them."

"How?" she asked. She shook her head. "What can I do?"

"Don't worry," God said. "I won't be sending you back home with another message that people can ignore or twist to suit themselves. It's too late for that kind of thing anyway." God shifted on his throne and looked at her with his head cocked to one side. "You'll borrow some of my power," he said. "You'll arrange it so that people treat one another better and treat their environment more sensibly. You'll give them a better chance to survive than they've given themselves. I'll lend you the power, and you'll do this." He paused, but this time she could think of nothing to say. After a while, he went on.

"When you've finished your work, you'll go back and live among them again as one of their lowliest. You're the one who will decide what that will mean, but whatever you decide is to be the bottom level of society, the lowest class or caste or race, that's what you'll be."

This time when he stopped talking, Martha laughed. She felt overwhelmed with questions, fears, and bitter laughter, but it was the laughter that broke free. She needed to laugh. It gave her strength somehow.

"I was born on the bottom level of society," she said. "You must have known that."

God did not answer.

"Sure you did." Martha stopped laughing and managed, somehow, not to cry. She stood up, stepped toward God. "How could you not know? I was born poor, black, and female to a fourteen-year-old mother who could barely read. We were homeless half the time while I was growing up. Is that bottom-level enough for you? I was born on the bottom, but I didn't stay there. I didn't leave my mother there, either. And I'm not going back there!"

Still God said nothing. He smiled.

Martha sat down again, frightened by the smile, aware that she had been shouting—shouting at God! After a while, she whispered, "Is that why you chose me to do this . . . this work? Because of where I came from?"

"I chose you for all that you are and all that you are not," God said. "I could have chosen someone much poorer and more downtrodden. I chose you because you were the one I wanted for this."

Martha couldn't decide whether he sounded annoyed. She couldn't decide whether it was an honor to be chosen to do a job so huge, so poorly defined, so *impossible*.

"Please let me go home," she whispered. She was instantly ashamed of herself. She was begging, sounding pitiful, humiliating herself. Yet these were the most honest words she'd spoken so far.

"You're free to ask me questions," God said as though he hadn't heard her plea at all. "You're free to argue and think and investigate all of human history for ideas and warnings. You're free to take all the time you need to do these things. As I said earlier, you're truly free. You're even free to be terrified. But I assure you, you will do this work."

Martha thought of Job, Jonah, and Noah. After a while, she nodded.

"Good," God said. He stood up and stepped toward her. He was at least twelve feet high and inhumanly beautiful. He literally glowed. "Walk with me," he said.

And abruptly, he was not twelve feet high. Martha never saw him change, but now he was her size—just under six feet—and he no longer glowed. Now when he looked at her, they were eye to eye. He did look at her. He saw that something was disturbing her, and he asked, "What is it now? Has your image of me grown feathered wings or a blinding halo?"

"Your halo's gone," she answered. "And you're smaller. More normal."

"Good," he said. "What else do you see?"

"Nothing. Grayness."

"That will change."

It seemed that they walked over a smooth, hard, level surface, although when she looked down, she couldn't see her feet. It was as though she walked through ankle-high, ground-hugging fog.

"What are we walking on?" she asked.

"What would you like?" God asked. "A sidewalk? Beach sand? A dirt road?"

"A healthy, green lawn," she said, and was somehow not surprised to find herself walking on short, green grass. "And there should be trees," she said, getting the idea and discovering she liked it. "There should be sunshine—blue sky with a few clouds. It should be May or early June."

And it was so. It was as though it had always been so. They were walking through what could have been a vast city park.

Martha looked at God, her eyes wide. "Is that it?" she whispered. "I'm supposed to change people by deciding what they'll be like, and then just . . . just saying it?"

"Yes," God said.

And she went from being elated to—once again—being terrified. "What if I say something wrong, make a mistake?"

"You will."

"But . . . people could get hurt. People could die."

God went to a huge deep red Norway maple tree and sat down beneath it on a long wooden bench. Martha realized that he had created both the ancient tree and the comfortable-looking bench only a moment before. She knew this, but again, it had happened so smoothly that she was not jarred by it.

"It's so easy," she said. "Is it always this easy for you?"

God sighed. "Always," he said.

She thought about that—his sigh, the fact that he looked away into the trees instead of at her. Was an eternity of absolute ease just another name for hell? Or was that just the most sacrilegious thought she'd had so far? She said, "I don't want to hurt people. Not even by accident."

God turned away from the trees, looked at her for several seconds, then said, "It would be better for you if you had raised a child or two."

Then, she thought with irritation, he should have chosen someone who'd raised a child or two. But she didn't have the courage to say that. Instead, she said, "Won't you fix it so I don't hurt or kill anyone? I mean, I'm new at this. I could do something stupid and wipe people out and not even know I'd done it until afterward."

"I won't fix things for you," God said. "You have a free hand."

She sat down next to him because sitting and staring out into the endless park was easier than standing and facing him and asking him questions that she thought might make him angry. She said, "Why should it be my work? Why don't you do it? You know how. You could do it without making mistakes. Why make me do it? I don't know anything."

"Quite right," God said. And he smiled. "That's why."

She thought about this with growing horror. "Is it just a game to you, then?" she asked. "Are you playing with us because you're bored?"

God seemed to consider the question. "I'm not bored," he said. He seemed pleased somehow. "You should be thinking about the changes you'll make. We can talk about them. You don't have to just suddenly proclaim."

She looked at him, then stared down at the grass, trying to get her thoughts in order. "Okay. How do I start?"

"Think about this: What change would you want to make if you could make only one? Think of one important change."

She looked at the grass again and thought about the novels she had written. What if she were going to write a novel in which human beings had to be changed in only one positive way? "Well," she said after a while, "the growing population is making a lot of the other problems worse. What if people could only have two children? I mean, what if people who wanted children could only have two, no matter how many more they wanted or how many medical techniques they used to try to get more?"

"You believe the population problem is the worst one, then?" God asked.

"I think so," she said. "Too many people. If we solve that one, we'll have more time to solve other problems. And we can't solve it on our own. We all know about it, but some of us won't admit it. And nobody wants some big government authority telling them how many kids to have." She glanced at God and saw that he seemed to be listening politely. She wondered how far he would let her go. What might offend him. What might he do to her if he were offended? "So everyone's reproductive system shuts down after two kids," she said. "I mean, they get to live as long as before, and they aren't sick. They just can't have kids anymore."

"They'll try," God said. "The effort they put into building pyramids, cathedrals, and moon rockets will be as nothing to the effort they'll put into trying to end what will seem to them a plague of barrenness. What about people whose children die or are seriously disabled? What about a woman whose first child is a result of rape? What about surrogate motherhood? What about men who become fathers without realizing it? What about cloning?"

Martha stared at him, chagrined. "That's why you should do this. It's too complicated."

Silence.

"All right," Martha sighed and gave up. "All right. What if even with accidents and modern medicine, even something like cloning, the two-kid limit holds? I don't know how that could be made to work, but you do."

"It could be made to work," God said, "but keep in mind

that you won't be coming here again to repair any changes you make. What you do is what people will live with. Or in this case, die with."

"Oh," Martha said. She thought for a moment, then said, "Oh, no."

"They would last for a good many generations," God said. "But they would be dwindling all the time. In the end, they would be extinguished. With the usual diseases, disabilities, disasters, wars, deliberate childlessness, and murder, they wouldn't be able to replace themselves. Think of the needs of the future, Martha, as well as the needs of the present."

"I thought I was," she said. "What if I made four kids the maximum number instead of two?"

God shook his head. "Free will coupled with morality has been an interesting experiment. Free will is, among other things, the freedom to make mistakes. One group of mistakes will sometimes cancel another. That's saved any number of human groups, although it isn't dependable. Sometimes mistakes cause people to be wiped out, enslaved, or driven from their homes because they've so damaged or altered their land or their water or their climate. Free will isn't a guarantee of anything, but it's a potentially useful tool—too useful to erase casually."

"I thought you wanted me to put a stop to war and slavery and environmental destruction!" Martha snapped, remembering the history of her own people. How could God be so casual about such things?

God laughed. It was a startling sound—deep, full, and, Martha thought, inappropriately happy. Why would this particular subject make him laugh? Was he God? Was he Satan? Martha, in spite of her mother's efforts, had not been able to believe in the literal existence of either. Now, she did not know what to think—or what to do.

God recovered himself, shook his head, and looked at Martha. "Well, there's no hurry," he said. "Do you know what a nova is, Martha?"

Martha frowned. "It's . . . a star that explodes," she said, willing, even eager, to be distracted from her doubts.

"It's a pair of stars," God said. "A large one—a giant—and a small, very dense dwarf. The dwarf pulls material from the giant. After a while, the dwarf has taken more material than it can control, and it explodes. It doesn't necessarily destroy itself, but it does throw off a great deal of excess material. It makes a very bright, violent display. But once the dwarf has quieted down, it begins to siphon material from the giant again. It can do this over and over. That's what a nova is. If you change it—move the two stars farther apart or equalize their density, then it's no longer a nova."

Martha listened, catching his meaning even though she didn't want to. "Are you saying that if . . . if humanity is changed, it won't be humanity anymore?"

"I'm saying more than that," God told her. "I'm saying that even though this is true, I will permit you to do it. What you decide should be done with humankind *will* be done. But whatever you do, your decisions will have consequences. If you limit their fertility, you will probably destroy them. If you limit their competitiveness or their inventiveness, you might destroy their ability to survive the many disasters and challenges that they must face."

Worse and worse, Martha thought, and she actually felt nauseous with fear. She turned away from God, hugging herself, suddenly crying, tears streaming down her face. After a while, she sniffed and wiped her face on her hands, since she had nothing else. "What will you do to me if I refuse?" she asked, thinking of Job and Jonah in particular.

"Nothing." God didn't even sound annoyed. "You won't refuse."

"But what if I do? What if I really can't think of anything worth doing?"

"That won't happen. But if it did somehow, and if you asked, I would send you home. After all, there are millions of human beings who would give anything to do this work."

And, instantly, she thought of some of these—people who would be happy to wipe out whole segments of the population whom they hated and feared, or people who would set up vast tyrannies that forced everyone into a single mold, no matter how much suffering that created. And what about those who would treat the work as fun—as nothing more than a good-guys-versus-bad-guys computer game, and damn the consequences. There were people like that. Martha knew people like that.

But God wouldn't choose that kind of person. If he was God. Why had he chosen her, after all? For all of her adult life, she hadn't even believed in God as a literal being. If this terrifyingly powerful entity, God or not, could choose her, he could make even worse choices.

After a while, she asked, "Was there really a Noah?"

"Not one man dealing with a worldwide flood," God said. "But there have been a number of people who've had to deal with smaller disasters."

"People you ordered to save a few and let the rest die?"

"Yes," God said.

She shuddered and turned to face him again. "And what then? Did they go mad?" Even she could hear the disapproval and disgust in her voice.

God chose to hear the question as only a question. "Some took refuge in madness, some in drunkenness, some in sexual license. Some killed themselves. Some survived and lived long, fruitful lives."

Martha shook her head and managed to keep quiet.

"I don't do that any longer," God said.

No, Martha thought. Now he had found a different amusement. "How big a change do I have to make?" she asked. "What will please you and cause you to let me go and not bring in someone else to replace me?"

"I don't know," God said, and he smiled. He rested his head back against the tree. "Because I don't know what you will do. That's a lovely sensation—anticipating, not knowing."

"Not from my point of view," Martha said bitterly. After a while, she said in a different tone, "Definitely not from my point of view. Because I don't know what to do. I really don't."

"You write stories for a living," God said. "You create

characters and situations, problems and solutions. That's less than I've given you to do."

"But you want me to tamper with real people. I don't want to do that. I'm afraid I'll make some horrible mistake."

"I'll answer your questions," God said. "Ask."

She didn't want to ask. After a while, though, she gave in. "What, exactly, do you want? A utopia? Because I don't believe in them. I don't believe it's possible to arrange a society so that everyone is content, everyone has what he or she wants."

"Not for more than a few moments," God said. "That's how long it would take for someone to decide that he wanted what his neighbor had—or that he wanted his neighbor as a slave of one kind or another, or that he wanted his neighbor dead. But never mind. I'm not asking you to create a utopia, Martha, although it would be interesting to see what you could come up with."

"So what are you asking me to do?"

"To help them, of course. Haven't you wanted to do that?"

"Always," she said. "And I never could in any meaningful way. Famines, epidemics, floods, fires, greed, slavery, revenge, stupid, stupid wars . . ."

"Now you can. Of course, you can't put an end to all of those things without putting an end to humanity, but you can diminish some of the problems. Fewer wars, less covetousness, more forethought and care with the environment . . . What might cause that?"

She looked at her hands, then at him. Something had occurred to her as he spoke, but it seemed both too simple and too fantastic, and to her personally, perhaps, too painful. Could it be done? Should it be done? Would it really help if it were done? She asked, "Was there really anything like the Tower of Babel? Did you make people suddenly unable to understand each other?"

God nodded. "Again, it happened several times in one way or another."

"So what did you do? Change their thinking somehow, alter their memories?"

"Yes, I've done both. Although before literacy, all I had to do was divide them physically, send one group to a new land or give one group a custom that altered their mouths—knocking out the front teeth during puberty rites, for instance. Or give them a strong aversion to something others of their kind consider precious or sacred or—"

To her amazement, Martha interrupted him. "What about changing people's . . . I don't know, their brain activity. Can I do that?"

"Interesting," God said. "And probably dangerous. But you can do that if you decide to. What do you have in mind?"

"Dreams," she said. "Powerful, unavoidable, realistic dreams that come every time people sleep."

"Do you mean," God asked, "that they should be taught some lesson through their dreams?"

"Maybe. But I really mean that somehow people should spend a lot of their energy in their dreams. They would have their own personal best of all possible worlds during their dreams. The dreams should be much more realistic and intense than most dreams are now. Whatever people love to do most, they should dream about doing it, and the dreams should change to keep up with their individual interests. Whatever grabs their attention, whatever they desire, they can have it in their sleep. In fact, they can't avoid having it. Nothing should be able to keep the dreams away—not drugs, not surgery, not anything. And the dreams should satisfy much more deeply, more thoroughly, than reality can. I mean, the satisfaction should be in the dreaming, not in trying to make the dream real."

God smiled. "Why?"

"I want them to have the only possible utopia." Martha thought for a moment. "Each person will have a private, perfect utopia every night—or an imperfect one. If they crave conflict and struggle, they get that. If they want peace and love, they get that. Whatever they want or need comes to them. I think if people go to a . . . well, a private heaven every night, it might take the edge off their willingness to spend their waking hours trying to dominate or destroy one another." She hesitated. "Won't it?"

God was still smiling. "It might. Some people will be taken over by it as though it were an addictive drug. Some will try to fight it in themselves or others. Some will give up on their lives and decide to die because nothing they do matters as much as their dreams. Some will enjoy it and try to go on with their familiar lives, but even they will find that the dreams interfere with their relations with other people. What will humankind in general do? I don't know." He seemed interested, almost excited. "I think it might dull them too much at first—until they're used to it. I wonder whether they can get used to it."

Martha nodded. "I think you're right about it dulling them. I think at first most people will lose interest in a lot of other things—including real, wide-awake sex. Real sex is risky to both the health and the ego. Dream sex will be fantastic and not risky at all. Fewer children will be born for a while."

"And fewer of those will survive," God said.

"What?"

"Some parents will certainly be too involved in dreams to take care of their children. Loving and raising children is risky, too, and it's hard work.

"That shouldn't happen. Taking care of their kids should be the one thing that parents want to do for real in spite of the dreams. I don't want to be responsible for a lot of neglected kids."

"So you want people—adults and children—to have nights filled with vivid, wish-fulfilling dreams, but parents should somehow see child care as more important than the dreams, and the children should not be seduced away from their parents by the dreams, but should want and need a relationship with them as though there were no dreams?"

"As much as possible." Martha frowned, imagining what it might be like to live in such a world. Would people still read books? Perhaps they would to feed their dreams. Would she still be able to write books? Would she want to?

What would happen to her if the only work she had ever cared for was lost? "People should still care about their families and their work," she said. "The dreams shouldn't take away their self-respect. They shouldn't be content to dream on a park bench or in an alley. I just want the dreams to slow things down a little. A little less aggression, as you said, less covetousness. Nothing slows people down like satisfaction, and this satisfaction will come every night."

God nodded. "Is that it, then? Do you want this to happen."

"Yes. I mean, I think so."

"Are you sure?"

She stood up and looked down at him. "Is it what I should do? Will it work? Please tell me."

"I truly don't know. I don't want to know. I want to watch it all unfold. I've used dreams before, you know, but not like this."

His pleasure was so obvious that she almost took the whole idea back. He seemed able to be amused by terrible things. "Let me think about this," she said. "Can I be by myself for a while?"

God nodded. "Speak aloud to me when you want to talk. I'll come to you."

And she was alone. She was alone inside what looked and felt like her home—her little house in Seattle, Washington. She was in her living room.

Without thinking, she turned on a lamp and stood looking at her books. Three of the walls of the room were covered with bookshelves. Her books were there in their familiar order. She picked up several, one after another—history, medicine, religion, art, crime. She opened them to see that they were, indeed, her books, highlighted and written in by her own hand as she researched this novel or that short story.

She began to believe she really was at home. She had had some sort of strange waking dream about meeting with a God who looked like Michelangelo's *Moses* and who ordered her to come up with a way to make humanity a less self-destructive species. The experience felt completely, un-nervingly real, but it couldn't have been. It was too ridiculous.

She went to her front window and opened the drapes. Her house was on a hill and faced east. Its great luxury was that it offered a beautiful view of Lake Washington just a few blocks down the hill.

But now, there was no lake. Outside was the park that she had wished into existence earlier. Perhaps twenty yards from her front window was the big red Norway maple tree and the bench where she had sat and talked with God.

The bench was empty now and in deep shadow. It was getting dark outside.

She closed the drapes and looked at the lamp that lit the room. For a moment, it bothered her that it was on and using electricity in this Twilight Zone of a place. Had her house been transported here, or had it been duplicated? Or was it all a complex hallucination?

She sighed. The lamp worked. Best to just accept it. There was light in the room. There was a room, a house. How it all worked was the least of her problems.

She went to the kitchen and there found all the food she had had at home. Like the lamp, the refrigerator, the electric stovetop, and the ovens worked. She could prepare a meal. It would be at least as real as anything else she'd run across recently. And she was hungry.

She took a small can of solid white albacore tuna and containers of dill weed and curry power from the cupboard and got bread, lettuce, dill pickles, green onions, mayonnaise, and chunky salsa from the refrigerator. She would have a tuna-salad sandwich or two. Thinking about it made her even hungrier.

Then she had another thought, and she said aloud, "May I ask you a question?"

And they were walking together on a broad, level dirt pathway bordered by dark, ghostly silhouettes of trees. Night had fallen, and the darkness beneath the trees was impenetrable. Only the pathway was a ribbon of pale light—starlight and moonlight. There was a full moon, brilliant, yellow-white, and huge. And there was a vast canopy of stars. She had seen the night sky this way only a few times in her life. She had always lived in cities where the lights and the smog obscured all but the brightest few stars.

She looked upward for several seconds, then looked at God and saw, somehow, without surprise, that he was black now, and clean-shaven. He was a tall, stocky black man wearing ordinary, modern clothing—a dark sweater over a white shirt and dark pants. He didn't tower over her, but he was taller than the human-sized version of the white God had been. He didn't look anything like the white Moses-God, and yet he was the same person. She never doubted that.

"You're seeing something different," God said. "What is it?" Even his voice was changed, deepened.

She told him what she was seeing, and he nodded. "At some point, you'll probably decide to see me as a woman," he said.

"I didn't decide to do-this," she said. "None of it is real, anyway."

"I've told you," he said. "Everything is real. It's just not as you see it."

She shrugged. It didn't matter—not compared to what she wanted to ask. "I had a thought," she said, "and it scared me. That's why I called you. I sort of asked about it before, but you didn't give me a direct answer, and I guess I need one."

He waited.

"Am I dead?"

"Of course not," he said, smiling. "You're here."

"With you," she said bitterly.

Silence.

"Does it matter how long I take to decide what to do?"

"I've told you, no. Take as long as you like."

That was odd, Martha thought. Well, everything was odd. On impulse, she said, "Would you like a tuna-salad sandwich?"

"Yes," God said. "Thank you."

They walked back to the house together instead of simply

appearing there. Martha was grateful for that. Once inside, she left him sitting in her living room, paging through a fantasy novel and smiling. She went through the motions of making the best tuna-salad sandwiches she could. Maybe effort counted. She didn't believe for a moment that she was preparing real food or that she and God were going to eat it.

And yet, the sandwiches were delicious. As they ate, Martha remembered the sparkling apple cider that she kept in the refrigerator for company. She went to get it, and when she got back to the living room, she saw that God had, in fact, become a woman.

Martha stopped, startled, then sighed. "I see you as female now," she said. "Actually, I think you look a little like me. We look like sisters." She smiled wearily and handed over a glass of cider.

God said, "You really are doing this yourself, you know. But as long as it isn't upsetting you, I suppose it doesn't matter."

"It does bother me. If I'm doing it, why did it take so long for me to see you as a black woman—since that's no more true than seeing you as a white or a black man?"

"As I've told you, you see what your life has prepared you to see." God looked at her, and for a moment, Martha felt that she was looking into a mirror.

Martha looked away. "I believe you. I just thought I had already broken out of the mental cage I was born and raised in—a human God, a white God, a male God . . ."

"If it were truly a cage," God said, "you would still be in it, and I would still look the way I did when you first saw me."

"There is that," Martha said. "What would you call it then?"

"An old habit," God said. "That's the trouble with habits. They tend to outlive their usefulness."

Martha was quiet for a while. Finally she said, "What do you think about my dream idea? I'm not asking you to foresee the future. Just find fault. Punch holes. Warn me."

God rested her head against the back of the chair. "Well, the evolving environmental problems will be less likely to cause wars, so there will probably be less starvation, less disease. Real power will be less satisfying than the vast, absolute power they can possess in their dreams, so fewer people will be driven to try to conquer their neighbors or exterminate their minorities. All in all, the dreams will probably give humanity more time than it would have without them."

Martha was alarmed in spite of herself. "Time to do what?"

"Time to grow up a little. Or at least, time to find some way of surviving what remains of its adolescence." God smiled. "How many times have you wondered how some especially self-destructive individual managed to survive adolescence? It's a valid concern for humanity as well as for individual human beings."

"Why can't the dreams do more than that?" she asked. "Why can't the dreams be used not just to give them their heart's desire when they sleep, but to push them toward some kind of waking maturity? Although I'm not sure what species maturity might be like."

"Exhaust them with pleasure," God mused, "while teaching them that pleasure isn't everything."

"They already know that."

"Individuals usually know that by the time they reach adulthood. But all too often, they don't care. It's too easy to follow bad but attractive leaders, embrace pleasurable but destructive habits, ignore looming disaster because maybe it won't happen after all—or maybe it will only happen to other people. That kind of thinking is part of what it means to be adolescent."

"Can the dreams teach—or at least promote—more thoughtfulness when people are awake, promote more concern for real consequences?

"It can be that way if you like."

"I do. I want them to enjoy themselves as much as they can while they're asleep, but to be a lot more awake and aware when they are awake, a lot less susceptible to lies, peer pressure, and self-delusion."

"None of this will make them perfect, Martha."

Martha stood looking down at God, fearing that she had

missed something important, and that God knew it and was amused. "But this will help?" she said. "It will help more than it will hurt."

"Yes, it will probably do that. And it will no doubt do other things. I don't know what they are, but they are inevitable. Nothing ever works smoothly with humankind."

"You like that, don't you?"

"I didn't at first. They were mine, and I didn't know them. You cannot begin to understand how strange that was." God shook her head. "They were as familiar as my own substance, and yet they weren't."

"Make the dreams happen," Martha said.

"Are you sure?"

"Make them happen."

"You're ready to go home, then."

"Yes."

God stood and faced her. "You want to go. Why?"

"Because I don't find them interesting in the same way you do. Because your ways scare me."

God laughed—a disturbing laugh now. "No, they don't," she said. "You're beginning to like my ways."

After a time, Martha nodded. "You're right. It did scare me at first, and now it doesn't. I've gotten used to it. In just the short time that I've been here, I've gotten used to it, and I'm starting to like it. That's what scares me."

In mirror image, God nodded, too. "You really could have stayed here, you know. No time would pass for you. No time has passed."

"I wondered why you didn't care about time."

"You'll go back to the life you remember, at first. But soon, I think you'll have to find another way of earning a living. Beginning again at your age won't be easy."

Martha stared at the neat shelves of books on her walls. "Reading will suffer, won't it—pleasure reading, anyway?"

"It will—for a while, anyway. People will read for information and for ideas, but they'll create their own fantasies. Did you think of that before you made your decision?"

Martha sighed. "Yes," she said. "I did." Sometime later, she added, "I want to go home."

"Do you want to remember being here?" God asked.

"No." On impulse, she stepped to God and hugged her—hugged her hard, feeling the familiar woman's body beneath the blue jeans and black T-shirt that looked as though it had come from Martha's own closet. Martha realized that somehow, in spite of everything, she had come to like this seductive, childlike, very dangerous being. "No," she repeated. "I'm afraid of the unintended damage that the dreams might do."

"Even though in the long run they'll almost certainly do more good than harm?" God asked.

"Even so," Martha said. "I'm afraid the time might come when I won't be able to stand knowing that I'm the one who caused not only the harm, but the end of the only career I've ever cared about. I'm afraid knowing all that might drive me out of my mind someday. She stepped away from God, and already God seemed to be fading, becoming translucent, transparent, gone.

"I want to forget," Martha said, and she stood alone in her living room, looking blankly past the open drapes of her front window at the surface of Lake Washington and the mist that hung above it. She wondered at the words she had just spoken, wondered what it was she wanted so badly to forget.

Wild Thing

Charles Coleman Finlay

Charles Coleman Finlay [home.earthlink.net/~ccfinlay/ personal.html] lives in Columbus, Ohio. Currently, he serves as Administrator for the Online Writing Workshop for SF and Fantasy, and writes SF and fantasy short stories for magazines such as F&SF. Autobiographical fragments on his website include: "Charlie was smart but funny-looking and used to drag home odd, smelly things like musty yellowed paperbacks," and "Charles Coleman Finlay worked for John Galipault at the Aviation Safety Institute (a forerunner of Europe's Eucare safety project), briefly served as a studio assistant for porcelain artist Curtis Benzle, and studied Constitutional history with Saul Cornell, helping to research The Other Founders.*" He has published some excellent fiction in recent years and is definitely an up-and-coming writer.*

"Wild Thing" was published in Fantasy & Science Fiction, *which had a particularly strong year in 2003. It is an Arthurian fantasy, about two supernatural creatures and the Holy Grail, and shows that even in such a conventional fantasy setting a strong and lively new telling is possible.*

Chrétien sows the seed
of a story he only begins,
and lodges it in such fertile loam
it's bound to bring a good yield.
—PERCEVAL (LE CONT DU GRAAL)

He was the sort of boy who always had a stick in his hand unless he chanced to have a stone. Today he held one of each as he ran in the mote-stirred sunlight. He skirted the plashes of water, pressed through the bulrushes, and paused on a small rise with his head cocked alertly.

"He's a nuisance," Howl muttered, sitting on a branch.

"I like him," Pooka whispered from his perch beside Howl.

"He's a mud-spattered, ratty-haired, goat-footed, frog-legged, spider-fingered, stick-swinging, rock-throwing nuisance."

"That's exactly why I like him."

Pooka snatched a ball of sunlight from the air and spun it, thrust fingers in his mouth and emitted a bird-loud whistle. He tumbled backward off the branch, landing on his feet just as the rock clipped Howl on the temple. Tiny periwinkle trousers cartwheeled through the air and Howl crashed upside down in the bushes. Pooka laughed.

A stick javelined into the leaves, resulting in a cry of "Oof!" Before Pooka could react, the boy landed on the pile and grabbed Howl.

"I got you!"

"Oh no you don't," Pooka answered, but not so the lad could hear him. He and Howl were almost as tall as human toddlers, but thinner and much lighter. Buzzing like a hive of hornets, Pooka jumped on the wild boy's head, drew his

74

little dagger, and inflicted several quick pricks across the scalp and neck.

The boy flailed his hand at the back of his head. "Eyah!"

"*Bzzzzzzz,*" Pooka hummed as he jabbed again and again.

Dropping Howl, the boy leapt up and ran away. Pooka clung to a handful of his hair, bouncing wildly on the boy's shoulder and buzzing with all his might. On impulse, he sawed through the strands with his blade rather than let go. Then he flitted to the ground and ran back to Howl's side.

His companion sat there, massaging a knot on the side of his head. "Why'd you do that? It was close—he nearly caught me!"

"He saw you," Pooka said.

"Did not! He heard your stupid whistle and caught that flash of glamour, didn't he?"

Pooka held out his hand, hauling Howl to his feet. "He hit you with the stick after you fell off the branch. Once he spotted you, he kept sight of you."

"But—"

"And snatched you with that first nab of his too. Quick hands. What're the chances of that?"

Howl wrinkled his brow. The two of them looked over at the boy, who, not so far away, still spun in circles brushing wildly at the back of his head.

"So he's of the blood?" Howl asked. "Related to us?"

"If he's mud-spattered, ratty-haired, and frog-legged, then he must be related to you." Pooka plucked a dappled pink foxglove blossom and twirled it on his finger. "Mind you, I'm rather handsome."

Howl scowled, his frown forming a crevice across his face. "His father, you think? There's no father around the farm I've seen."

"Mother, or I've missed my guess." Pooka dropped the blossom and begin twisting the long strands of the hair he'd cut off. "There's no shine about her, but she tends to that tidy hedge of gorse around the house. I can't find a way through it and I've tried more than once. She knows what she's about, that one. Here you go." He tossed one braided loop to Howl.

"What is it?"

"A necklace woven from the boy's hair." He finished the other and draped it over his own head. "A recompense for the tumble you took and a token for good luck."

Howl was wiggling the necklace over his pointy, out-thrust ears when he froze. "Look at that, will you."

The boy stared straight at them. Pooka sank into the brush, followed by Howl. The dirt smelled of slugs and beetles, but not enough to cause complaint. They peeked out over the leaves. The boy was creeping in their direction with a new stick in his hand.

"The nuisance," Howl grumbled, pulling the necklace down tight and crawling backward. "We ought to tell the king."

"Wouldn't you rather stay here and play?" Pooka asked.

But he too had noticed something wrong, vibrations all the way out at the end of a web that had nothing to do with this boy, and he felt a faint need to deliver the news to those who might do something about it, so he shimmied off through the undergrowth after Howl.

No path led where Pooka and Howl went, for the crossing they sought shifted constantly. In time they found it at a spot on the river where freshets of water jetted white over moss-slick rocks.

Having found it, they couldn't bring themselves to cross and sat on the high bank gazing into the twilight. Though it was summer—it was always summer on the other side—autumn tinged the forest leaves, russets and honey-golds and crisp tawny scattered among the green.

"I told you we should come to see the King," Howl said. "Told you there was something wrong."

Pooka's heart fluttered like a hummingbird at some dry blossom. "Whatever's wrong there, they don't need us to bring the news. They *know*."

"We should go find out," Howl said without enthusiasm.

They sat, hands folded, unmoving. If they waited long enough, Pooka thought, perhaps the leaves would change back.

Horns sounded in the distance.

"Let's hide," Pooka suggested. "Until we see our company."

"I'm all for that," Howl replied, and they tucked into the hollow trunk of a tree. It had the sharp dry smell of squirrels and empty shells, though not enough to be annoying. The horns echoed off the trees, closer and yet closer still, until Pooka and Howl peered from the crack. The riders came over the hills, mounted on horses no bigger than greyhounds, pearly white, sleek and lean. They were clad in silver armor, as radiant and multicolored as the shells of beetles glistening in the liquid Sun. Scarlet and verdant banners hung limp on their long lances, and riderless mounts jostled among them. The Herald, resplendent in his turquoise and orange butterfly-wing surcoat, reined in his horse at the edge of the river and blew a series of notes that made Pooka tremble. The leaves on the trees shivered too. Across the water, a few fell loose, and fluttered to the ground, some slowly, some quick. Then the riders surged past the Herald and crossed the turbulent river, the hooves of their mounts barely splashing on the surface.

The Herald turned his head toward the hollow tree, sniffing. "Who spies on us? These are days when spies may suffer death."

Howl slipped out of the tree at once and bowed so deeply his forelock dragged the ground. "O most gracious and courteous Lord Herald, munificently martial and majestically eloquent voice of the King—"

"On with it," the Herald snapped. "What is your name?"

"A poor and solitary creature like myself requires no name."

"Not so solitary, I think. There's another mouse who shares your hole." His face was grim beneath its mantis carapace as he peered at Pooka's hiding place. "Show yourself!"

Pooka emerged from the crevice, bending slightly at the waist. "It's a good day to be out riding, isn't it?"

"Ah," the Herald said. "Not a mouse, but a toad." He measured the passage of the army as it crossed the water. Pooka considered running, but the horse made that impractical.

"Forgive my unpardonable ignorance, my Lord Herald," Howl said. "But from what battle do you come? And what danger is it, that stretches thus into mortal lands?"

"Some things should not be spoken of on this side of the water." He laid his horn across his lap and reached down to Howl. "Come, little neighbor, cross the stream with me and all your questions shall be answered though I do not speak a word."

Howl accepted the hand, climbed up, and straddled the horse's neck. "Is that a riddle, your elevated Lordship?"

"'Tis no riddle, for it has no solution. Come, you too, Master Toad." A star of light glinted in the nicked edge of the Herald's lance. "Hop up behind."

"Breeeeep," Pooka croaked, more like a frog than a toad. He took the proffered hand and slid across the rump.

The last of the army flashed past, cheerless and silent, eyes as hard as gems. The trailing riders herded more empty mounts bearing broken, bloodied armor. Then the Herald raised the horn to his lips again, blared one last doleful note, and prodded his mount to close the rear.

Pooka shivered in the cool air above the river and shut his ears against the despondent babble of the voices in the water. When they came to the far shore, the air rippled like pebbles breaking the surface of a still pond as they passed.

He sucked in his breath. The lambent radiance that lit the land beyond the river had always been yellow as butter and as sweet. Something had curdled it, made it sour on his tongue. As the other riders veered away, disappearing like shadows among the trees, the Herald rode straight for the dingle of the King. The branches of the trees that encircled the rim of the vale drooped as if weeping.

"Aiieee!" Howl cried.

"Hush, little neighbor," the Herald said gently.

Pooka tried to lean around the Herald to see the source of Howl's dismay. The horse stopped beneath the white-blossomed hawthorn in the center of the bowl. Its teardrop petals fell in silent profusion at the stirring of the breeze.

Howl slipped to the ground and dropped to his knees, tearing at his chest, his hair. Pooka dismounted and saw the cause.

The Pale Lady, dressed in mourning green, sat beneath the hawthorn tree. Next to her lay the body of the King, a giant in death, a grassy tumulus of corpse with the scales of his armor slipping off as lichen-covered slabs of stone. He had grown large, larger even than the human proportions he and his Lady held in life. His head was missing. Reddish water trickled from the stump of his neck, staining the rocks with rust as it soaked into the ground.

A small pile of untouched toadstools lay at the Lady's side. Her tail slipped from under her skirts as she stirred. She rearranged herself to sit upon it again. She *was* disturbed, thought Pooka, despite her placid appearance, to let her tail show even for a moment.

The Herald bowed low before her, pretending not to notice the slip. She bid him rise.

"Lord Herald," she said. "Do you bring good company to soothe bad news or bad company to moderate our joy?"

"I bring company by chance for chance did not accompany our purpose. We recovered neither head nor Hallows."

"Did you accomplish nothing?"

"We died, m'Lady. That is nothing enough for those who died."

"But not enough to win the day."

He bowed low again. "There will be many other days to win but death is the final loss, and we are not a people given to finalities. Is it not enough that the Usurper-Thief is sorely wounded?"

"The King did that to his brother ere *he* died, not you."

Pooka tensed at that news. When brother fought brother, everyone suffered. More so when the one was King and the other wished to be.

"Yes," the Herald replied. "But the fact remains that he is injured, high upon his thigh, and all the life may yet leak out of him. If he did not have the stolen Hallows—the Cup and Platter—he'd be dead already."

"If he did not have the Hallowed Lance and Sword, you'd not fear to press your attack unto victory."

The Herald hesitated, drawing his breath before he spoke. "He no longer has the sword. He lost it crossing the lake and it has been passed into the safekeeping of a mortal's hands for a time so that it cannot be used against us."

The Lady's frown at this news was loathsome to behold. "But neither can we wield it to our strength."

The Herald did not answer.

"So by what chance do you bring our friends to visit?" She waved her lily-white fingers toward Pooka and Howl. Her hand made the sound of tiny bells as it passed through the air.

"I found them spying on the other side of the ford. I don't think they serve the Usurper-Turncoat"—Howl gasped at the suggestion "—but they have a mortal stink about them."

She stared at Pooka. Her eyes lingered on his throat, making it hard for him to breathe. "Your bravery and sacrifice are noted," she said to the Herald. "We shall continue our conversation later."

"M'Lady," he replied, and thus dismissed, departed. His mount trotted along at his side with canine obedience.

"Most radiant and glorious Lady," sniffled Howl, wiping tears away from reddened eyes, "your splendor is the sole light shining in this hour of our perpetual darkness. Believe not any slander that would place *me* at the side of the Usurper-Killer."

She beckoned him. Invisible chimes stirred at the movement of her hand. She placed one translucent fingernail on the braid of hair where it touched the hollow of his neck. "What's this?"

"What? This?" Howl's hands leapt to cover his throat. "It was a foolish fancy, a simple whim, a mere caprice—a gift from him!" He pointed at Pooka, who shifted from foot to foot. "It's a worthless trifle, taken from some unwitting mortal."

"Not so worthless, nor so mortal," she said. "This comes from one who shares our blood. Will you give it to me, neighbor?"

Pooka glanced off into the trees. Silver armor stippled the viridescent shadows. If he ran, he'd be running out of one trouble into worse.

"Such a pathetic token is not worthy of my Lady's grace," Howl said. He gripped the necklace like an asp as he handed it to her.

She slipped it over her wrist and inhaled sharply.

Pooka's mouth flew open. "If it tickles you, Lady, then you shouldn't wear it."

"You think that chance alone brought this to me?" she asked, her fingertip stroking the strands.

"No, I think I did."

"And where did the impulse arise to cut off those strands, and what prompted you to visit our domain again after so very long away?"

Pooka clamped his mouth down shut.

"Though truly I knew not what I sought when I reached out beyond our land—" Silver bracelets jangled as she stretched her bare arm. "—I exerted all my power to find and bring some key to unlock the cage of our predicament. And here it is."

"Then your magic failed," Pooka said.

"How's that?"

"Strands of hair form a lock, not a key."

She smiled, chill as an autumn morning. "Nevertheless. The Usurper-Betrayer who did this—" She flicked one finger at the green mound of the king—*ping!* "—is not the first to forsake us for the mortal world."

"No," Pooka admitted. "He's merely the first to take the four sacred Hallows, the head of his brother, and the crown of the kingdom along for the visit."

"Don't talk to the Lady that way!" Howl screamed, knocking Pooka over. He rolled as he hit the ground and landed on his feet, hands fisted.

"Stay!" the Lady commanded. "He speaks the truth, though he dresses it in shabby garb. And truth or lies, I would have no more violence between our folk within the borders of our land until this fratricide has been answered for."

The scent of chamomile invaded the air, stealing Pooka's anger. "That necklace was made by my own hand, Lady, and given for luck's sake. This is unlucky on us all. I ask for its return."

She smiled, as cold as frost. "But you're right. Hair can form nothing else but a locket. Let me bend the locket's hinge and gaze upon the mortal portrait painted within before I return it to you."

Without waiting for his reply, she lifted it from her wrist and held it up to the jaundiced light. With one word, it turned freely, a spinning wheel in her palm. With a second word, it glowed. A third word, and it opened like a tiny window.

The Pale Lady stared at the scenes inside the shining ring, eyes unblinking, ruby lips agape.

Pooka stepped closer, curling his toes in the brown-tipped clover blossoms. He saw the wild boy, grown up into a man, dressed in warrior's armor and seated at a great round table. He saw the boy-knight rise and leave the table and come to the shore of a lake. He saw the dead King's brother, crown upon his head, in a boat on that fish-thronged lake between two worlds. The boy crossed over the lake to enter the castle where the King's brother and all his traitorous retinue feasted. The Cup sat on the table. The King's own head, resting on the sacred Platter that preserved and sustained its coherent mind and tongue, opened its mouth to speak. Pooka strained forward to hear the King's words—

—and the little window snapped shut.

The Lady sighed and closed her eyes. Pooka blinked moisture into his own.

"He's the one, isn't he," Howl said, crowded in at Pooka's shoulder, and Pooka knew he meant the lad. "As one of us, he can reach the castle. As a mortal, he can break the spell and heal the Usurper-Knave."

She smiled, opaque as ice. "Perhaps." She offered him the braid of hair. "Here is your trifle."

"I don't want it," Howl blurted. He crossed his arms and scrunched his shoulders.

She turned her eyes on Pooka. "I'll happily trade it for yours, my diminutive Lord."

"No," he muttered and took a step back. He didn't like what he saw coming. "Mine's much nicer. Think I'll keep it."

"You must bring me the boy," she said, and spoke the word of geas. It was binding, as if she'd fastened a silver chain about their ankles.

Somewhere among the stones on the mound of the dead king, a single cricket chirped its lonely dirge.

The mortal Sun hid behind a vast gray canopy of clouds as the green tongues of the trees whispered to one another in the searching wind. The air was redolent with the scent of rain.

"She only called me 'neighbor,'" Howl sniffed. "She called you 'Lord'—and you were rude to her!"

"Meaningless flattery," Pooka replied.

"How can you say that? She's the Lady of our King."

"Noble is as noble does. Mortals set out saucers of fresh cream for me, no matter what they call me. She called me 'Lord' but didn't offer me a single toadstool."

Howl swallowed wistfully. "And she wasn't eating them either. I can still smell them." He sighed, lifting his head. "Are you sure he's the same boy? That we saw at the farmhouse and in the woods? He looks so much bigger."

"Time passes that way in the other country. And mortal lives pass that way here. Another reason not to trample on them—they're gone so quickly as it is."

"We have to catch him though, when he comes this way, and take him to the Lady."

Pooka grunted. "You do what you want, but I'm not going to help," he said, but as he said it, the invisible chain tugged tight against his ankle.

Something crashed through the brush above them on the hillside. Reddish-brown flashed between the black-brown trunks and two large does burst into view. The boy dashed after them, keeping pace, leaping to one side and then the other, slapping their hindquarters with his bare palms, driving them.

Howl hopped on a branch and trilled stridently like a wren—if the wren were the size of a chicken and had a bad throat cold, Pooka thought, peeking from the bushes. But it caught the boy's attention. He dug his heels into the moldered leaves as the deer bounded off through the trees and disappeared. He stared at the branch, but didn't seem to see Howl. His hand was cocked to throw, but empty.

Howl whistled again, cleared his throat, and shimmered into visibility. "Hello."

The boy retreated. "Are you bird or devil?"

"Neither," Howl replied. "But I would be your friend."

"That's what the spider told the fly," Pooka murmured, rubbing hard where the chain of geas felt the weakest. He wasn't going to be bound if he could help it.

The boy straightened. "Mother says that I must never hurt the birds, for God sees even one sparrow fall. But she says that if I see a devil, I must flee from it. Are you a bird or a devil," he paused, leaning forward, trying to peer through the veil of glamour. "Or are you a boy like me?"

Howl nodded enthusiastically. "I'm a boy like you."

The wild boy traced fingertips over his bare chin. "You're very hairy for a boy."

"Not to mention ugly," Pooka muttered.

Howl jutted out his curly beard. "Where I come from, all the children have beards."

"Really?" asked the boy. "Do they get them from their fathers?"

"Yes," Howl said. "Everyone has one."

"Beards or fathers?"

"Both. You could have one of each if you wished. Would you like to go see?"

The boy stepped forward, eagerness and hope written clearly on his face. There was such a loneliness in the sharp, intense eyes, just waiting to be filled. The wind gusted, shaking the trees as the boy willingly followed Howl.

Pooka popped out of the bushes. "Boo! Go away!"

The boy jumped. "Who're you?"

"He's trouble," Howl said.

"I'm a devil!" Pooka growled as fiercely as he could. He thought that maybe devils were some kind of large and dangerous bird, so he clawed his hands and flashed glamour at the fingertips to make them look like talons. "Now scat! Run away! Run for your life!"

"He's just playing games," Howl sneered. "Ignore him. We all do."

The mortal boy looked at Pooka, glanced at Howl, looked at Pooka some more, and then laughed. "I like games but it's boring playing them by myself. You're a funny boy."

Pooka kicked the boy in the shin. "Do you think that's funny? Run!"

"Hey!" The boy bent over to rub his leg.

The trees shook furiously in the wind. A drop of water fell out of the sky and landed splat on Pooka's pointed nose. Then another fell. They all looked up.

"If we go where the other children are," Howl cried above the din, "we shall all stay dry!"

The boy opened his mouth to answer.

Pooka hammered his toe into the boy's shin again. "You're a snail in a pail and you can't catch me," he taunted, and took off running in the direction of the farm where the boy lived.

Big fat raindrops falling sideways spattered him as he ran. He looked over his shoulder and saw the boy right beside him.

"You're not very fast," the lad said, grinning.

So Pooka tripped him. The boy stumbled, but kept his

feet. Pooka shifted direction and ran downhill to pick up speed. The important thing was to get him away from Howl and keep him away from the Lady.

The wind whistled up a pitch, stripping the branches. The lacerated leaves swirled around Pooka like so many fingers. He glanced over his shoulder and the boy was right behind, the tip of his tongue poking from the corner of his mouth as he lunged with his hand outstretched.

"I'm going to catch you!"

"Not like that, you won't," Pooka said, but he barely evaded the boy's grasp by swinging from a low-slung branch and landing on a fallen tree. "Turtle on a log, head in the fog, that's you."

He turned, his soles gripping the rough bark as he ran the length of the trunk and jumped off the end. The boy vaulted the barrier and kept after him.

Thunder crashed and rain fell in a deluge. It became impossible to see more than a few yards forward or back, the rest of the world cut off by a curtain of threaded raindrops. The slope turned to mud beneath their feet, rivulets carrying away the soil before they could stand on it. The wind off the hilltop buffeted them sideways two steps for every one they took forward.

A fear seized Pooka more strongly than the wind—the boy might actually catch him. For though the rain fell hard enough to sting, the boy did not relent. Pooka, who had never been caught by a mortal and who had no desire to satisfy anyone's wishes but his own, concentrated only on escape.

The wind surged again. Branches cracked and fell from the trees on either side of them. The air sizzled as if on fire, and then lightning flashed, striking a giant tree in front of them. A great gust of wind blew at the same time, knocking it over. Its roots ripped free of the sodden ground with a massive, sucking *pop,* spraying wet clumps of dirt and pebbles everywhere. Seeing his chance, Pooka grasped a sundered root and rode it into the air as the tree tilted over and fell. Then he ran along the trunk as it fell shuddering into place. He didn't notice the river gushing beneath him until he was more than halfway across, and then he screeched and leapt at once—

—and fell, soaked to the bone, covered in mud, into a dry land of summer under a sky as yellow as the contents of a chamber pot and as sour to the tongue. He spit, noticing the harshness of the noise in the sudden silence.

The Herald stood there, wearing a turquoise and mallow-blossom-colored cape. Parts of it were faded, like dust knocked off a butterfly's wing. One arm was bound up in a sling. He'd been in another battle.

"Do not feel bad, Toad," the Herald said. "The Lady always receives what she desires."

"Yes," Pooka mumbled. He felt the invisible cuff of geas unlatch and fall away from his ankle, fulfilled. "May she desire warts."

A surprised grunt preceded the boy as he splashed out of nothingness trailed by mist and landed on the grassy bank. He crouched down low and gazed all around, confused.

The Herald bowed to the boy. "Welcome, O Ephemera of Most Everlasting Importance. Shall we go see the Lady of the Dingle? She awaits us."

He extended the sharp plane of his hand like an arrow. It pointed through the gray forest toward the hollow at the heart of the country.

The white blossoms had all fallen from the hawthorn tree. It was covered with stunted, shriveled fruit suspended in some state that might never ripen into seed.

A carpet of woolly thyme blanketed the King's mound. Pale blue forget-me-nots, their washed-out blossoms frayed around the edges, formed a sash across the hummock's waist. The moss-covered stones had weathered some, sinking into the soil. Between the mound and the tree, the Lady rested, her emerald garb deepened into a dark and stony jade shot through with near-black veins. Piles of toadstools lay heaped around her, all untouched, some so old they had decayed. She still was not well. But Pooka had no appetite either.

"Welcome," she said to the boy. "Your mother is a dear cousin of mine and so I bid you welcome. Will you have a seat upon our humble sward?"

She waved her hand in a single graceful arc that sounded like fingers strumming a harp's strings. The boy started at the noise, but sat down. "You look a bit like my mother," he said.

Pooka lifted his chin. "So how's the Usurper-Victor doing these days?"

The Lady's smile froze for a brief second. "I have not overlooked you, my most inquisitive, acquisitive little Lordling. The Unctuous-Usurper bleeds with an unsalvable wound. His retinue drowns their despair in preemptive feasts of false celebration. Come!" She patted her hand on the ground beside her—taps on a cymbal. "Sit beside us and advise us."

Pooka plopped down beside the boy and crossed his legs. "I'm comfy here."

She arched her eyebrows, then looked through him as if he no longer existed and turned all her attention to the boy. "I say welcome again, my young cousin and most perceptive Lord. It is past time we met, although it is perhaps not yet too late. Will you tell me your name?"

"Don't do it!" Pooka shouted. "Or, if you do, first offer to trade your name for hers. Then you'll have equal power over her."

"Hush," the Lady smiled. "My little neighbor has a mouth whose capacity far exceeds the size of his simple brain. Some things that fall out of it belong at the other end of the tunnel that passes through him."

The boy looked at both of them, puzzled. "But if you know my mother, then you know that she gave me no name. She says that I am better off without one."

Pooka laughed. She did know what she was about, that one. He started to have hope for the boy after all.

"Then we shall follow the guidance of your little counselor," the Lady said, "and offer things besides our names to one another in trade. Do you wish to play?"

The Herald returned—though Pooka had not noticed him leave—bearing a tray that contained a loaf of fresh bread. The aroma drifting from it smelled of wheatfields and honey. A small pitcher rested beside it, and though Pooka could not see the fluid inside, the scent of wild blackberries nearly made him dizzy.

"Thank you, but no," the Lady said, smiling up at the Herald. "I find no appetite within."

"I'm hungry!" the boy cried.

"Don't take it." Pooka thrust out his hand. "Don't even take one bite."

"Be silent!" the Lady said. "My buzzing pipsqueak of a distant relative is far too big for his breeches, and should consider pulling the waistband up over his head until he can grow into them. In the meantime, pay no more attention to his noise than you would any other sound from the seat of someone's pants. May I offer you food or drink?"

The boy licked his lips, his eyes quickly calculating the size of his hunger and the worth of the loaf. "Give me half. Mother says it's never polite to take more than half."

She broke the bread—a bell sounded, a deep toll that hung in the air—and handed half the loaf to him. He broke a morsel off with his fingers, sighing as he swallowed.

"In exchange for half a loaf of bread," the Lady closed her hand in the air and the bell stopped, "I'll take half your wit."

"Oh, fool!" Pooka cried. He stared into the boy's eyes and saw them dull by half, shining water eclipsed by thick clouds. The boy shook his head, like someone chasing away an insect, then shoved the rest of the bread into his mouth. Crumbs spilled out the sides as he chewed.

"A fair deal for fairy bread bestowed upon a mortal," the Lady said. "My dear cousin's dearer child, is there anything else your heart desires?"

"Yes," the boy answered, crumbs on his cheek.

"Be careful," Pooka warned. "Ask only for—"

"Be quiet, my pestilential and profligate unwelcome acquaintance!"

"I want . . . I want. . . ." The boy couldn't find the words, wrinkling his forehead in dismay. He made a throwing motion with his hand.

"You want true aim?"

"Yes! It's . . . *fun*. I like it."

"So be it," the Lady said. She curved her hand in the air around an invisible spear—a sound shot through it like a distant trumpet when she cast. "Your missiles shall never miss their bull's-eye. But in exchange, all your choices shall fly wide of their intended targets."

The Herald smiled and murmured, "Yes, let the Usurper-Beggar beg for the boy's aid now."

A bee's stinger of pain lodged in Pooka's heart. "Let him choose to help you; that would be fair reward for a fairy gift."

She folded her hands on her lap, ignoring Pooka. The pale flesh of her bosom trembled lightly like milk in a bucket. "Is there anything else you'd like to have?" she asked the boy. "Some third request?"

She shifted as she awaited his answer. The folds of her dress rippled beneath her.

Pooka leaned over and whispered in the boy's ear. The boy nodded. "Lady," he started, just as Pooka had told him. "Your tail is showing! How do you come to have a cow's tail?"

"No, no—" Pooka said.

One hand clutched the cloth at her bosom, while the other swept the tail out of sight—the cacophonous clangor of a shelf full of pans as it collapsed.

"—no! You were supposed to say *'your garter's showing'* so she'd owe you a favor. Ach!" Pooka buried his face in his palms.

"Get out of here, get out of my sight!" the Lady hissed, humiliated and enraged. Pooka's ears twitched and he looked up. The Herald bent to soothe her but she smacked the tray, spilling the pitcher. "You take that dead scrap of animated flesh, and that miserable, ill-mannered, buck-toothed, scabrous rat—"

Pooka didn't wait for her to finish. He grabbed the boy's hand and dragged him to his feet. "She dismissed us—run for the river, faster than you've ever run before!"

They ran. Before they surmounted the lip of the dingle, a

tocsin sounded behind them, hackling the hairs on Pooka's back. The shades of warriors descended from the trees and hurried toward the vale in answer to the summons.

"This way," Pooka shouted.

He heard the sound of water over rocks before he burst from the edge of the forest with the boy behind him. The top of the tree-bridge still emerged from a fog that blanketed the river. He pushed the boy ahead first, turning to see how much time they had.

Not much. Lance-bearing warriors, some already in armor, stepped out from between the trees. The horns sounded again.

The boy climbed the tree, passed through the veil of mist, and disappeared. Pooka mounted the branches more nimbly, pausing when he reached the top. The horns fell silent.

"Halt, you dirt-grubbing, hole-dwelling, curd-licking—"

The Lady herself strode forward, the Herald at her side. Pooka cupped his hands to his mouth.

"Mooooooo!"

Her face froze, speechless before she could speak a word of binding. Pooka turned and plunged after the boy.

The pale light transmuted to sudden gray darkness, warmth dissolved in wetness, and the silence relented to the keening wind, while raindrops pounded on the drumheads of a million leaves. The flooding river thrust against the fallen tree, splashing over it, rocking it violently from side to side. Pooka gripped the branches like handles to balance himself as he stepped fitfully toward the other side. When he reached the middle of the tree-bridge, something roared upstream. A muddy, churning, foam-flecked wall of water charged down between the riverbanks. Pooka had just one second to leap for the mortal shore.

He was caught by the boy's outstretched hand and dragged to the high bank as the flood-surge ripped the tree away behind him.

They found Howl searching for them and they all took shelter in a mostly damp spot under an overhanging ledge of rock. It smelled of muddy decay and green things drowning, enough to make you sad if you granted it too much attention.

The boy told Howl everything that had happened. Pooka picked the caked mud off his arms and legs. He winced as clumps of hair came off with it. Meanwhile, the rain stopped, the sky cleared, and a seemingly sourceless saffron light illuminated the land.

"But you were scarcely gone at all," Howl said.

Pooka held his hands open. "Things are like that when you travel to the other country."

"We won't be allowed back, will we?" Howl asked, and Pooka shook his head. "What do you think will happen?"

"I don't know."

They sat there as water dripped from the branches and the ledge above them until the world passed into darkness. The boy looked up and pointed at the first star shining in the sky. "I better be going home. Mother will be growing worried." Then he sighed. "Can I come play again tomorrow? It's been very fun having other children to talk to and play with."

"Yes," Howl assured him. "We'll go back to see the Lady—"

Pooka grabbed the star's twinkle and patted it into a walnut-sized sphere of glamour. Then he took the braid of hair from around his neck and tied up the ball in a bow. He held it out for the boy. "Here's a gift for you."

The boy's eyes regained some of their luster. "Oh, thank you!"

Pooka pulled it back again. "But, you mustn't unwrap it until you are in sight of your home. Will you promise?"

"Yes," the boy answered solemnly.

Pooka handed it to him. "You'd better run. We'll see you tomorrow."

"Farewell." The lad jogged off smiling. He disappeared from sight, and there was only the sound of his feet slapping the mud, then even that was gone.

"What did you give him?" Howl asked.

"Forgetfulness," Pooka said. He could see the future

clearly, the wild boy growing up now to serve a human king for his brief blossoming of years as the seelie kingdom sickened and failed. But so be it. "He won't remember meeting the Lady, what he gained or lost, or anything else that happened to him today."

Howl crouched forward, elbows on knees, bearded chin on his knuckles. He could see that future too. "Do you have any forgetfulness left to spare for me?"

"Alas." Pooka sighed. "I've given it all away."

The knight skirted the heavy grove of trees, pressed through the thicket, and paused at the hilltop, his head cocked alertly. His eye passed over Pooka and Howl as they ran along the branches of the tree, then snapped back to them again.

"That's not the same wild boy," Howl said. "Is it?"

"He's changed," Pooka whispered. "But it's him—he's seen us."

"I beseech you," the knight said, "in the name of the Father, Son, and Holy Spirit to help me find my way."

"In the name of who?" Howl muttered.

But Pooka seated himself upon a limb. "What is your name, good sir?"

"Percival," he answered proudly, his hand tapping his armored chest. "A knight of the Round Table in the hall at Camelot."

"Ah," Pooka said, a little sadly at the loss implied by such a gain. He pointed down the right hand road. "Follow this trail until you reach a beautiful river, follow the river until you find a man fishing from a boat, and follow that man across the river to his castle to find what you seek."

Reaching into his bag, Percival said, "God's blessing fall on you. May I give you a token for your trouble?"

Howl stroked his beard and leaned eagerly forward. But Pooka said, "No, we've taken enough from you already." He sniffed hard, then spun glamour around them to make them disappear.

Percival's startled expression was followed quickly by his

hand marking the sign of the cross. A moment later, however, he turned his charger down the right hand path.

A brisk winter wind stirred through the trees as they watched him go. Pooka hugged himself, shivering like someone who did not expect to see another summer.

Closing Time

❧～❧

Neil Gaiman

Neil Gaiman [www.neilgaiman.com] lives in Menominee, Wisconsin, and travels incessantly. His publications and accomplishments are too numerous to list. For over twenty years as a professional writer, Neil Gaiman has been one of the top writers in modern comics. He is the creator and writer of monthly DC Comics horror-weird series, Sandman, of which Norman Mailer said, "Along with all else, Sandman is a comic strip for intellectuals, and I say it's about time." He is now a bestselling novelist whose most recent novel for adults, American Gods, was awarded the Hugo, Nebula, Bram Stoker, SFX, and Locus awards, while his children's novel Coraline has been an international bestseller and an enormous critical success. Neil Gaiman is a star. In 2004 Mirror Mask, a film written by Neil Gaiman and directed by Dave McKean, will be released. Some of his short fiction is collected in Angels and Visitations (1993) and Smoke and Mirrors: Short Fictions and Illusions (1998).

"Closing Time," from McSweeney's Thrilling Tales, is a classic tale told to elderly men in a club, with a twist ending. It is an ambiguous ghost story, not overtly fantasy, but with a weird twist that makes it uncanny. It reminds us of the fiction of Gene Wolfe and Robert Aickman.

There are still clubs in London. Old ones, and mock-old, with elderly sofas and crackling fireplaces, newspapers, and traditions of speech or of silence, and new clubs, the Groucho and its many knockoffs, where actors and journalists go to be seen, to drink, to enjoy their glowering solitude, or even to talk. I have friends in both kinds of club, but am not myself a member of any club in London, not anymore.

Years ago, half a lifetime, when I was a young journalist, I joined a club. It existed solely to take advantage of the licensing laws of the day, which forced all pubs to stop serving drinks at eleven PM, closing time. This club, the Diogenes, was a one-room affair located above a record shop in a narrow alley just off the Tottenham Court Road. It was owned by a cheerful, chubby, alcohol-fueled woman called Nora, who would tell anyone who asked and even if they didn't that she'd called the club the Diogenes, darling, because she was still looking for an honest man. Up a narrow flight of steps, and, at Nora's whim, the door to the club would be open, or not. It kept irregular hours.

It was a place to go once the pubs closed, that was all it ever was, and despite Nora's doomed attempts to serve food or even to send out a cheery monthly newsletter to all her club's members reminding them that the club now served food, that was all it would ever be. I was saddened several years ago when I heard that Nora had died; and I was struck, to my surprise, with a real sense of desolation last month when, on a visit to England, walking down that alley, I tried to figure out where the Diogenes Club had been, and looked first in the wrong place, then saw the faded green cloth awnings shading the windows of a tapas restaurant above a mobile phone shop, and, painted on them, a stylized man in a barrel. It seemed almost indecent, and it set me remembering.

There were no fireplaces in the Diogenes Club, and no armchairs either, but still, stories were told there.

Most of the people drinking there were men, although women passed through from time to time, and Nora had recently acquired a glamorous permanent fixture in the shape of a deputy, a blonde Polish émigré who called everybody "darlink" and who helped herself to drinks whenever she got behind the bar. When she got drunk, she would tell us that she was by rights a countess, back in Poland, and swear us all to secrecy.

There were actors and writers, of course. Film editors, broadcasters, police inspectors, and drunks. People who did not keep fixed hours. People who stayed out too late, or who did not want to go home. Some nights there might be a dozen people there, or more. Other nights I'd wander in and I'd be the only person there—on those occasions I'd buy myself a single drink, drink it down, and then leave.

That night, it was raining, and there were four of us in the club after midnight.

Nora and her deputy were sitting up at the bar, working on their sitcom. It was about a chubby-but-cheerful woman who owned a drinking club, and her scatty deputy, an aristocratic foreign blonde who made amusing English mistakes. It would be like *Cheers*, Nora used to tell people. She named the comical Jewish landlord after me. Sometimes they would ask me to read a script.

The rest of us were sitting over by the window: an actor named Paul (commonly known as Paul-the-actor, to stop people confusing him with Paul-the-police-inspector or Paul-the-struck-off-plastic-surgeon, who were also regulars), a computer gaming magazine editor named Martyn, and me. We knew each other vaguely, and the three of us sat at a table by the window and watched the rain come down, misting and blurring the lights of the alley.

There was another man there, older by far than any of the three of us. He was cadaverous, and gray-haired and painfully thin, and he sat alone in the corner and nursed a single whiskey. The elbows of his tweed jacket were patched with brown leather, I remember that quite vividly.

He did not talk to us, or read, or do anything. He just sat, looking out at the rain and the alley beneath, and, sometimes, he sipped his whisky without any visible pleasure.

It was almost midnight, and Paul and Martyn and I had started telling ghost stories. I had just finished telling them a sworn-true ghostly account from my school days: the tale of the Green Hand. It had been an article of faith at my prep school that there was a disembodied, luminous hand that was seen, from time to time, by unfortunate schoolboys. If you saw the Green Hand you would die soon after. Fortunately, none of us were ever unlucky enough to encounter it, but there were sad tales of boys there before our time, boys who saw the Green Hand and whose thirteen-year-old hair had turned white overnight. According to school legend they were taken to the sanatorium, where they would expire after a week or so without ever being able to utter another word.

"Hang on," said Paul-the-actor. "If they never uttered another word, how did anyone know they'd seen the Green Hand? I mean, they could have seen anything."

As a boy, being told the stories, I had not thought to ask this, and now that it was pointed out to me it did seem somewhat problematic.

"Perhaps they wrote something down," I suggested, a bit lamely.

We batted it about for a while, and agreed that the Green Hand was a most unsatisfactory sort of ghost. Then Paul told us a true story about a friend of his who had picked up a hitchhiker, and dropped her off at a place she said was her house, and when he went back the next morning, it turned out to be a cemetery. I mentioned that exactly the same thing had happened to a friend of mine as well. Martyn said that it had not only happened to a friend of his, but, because the hitchhiking girl looked so cold, the friend had lent her his coat, and the next morning, in the cemetery, he found his coat all neatly folded on her grave.

Martyn went and got another round of drinks, and we wondered why all these ghost-women were zooming around the country all night and hitchhiking home, and

Martyn said that probably living hitchhikers these days were the exception, not the rule.

And then one of us said, "I'll tell you a true story, if you like. It's a story I've never told a living soul. It's true—it happened to me, not to a friend of mine—but I don't know if it's a ghost story. It probably isn't."

This was over twenty years ago. I have forgotten so many things, but I have not forgotten that night, nor how it ended.

This is the story that was told that night, in the Diogenes Club.

I was nine years old, or thereabouts, in the late 1960s, and I was attending a small private school not far from my home. I was only at that school less than a year—long enough to take a dislike to the school's owner, who had bought the school in order to close it, and to sell the prime land on which it stood to property developers, which, shortly after I left, she did.

For a long time—a year or more—after the school closed the building stood empty before it was finally demolished and replaced by offices. Being a boy, I was also a burglar of sorts, and one day before it was knocked down, curious, I went back there. I wriggled through a half-opened window and walked through empty classrooms that still smelled of chalk dust. I took only one thing from my visit, a painting I had done in Art of a little house with a red doorknocker like a devil or an imp. It had my name on it, and it was up on a wall. I took it home.

When the school was still open I walked home each day, through the town, then down a dark road cut through sandstone hills and all grown over with trees, and past an abandoned gatehouse. Then there would be light, and the road would go past fields, and finally I would be home.

Back then there were so many old houses and estates, Victorian relics that stood in an empty half-life awaiting the bulldozers that would transform them and their ramshackle grounds into blandly identical landscapes of desirable modern residences, every house neatly arranged side by side around roads that went nowhere.

The other children I encountered on my way home were, in my memory, always boys. We did not know each other, but, like guerrillas in occupied territory, we would exchange information. We were scared of adults, not each other. We did not have to know each other to run in twos or threes or in packs.

The day that I'm thinking of, I was walking home from school, and I met three boys in the road where it was at its darkest. They were looking for something in the ditches and the hedges and the weed-choked place in front of the abandoned gatehouse. They were older than me.

"What are you looking for?"

The tallest of them, a beanpole of a boy, with dark hair and a sharp face, said, "Look!" He held up several ripped-in-half pages from what must have been a very, very old pornographic magazine. The girls were all in black and white, and their hairstyles looked like the ones my great-aunts had in old photographs. The magazine had been ripped up, and fragments of it had blown all over the road and into the abandoned gatehouse front garden.

I joined in the paper chase. Together, the three of us retrieved almost a whole copy of *The Gentleman's Relish* from that dark place. Then we climbed over a wall, into a deserted apple orchard, and looked at it. Naked women from a long time ago. There is a smell, of fresh apples, and of rotten apples moldering down into cider, which even today brings back the idea of the forbidden to me.

The smaller boys, who were still bigger than I was, were called Simon and Douglas, and the tall one, who might have been as old as fifteen, was called Jamie. I wondered if they were brothers. I did not ask.

When we had all looked at the magazine, they said, "We're going to hide this in our special place. Do you want to come along? You mustn't tell, if you do. You mustn't tell anyone."

They made me spit on my palm, and they spat on theirs, and we pressed our hands together.

Their special place was an abandoned metal water tower, in a field by the entrance to the lane near to where I lived. We climbed a high ladder. The tower was painted a dull green on the outside, and inside it was orange with rust that covered the floor and the walls. There was a wallet on the floor with no money in it, only some cigarette cards. Jamie showed them to me: each card held a painting of a cricketer from a long time ago. They put the pages of the magazine down on the floor of the water tower, and the wallet on top of it.

Then Douglas said, "I say we go back to the Swallows next."

My house was not far from the Swallows, a sprawling manor house set back from the road. It had been owned, my father had told me once, by the Earl of Tenterden, but when he had died his son, the new earl, had simply closed the place up. I had wandered to the edges of the grounds, but had not gone farther in. It did not feel abandoned. The gardens were too well cared for, and where there were gardens there were gardeners. Somewhere there had to be an adult.

I told them this.

Jamie said, "Bet there's not. Probably just someone who comes in and cuts the grass once a month or something. You're not scared, are you? We've been there hundreds of times. Thousands."

Of course I was scared, and of course I said that I was not. We went up the main drive, until we reached the main gates. They were closed, and we squeezed beneath the bars to get in.

Rhododendron bushes lined the drive. Before we got to the house there was what I took to be a groundskeeper's cottage, and beside it on the grass were some rusting metal cages, big enough to hold a hunting dog, or a boy. We walked past them, up to a horseshoe-shaped drive and right up to the front door of the Swallows. We peered inside, looking in the windows, but seeing nothing. It was too dark inside.

We slipped around the house, into a rhododendron

thicket and out again, into some kind of fairyland. It was a magical grotto, all rocks and delicate ferns and odd, exotic plants I'd never seen before: plants with purple leaves, and leaves like fronds, and small half-hidden flowers like jewels. A tiny stream wound through it, a rill of water running from rock to rock.

Douglas said, "I'm going to wee-wee in it." It was very matter-of-fact. He walked over to it, pulled down his shorts, and urinated in the stream, splashing on the rocks. The other boys did it too, both of them pulling out their penises and standing beside him to piss into the stream.

I was shocked. I remember that. I suppose I was shocked by the joy they took in this, or just by the way they were doing something like that in such a special place, spoiling the clear water and the magic of the place, making it into a toilet. It seemed wrong.

When they were done, they did not put their penises away. They shook them. They pointed them at me. Jamie had hair growing at the base of his.

"We're cavaliers," said Jamie. "Do you know what that means?"

I knew about the English Civil War, Cavaliers (wrong but romantic) versus Roundheads (right but repulsive), but I didn't think that was what he was talking about. I shook my head.

"It means our willies aren't circumcised," he explained. "Are you a cavalier or a roundhead?"

I knew what they meant now. I muttered, "I'm a round-head."

"Show us. Go on. Get it out."

"No. It's none of your business."

For a moment, I thought things were going to get nasty, but then Jamie laughed, and put his penis away, and the others did the same. They told dirty jokes to each other then, jokes I really didn't understand at all, for all that I was a bright child, but I heard them and remembered them, and several weeks later was almost expelled from school for telling one of them to a boy who went home and told it to his parents.

The joke had the word fuck in it. That was the first time I ever heard the word, in a dirty joke in a fairy grotto.

The principal called my parents into the school, after I got in trouble, and said that I'd said something so bad they could not repeat it, not even to tell my parents what I'd done.

My mother asked me, when they got home that night.

"Fuck," I said.

"You must never, ever say that word," said my mother. She said this very firmly, and quietly, and for my own good. "That is the worst word anyone can say." I promised her that I wouldn't.

But after, amazed at the power a single word could have, I would whisper it to myself, when I was alone.

In the grotto, that autumn afternoon after school, the three big boys told jokes and they laughed and they laughed, and I laughed too, although I did not understand any of what they were laughing about.

We moved on from the grotto. Out into the formal gardens, and over a small bridge that crossed a pond; we crossed it nervously, because it was out in the open, but we could see huge goldfish in the blackness of the pond below, which made it worthwhile. Then Jamie led Douglas and Simon and me down a gravel path into some woodland.

Unlike the gardens, the woods were abandoned and unkempt. They felt like there was no one around. The path was grown over. It led between trees, and then, after a while, into a clearing.

In the clearing was a little house.

It was a playhouse, built perhaps forty years earlier for a child, or for children. The windows were Tudor-style, leaded and crisscrossed into diamonds. The roof was mock-Tudor. A stone path led straight from where we were to the front door.

Together, we walked up the path to the door.

Hanging from the door was a metal knocker. It was painted crimson, and had been cast in the shape of some kind of imp, some kind of grinning pixie or demon, cross-legged, hanging by its hands from a hinge. Let me see . . .

how can I describe this best: it wasn't a good thing. The expression on its face, for starters. I found myself wondering what kind of a person would hang something like that on a playroom door.

It frightened me, there in that clearing, with the dusk gathering under the trees. I walked away from the house, back to a safe distance, and the others followed me.

"I think I have to go home now," I said.

It was the wrong thing to say. The three of them turned and laughed and jeered at me, called me pathetic, called me a baby. They weren't scared of the house, they said.

"I dare you!" said Jamie. "I dare you to knock on the door."

I shook my head.

"If you don't knock on the door," said Douglas, "you're too much of a baby ever to play with us again."

I had no desire ever to play with them again. They seemed like occupants of a land I was not yet ready to enter. But still, I did not want them to think me a baby.

"Go on. We're not scared," said Simon.

I try to remember the tone of voice he used. Was he frightened too, and covering it with bravado? Or was he amused? It's been so long. I wish I knew.

I walked slowly back up the flagstone path to the house. I reached up, grabbed the grinning imp in my right hand, and banged it hard against the door.

Or rather, I tried to bang it hard, just to show the other three that I was not afraid at all. That I was not afraid of anything. But something happened, something I had not expected, and the knocker hit the door with a muffled sort of a thump.

"Now you have to go inside!" shouted Jamie. He was excited. I could hear it. I found myself wondering if they had known about this place already, before we came. If I was the first person they had brought there.

But I did not move.

"You go in," I said. "I knocked on the door. I did it like you said. Now you have to go inside. I dare you. I dare all of you."

I wasn't going in. I was perfectly certain of that. Not then. Not ever. I'd felt something move; I'd felt the knocker twist under my hand as I'd banged that grinning imp down on the door. I was not so old that I would deny my own senses.

They said nothing. They did not move.

Then, slowly, the door fell open. Perhaps they thought that I, standing by the door, had pushed it open. Perhaps they thought that I'd jarred it when I knocked. But I hadn't. I was certain of it. It opened because it was ready.

I should have run, then. My heart was pounding in my chest. But the devil was in me, and instead of running I looked at the three big boys at the bottom of the path, and I simply said, "Or are you scared?"

They walked up the path toward the little house.

"It's getting dark," said Douglas.

Then the three boys walked past me, and one by one, reluctantly perhaps, they entered the playhouse. A white face turned to look at me as they went into that room, to ask why I wasn't following them in, I'll bet. But as Simon, who was the last of them, walked in, the door banged shut behind them, and I swear to God I did not touch it.

The imp grinned down at me from the wooden door, a vivid splash of crimson in the gray gloaming.

I walked around to the side of the playhouse and peered in through all the windows, one by one, into the dark and empty room. Nothing moved in there. I wondered if the other three were inside hiding from me, pressed against the wall, trying their damnedest to stifle their giggles. I wondered if it was a big-boy game.

I didn't know. I couldn't tell.

I stood there in the courtyard of the playhouse, while the sky got darker, just waiting. The moon rose after a while, a big autumn moon the color of honey.

And then, after a while, the door opened, and nothing came out.

Now I was alone in the glade, as alone as if there had never been anyone else there at all. An owl hooted, and I realized that I was free to go. I turned and walked away, following a different path out of the glade, always keeping my distance from the main house. I climbed a fence in the moonlight, ripping the seat of my school shorts, and I walked—not ran, I didn't need to run—across a field of barley stubble, and over a stile, and into a flinty lane that would take me, if I followed it far enough, all the way to my house.

And soon enough, I was home.

My parents had not been worried, although they were irritated by the orange rust-dust on my clothes, by the rip in my shorts. "Where were you, anyway?" my mother asked.

"I went for a walk," I said. "I lost track of time."

And that was where we left it.

It was almost two in the morning. The Polish countess had already gone. Now Nora began, noisily, to collect up the glasses and ashtrays, and to wipe down the bar. "This place is haunted," she said, cheerfully. "Not that it's ever bothered me. I like a bit of company, darlings. If I didn't, I wouldn't have opened the club. Now, don't you have homes to go to?"

We said our good nights to Nora and she made each of us kiss her on her cheek, and she closed the door of the Diogenes Club behind us. We walked down the narrow steps past the record shop, down into the alley and back into civilization.

The underground had stopped running hours ago, but there were always night buses, and cabs still out there for those who could afford them. (I couldn't. Not in those days.)

The Diogenes Club itself closed several years later, finished off by Nora's cancer, and, I suppose, by the easy availability of late-night alcohol once the English licensing laws were changed. But I rarely went back after that night.

"Was there ever," asked Paul-the-actor, as we hit the street, "any news of those three boys? Did you see them again? Or were they reported as missing?"

"Neither," said the storyteller. "I mean, I never saw them again. And there was no local manhunt for three missing boys. Or if there was, I never heard about it."

"Is the playhouse still there?" asked Martyn.

"I don't know," admitted the storyteller.

"Well," said Martyn, as we reached the Tottenham Court Road, and headed for the night bus stop, "I for one do not believe a word of it."

There were four of us, not three, out on the street long after closing time. I should have mentioned that before. There was still one of us who had not spoken, the elderly man with the leather elbow-patches, who had left the club when the three of us had left. And now he spoke for the first time.

"I believe it," he said, mildly. His voice was frail, almost apologetic. "I cannot explain it, but I believe it. Jamie died, you know, not long after Father did. It was Douglas who wouldn't go back, who sold the old place. He wanted them to tear it all down. But they kept the house itself, the Swallows. They weren't going to knock that down. I imagine that everything else must be gone by now."

It was a cold night, and the rain still spat occasional drizzle. I shivered, but only because I was cold.

"Those cages you mentioned," he said. "By the driveway. I haven't thought of them in fifty years. When we were bad he'd lock us up in them. We must have been bad a great deal, eh? Very naughty, naughty boys."

He was looking up and down the Tottenham Court Road, as if he were looking for something. Then he said, "Douglas killed himself, of course. Ten years ago. When I was still in the bin. So my memory's not as good. Not as good as it was. But that was Jamie all right, to the life. He'd never let us forget that he was the oldest. And you know, we weren't ever allowed in the playhouse. Father didn't build it for us." His voice quavered, and for a moment I could imagine this pale old man as a boy again. "Father had his own games."

And then he waved his arm and called "Taxi!" and a taxi pulled over to the curb. "Brown's Hotel," said the man, and he got in. He did not say good night to any of us. He pulled shut the door of the cab.

And in the closing of the cab door I could hear too many other doors closing. Doors in the past, which are gone now, and cannot be reopened.

Catskin

Kelly Link

Kelly Link [www.kellylink.net] lives in Northampton, Massachusetts. She and her partner Gavin Grant are the publishers of Small Beer Press, one of the more distinguished small presses in the field, and of Lady Churchill's Rosebud Wristlet, *a literary magazine (zine) with a bent toward the fantastic. She is one of the best of the younger fiction writers in the field. Her self-published collection of stories,* Stranger Things Happen, *has been widely and deservedly praised. In 2003 she edited the cross genre/slipstream anthology,* Trampoline. *She doesn't hesitate to identify herself as a genre writer. "I still think of myself, if not as a science fiction writer, then as a wanna-be science fiction writer. It frustrates me when people try to very narrowly define things. There's no point to it ... So I reached a certain point where I just thought, 'I'm going to define genre very loosely ... I'll call it genre to suit myself,'" she says in an interview with Gabriel J. Mesa [www.milkofmedusa.com/article_link.htm]. "As for fantasy, I don't know why I write it. It was the first kind of story that I read."*

"Catskin," another story from McSweeney's Thrilling Tales, *is a real fantasy story, with all the fascination and horror of a fairy tale but with a slightly postmodern ending. It has a fine literary fairy tale feel to it and lovely surreal imagery.*

Cars went in and out of the witch's house all day long. The windows stayed open, and the doors, and there were other doors, cat-sized and private, in the walls and up in the attic. The cats were large and sleek and silent. No one knew their names, or even if they had names, except for the witch.

Some of the cats were cream-colored and some were brindled. Some were black as beetles. They were about the witch's business. Some came into the witch's bedroom with live things in their mouths. When they came out again, their mouths were empty.

The cats trotted and slunk and leapt and crouched. They were busy. Their movements were catlike, or perhaps clockwork. Their tails twitched like hairy pendulums. They paid no attention to the witch's children.

The witch had three living children at this time, although at one time she had had dozens, maybe more. No one, certainly not the witch, had ever bothered to tally them up. But at one time the house had bulged with cats and babies.

Now, since witches cannot have children in the usual way—their wombs are full of straw or bricks or stones, and when they give birth, they give birth to rabbits, kittens, tadpoles, houses, silk dresses, and yet even witches must have heirs, even witches wish to be mothers—the witch had acquired her children by other means: she had stolen or bought or made them.

She'd had a passion for children with a certain color of red hair. Twins she had never been able to abide (they were the wrong kind of magic) although she'd sometimes attempted to match up sets of children, as though she had been putting together a chess set, and not a family. If you were to say *a witch's chess set*, instead of *a witch's family*, there would be some truth in that. Perhaps this is true of other families as well.

One girl she had grown like a cyst, upon her thigh. Other children she had made out of things in her garden, or bits of trash that the cats brought her: aluminum foil with strings of chicken fat still crusted to it, broken television sets, cardboard boxes that the neighbors had thrown out. She had always been a thrifty witch.

Some of these children had run away and others had died. Some of them she had simply misplaced, or accidentally left behind on buses. It is to be hoped that these children were later adopted into good homes, or reunited with their natural parents. If you are looking for a happy ending in this story, then perhaps you should stop reading here and picture these children, these parents, their reunions.

Are you still reading? The witch, up in her bedroom, was dying. She had been poisoned by an enemy, a witch, a man named Lack. The child Finn, who had been her food taster, was dead already and so were three cats who'd licked her dish clean. The witch knew who had killed her and she snatched pieces of time, here and there, from the business of dying, to make her revenge. Once the question of this revenge had been settled to her satisfaction, the shape of it like a black ball of twine in her head, she began to divide up her estate between her three remaining children.

Flecks of vomit stuck to the corners of her mouth, and there was a basin beside the foot of the bed which was full of black liquid. The room smelled like cats' piss and wet matches. The witch panted as if she were giving birth to her own death.

"Flora shall have my automobile," she said, "and also my purse, which will never be empty, so long as you always leave a coin at the bottom, my darling, my spendthrift, my profligate, my drop of poison, my pretty, pretty Flora. And when I am dead, take the road outside the house and go west. There's one last piece of advice."

Flora, who was the oldest of the witch's living children, was red-headed and stylish. She had been waiting for the witch's death for a long time now, although she had been patient. She kissed the witch's cheek and said, "Thank you, Mother."

The witch looked up at her, panting. She could see Flora's life, already laid out, flat as a map. Perhaps all mothers can see as far.

"Jack, my love, my bird's nest, my bite, my scrap of porridge," the witch said, "you shall have my books. I won't have any need of books where I am going. And when you leave my house, strike out in an an easterly direction and you won't be any sorrier than you are now."

Jack, who had once been a little bundle of feathers and twigs and eggshell all tied up with a tatty piece of string, was a sturdy lad, almost full grown. If he knew how to read, only the cats knew it. But he nodded and kissed his mother, one kiss on each staring eye, and one on her gray lips.

"And what shall I leave to my boy Small?" the witch said, convulsing. She threw up again in the basin. Cats came running, leaning on the lip of the basin to inspect her vomitus. The witch's hand dug into Small's leg.

"Oh, it is hard, hard, so very hard, for a mother to leave her children (though I have done harder things). Children need a mother, even such a mother as I have been." She wiped at her eyes, and yet it is a fact that witches cannot cry.

Small, who still slept in the witch's bed, was the youngest of the witch's children. (Perhaps not as young as you think.) He sat upon the bed, and although he didn't cry, it was only because witches' children have no one to teach them the use of crying. His heart was breaking.

Small was ten years old and he could juggle and sing and every morning he brushed and plaited the witch's long, silky hair. Surely every mother must wish for a boy like Small, a curly-headed, sweet-breathed, tenderhearted boy like Small, who can cook a fine omelet, and who has a good strong singing voice as well as a gentle hand with a hairbrush.

"Mother," he said, "if you must die, then you must die. And if I can't come along with you, then I'll do my best to live and make you proud. Give me your hairbrush to remember you by, and I'll go make my own way in the world."

"You shall have my hairbrush, then," said the witch to Small, looking, and panting, panting. "And I love you best of all. You shall have my tinderbox and my matches, and also my revenge, and you will make me proud, or I don't know my own children."

"What shall we do with the house, Mother?" said Jack. He said it as if he didn't care.

"When I am dead," the witch said, "this house will be of no use to anyone. I gave birth to it—that was a very long time ago—and raised it from just a dollhouse. Oh, it was the most dear, most darling dollhouse ever. It had eight rooms and a tin roof, and a staircase that went nowhere at all. But I nursed it and rocked it to sleep in a cradle, and it grew up to be a real house, and see how it has taken care of me, its parent, how it knows a child's duty to its mother. And perhaps you can see how it is now, how it pines, how it grows sick to see me dying like this. Leave it to the cats. They'll know what to do with it."

All this time the cats have been running in and out of the room, bringing things and taking things away. It seems as if they will never slow down, never come to rest, never nap, never have the time to sleep, or to die, or even to mourn. They have a certain proprietary look about them, as if the house is already theirs.

The witch vomits up mud, fur, glass buttons, tin soldiers, trowels, hat pins, thumbtacks, love letters (mislabeled or sent without the appropriate amount of postage and never read), and a dozen regiments of red ants, each ant as long and wide as a kidney bean. The ants swim across the perilous stinking basin, clamber up the sides of the basin, and go marching across the floor in a shiny ribbon. They are carrying pieces of time in their mandibles. Time is heavy, even in such small pieces, but the ants have strong jaws, strong legs. Across the floor they go, and up the wall, and out the window. The cats watch, but don't interfere. The witch gasps and coughs and then lies still. Her hands beat against the bed once and then are still. Still the children wait, to make sure that she is dead, and that she has nothing else to say.

In the witch's house, the dead are sometimes quite talkative.

But the witch has nothing else to say at this time.

The house groans and all the cats begin to mew piteously, trotting in and out of the room as if they have dropped something and must go and hunt for it—they will never find it—and the children, at last, suddenly know how to cry, but the witch is perfectly still and quiet. There is a tiny smile on her face, as if everything has happened exactly to her satisfaction. Or maybe she is looking forward to the next part of the story.

The children buried the witch in one of her half-grown dollhouses. They crammed her into the downstairs parlor, and knocked out the inner walls so that her head rested on the kitchen table in the breakfast nook, and her ankles threaded through a bedroom door. Small brushed out her hair, and, because he wasn't sure what she should wear now that she was dead, he put all her dresses on her, one over the other over the other, until he could hardly see her white limbs at all, beneath the stack of petticoats and coats and dresses. It didn't matter: Once they'd nailed the dollhouse shut again, all they could see was the red crown of her head in the kitchen window, and the worn-down heels of her dancing shoes knocking against the shutters of the bedroom window.

Jack, who was handy, rigged a set of wheels for the dollhouse, and a harness so that it could be pulled. They put the harness on Small, and Small pulled and Flora pushed, and

Jack talked and coaxed the house along, over the hill, down to the cemetery, and the cats ran along beside them.

The cats are beginning to look a bit shabby, as if they are molting. Their mouths look very empty. The ants have marched away, through the woods, and down into town, and they have built a nest on your yard, out of the bits of time. And if you hold a magnifying glass over their nest, to see the ants dance and burn, Time will catch fire and you will be sorry.

Outside the cemetery gates, the cats had been digging a grave for the witch. The children tipped the dollhouse into the grave, kitchen window first. But then they saw that the grave wasn't deep enough, and the house sat there on its end, looking uncomfortable. Small began to cry (now that he'd learned how, it seemed he would spend all his time practicing), thinking how horrible it would be to spend one's death, all of eternity, upside down and not even properly buried, not even able to feel the rain when it beat down on the exposed shingles of the house, and seeped down into the house and filled your mouth and drowned you, so that you had to die all over again, every time it rained.

The dollhouse chimney had broken off and fallen on the ground. One of the cats picked it up and carried it away, like a souvenir. That cat carried the chimney into the woods and ate it, a mouthful at a time, and passed out of this story and into another one. It's no concern of ours.

The other cats began to carry up mouthfuls of dirt, dropping it and mounding it around the house with their paws. The children helped, and when they'd finished, they'd managed to bury the witch properly, so that only the bedroom window was visible, a little pane of glass like an eye at the top of a small dirt hill.

On the way home, Flora began to flirt with Jack. Perhaps she liked the way he looked in his funeral black. They

talked about what they planned to be, now that they were
grown-up. Flora wanted to find her parents. She was a
pretty girl; someone would want to look after her. Jack said
he would like to marry someone rich. They began to make
plans.

Small walked a little behind, slippery cats twining around
his ankles. He had the witch's hairbrush in his pocket, and
his fingers slipped around the figured horn handle for comfort.

The house, when they reached it, had a dangerous, grief-
stricken look to it, as if it was beginning to pull away from
itself. Flora and Jack wouldn't go back inside. They
squeezed Small lovingly, and asked if he wouldn't want to
come along with them. He would have liked to, but who
would have looked after the witch's cats, the witch's revenge? So he watched as they drove off together. They went
north. What child has ever heeded a mother's advice?

Jack hasn't even bothered to bring along the witch's library:
He says there isn't space in the trunk for everything. He'll
rely on Flora and her magic purse.

Small sat in the garden, and ate stalks of grass when he was
hungry, and pretended that the grass was bread and milk
and chocolate cake. He drank out of the garden hose. When
it began to grow dark, he was lonelier than he had ever been
in his life. The witch's cats were not good company. He said
nothing to them and they had nothing to tell him, about the
house, or the future, or the witch's revenge, or about where
he was supposed to sleep. He had never slept anywhere except in the witch's bed, so at last he went back over the hill
and down to the cemetery.

Some of the cats were still going up and down the grave,
covering the base of the mound with leaves and grass,
birds' feathers and their own loose fur. This looked
strange, but it was a soft sort of nest to lie down on, Small

discovered. The cats were still busy when he fell asleep—
cats are always busy—cheek pressed against the cool glass
of the bedroom window, hand curled in his pocket around
the hairbrush, but in the middle of the night, when he
woke up, he was swaddled, head to foot, in warm, grass-
scented cat bodies.

A tail is curled around his chin like a scarf, and all the bodies are soughing breath in and out, whiskers and paws
twitching, silky bellies rising and falling. All the cats are
sleeping a frantic, exhausted, busy sleep, except for one, a
white cat who sits near his head, looking down at him.
Small has never seen this cat before, and yet he knows her,
the way that you know the people who visit you in dreams:
She's white everywhere, except for reddish tufts and frills at
her ears and tail and paws, as if someone has embroidered
her with fire around the edges.

"What's your name?" Small says. He's never talked to the
witch's cats before.

The cat lifts a leg and licks herself in a private place. Then
she looks at him. "You may call me Mother," she says.

But Small shakes his head. He can't call the cat that.
Down under the blanket of cats, under the pane of window
glass, the witch's Spanish heel is drinking in moonlight.

"Very well then, you may call me The Witch's Revenge," the cat says. Her mouth doesn't move, but he
hears her speak inside his head. Her voice is furry and
sharp, like a blanket made out of needles. "And you may
comb my fur."

Small sits up, displacing sleepy cats, and lifts the brush
out of his pocket. The bristles have left rows of little holes
indented in the pink palm of his hand, like some sort of
code. If he could read the code, it would say: Comb my fur.

Small combs the fur of The Witch's Revenge. There's
grave dirt in the cat's fur, and one or two red ants, who
drop and scurry away. The Witch's Revenge bends her head
down to the ground, snaps them up in her jaws. The heap of

cats around them is yawning and stretching. There are things to do.

"You must burn her house down," The Witch's Revenge says. "That's the first thing."

Small's comb catches a knot, and The Witch's Revenge turns and nips him on the wrist. Then she licks him in the tender place between his thumb and his first finger. "That's enough," she says. "There's work to do."

So they all go back to the house, Small stumbling in the dark, moving farther and farther away from the witch's grave, the cats trotting along, their eyes lit like torches, twigs and branches in their mouths, as if they plan to build a nest, a canoe, a fence to keep the world out. The house, when they reach it, is full of lights, and more cats, and piles of tinder. The house is making a noise, like an instrument that someone is breathing into. Small realizes that all the cats are mewing, endlessly, as they run in and out the doors, looking for more kindling. The Witch's Revenge says, "First we must latch all the doors."

So Small shuts all the doors and windows on the first floor, and The Witch's Revenge shuts the catches on the secret doors, the cat doors, the doors in the attic, and up on the roof, and the cellar doors. Not a single secret door is left open. Now all the noise is on the inside, and Small and The Witch's Revenge are on the outside.

All the cats have slipped into the house through the kitchen door. There isn't a single cat in the garden. Small can see the witch's cats through the windows, arranging their piles of twigs. The Witch's Revenge sits beside him, watching. "Now light a match and throw it in," says The Witch's Revenge.

Small lights a match. He throws it in. What boy doesn't love to start a fire?

"Now shut the kitchen door," says The Witch's Revenge, but Small can't do that. All the cats are inside. The Witch's Revenge stands on her hind paws and pushes the kitchen door shut. Inside, the lit match catches something on fire. Fire runs along the floor and up the kitchen walls. Cats catch fire, and run into the other rooms of the house. Small can see all this through the windows. He stands with his face against the glass, which is cold, and then warm, and then hot. Burning cats with burning twigs in their mouths press up against the kitchen door, and the other doors of the house, but all the doors are locked. Small and The Witch's Revenge stand in the garden and watch the witch's house and the witch's books and the witch's sofas and the witch's cooking pots and the witch's cats, her cats, too, all her cats burn.

You should never burn down a house. You should never set a cat on fire. You should never watch and do nothing while a house is burning. You should never listen to a cat who says to do any of these things. You should listen to your mother when she tells you to come away from watching, to go to bed, to go to sleep. You should listen to your mother's revenge.

You should never poison a witch.

In the morning, Small woke up in the garden. Soot covered him in a greasy blanket. The Witch's Revenge, white and red and clean-smelling, was curled up asleep on his chest. The witch's house was still standing, but the windows had melted and run down the front of the house.

The Witch's Revenge, waking, licked Small clean with her small sharkskin tongue. She demanded to be combed. Then she went into the house and came out, carrying a little bundle. It dangled, boneless, from her mouth, like a kitten.

It is a catskin, Small sees, only there is no longer a cat inside it.

* * *

He picked it up and something shiny fell out of the loose light skin. It was a piece of gold, sloppy, slippery with fat. The Witch's Revenge brought out dozens and dozens of catskins, and there was a gold piece in every skin. While Small counted his fortune, The Witch's Revenge bit off one of her own claws, and pulled one long witch hair out of the witch's comb. She sat up, like a tailor, cross-legged in the grass, and began to stitch up a bag, out of the many catskins.

Small shivered. There was nothing to eat for breakfast but grass, and the grass was black and cooked.

"Are you cold?" said The Witch's Revenge. She put the bag aside, and picked up another catskin, a fine black one. She slit a sharp claw down the middle. "We'll make you a warm suit."

She used the coat of a black cat, and the coat of a calico cat, and she put a trim around the paws, of gray and white striped fur.

While she did this, she said to Small, "Did you know that there was once a battle, fought on this very patch of ground?"

Small shook his head no.

"Wherever there's a garden," The Witch's Revenge said, scratching with one paw at the ground, "I promise you there are people buried down under it. Look here." She plucked up a little brown clot, put it in her mouth, and cleaned it with her tongue.

When she spat the little circle out again, Small saw it was an ivory regimental button. The Witch's Revenge dug more buttons out of the ground—as if buttons of ivory grew in the ground—and sewed them onto the catskin. She fashioned a hood with two eyeholes and a set of fine whiskers, and sewed four fine cat tails to the back of the suit, as if the one that grew there wasn't good enough for Small. She threaded a bell on each one. "Put this on," she said to Small.

He does and the bells chime and The Witch's Revenge laughs. "You make a fine-looking cat," she says. "Any mother would be proud."

The inside of the catsuit is soft and a little sticky against Small's skin. When he puts the hood over his head, the world disappears. He can only see the vivid corners of it through the eyeholes—grass, gold, the cat who sits cross-legged, stitching up her sack of skins—and air seeps in, down at the loosely sewn seam, where the skin droops and sags over his chest and around the gaping buttons. Small holds his tails in his clumsy fingerless paw, like a handful of eels, and swings them back and forth to hear them ring. The sound of the bells and the sooty, cooked smell of the air, the warm stickiness of the suit, the feel of his new fur against the ground: He falls asleep and dreams that hundreds of ants come and lift him and gently carry him off to bed.

When Small tipped his hood back again, he saw that The Witch's Revenge had finished with her needle and thread. Small helped her fill the bag with the gold pieces. The Witch's Revenge stood up on her hind legs, took the bag between her paws, and swung it over her shoulders. The gold coins went sliding against each other, mewling and hissing. The bag dragged along the grass, picking up ash, leaving a green trail behind it. The Witch's Revenge strode along as if she were carrying a sack of air.

Small put the hood on again, and he got down on his hands and knees. And then he trotted after The Witch's Revenge. They left the garden gate wide open, and went into the forest, toward the house where the witch Lack lives.

The forest is smaller than it used to be. Small is growing, but the forest is shrinking. Trees have been cut down. Houses have been built. Lawns rolled, roads laid. The Witch's Revenge and Small walked alongside one of the roads. A school bus rolled by: The children inside looked out their windows and laughed when they saw The Witch's Revenge striding along, and at her heels, Small, in his catsuit. Small lifted his head and peered out of his eyeholes after the school bus.

"Who lives in these houses?" he asked The Witch's Revenge.

"That's the wrong question, Small," said The Witch's Revenge, looking down at him and striding along.

Miaow, the catskin bag says. Clink.

"What's the right question then?" Small said.

"Ask me who lives under the houses," The Witch's Revenge said.

Obediently, Small said, "Who lives under the houses?"

"What a good question!" said The Witch's Revenge. "You see, not everyone can give birth to their own house. Most people give birth to children instead. And when you have children, you need houses to put them in. So children and houses: most people give birth to the first and have to build the second. The houses, that is. A long time ago, when men and women were going to build a house, they would dig a hole first. And they'd make a little room—a little, wooden, one-room house—in the hole. And they'd steal, or buy, a boy or a girl to put in the house in the hole, to live there. And then they built their house over that first little house."

"Did they make a door in the lid of the little house?" Small said.

"They did not make a door," said The Witch's Revenge.

"But then how did the girl or the boy climb out?" Small said.

"The boy or the girl stayed in that little house," said The Witch's Revenge. "They lived there all their life, and they are living in those houses still, under the other houses where the people live, and the people who live in the houses above may come and go as they please, and they don't ever think about how there are little houses with children sitting in little rooms, under their feet."

"But what about the mothers and fathers?" Small asked. "Didn't they ever go looking for their boys and girls?"

"Ah," said The Witch's Revenge. "Sometimes they did and sometimes they didn't. And after all, who was living under *their* houses? But that was a long time ago. Now people mostly bury a cat when they build their house, instead of a child. That's why we call cats *house cats*. Which is why we must walk along smartly. As you can see, there are houses under construction here."

And so there are. They walk by clearings where men are digging little holes. First Small puts his hood back and walks on two legs, and then he puts on his hood again, and goes on all fours: He makes himself as small and slinky as possible, just like a cat. But the bells on his tails jounce and the coins in the bag that The Witch's Revenge carries go clink, miaow, and the men stop their work and watch them go by.

How many witches are there in the world? Have you ever seen one? Would you know a witch if you saw one? And what would you do if you saw one? For that matter, do you know a cat when you see one? Are you sure?

Small followed The Witch's Revenge. Small grew calluses on his knees and the pads of his fingers. He would have liked to carry the bag sometimes, but it was too heavy. How heavy? You would not have been able to carry it, either.

They drank out of streams. At night they opened the catskin bag and climbed inside to sleep, and when they were hungry they licked the coins, which seemed to sweat golden fat, and always more fat. As they went, The Witch's Revenge sang a song:

> I had no mother
> and my mother had no mother
> and her mother had no mother
> and her mother had no mother
> and her mother had no mother
> and you have no mother
> to sing you
> this song

The coins in the bag sang along, miaow, miaow, and the bells on Small's tails kept the rhythm.

* * *

Every night Small combs The Witch's Revenge's fur. And every morning The Witch's Revenge licks him all over, not neglecting the places behind his ears, and at the backs of his knees. And then he puts the catsuit back on, and she grooms him all over again.

Sometimes they were in the forest, and sometimes the forest became a town, and then The Witch's Revenge would tell Small stories about the people who lived in the houses, and the children who lived in the houses under the houses. Once, in the forest, The Witch's Revenge showed Small where there had once been a house. Now there was only the stones of the foundation, covered in soft green moss, and the chimney stack, propped up with fat ropes and coils of ivy.

The Witch's Revenge rapped on the grassy ground, moving clockwise around the foundation, until both she and Small could hear a hollow sound.

The Witch's Revenge dropped to all fours and clawed at the ground, tearing it up with her paws and biting at it, until they could see a little wooden roof. The Witch's Revenge knocked on the roof, and Small lashed his tails nervously.

"Well," said The Witch's Revenge, "shall we take off the roof and let the poor child go?"

Small crept up close to the sunken roof. He put his ear against it and listened, but he heard nothing at all. "There's no one in there," he said.

"Maybe they're shy," said The Witch's Revenge. "Shall we let them out, or shall we leave them be?"

"Let them out!" said Small, but what he meant to say was, "Leave them alone!" Or maybe he said "Leave them be!" although he meant the opposite. The Witch's Revenge looked at him, and Small thought he heard something then—beneath him where he crouched, frozen—very faint: a scrabbling at the dirty, moldering roof.

Small sprang away. The Witch's Revenge picked up a stone and brought it down hard, caving the roof in. When they peered inside, there was nothing except blackness and a faint, dry smell. They waited, sitting on the ground, to see what might come out, but nothing came out, and after a while, The Witch's Revenge picked up her catskin bag, and they set off again.

For several nights after that, Small dreamed that someone, something, small and thin and cold and dirty, was following them. One night it crept away again, and Small never knew where it went. But if you come to that part of the forest, where they sat and waited by the stone foundation, perhaps you will meet the thing that they set free.

No one knew the reason for the quarrel between the witch Small's mother and the witch Lack, although the witch Small's mother had died for it. The witch Lack was a handsome man and he loved his children dearly. He had stolen them out of the cribs and beds of palaces and manors and harems. He dressed his children in silk, as befitted their station, and they wore gold crowns and ate off gold plates. They drank from cups of gold. Lack's children, it was said, lacked nothing.

Perhaps the witch Lack had made some remark about the way the witch Small's mother was raising her children, or perhaps the witch Small's mother had boasted of her children's red hair. But it might have been something else. Witches are proud and they like to quarrel.

When Small and The Witch's Revenge came at last to the house of the witch Lack, The Witch's Revenge said to Small, "Look at this monstrosity! I've produced finer turds and buried them under leaves. And the smell, like an open sewer! How can his neighbors stand the stink?"

Male witches have no wombs, and must come by their houses in other ways, or else buy them from female witches. But Small thought it was a very fine house. There was a prince or a princess at each window staring down at him, as he sat on his haunches in the driveway, beside The Witch's

Revenge. He said nothing, but he missed his brothers and sisters.

"Come along," said The Witch's Revenge. "We'll go a little ways off and wait for the witch Lack to come home."

Small followed The Witch's Revenge back into the forest, but in a little while, two of the witch Lack's children came out of the house, carrying baskets made of gold. They went into the forest as well and began to pick blackberries.

The Witch's Revenge and Small sat in the briar and watched.

Small was thinking of his brothers and sisters. He thought of the taste of blackberries, the feel of them in his mouth, which was not at all like the taste of fat. Deep in the briar, the hood of his catsuit thrown back, he pressed his face against the briar, a berry plumped against his lips. The wind went through the briar and ruffled his fur and raised gooseflesh on his skin beneath the fur.

The Witch's Revenge nestled against the small of Small's back. She was licking down a lump of knotted fur at the base of his spine. The princesses were singing.

Small decided that he would live in the briar with The Witch's Revenge. They would live on berries and spy on the children who came to pick them, and The Witch's Revenge would change her name. The name Mother was in his mouth, along with the sweet taste of the blackberries.

"Now you must go out," said The Witch's Revenge, "and be kittenish. Be playful. Chase your tail. Be shy, but don't be too shy. Don't talk to them. Let them pet you. Don't bite."

She pushed at Small's rump, and Small tumbled out of the briar, and sprawled at the feet of the witch Lack's children.

The Princess Georgia said, "Look! It's a dear little cat!"

Her sister Margaret said doubtfully, "But it has five tails. I've never seen a cat that needed so many tails. And its skin is done up with buttons and it's almost as large as you are."

Small, however, began to caper and prance. He swung his tails back and forth so that the bells rang out and then he pretended to be alarmed by this. First he ran away from his tails and then he chased his tails. The two princesses put down their baskets, half-full of blackberries, and spoke to him, calling him a silly puss.

At first he wouldn't go near them. But slowly he pretended to be won over. He allowed himself to be petted and fed blackberries. He chased a hair ribbon and he stretched out to let them admire the buttons up and down his belly. Princess Margaret's fingers tugged at his skin, then she slid one hand in between the loose catskin and Small's boy skin. He batted her hand away with a paw, and Margaret's sister Georgia said knowingly that cats didn't like to be petted on their bellies.

They were all good friends by the time The Witch's Revenge came out of the briar, standing on her hind legs and singing:

> *I have no children*
> *and my children*
> *have no children*
> *and their children*
> *have no children*
> *and their children*
> *have no whiskers*
> *and no tails*

At this sight, the Princesses Margaret and Georgia began to laugh and point. They had never heard a cat sing, or seen a cat walk on its hind legs. Small lashed his five tails furiously, and all the fur of the catskin stood up on his arched back, and they laughed at that too.

When they came back from the forest, with their baskets piled with berries, Small was stalking close at their heels, and The Witch's Revenge came walking just behind. But she left the bag of gold hidden in the briar.

That night, when the witch Lack came home, his hands were full of gifts for his children. One of his sons ran to meet him at the door and said, "Come and see what followed Margaret and Georgia home from the forest! Can we keep them?"

And the table had not been set for dinner, and the children of the witch Lack had not sat down to do their homework, and in the witch Lack's throne room, there was a cat with five tails, spinning in circles, while a second cat sat impudently upon his throne, and sang:

> Yes!
> your father's house
> is the shiniest
> brownest largest
> the most expensive
> the sweetest-smelling
> house
> that has ever
> come out of
> anyone's
> ass

The witch Lack's children began to laugh at this, until they saw the witch, their father, standing there. Then they fell silent. Small stopped spinning.

"You!" said the witch Lack.

"Me!" said The Witch's Revenge, and sprang from the throne. Before anyone knew what she was about, her jaws were fastened about the witch Lack's neck, and then she ripped out his throat. Lack opened his mouth to speak and his blood fell out, making The Witch's Revenge's fur more red, now, than white. The witch Lack fell down dead, and red ants went marching out of the hole in his neck and the hole of his mouth, and they held pieces of time in their jaws as tightly as The Witch's Revenge had held Lack's throat in hers. But she let Lack go and left him lying in his blood on the floor, and she snatched up the ants and ate them, quickly, as if she had been hungry for a very long time.

While this was happening, the witch Lack's children stood and watched and did nothing. Small sat on the floor, his tails curled about his paws. Children, all of them, they did nothing. They were too surprised. The Witch's Revenge, her belly full of ants and time, her mouth stained with blood, stood up and surveyed them.

"Go and fetch me my catskin bag," she said to Small.

Small found that he could move. Around him, the princes and princesses stayed absolutely still. The Witch's Revenge was holding them in her gaze.

"I'll need help," Small said. "The bag is too heavy for me to carry."

The Witch's Revenge yawned. She licked a paw and began to pat at her mouth. Small stood still.

"Very well," she said. "Take those big strong girls, the Princesses Margaret and Georgia, with you. They know the way."

The Princesses Margaret and Georgia, finding that they could move again, began to tremble. They gathered their courage and they went with Small, the two girls holding each other's hands, out of the throne room, not looking down at the body of their father, the witch Lack, and back into the forest.

Georgia began to weep, but the Princess Margaret said to Small: "Let us go!"

"Where will you go?" said Small. "The world is a dangerous place. There are people in it who mean you no good." He threw back his hood, and the Princess Georgia began to weep harder.

"Let us go," said the Princess Margaret. "My parents are the king and queen of a country not three days' walk from here. They will be glad to see us again."

Small said nothing. They came to the briar, and he sent the Princess Georgia in, to hunt for the catskin bag. She came out scratched and bleeding, the bag in her hand. It had caught on the briars and the end had ripped. Gold coins dripped out, like glossy drops of fat, falling on the ground.

"Your father killed my mother," said Small.

"And that cat, your mother's devil, will kill us, or worse," said Princess Margaret. "Let us go!"

Small lifted the catskin bag. There were no coins in it

now. The Princess Georgia was on her hands and knees, scooping up coins and putting them into her pockets.

"Was he a good father?" Small asked.

"He thought he was," Princess Margaret said. "But I'm not sorry he's dead. When I grow up, I will be queen. I'll make a law to put all the witches in the kingdom to death, and all their cats, as well."

At this, Small became afraid. He took up the catskin bag and ran back to the house of the witch Lack, leaving the two princesses in the forest. And whether they made their way home to the Princess Margaret's parents, or whether they fell into the hands of thieves, or whether they lived in the briar, or whether the Princess Margaret grew up and kept her promise and rid her kingdom of witches and cats, Small never knew, and neither do I, and neither shall you.

When he came back into the witch Lack's house, The Witch's Revenge saw at once what had happened. "Never mind," she said.

There were no children, no princes and princesses, in the throne room. The witch Lack's body still lay on the floor, but The Witch's Revenge had skinned it like a coney, and sewn up the skin into a bag. The bag wriggled and jerked, the sides heaving as if the witch Lack were still alive somewhere inside. The Witch's Revenge held the witchskin bag in one hand, and with the other, she was stuffing a cat into the neck of the skin. The cat wailed as it went into the bag. The bag was full of wailing. But the discarded flesh of the witch Lack lolled, slack.

There was a little pile of gold crowns on the floor beside the flayed corpse, and transparent, papery things which blew about the room, on a current of air, surprised looks on the thin, shed faces.

Cats were hiding in the corners of the room, and under the throne. "Go catch them," said The Witch's Revenge. "But leave the three prettiest alone."

"Where are the witch Lack's children?" Small said.

The Witch's Revenge nodded around the room. "As you see," she said, "I've slipped off their skins, and they were all cats underneath. They're as you see now, but if we were to wait a year or two, they would shed these skins as well and become something new. Children are always growing."

Small chased the cats around the room. They were fast, but he was faster. They were nimble, but he was nimbler. He had worn a catsuit for longer. He drove the cats down the length of the room, and The Witch's Revenge caught them and dropped them into her bag. At the end, there were only three cats left in the throne room, and they were as pretty a trio of cats as anyone could ask for. All the other cats were inside the bag.

"Well done, and quickly done, too," said The Witch's Revenge, and she took her needle and stitched shut the neck of the bag. The skin of the witch Lack smiled up at Small, and a cat put its head through his slack, stained mouth, wailing. But The Witch's Revenge sewed Lack's mouth shut too, and the hole on the other end, where a house had come out. She left only his earholes and his eyeholes and his nostrils, which were full of fur, rolled open so that the cats could breathe.

The Witch's Revenge slung the skin full of cats over her shoulder and stood up.

"Where are you going?" Small said.

"These cats have mothers and fathers," The Witch's Revenge said. "They have mothers and fathers who miss them very much."

She gazed at Small. He decided not to ask again. So he waited in the house, with the two princesses and the prince in their new catsuits, while The Witch's Revenge went down to the river. Or perhaps she took them down to the market and sold them. Or maybe she took each cat home, to its own mother and father, back to the kingdom where it had been born. Maybe she wasn't so careful to make sure that each child was returned to the right mother and father. After all, she was in a hurry, and cats look very much alike at night.

No one saw where she went: but the market is closer than the palaces of the kings and queens whose children had been stolen by the witch Lack, and the river is closer still.

When The Witch's Revenge came back to Lack's house, she looked around her. The house was beginning to stink very badly. Even Small could smell it now.

"I suppose the Princess Margaret let you fuck her," said The Witch's Revenge, as if she had been thinking about this while she ran her errands. "And that is why you let them go. I don't mind. She was a pretty puss. I might have let her go myself."

She looked at Small's face and saw that he was confused. "Never mind," she said.

She had a length of string in her paw, and a cork, which she greased with a piece of fat she had cut from the witch Lack. She threaded the cork on the string, calling it a good, quick little mouse, and greased the string as well, and she fed the wriggling cork to the tabby who had been curled up in Small's lap. And in a little while, when she had the cork again, she greased it again, and fed it to the little black cat, and then she fed it to the cat with two white forepaws, so that she had all three cats upon her string.

She sewed up the rip in the catskin bag, and Small put the gold crowns in the bag, and it was nearly as heavy as it had been before. The Witch's Revenge carried the bag, and Small took the greased string, holding it in his teeth, so the three cats were forced to run along behind him, as they left the house of the witch Lack.

Small strikes a match, and he lights the house of the dead witch, Lack, on fire, as they leave. But shit burns slowly, if at all, and that house might be burning still, if someone hasn't gone and put it out. And maybe, someday, someone will go fishing in the river near that house, and hook their line on a bag full of princes and princesses, wet and sorry and wriggling in their catsuit skins—that's one way to catch a husband or a wife.

* * *

Small and The Witch's Revenge walked without stopping and the three cats came behind them. They walked until they reached a little village very near where the witch Small's mother had lived and there they settled down in a room The Witch's Revenge rented from a butcher. They cut the greased string, and bought a cage and hung it from a hook in the kitchen. They kept the three cats in it, but Small bought collars and leashes, and sometimes he put one of the cats on a leash and took it for a walk around the town.

Sometimes he wore his own catsuit, and went out prowling, but The Witch's Revenge used to scold him if she caught him dressed like that. There are country manners and there are town manners, and Small was a boy about town now.

The Witch's Revenge kept house. She cleaned and she cooked and she made Small's bed in the morning. Like all of the witch's cats, she was always busy. She melted down the gold crowns in a stewpot, and minted them into coins. She opened an account in a bank, and she enrolled Small in a private academy.

The Witch's Revenge wore a silk dress and gloves and a heavy veil, and ran her errands in a fine carriage, Small at her side. She bought a piece of land to build a house on, and she sent Small off to school every morning, no matter how he cried. But at night she took off her clothes and slept on his pillow and he combed her red and white fur.

Sometimes at night, she twitched and moaned, and when he asked her what she was dreaming, she said, "There are ants! Can't you comb them out? Be quick and catch them if you love me."

But there were never any ants.

One day when Small came home, the little cat with the white front paws was gone. When he asked The Witch's Revenge, she said that the little cat had fallen out of the cage and through the open window and into the garden and before The Witch's Revenge could think what to do, a crow had swooped down and carried the little cat off. They moved into their new house a few months later, and Small was always very careful when he went in and out the doorway, imagining the little cat, down there in the dark, under the doorstep, under his foot.

Small got bigger. He didn't make any friends in the village, or at his school, but when you're big enough, you don't need friends.

One day while he and The Witch's Revenge were eating their dinner, there was a knock at the door. When he opened the door, there stood Flora and Jack, looking very shabby and thin. Jack looked more than ever like a bundle of sticks.

"Small!" said Flora. "How tall you've become!" She burst into tears, and wrung her beautiful hands. Jack said, looking at The Witch's Revenge, "And who are you?"

The Witch's Revenge said to Jack, "Who am I? I'm your mother's cat, and you're a handful of dry sticks in a suit two sizes too large. But I won't tell anyone if you won't tell, either."

Jack snorted at this, and Flora stopped crying. She began to look around the house, which was sunny and large and well appointed.

"There's room enough for both of you," said The Witch's Revenge, "if Small doesn't mind."

Small thought his heart would burst with happiness to have his family back again. He showed Flora to one bedroom and Jack to another. And then they went downstairs and had a second dinner, and Small and The Witch's Revenge listened, and the cats in their hanging cage listened, while Flora and Jack recounted their adventures.

A pickpocket had taken Flora's purse, and they'd sold the witch's automobile, and lost the money in a game of cards. Flora had found her parents, but they were a pair of old scoundrels who had no use for her. (She was too old to sell again. She would have realized what they were up to.) She'd gone to work in a department store, and Jack had sold tickets in a movie theater. They'd quarreled and made up, and then fallen in love with other people, and had many disappointments. At last they had decided to go home to the witch's house and see if it would do for a squat, or if there was anything left to carry away and sell.

But the house, of course, had burned down. As they argued about what to do next, Jack had smelled Small, his brother, down in the village. So here they were.

"You'll live here, with us," Small said.

Jack and Flora said they could not do that. They had ambitions, they said. They had plans. They would stay for a week, or two weeks, and then they would be off again. The Witch's Revenge nodded and said that this was sensible.

Every day Small came home from school and went out again, with Flora, on a bicycle built for two. Or he stayed home and Jack taught him how to hold a coin between two fingers, and how to follow the egg as it moved from cup to cup. The Witch's Revenge taught them to play bridge, although Flora and Jack couldn't be partners. They quarreled with each other as if they were husband and wife.

"What do you want?" Small asked Flora one day. He was leaning against her, wishing he were still a cat, and could sit in her lap. She smelled of secrets. "Why do you have to go away again?"

Flora patted Small on the head. She said, "What do I want? To never have to worry about money. I want to marry a man and know that he'll never cheat on me, or leave me." She looked at Jack as she said this.

Jack said, "I want a rich wife who won't talk back, who doesn't lie in bed all day, with the covers pulled up over her head, weeping and calling me a bundle of twigs." And he looked at Flora when he said this.

The Witch's Revenge put down the sweater that she was knitting for Small. She looked at Flora and she looked at Jack and then she looked at Small.

Small went into the kitchen and opened the door of the hanging cage. He lifted out the two cats and brought them to Flora and Jack. "Here," he said. "A husband for you, Flora, and a wife for Jack. A prince and a princess, and both of them beautiful, and well brought up, and wealthy, no doubt."

Flora picked up the little tomcat and said, "Don't tease at me, Small! Whoever heard of marrying a cat!"

The Witch's Revenge said, "The trick is to keep their catskins in a safe hiding place. And if they sulk, or treat you badly, sew them back into their catskin and put them into a bag and throw them in the river."

Then she took her claw and slit the skin of the tabby-colored catsuit, and Flora was holding a naked man. Flora shrieked and dropped him on the ground. He was a handsome man, well made, and he had a princely manner. He was not a man whom anyone would ever mistake for a cat. He stood up and made a bow, very elegant, for all that he was naked. Flora blushed, but she looked pleased.

"Go fetch some clothes for the prince and the princess," The Witch's Revenge said to Small. When he got back, there was a naked princess hiding behind the sofa, and Jack was leering at her.

A few weeks after that, there were two weddings, and then Flora left with her new husband, and Jack went off with his new wife. Perhaps they lived happily ever after.

The Witch's Revenge said to Small, that night at dinner, "We have no wife for you."

Small shrugged. "I'm still too young," he said.

But try as hard as he can, Small is getting older now. The catskin barely fits across his shoulders. The buttons strain when he fastens them. His grown-up fur—his people fur—is coming in. At night he has dreams.

The witch his mother's Spanish heel beats against the pane of glass. The princess hangs in the briar. She's holding up her dress, so he can see the cat fur down there. Now she's under the house. She wants to marry him, but the house will fall down if he kisses her. He and Flora are children again, in the witch's house. Flora lifts up her skirt and says, See my pussy? There's a cat down there, peeking out at him, but it doesn't look like any cat he's ever seen. He says to Flora, I have a pussy too. But his isn't the same.

At last he knows what happened to the little, starving, naked thing in the forest, where it went. It crawled into his catskin, while he was asleep, and then burrowed into his own skin, and now it is nestled in his chest, still cold and lonely and hungry. It is eating him from the inside, and getting bigger, and one day there will be no Small left at all, only that nameless, hungry child, wearing a Small skin.

Small moans in his sleep.

There are ants in The Witch's Revenge's skin, leaking out of her seams, and they march down into the sheets and pinch at him, down into his private places, down where his fur is growing in, and it hurts, it aches and aches. He dreams that The Witch's Revenge wakes now, and comes and licks him all over, until the pain melts, the pane of glass melts, and the ants march away again, on their long, greased thread.

"What do you want?" says The Witch's Revenge.

Small is no longer dreaming. He says, "I want my mother!"

Light from the moon comes down through the window over their bed. The Witch's Revenge is very beautiful—she looks like a queen, like a knife, like a burning house, a cat—in the moonlight. Her fur shines. Her whiskers stand out like pulled stitches, wax, and thread. The Witch's Revenge says, "Your mother is dead."

"Take off your skin," Small says. He's crying and The Witch's Revenge licks his tears away. Small's skin pricks all over, and down under the house, something small wails and wails. "Give me back my mother," he says.

"What if I'm not as beautiful as you remember?" says his mother, the witch, The Witch's Revenge. "I'm full of ants. Take off my skin, and all the ants will spill out, and there will be nothing left of me."

Small says, "Why have you left me all alone?"

His mother the witch says, "I've never left you alone, not even for a minute. I sewed up my death in a catskin so I could stay with you."

"Take it off! Let me see you!" Small says.

The Witch's Revenge shakes her head and says, "Tomorrow night. Ask me again, tomorrow night. How can you ask me for such a thing, and how can I say no to you? Do you know what you're asking me for?"

All night long, Small combs his mother's fur. His fingers are looking for the seams in her catskin. When The Witch's Revenge yawns, he peers inside her mouth, hoping to catch a glimpse of his mother's face. He can feel himself becoming smaller and smaller. In the morning he will be so small that when he tries to put his catskin on, he can barely do up the buttons. He'll be so small, so sharp, you might mistake him for an ant, and when The Witch's Revenge yawns, and opens her mouth, he'll creep inside, he'll go down into her belly, he'll go find his mother. If he can, he will help his mother cut her catskin open so that she can get out again, and if she won't come out, then he won't either. He thinks he'll live there, the way that sailors sometimes live inside the belly of fish who have eaten them, and keep house for his mother inside the house of her skin.

This is the end of the story. The Princess Margaret grows up to kill witches and cats. If she doesn't, then someone else will have to do it. There is no such thing as witches, and there is no such thing as cats, either, only people dressed up in catskin suits. They have their reasons, and who is to say that they might not live that way, happily ever after, until the ants have carried away all of the time that there is, to build something new and better out of it?

Dragon's Gate

~~~~~~

Pat Murphy

Pat Murphy [www.brazenhussies.net/murphy] lives in San Francisco, California. She has been publishing science fiction stories and novels since the 1970s and fantasy for at least the last decade. Her most famous novel is The Falling Woman *(1987). Some of her stories are collected in* Points of Departure *(1990). "When I'm not writing science fiction," she says, "I write for the Exploratorium, San Francisco's museum of science, art, and human perception." She also co-writes an occasional science column for* Fantasy & Science Fiction. *She teaches writing, and is co-founder of the James Tiptree, Jr. Awards for feminist and gender-bending SF (and for the last decade has been travelling to SF conventions in support of these awards). She travels for readings and public appearances with her writer friends Lisa Goldstein and Michaela Roessner Herman, and they call themselves the Brazen Hussies.*

"Dragon's Gate" was published in Fantasy & Science Fiction, *and is a first-class dragon story with a feminist fairy tale structure and several layers of gentle irony. It is particularly impressive to see Murphy gracefully handling the conventional furniture of fantasy, yet producing striking and unusual effects.*

My name is Alita, which means "girl to be trusted." My mother calls me Al. If anyone asks, I tell them it's short for Alonzo, a solid masculine name. At fifteen years of age, I can pass for a boy on the verge of manhood. I dress in men's clothing, preferring tunic and breeches to petticoats and skirts.

My mother plays the harp and sings ballads; I am a storyteller. I know common folk stories (rife with bawdy asides and comic characters), heroic tales favored by the nobility (usually involving handsome princes, beautiful princesses, and courtly love), and morality tales (favored by the clergy, but not by many others). I know how a story should go.

The story that I tell you now is unruly and difficult. It refuses to conform to any of the traditional forms. This story wanders like sheep without a shepherd. It involves a prince and a dragon, but not until later. There will be magic and wishes and . . . well, I'll get to all that presently.

I begin my story in the mountain town of Nabakhri, where shepherds and weavers gather each fall. The shepherds come down from the mountains to sell their wool; the weavers come up from the lowlands to buy. My mother and I come to the festival to entertain the lot of them.

Twilight was falling when my mother and I reached the town. We had been traveling for two days, beginning our journey in the warm valley where the Alsi River ran. There, people grew rice and millet and wore bright colorful clothing. In Nabakhri, people grew barley and potatoes, herded goats and sheep, and wore heavy woolen clothing.

The trail that led to town was steep, better suited for goats than for our pony. The evening breeze blew from the great glacier that filled the valley to the west of Nabakhri. Our pony's breath made clouds in the cold, crisp air.

At the edge of town, we waited for a flock of sheep to cross the main path. The sheep bleated in protest as dogs nipped at their heels. One of the shepherds, an older man in a ragged cloak, glanced at us. He smiled as he noted my mother's harp, slung on the side of our pony's pack. "Musicians!" he said. "Are you looking for an inn?"

I nodded. After the long summer alone in the mountains, shepherds are eager for music and good company.

"The inns in the center of the village are full," he said. "Try Sarasri's place. West side of the village, overlooking the glacier. Good food, good drink."

Someone shouted from the direction in which the man's flock was disappearing. The man lifted a hand in farewell and hurried after his sheep.

Sarasri's was a sprawling, ramshackle inn on the edge of town. We hitched the pony by the open door to the tavern, where the air was rich with the scent of lamb stew and fried bread. The barmaid called for Sarasri, the innkeeper.

Sarasri, a stout, round-faced woman, hurried from the kitchen, drying her hands on her apron. In the lowlands, it's unusual for a woman to run an inn, but women from the mountain tribes often go into business for themselves.

"We're looking for a room," I said, but she was shaking her head before the words were out of my mouth.

"Alas, young fellow, there are too many travelers this year," she said. "I don't know that there's a room left anywhere in town."

My mother was not listening. She was looking past Sarasri into the tavern. "What do you think I should play tonight, Al?" she asked me. "It looks like there'll be quite a crowd." She smiled at Sarasri—my mother has a smile that could melt the snow on a mountaintop ten miles distant. "You have such a lovely inn," she said warmly and sincerely.

My mother is warm-hearted and guileless—traits that serve her in good stead. When my father read fortunes with the Tarot cards, my mother was always represented by the Fool, a young man in motley who is about to dance over the edge of a cliff. The Fool is a divine innocent, protected by angels. If he tripped over the cliff's edge, he would fall into a haystack.

Sarasri glanced at my mother. "You are musicians? It would be nice to have music in the tavern tonight." She frowned, thinking hard. "I do have one small room. . . ."

The room was used for storage—burlap sacks of potatoes and baskets filled with wool were stacked against one wall. The remaining space was barely big enough for a bed and a table. The window overlooked the glacier—at least we would not wake in the morning to the clamor of the village.

"Good enough?" I asked my mother.

"This is just wonderful." My mother would be comfortable in a stable stall, as long as she had her harp to play.

My father, a conjurer skilled at illusions and fortune telling, had died three years ago, when I was a girl of twelve. After his death, it fell to me to attend to practical details of life, as my mother was ill-suited to such a task. I did my best to take care of her.

When the weather was warm, we traveled from town to town. Wherever there was a festival, we performed in the taverns, passing the hat for our keep. In the cold months, we stayed in the lowlands, in the small village where my mother was born.

That evening, in Sarasri's tavern, my mother sang for an appreciative (and drunken) crowd of shepherds. Following my mother's performance, I told the tale of King Takla and the ice woman. With the glacier so near, I thought it appropriate to tell a story about the ice women.

Ice women are, of course, cousins of the river women. River women, as every lowlander knows, are magical creatures that take the form of beautiful maidens with green eyes and long hair the color of new leaves. Ice women are just as beautiful, but their eyes are as blue as the ice in the deep glacial caves and their hair is as white as new snow. Just as the river women inhabit the rivers, the ice women live in the high mountain glaciers.

King Takla, the ruler of a small kingdom high in the mountains, was hunting for mountain goats when he found a woman sleeping in a hollow in the glacier. She lay on the bare ice, covered with a white shawl woven of wool as fine and delicate as the first splinters of winter frost on the stones of the mountain. Only her beautiful face was exposed to the cold mountain air.

Takla recognized that she was not an ordinary woman. He knew, as all the hill folks know, that taking an ice woman's shawl gave a man power over her. He snatched up the shawl, revealing the ice woman's naked body. Ah, she was beautiful. Her skin was as smooth and pale as the ice on which she rested. Her face was that of a sleeping child, so innocent and pure.

Takla hid the shawl in his hunting pack. Then, captivated by the woman's beauty, Takla lay beside her on the ice, kissing her pale face, caressing her naked breasts, stroking her thighs.

When she woke and stared at him with cool blue eyes, he spoke to her, saying "You will be my queen, beautiful one." Though she struggled to escape, he grasped her arms and pulled her close to him. Overcome with passion for this pale maiden, he forced himself upon her.

Then Takla wrapped her in his hunting cloak and took her back to his castle to become his queen. He dressed her in fine clothing and adorned her with glittering gems. Her beauty surpassed that of any mortal woman, but she never smiled and she seldom spoke. When she did, her voice was as soft as the sound of wind-blown ice crystals whispering over the snow.

"I must go home," she told Takla. "My mother will miss me. My sisters will miss me."

"You have a husband now," he told her. "Your mother will get over it. And if your sisters are as beautiful as you are, they must come to court and find husbands here." He kissed her pale face.

There are different ways one could tell this tale. In the tavern, I told it from King Takla's point of view, describing the ice woman's beauty, the allure of her naked body. A magical being captivates a man against his will. She is a lovely temptress. Unable to control his passion, the man takes possession of her.

In this version of the story, King Takla is helpless, a strong man stricken by love. In this version, Takla is an honest man in his way—he marries the ice woman, takes her for his queen. What more could any woman want?

I think that the ice woman would tell a very different version of the story. She was sleeping peacefully, bothering no one, when the king raped and abducted her, taking her away from her home and her sisters.

This version of the story would not be as popular in the tavern, but I think about it often, particularly when we perform in a tavern filled with soldiers. I am aware that my mother is a beautiful woman and that the soldiers admire more than her music. Because I dress as a young man, I avoid the soldiers' leers.

Of course, the tale of King Takla does not end with his capture of the ice woman. A man who takes a magical creature to his bed must face the consequences of his action.

After Takla brought the ice woman to his castle, bluewhite lights flickered over the ice fields at night. The glacier moaned and creaked as the ice shifted and people said that the ice women were talking among themselves. A year passed and the ice woman bore King Takla a son—a sturdy child with his father's red hair and his mother's piercing blue eyes.

Not long after his son's birth, King Takla went hunting alone in the mountains. While following a path that led beside the glacier, he saw a white mountain goat, standing a hundred yards away on the ice. He shot an arrow, and the beast fell.

Takla made his way across the ice to where the goat had stood. But when he reached the place where the goat had fallen, he found nothing but ice. A trick of the ice women, he thought, and turned to retrace his steps to the rocky mountain slope. A tall woman with white hair blocked his way.

"King Takla," she said. "You must set my daughter free."

Takla studied the woman. This woman was older than his wife, but just as beautiful. The same fair features, the same piercing blue eyes, the same beautiful body.

"Your daughter is my wife and the mother of my son," he said.

"I will reward you handsomely if you let her go," said the woman. She held out a silver hunting horn. "Release my daughter and sound the horn—and I will come and grant you a wish. Three times I will come when the horn is sounded and three wishes I will grant." She held the instrument up so that the king could admire its fine workmanship and contemplate what wishes he might make.

Takla studied the horn and considered the woman's offer. He had, over the passing year, grown weary of his wife's unsmiling silence. Yes, she was beautiful, but he had begun to admire one of his wife's ladies in waiting, a fiery beauty with auburn hair and dark brown eyes. If he accepted the ice woman's offer, his wife would return to her people, leaving him free to marry again. With the ice woman's help, he could become more powerful.

Takla smiled and took the horn from the woman's hand. She stepped aside and he returned to his castle.

He took his wife's white shawl from the trunk where it had been hidden for the past year. When he entered his wife's chambers, she was suckling his infant son. She saw the shawl in his hands and her blue eyes widened. She handed the baby to her lady in waiting, the beauty who had captured the king's attention.

"What have you brought me?" the king's wife asked softly.

"Your mother gave me a gift." The king lifted the horn. "Three wishes will be mine, in exchange for one wish of hers. Her wish is that I set you free."

The king's wife took the shawl from his hands and wrapped it around her shoulders. Without a word, she left the room, running through the corridor, down the stairs, and out to the glacier. She was never seen again.

Takla smiled at the lady in waiting, then kissed his son on the forehead. Since the lady held his son cradled in her arms, bestowing this sign of fatherly affection afforded the king an opportunity to admire her bosom.

Filled with joy and thoughts of continuing power, Takla

took the hunting horn and left the castle, climbing to a rock outcropping that overlooked the glacier, the castle, the pass, and the valley.

The Sun was dipping toward the horizon in the west. Takla looked out over his kingdom and thought of his first wish.

He put the horn to his lips and blew. A blue light flickered in the glacier below, then the ice woman stood before him. "What is your wish?" she asked.

"I wish that I may remain above all others as I am now and that my reign will last as long as the stones of the mountain."

The ice woman smiled and lifted her hand. The silver horn fell from the king's hand as a transformation took place. The king became stone, a royal statue gazing over the kingdom.

"As you wish, you will stay here, above all others," the ice woman said. "Your reign will last as long as the stones of the mountain. Until the wind and the weather wear you away, you will reign over this place."

Among the mountain people, there is a saying. "Like a gift of the ice women," they say about presents that end up costing the recipient dearly. It is best not to meddle in magical matters. One must not trust a gift of the ice women.

I had just reached the end of the story when the wind blew the tavern door open. At the time, I thought that was a stroke of good luck; the blast of cold air made my listeners shiver and appreciate the story all the more. "A gift of the ice women," I said, and the crowd laughed.

I passed among the shepherds, gathering coins from those who had enjoyed the tale. When I walked near the kitchen door, I saw that Sarasri was frowning. She spoke to me as I passed. "That's not a good tale to tell so close to the glacier. You'd best keep your shutters closed tonight. The ice women won't like it that you're talking about them."

I was a humble storyteller, far beneath the notice of magical creatures. I didn't think that the ice women would concern themselves with my doings. Still, I followed Sarasri's advice that night. I closed the shutters—not to keep out the ice women, but rather to keep out the cold. Unfortunately the wooden shutters were warped. Though I closed them as tightly as I could, a cold draft blew through the gap between them.

I did not sleep well. I could hear the glacier groaning and creaking as the ice shifted and moved. I was glad when the first light of dawn crept through the gap in the shutters, casting a bright line on my mother, who slept soundly beside me.

Quietly, I dressed and went down to the street. The weather had grown colder and the rocky paths were slick with frost. At a baker's shop I bought sweet buns for our breakfast. The buns were warm against my hands as I carried them back to our room.

When I entered the room, I called to my mother to wake her, but she did not move. I shook her, and still she did not wake. "Mother," I called to her. "Mother?"

She would not wake up. I found Sarasri in the kitchen and she sent a boy to find a healer. I sat by my mother's side, breakfast forgotten.

The healer, an old woman with white hair, sat on the edge of my mother's bed and felt my mother's cheek. She held a silver spoon beneath my mother's nose and watched to see that my mother's breath fogged the silver. She stroked my mother's hand and called to her. Then she shook her head and said, "Ice sickness."

I stared at her. "What do you mean?"

"It comes from the wind off the glacier," Sarasri said. She frowned unhappily. "That's what comes of telling tales about the women of the ice."

"Those who get the ice sickness sleep peacefully until they waste away," the healer said.

I stared at my mother. Her face was so calm and peaceful in sleep. It was hard to believe that anything was amiss. "What can I do?"

"There is one cure," the healer said.

"What is it?" I asked.

"Three drops of dragon's blood. Place them in her mouth and they'll warm her back to life." The healer shrugged. "But we have no dragon's blood and no hero to fetch it for us."

Sarasri shook her head sorrowfully. "As if a hero would help," she said. "How many have journeyed to Dragon's Gate, filled with pride and noble plans? Not a one has returned."

"Do you have to be a hero to fetch dragon's blood?" I asked. "We only need three drops of blood. The dragon doesn't have to die to give up three drops."

Sarasri frowned but the old healer nodded. "That's true," she said. "Slaying the dragon is not necessary, if you can get a bit of blood by some other means." She studied me. Her eyes were a brilliant blue, unfaded by her years. "Do you know anything about dragons?" she asked me.

"Only what I have learned from heroic tales," I said. "And that's not much. The dragon usually dies as soon as the prince shows up."

The old woman nodded. "Those tales are about princes, not about dragons. Those stories describe a dragon as a fire-breathing lizard with wings."

"Is that wrong?" I asked.

"It is not so much wrong as it is incomplete. The essence of a dragon is not in its appearance, but in its nature."

"What is its nature?"

"A dragon is an inferno of anger, blazing with fury, exploding with pain. A dragon is a beast of fire and passion, feeding on fear and hatred." The old woman stood and drew her woolen cloak around her shoulders. "Approached with fear, a dragon responds with fire."

"What if one does not approach with fear?" I asked.

She shrugged. "A difficult task to accomplish," she said. "But if it could be done, you might manage to start a conversation. I have heard that dragons like to talk. But they can smell a liar and that awakens their anger. Never lie to a dragon."

Perhaps this is where the story really begins. With my realization that I had to go to Dragon's Gate and return with three drops of blood from the dragon who had guarded the pass for the past hundred years.

I arranged for Sarasri to care for my mother. I left the pony in Sarasri's stables, since the way ahead was too rough and steep for the animal. Then I followed a footpath that led high into the hills.

Dragon's Gate was once known as Takla's Pass, named after King Takla, who married the ice woman. This mountain pass offered the shortest route from the lowlands to the trading cities on the Northern Sea. Long ago, caravans laden with carpets and spices and gems made their way through the mountains along this road. King Takla—and after him Takla's son, King Rinzen—charged merchants for safe passage.

All that changed a hundred years ago when good King Belen of the lowlands had, at the urging of rich merchants, sought to overthrow King Rinzen and put an end to his tolls. King Belen's army invaded the mountain kingdom. But a dragon released by some black magic drove back his army and closed the pass.

The dragon laid waste to the land. What had once been a thriving kingdom became a barren deserted land. Merchants from the lowlands banded together to offer a reward to any who could slay the dragon and open the road through the pass. But all the heroes who tried to win the reward perished in the attempt: burned by the dragon's fire, slashed by the dragon's claws.

Now merchants sent their goods through the desert and around the mountains to the south, a long and perilous journey. In the desert, bandits preyed on caravans and kidnapped merchants for ransom. But the possibility of being waylaid by bandits was better than the certainty of being killed by the dragon.

The path I took to Dragon's Gate was little better than a goat path. Winter avalanches had covered sections of the old trade route. Prickly shrubs had grown over the old road, and no one had cleared them away.

From Nabakhri, it was three days' hard travel to Dragon's Gate. The villages grew smaller and meaner as I traveled. People along the way asked me where I was going—and shook their heads grimly when they heard of my mission.

"Turn back, young man," they said. "You haven't a chance of succeeding."

The last village before the dragon's pass was little better than a collection of grimy huts clinging to the side of the mountain. There a tiny teahouse doubled as an inn. Three shepherds sat by the fire in the common room, dining on lentil stew, fried bread, and tea.

The innkeeper was a stout man with an impressive mustache and a head of hair as thick as the wool on the mountain sheep. "Are you lost?" he asked me. "There is nowhere to go on this trail."

I explained my mission. He served me dinner and sat with me while I ate.

"You say you must approach the dragon without fear," he said. "How can you do that? Only a fool would not fear the dragon."

It was a good question. As I climbed the mountain trails, I had been thinking about how to quell my fear.

"Some of the stories that I tell are very frightening," I told the innkeeper. "But I am not afraid when I tell these tales because I know they will end well. What I am doing now is worthy of a story. If I think of this as a story I am telling, I will not be afraid."

The innkeeper frowned. "But you don't know that there will be a happy ending to this story of yours."

"Of course there will be," I said. "I am telling the story, remember? Why would I tell my own story with an unhappy ending?"

The innkeeper shook his head. "It sounds like you are just fooling yourself."

I nodded. "Indeed I am. What better way to keep away fear?"

The innkeeper shook his head and poured me another cup of tea. He spent the rest of the evening telling me of heroes who went to slay the dragon and never returned.

When I left the village the next morning, I did my best to put this conversation out of my mind. It wasn't easy. Above me loomed the barren crags of Dragon's Gate. Black rocks, like pointed teeth, made sharp silhouettes against the blue sky. One outcropping bore a resemblance to a standing man. That, it was said, was all that remained of King Takla.

Late in the afternoon, I reached the ice field that surrounded the castle where the dragon lived. Over the years, the glacier had flattened the walls that surrounded the castle gardens and had engulfed the outbuildings. The castle's outer walls had collapsed under the pressure of the ice, but the castle keep, the structure's central fortress, still stood. One tall tower rose from the ice field. From where I stood, the tower was as big as my thumb, held at arm's length.

Cautiously I started across the ice fields toward the tower. I used my walking stick to test each patch of ice before trusting my weight to it. Once, the ice collapsed beneath my stick, sending up a spray of snow as it fell. At my feet, where my next step would have taken me, was a crevasse so deep that the bottom was lost in blue light and shadows. The crash of the ice shelf hitting the bottom of the crevasse reverberated through the glacier.

The wind cut through my cloak; I could not stop shivering. At first, my feet ached with the cold. After a time, they became numb. I thought about how it would feel to lie down on the ice, like the ice woman in the story of King Takla. It would be painful at first, but then I would grow numb. I could rest, sleeping as peacefully as my mother slept.

The sky darkened to a deep blue. The light that reflected from cracks deep in the ice was the same beautiful blue. In my weariness, I grew dizzy. Looking up at the sky seemed much the same as gazing down into the ice. My walking stick slipped and I stumbled, falling full length onto the ice. I turned over on my back to look up at the blue sky, grateful to be resting.

I thought about staying there, just for a while. But that would not do. No tavern crowd would pay good money to hear about a hero who gave up and lay down in the snow. So I got up and kept walking on feet that felt like wood.

At last, I reached the tower and circled it, looking for a way in. Halfway around, I discovered a gap in the tower wall. I ducked through the gap and found myself on an ice-slicked stairway. Narrow slits in the walls let in just enough light to reveal the stone steps. Beneath the layers of ice, I could see sconces that had once held torches. The walls were marked with soot where flames had licked the stone.

Though the castle walls blocked the wind, it was even colder in the castle than it had been outside. My teeth chattered; I could not stop shivering. I climbed the stairs slowly, taking care not to slip on the icy steps.

At the top of the stairs was a wide corridor. The walls were clear of ice and the air felt a little warmer. Looking down the corridor, I could see a glimmer of golden light, spilling from an open doorway. I walked toward it.

In the doorway, I stopped and stared, my heart pounding. I could feel fear scratching at the edges of my awareness, but I reminded myself that there would be a happy ending. There had to be a happy ending.

The dragon slept in the center of the great hall. The beast lay on what had once been a fine carpet—now tattered and scorched. The air stank of ashes and smoke. I could feel heat radiating from the beast, like the warmth from a banked fire.

To hold fear at bay, I stared at the dragon and imagined how I might describe the monster when I told this story. The dragon's body was like that of a terrible lizard, a lizard as large as a warhorse. Its wings—great leathery wings—stretched over its back. Its eyes were closed. Its mighty head rested on its front talons. I did not stare for too long at the dragon's jaws and powerful talons. Instead, I considered the rest of the room and decided how best to describe it when I was telling this story in a tavern.

This had once been a magnificent hall. The walls were dark with soot, but I could see paintings beneath the layer of grime. More than a hundred years ago, artists had decorated these walls. On the wall to my left, two men in hunting garb shot arrows at mountain goats, which were bounding away up the mountain. On the far side of the room, the wall was painted with a mountain landscape—the same mountain that lay outside the castle. But the artist had worked in a warmer and happier time. In the painting, wildflowers grew among the gray stones.

In the painting, the stones of the mountain formed a natural cave at the level of the floor. The rocks of the painted cave blended with the very real rocks of a great fireplace, large enough to hold a roasting ox.

Beside that fireplace, a skeleton sat slumped in a carved oak chair. A golden crown rested on the skull. Tatters of rich fabric clung to the bones. They fluttered in the breeze that blew through a large break in the wall to my right.

That wall had been shattered and its painting with it. I tried to imagine the blow that had shattered the wall, sending the stones tumbling inward and leaving a hole big enough to let the dragon pass through. Through the gap, I could see the glacier far below. The first stars of evening were appearing in the darkening sky. I shivered in the cool breeze.

"I smell an enemy," a voice growled.

I looked at the dragon. The beast had not moved, but its eyes were open now. They glowed like the embers of a fire. Colors shifted and flickered in their depths: gold and red and blue. "I know you are an enemy because you stink of the lowlands. You aren't a prince. You aren't a hero. What are you, and why have you come here?"

Be honest, I thought. Dragons can spot a liar. "A humble storyteller," I said.

"A storyteller?" The dragon lifted its head and studied me with glowing eyes. "How unusual. For the past hundred years, all my visitors have come to kill me. They march up the road from the lowlands with their soldiers following behind and their fear wakes me. I feel the shivering in their souls, the hatred in their hearts. I feel it burning and my own fire flares in response. And I shake off sleep and rise to do battle."

The dragon yawned, revealing a terrifying array of teeth. The beast stretched slowly, shaking out its great golden wings with a leathery rustle. Then the monster regarded me once again. "But you're not a hero. You are dressed as a boy, but I know by your smell that you are a girl. You are afraid, but not so very afraid. And you want something from me. What is it you want? Tell me, girl of the lowlands, why I shouldn't roast your bones with a single breath?"

As a storyteller, I have learned that everyone has a story. Not only that, but everyone has a story that they think should be told.

"I have a few reasons for coming here," I said carefully. "As a storyteller, I know many tales in which there are dragons. But those are stories about princes. And in every one of them, the dragon dies at the end of the tale. That doesn't seem right. I thought you might help me to tell a new sort of tale about dragons."

"Very tricky," said the dragon. "You hope to appeal to my vanity. And I notice that you said you had a few reasons and then you told me only one. You hope to intrigue me so that I'll decide you are interesting enough to spare."

When an audience catches you out, I have found it is best to acknowledge that they are right. If you deny it, they'll turn against you. "Have I succeeded?" I asked.

"Perhaps." The dragon continued to study me. "As long as I find you interesting, I will let you live. If I grow bored, I will roast you before I return to sleep. For now, I will spare you because you remind me of a wild girl I once knew." The dragon blinked slowly. "Would you like to hear about that wild girl? She was a lovely princess, until I destroyed her."

Not an entirely promising start. I reminded the dragon of a princess that it had destroyed. But at least the beast was not going to roast me immediately.

Though the heat radiated by the dragon had warmed me, my legs were trembling with weariness. I took a chance and asked, "Might I come in and sit while you tell the tale?"

The dragon stared at me, and for a moment I thought all was lost. Then the monster opened its jaws in a terrible grin. "Of course. I have forgotten the duties of a host. Come in. Sit down. There." The dragon lifted a talon and gestured to a bench beside the chair where the skeleton sat.

I crossed the room and sat on the bench, putting my pack on the stone floor beside me.

"You look cold," the dragon said. "Let me kindle a fire."

The beast opened its mouth and a blast of fire shot into the fireplace beside me. The half-burned logs, remnants of a long-dead fire, blazed.

"Alas, I have no food and drink to offer you," the dragon said. "The kitchens were crushed by the glacier long ago."

I opened my pack and took out a metal flask filled with brandy. "I have a bit of brandy. It's not the best, but I would be happy to share."

The dragon's toothy grin widened. "You drink and I will talk. I will tell the storyteller a story."

I sipped from the flask and felt the warmth of the brandy fill my throat and my chest.

"The wild girl was a princess," the dragon said. "A wild mountain princess more likely to be found hunting bandits than working her embroidery." The beast cocked its head, regarding me thoughtfully. "Tell me, what do you know of this castle, this kingdom?"

I chose my words carefully. "I know of King Takla, who built this castle and captured an ice woman for his queen."

"Very good," the dragon said. "Then you recognize that horn?"

I followed the dragon's gaze and saw a silver hunting horn, lying on the stone floor beside the royal skeleton. "King Takla's horn?" I asked.

"The very same. Blow it and the ice woman will grant your wish. But you must be very careful what you wish for."

I stared at the instrument in amazement. Though I had often told the story of King Takla, I had never thought about what happened to the horn.

"The wild princess of my story was the granddaughter of King Takla. Her father, King Rinzen, was the ruler of this mountain kingdom. He was a good king, noble and wise. Do you know of him?"

"I have heard of him," I admitted. The stories that I

knew all emphasized the wealth of King Rinzen and how unfair his tolls had been.

"What have you heard?"

"Far less than I wish to know. Far less than you could tell me."

"An evasive answer," the dragon said, studying me with those great glowing eyes. "You know, I have heard that storytellers are all liars."

"Not necessarily liars," I said. "But careful in choosing the right audience for a tale."

"And I am not the right audience for the lowland tales of King Rinzen," the dragon said.

I nodded.

"Very well. Then I will tell you a tale that you don't hear in the lowlands."

I tipped back my flask and took a swallow of brandy, grateful to have survived this long.

"The men and women of King Rinzen's court hunted in the hills—sometimes for wild goat for the king's table, and sometimes for the bandits who sought to prey on merchant caravans. Decades before, King Takla had driven away the worst of the bandit gangs. But keeping the pass free of robbers and rogues required constant vigilance. You know of all this, of course."

I shook my head. None of the stories told in the lowlands talked about the bandits that King Takla and King Rinzen had driven off. In the lowland tales, these two kings were accounted as no better than bandits themselves.

"I could tell you many fine stories about bandits, about their hidden treasures, their secret caves. But that will have to wait. Just now, I was telling you about King Rinzen's court. The king was fond of musicians and storytellers. Many came to the castle to perform for the court. In this very hall, minstrels played and bards told tales of adventure, while the king listened and rewarded them handsomely for their art."

The dragon paused and I thought the beast might have lost the thread of the story. "What about the princess?" I asked.

The dragon turned its gaze back to me, eyes narrowing. "I suggest that you let me tell this story in my own way," the beast growled.

"Of course," I said hastily. "As you wish. I just wondered about the princess."

"Yes, Princess Tara. One summer evening, Princess Tara came home late from an afternoon of hawking. She knew that a troupe of performers from the lowlands had come to entertain the king. They had come from the court of King Belen, sent by him to King Rinzen. That evening, there was to be a gala performance, but Tara was weary from the hunt. She sent her apologies to her father the king and she did not go to the court that evening. She dined on bread and cheese in her chambers, and went to her bed early.

"That night she woke to the screams of women and the clash of steel." The dragon's eyes were wide open now, glowing more brightly than before. "She pulled on her clothes and ran into the corridor. It was dark except for the glow of smoldering straw. A torch had fallen, igniting the straw that was strewn on the stone floor."

"What did she do?" I asked.

"She listened in the darkness. Someone was running toward her, scattering the burning straw beneath his feet. In the dim light, she recognized a young bard who had come to the castle a week before. His eyes were wild; he was bleeding from a cut over his eye.

" 'What is happening?' Tara called to him."

" 'Treachery,' he gasped. 'Belen's men are in the castle. There is fighting in the great hall.' Then he ran on, and he was gone.

"Tara rushed through the darkness, hurrying toward the great hall. There, the torches cast a crimson light over a terrible scene. The air was thick with the stench of newly spilled blood. Her father was slumped in the big oak chair by the fire. He had been stabbed in the back. By the door were more dead men—some were castle guards, some were men clad in minstrel garb. The festive cloak of one of the minstrels had been torn by a sword stroke, and Tara could see armor beneath the velvet."

The dragon fell silent. I stared at the skeleton in the chair by the fireplace. King Rinzen, still wearing his crown in death.

"What had happened?" I asked at last.

"Belen's troupe of performers was a troop of assassins. They had killed the king, fought the guard, and opened the gates to the soldiers outside.

"Tara ran to her father's side. She kissed his cold cheek and vowed that she would take revenge for what had happened that night. On the wall above the fireplace hung King Takla's great silver hunting horn, the gift of the ice woman. It had fallen from King Takla's hand when he turned to stone. No one had been bold enough to risk blowing it again. An object of beauty, power, and danger, it hung on the wall above the fireplace.

"Tara could hear the tramping of boots and the rattle of armor in the corridor. Her father was dead and Belen's men had taken the castle. Tara pushed a bench to a spot near the fire and stood on the bench to take down the horn."

I nodded, realizing with a shiver that I was sitting on that very bench.

The dragon continued, its voice low. "Tara put the horn to her lips and blew, sounding a high clear note that echoed from the stone walls. The wall of the tower cracked and crumbled. A wind from the ice fields blew through the breach in the wall. Through the opening, Tara could see the dark sky above and the pale ice below. A blue light rose from the glacier and flew to the tower. A tall woman with flowing white hair appeared before Tara. 'Why have you awakened me?' the woman asked."

"The ice woman," I said.

"Tara's great-grandmother, the mother of the maiden that Takla had stolen," the dragon said. "Tara met the woman's icy gaze. 'I need your aid,' the princess said. 'Belen's men have killed my father.'

" 'What do you want of me?' the ice woman said.

" 'I want the power to kill my enemies and drive them from our land. I want the strength to avenge my father.'

" 'Power and strength and passion,' the woman murmured. 'Death and vengeance. These are dangerous things and you are so young.'

" 'Tara fell to her knees before the woman. 'You must help me.'

"The woman touched Tara's cheek. Tara could feel her tears freezing at the ice woman's touch.

" 'I will grant your wish,' the ice woman said. 'Your heart will become ice; your passion, fire. And then you will have the power you need. But it troubles me to cast this spell on one so young. So I will also tell you how to break the spell and return to yourself. When the tears of your enemy melt the ice of your heart, you will become yourself once again. Until then, you will have your wish.'

"The woman's cold touch moved to Tara's breast, a searing chill that took her breath away. The woman stepped back. 'Now you will take the shape you need. You are filled with fire and passion, anger and pain. Let those dictate your form. You will have the power you seek and I will return to sleep.'

"The sorrow that had filled Tara at her father's death left her when her heart froze at the woman's touch. Rage and the desire for vengeance filled her.

"Transformation came with burning pain—a searing at her shoulders as wings formed; a blazing spasm as her back stretched, the bones creaking as they changed shape. Her jaws lengthened; her teeth grew sharp. Hands became claws." The dragon stretched its wings. Its claws flexed, making new tears in the carpet on which it lay. "Tara became a dragon," the beast said.

I stared at the dragon.

"Her breath was flame," Tara said. "Her scales shone like the coals of a fire, shifting and changing with each passing breeze. Now deep red, brighter than fresh blood; now flickering gold; now shining blue-white, like the heart of a flame." As the dragon spoke, her scales flickered and glowed.

"She spread her wings and flew, swooping low over the soldiers in the road. She opened her terrible jaws and her rage became a blast of fire. The men broke and ran. The horses, mad with fear, trampled the men as they fled. The soldiers died—so many died. In her rage, she did not distinguish between one fleeing figure and another. Belen's men burned in her flames, but so did people of her own castle. Stableboys and chambermaids, peasants and noblemen, fleeing Belen's men, fleeing the monster in the sky."

The dragon fell silent for a moment, then continued softly. "Now I live here in the castle. For a hundred years, I have lived here. Sometimes, heroes come to slay me—and I kill them instead." The dragon studied me with glowing eyes. I stared back, imagining what it would be like to be imprisoned in the body of a monster.

"Sometimes, my rage dies down, like a fire that is banked. But then someone filled with hate and fear stirs those ashes and the fire returns, as hot as ever.

"Now it is your turn, humble storyteller. Tell me a story and I will decide what to do with you."

I met the dragon's steady gaze. "I will tell you why I am here," I said. "This is not a story I would ordinarily tell, since most audiences favor stories about princes and dragons over stories about storytellers. But I think you will find it interesting. This story begins in a mountain town, one week ago. The town was having its harvest festival, and I traveled there with my mother."

I told her the story that you have already heard—about the inn on the edge of the glacier, about my mother's illness, about the healer who explained that three drops of dragon's blood would cure my mother of the illness inflicted by the ice woman. "Hope is what brings me here," I said. "Hope is what keeps me from fear and hatred."

The dragon's glowing eyes did not waver. "So you hope to slay me and take my blood?" the dragon rumbled.

"Slay you?" I laughed. The dragon stared at me, but it had been a long night. I had finished the flask of brandy and the dragon hadn't killed me yet. The idea that I planned to slay the dragon was so ridiculous that I couldn't help laughing. I pulled my dagger from my belt. The blade was half as long as one of the dragon's talons. "I suppose I planned to chop off your head with this?" I shook my head. "I'm no dragon slayer."

I thought of my mother's warm smile, of her honest heart. If only she could be here instead of me. She would smile and the dragon would know that this was a woman worth helping. "I had hoped that you might help my mother. That was all I hoped."

"Hope," the dragon repeated, her voice softening. "I remember feeling hope when I was human." The dragon's gaze moved from my face to the gap in the wall. "As a lowlander, you are my enemy. But it has been interesting talking with you this long night. It has reminded me of much that I had forgotten, over the passing years."

I glanced through the breach in the wall. A thin crescent Moon had risen over the glacier. The crackling fire in the fireplace beside me had burned to embers. While drinking brandy and talking with the dragon, I had lost track of time. It was nearly dawn.

"You came to me for help," she said. "What more will you do to save your mother? What will you give me in return for three drops of precious blood?"

I spread my hands. "What would you have me do?"

The dragon did not blink. "In memory of the wild girl that I once was, I will give you three drops of blood. But you must return after you take my blood to your mother. You must come back and keep me company for a time. Will you do that?"

"Yes," I said, without hesitation. "It's a bargain. As soon as my mother is well, I will return."

"Very well then," the dragon said, holding out a taloned paw.

I took a small metal vial from my pack. I reached out and took the dragon's talon in my hand. The scales burned against my skin. With my dagger, I pierced the scaly hide and let three drops of blood fall into the vial. They sizzled as they struck the metal.

"You have a long journey ahead of you," the dragon said. "You'd do well to rest before you begin."

As if I could sleep with a dragon at my side. Still, it did not seem wise to argue. I lay down on the carpet between the dragon and the embers of the fire. I pillowed my head on my pack, and closed my eyes. Weary from my long journey, drunk with brandy and success, I slept for a time.

When I woke, the Sun had risen over the glacier. The dragon was sleeping. As quietly as I could, I left the great hall and headed down the mountain.

I will spare you the account of my journey back to my mother's side. Suffice it to say that everyone along the trail was startled to see me, amazed to hear that I had succeeded in my quest.

At last, I reached the inn where my mother slept. Sarasri was astonished to see me. Though she had never believed that I would return, the good woman had been true to her promise. She had taken care of my mother. Pale and thin, my mother slept peacefully in the room where she had been stricken with the ice sickness.

Sarasri summoned the healer, and the old woman came to my mother's chambers. The healer smiled when she saw me.

"Three drops of dragon's blood," I said, holding out the vial.

"Very good," she said.

"Did you slay the dragon?" Sarasri asked, her eyes wide.

I shook my head. "The dragon told me a story and I told the dragon a story. The dragon gave me this blood on the condition that I return to Dragon's Gate when my mother is well."

The healer nodded. "Ah," she said, "you may very well have slain the dragon then."

I stared at the old woman. "I did not. She gave me this blood freely."

"Indeed—she gave it to you as an act of friendship. And that itself may slay the dragon. Dragons feed on hatred and fear. Acting out of love will weaken the beast."

"This act of kindness weakened the dragon?" I said. "That's not fair."

"Hate and fear nourish and strengthen a dragon. Love

and friendship erode that strength. Fair or not, it's the way things work." She shrugged. "The next hero may find an easy kill. I have heard that Prince Dexter of Erland will soon be going to Dragon's Gate. But that is no concern of yours."

The old woman took the vial of blood. Her touch was cold on my hand. Gently, she stroked my mother's hair, then wet my mother's lips with the dragon's blood.

As I watched, the color returned to my mother's cheeks. My mother parted her lips, sighed, then opened her eyes and blinked at me. "Al," she murmured. "It must be past breakfast time. I'm ravenous."

Sarasri clapped her hands together and hurried off to fetch food. I held my mother's hands, cold in my grip at first, then warming—and I told her all that had happened. She feasted on scones and fresh milk. And when I thought to look around for the healer, the old woman was gone.

My mother recovered quickly. By the evening, she was out of bed. By the next morning, she was asking what we would do next.

I knew that I had to return to the dragon's castle as soon as possible. The healer's words had left me uneasy. My mother was captivated by the dragon's story, and she said that she would go with me. With some effort, I persuaded her that it was more important that she write a ballad that told Tara's tale.

At last I prevailed. But not before I found out more information about Prince Dexter and his plans.

Erland was a kingdom to the north—a small, cold, barren place. Its population lived by fishing and hunting the great whales that lived in the Northern Seas. Princes were as common as fish heads in Erland. (The king of Erland was a virile man.) Prince Dexter, the youngest of the king's eight sons, had left Erland to seek his fortune.

A group of merchants in the lowlands had offered Dexter a great reward if he would slay the dragon. From the merchants' point of view, it was a very sensible move. If the prince failed, it cost them nothing. If he succeeded, the dragon's death opened an easy route to the trading ports—

and Dexter's reward would be nothing compared to the fortunes they would make.

From the prince's point of view—well, I confess, I do not understand the prince's point of view. It seems to me that there are easier ways to make your fortune than attempting to slay a dragon that has killed many heroes. But princes are raised on stories in which the dragon always dies. Like me, the prince believed in a happy ending.

Knowing that the prince would soon be going to Dragon's Gate, I set out on the trail. It was a long, difficult journey—though not as difficult as it had been the first time. It was not as cold as it had been before. As I climbed the pass to reach the castle, I saw a few wildflowers blooming among the gray stones of the mountain. They seemed like a good sign, until I looked down from my high vantagepoint and saw soldiers riding up the trail below me. Their banner was green and white, the colors of Erland.

I climbed the ice-slicked stairs of the castle and made my way to the great hall. The dragon lay where I had seen her last, stretched out on the tattered rug. But her scales were dull and lusterless.

"Tara!" I said. "Wake up!"

The dragon did not move. I threw myself on her great scaly neck. "Wake up!" I shouted again. "There is danger here."

I could feel the barest warmth through the scaly hide. The dragon's breathing was low and shallow.

I could hear the tramping of boots and the rattle of armor in the corridor. Prince Erland and his men had caught up with me. "Can you hear them?" I said. "Can you feel their fear? Can you feel the hatred in their hearts? They have come to kill you. You must wake up."

The dragon did not move.

The prince stepped into the room. His sword was drawn. For a moment I could not help but see the scene as I might have described it in a tale for the tavern crowd. A handsome prince lifted his sword against a terrible monster. But I could see the scene in another way as well: a beast of unearthly beauty, an enchanted princess enslaved and transformed by her own passion, dying for a kindness that had sapped her strength.

I pulled my dagger and stood between the prince and the dragon. The prince looked startled to see me. I could tell by his expression that this was not the way he expected the story to go. I have never heard a story in which anyone tries to protect a dragon.

"You must not kill this dragon," I told him. "She is an enchanted princess. She was weakened because she acted with great kindness. You must not slay her."

"Enchanted princess?" The prince frowned, staring at the sleeping dragon. "I'm not likely to kiss that. A woman capable of laying waste to a kingdom and driving soldiers before her like sheep is no wife for me."

Clearly he had heard too many stories of princes and enchanted princesses. I had suggested neither a kiss nor a royal wedding.

"I think I'd better just kill the beast," the prince was saying. "If you do not step aside, I will have to remove you."

I've told enough stories about princes to know that is what they are trained to do—slay monsters and marry princesses. This prince, like others of his kind, was not a man inclined to change direction quickly.

"I will not step aside," I said, holding out my dagger.

The prince was, however, trained to fight. I was not. With a flick of his sword, the prince struck my dagger aside, stepped in, twisted it from my hands, and tossed it into the corner. Then he lifted his sword.

I fell on the dragon's neck so that the prince could not strike the sleeping dragon without striking me. "Wake up," I murmured to Tara, my eyes filling with tears. It was too much; it was not fair. "You must save yourself." My tears spilled over, dropping onto the beast's neck, trickling over the dull scales.

Where the tears touched, the scales shone with a new brilliance, a blue-white light so bright it dazzled my eyes. The dragon shuddered beneath me. I released my hold on her neck, scrambling away.

The brilliant light—ten times brighter than sunlight on

the ice fields—enveloped the dragon. I squinted through my tears at the light. I could see a shadow in the glare, a dark shape that changed as I strained to see what it was.

The light faded, and I blinked, my eyes still dazzled. A woman stood on the tattered rug. Her eyes were as blue as glacial ice. Her hair was the color of flames. She was dressed in an old-fashioned hunting tunic and breeches. Her hand was on the sword at her belt, and I was certain that she knew how to use it. Much experience with bandits, I suspected.

Tara sat by the fire that the soldiers had built, watching the flames.

"Of course, you can claim your reward," I told the prince. "The merchants asked that you do away with the dragon—and you achieved that end. Your men can testify to it: The dragon is gone."

"That's true," the prince agreed.

"It is the way the story had to go," I explained to the prince. "My tears melted the ice in her heart and she returned to her true form."

"And now what happens?" The prince was studying Tara thoughtfully.

Tara turned from contemplating the fire and met his gaze. "Now I return my kingdom to its former glory. With the dragon gone, my people will return." She smiled. "It will take time, but there's no rush."

"You will need help," the prince said. "Such a lovely princess should not rule alone. Perhaps. . . ."

"Perhaps you should remember your own thoughts, as you prepared to slay a dragon," Princess Tara said, still smiling. "A woman capable of laying waste to a kingdom and driving soldiers before her like sheep is no wife for you."

She turned her gaze back to the fire. "My people will return, and so will the bandits. We will hunt the bandits in the hills and the merchants will pay a toll to pass this way."

"Perhaps you'd best not tell the merchants that part just yet," I advised the prince.

Is the story done yet? Not quite. There is still King Takla's horn to account for. That evening, I stood by the glacier and I blew that horn. I saw a flash of blue light over the ice, and then a beautiful woman wrapped in a white shawl stood before me. Her eyes looked familiar—a beautiful, piercing blue. Her hair was white, and she smiled with recognition when she saw me.

"You have called me," the ice woman said. "What do you wish?"

I held out the horn. "Only to return this horn," I said. "Nothing more."

The ice woman studied me. "No other wishes? You do not wish for wealth or fame or glory?"

I smiled and shook my head.

"You dress as a man, yet you are a woman. Would you wish to be a man?"

I thought about Princess Tara, a woman who hunted for bandits and claimed her own kingdom, and shook my head. "I have no wish to make," I said. Then I asked, "How is your daughter?"

"Very well," she said. "She was pleased to return to her home."

I nodded. "Of course she would be."

"How is your mother?" the ice woman asked.

"Doing well. Writing a ballad about Tara."

She took the horn from my extended hand. "You did very well," she said then. "I am glad that you could help my great-granddaughter, Tara."

I bowed to her. "I am grateful to have been of service." When I looked up, she was gone.

I returned to Sarasri's inn in Nabakhri, where my mother waited. I reached the inn early in the afternoon. I went looking for my mother and found her in the kitchen. Sarasri was kneading bread and my mother was playing the harp and keeping her company.

The kitchen was warm. A pot of lamb stew bubbled on the fire. The yeasty scent of bread filled the air. "Al is back!" Sarasri shouted when she saw me. My mother abandoned her music and hugged me. Sarasri heaped lamb stew in a bowl and insisted that I eat it all.

"My wonderful child," my mother said. "You must tell us all that has happened since you left here."

I shook my head, my mouth filled with stew. "Tonight," I said. "I will tell the tale tonight."

The tavern was full that night. People had heard of my mother's illness, of my trip to Dragon's Gate and my return with dragon's blood, of my return to Dragon's Gate to keep my promise.

I smiled at the crowd. Dressed in tunic and breeches, returning in triumph from Dragon's Gate, I knew the story that they expected. It was the story of Al, a heroic young man who confronts a monster.

"My name is Alita," I said. "And that means 'a girl to be trusted.' Some of you know me as Al and think that I am a young man. But the world is filled with illusions—as I learned when I met the dragon. Let me tell you my story."

One Thing about the Night

~~~~

Terry Dowling

*Terry Dowling [eidolon.net/homesite.html?section_name=
terry_dowling] lives in Hunters Hill, Australia, and is one
of the best prose stylists in science fiction and fantasy. His
short fiction is widely published in Australia and has appeared in* Fantasy & Science Fiction, SciFiction, *and* Interzone. *Although he has never written a novel, his SF stories
have been collected in eight volumes in Australia since
1990, most famously in the Tom Rynosseros series, and his
influences are most saliently the stories of J. G. Ballard,
Ray Bradbury, and Jack Vance. He was presented with the
special Convenor's Award for Excellence at the 1999 Aure-
alis Awards for* Antique Futures: The Best of Terry Dowling.
*In addition a critic and reviewer, and an anthologist, Dowl-
ing is also a musician and songwriter, with eight years of appearances on Australia's longest-running television program,
ABC's* Mr. Squiggle & Friends. *Presently, he teaches creative
writing in Sydney and Perth.*

"One Thing about the Night" was published in The Dark,
*edited by Ellen Datlow, a distinguished original anthology
of horror and the supernatural. It is a polished and slickly
told story of supernatural research, with rational scientific
arguments and a finely tuned atmosphere that is the hall-
mark of the master craftsman. It somehow manages to be
both authentically horrific and optimistic. It is an interesting
comparison to the Neil Gaiman story, earlier in this book.*

Like the good friend he was, Paul Vickrey had kept to our first rule. He'd told me nothing about the Janss place, hadn't dared mention that name in his e-mail, but what precious few words there were brought me halfway around the world nineteen hours after it reached me.

Access to hexagonal prime natural.
Owner missing. Come soonest.

Suitably vague, appropriately cautious in these spying, prying, hacker-cracker times, "prime natural" would have been enough to do it. But hexagonal! Paul had *seen* this six-sided mirror room firsthand, had verified as far as anyone reasonably could that it was probably someone's personal, private, secret creation, and not the work of fakers, frauds, or proven charlatans muddying the waters, salting the lode, exploiting both would-be experts and the gullible.

The complete professional, Paul had even arranged for an independent observer for us. Connie Peake stood with Paul Vickrey and me in the windy afternoon before 67 Ferry Street, the red-brick, suburban home overlooking the lawns and Moreton Bay Figs of Putney Park, which in turn looked out over the Parramatta River. She promised to be a natural in that other sense: someone with a healthy curiosity, an open and scientific mind, and a respected position in a local IT business, recommended to Paul by a mutual friend as someone unfamiliar with the whole notion of psychomantiums and willing to help.

And now Paul was briefing her, giving her much of what he'd given me on our way from the airport. The Janss place would have been an ordinary enough, single-storied house except that its missing owner had bricked up his windows a year ago. At least a year, Paul was telling her, because it was all behind window frames and venetian blinds before then. Finally one of those venetians had fallen, revealing an inner wall of gray brickwork beyond, making 67 Ferry Street an eyesore and its reclusive owner an increasingly mysterious and unpopular neighbor.

"Seems Janss was a nice enough guy at one time," Paul was saying. "Friendly, always obliging. When he lost his wife and kids in the car accident, he went funny. He bricked up the windows, never answered the door. He abandoned the shed he was building in the yard, though he moved his bed out there and prepared meals and slept in the finished half. The neighbors still saw him around the place until two months ago."

"Surely local authorities did something," Connie Peake said. "Contravening building ordinances like this." We hadn't known her long, but Connie definitely seemed the sort of person who used words like "contravening."

"They never knew," Paul told her. "Not till the blinds in the living-room window there fell—in what used to be the living room anyway. Finally, neighbors did phone it in. The council investigated, and my contact arranged for me to be there soon afterward, as Janss's solicitor."

Which he wasn't, of course, but Paul was hardly going to tell Connie that. Who was to know that Janss hadn't had one since the inquest three years ago? Bringing me from the airport, Paul had explained that there was a sister in Perth who had come over for the funeral but seemed to have moved since then.

"A neighbor convinced them that they should break in, in case Janss had had a stroke or something and was lying there. He wasn't. The place was abandoned. So they fitted a new lock and stuck an inspection notice on the back door. My contact told me about the room."

"And now you have a key." His sangfroid had, quite frankly, astonished me.

"I do. If anyone challenges me on it, I'll say Janss and I had a verbal agreement. No paperwork yet."

"Provided he doesn't turn up."

"Provided that, though I'd just say someone phoned

claiming to be him. Very thin, I know, but it's worth it. We have a window of opportunity here, Andy."

I could only agree. Hearing him talk to Connie now, I marveled yet again at how my only contact in this part of the world, a middle-aged former lawyer normally busy running his antique business, just happened to learn of this particular house halfway across the city, not through his usual antique-market channels but through an acquaintance who knew something about his interest in mirrored rooms.

"I'd like to see it," Connie Peake said, as if tracking my thoughts. "It's cool out here."

It was. A chill autumn wind was blowing across the river from the southwest. The big trees in the park across Ferry Street took most of the force, heaving and churning under a rapidly growing overcast, but screened off much of the lowering sun as well.

"Of course," Paul said. "We have to go around back. There's no front door anymore."

Connie frowned. "But—oh, it's bricked up, too."

The comment brought a thrill. More than Paul's e-mail, more than seeing the dull-gray Besser bricks behind the window glass in the red-brick wall where the living room used to be. There was a prime hexagonal in there, in all likelihood a genuine psychomantium and more.

Eric Janss had let the trees and bushes in his driveway and backyard grow tall. No curious neighbors could peer over their fences at us. Anyone seeing us arrive would be left with impressions of three well-dressed, professional-looking people talking out front, obviously there in some official capacity and driven inside because of the deteriorating weather.

Paul unlocked the sturdy back door and we stepped into an ordinary enough combination laundry-bathroom. There was a washing machine, sink, drier, and water heater to one side, a toilet and a shower stall to the other. What looked like a closed sliding door at the end led deeper into the house.

"It gets stranger from here," Paul said for Connie's benefit, closing and locking the back door behind us. "I'll have to go first."

At one time, the sliding door would have led into a kitchen. Now, as Paul drew it aside, it revealed a short, dim passage of the same drab Besser brick we'd seen behind the front windows. At the end of its barely two-meter length was another door, made of wood, painted matte black. Paul switched on his torch, waited till we were all in the passage, and slid the first door shut behind us.

"So most of the house is dead space or solid?" I asked, again for Connie's benefit.

"We can't know without demolition or soundings, Andy. Janss probably brought in the mirrors through the French windows facing the yard, then bricked them up behind the frames. None of this is the original house plan. He pulled down interior load-bearing walls, pulled up flooring, and anchored the new construction in concrete."

"And the neighbors never knew?" I said. "Never saw him bringing in bricks or heard him doing renovations?"

"Apparently not. He was just the reclusive, recently bereaved neighbor. Maybe he brought in stuff late at night or waited till people went on holidays. Who would have known? You saw how overgrown the driveway and backyard are."

"Can we get on with this please, Mr. Vickrey . . . Paul?" Connie said. 'I'm supposed to be back at the office by five. You wanted me to see the room!'

She didn't mean it peevishly. She just had things to do; things no doubt set out very meticulously in a busily filled diary. In another life she might have been a relaxed, even pretty, woman. But not here, not now, not this Connie.

"Of course," Paul said, and moved past us to push on the inner door. It opened with a spring-loaded snick.

Other torches shone back at us immediately, dozens, hundreds of them, in a sudden rush of stars. It was like walking onto a television set, that kind of dramatic, overlit intensity.

It was the single eye of Paul's torch, of course, thrown back at us a thousandfold from the mirror walls of Eric Janss's secret room.

"Oh my!" Connie said. "It's all mirrors!"

Paul, bless him, had been right. This was a prime and, with any luck, a true prime natural.

We stood inside a hexagonal room at least five meters in diameter but seeming larger because of the floor-to-ceiling mirror walls on all six sides. Even the wall behind us was mirrored, the door set flush in it as a hairline rectangle and barely visible, spring-latched to open at the slightest touch from either side. The floor was dark, varnished timber, but with little resilience to it; probably laid over concrete. The two-and-a-half-meter ceiling was matte black with a recessed light-fitting at its center. The only other features were an old-style bentwood chair and the reed-thin shaft of a candle stand next to it, a waist-high, wrought-iron affair and empty now. Whatever candle it had last held had burned right down. The chair and stand were at the room's midpoint.

Paul crossed to where two mirror walls came together and pressed a tiny switch concealed in the join. Soft yellow light from the ceiling fixture confirmed the reality, sent images of us curving away on all sides. What had already been a moderately large room now went on forever, every wall the wall of another room just like it, then another and another and another, on and on. It was as if you stood in, yes, a maze, or on a plain, or at the junction of promenades like those on the space station in Kubrick's *2001*, arching and curving off. *Very large array* came to mind. It was startling, riveting, overwhelming, all those linked, hexagonal chambers, all those countless Pauls, Connies, and Andys sweeping away in an infinite regress. You *knew* the room ended right there, hard and cold at silvered glass, yet that was nonsense now, impossible. We were at the center of a universe.

"You see why I e-mailed you, Andy," Paul said.

Connie Peake had her notepad out, checking the word Paul had given her earlier. "And this is a . . . psychomantium?"

"Probably is," Paul answered. "There are other theories."

"Psychomantium covers it," I said, trying to cue Paul to hold back, but it only made Connie more curious.

"No. Please, Mr. Galt—Andy—you wanted me here as observer for this first entry. What is a psychomantium? What are these other theories?"

"It'll bias you, Connie. You're meant to report only on what you see today, what is actually here in case the site ever becomes—"

"I know. But you and Mr. Vickrey both know I'm going to do a Net search the minute I get back to the office. You might as well tell me."

"All right. But help us here, please. Just observe. You can go verify whatever you want and bring questions later. Paul, best guess, how long have we got?"

Paul shook his head. "Can't say. It's not being treated as a crime scene. Janss has disappeared, but there's no suggestion of foul play. He may have just gone off."

"But you don't think so," Connie said. "Look, I'm trying to be of use. Say I've done a Net search already. What's a psychomantium?"

Another time I might have resented the presence of this officious young woman, but not now. It was good to be challenged on the fundamentals, especially on the fundamentals. Instead of pleading jet lag and letting Paul deal with her questions, I kept my attention on the earnest face, not wanting her to see Paul and me exchange glances, and didn't hesitate.

"Okay. Psychomancy was originally telling fortunes by gazing into people's souls. Catoptromancy was scrying using mirrors. The Victorians were especially fond of combining the two: building mirrored rooms so they could contact spirits of the dead. Mirrors are traditionally meant to trap the souls of the departed and act as doorways to the other side; that's why they used to be covered or removed when someone died. A psychomantium is a mirrored room built for that purpose."

"You believe this?"

Again I didn't look at Paul. This was the way to go and I hoped he'd see that it was.

"That they existed and still exist today, yes. That they permit communication with the dead, no. But others believe it, and I've been collecting psychomantia, mainly the modern ones."

"What, as oddments? Curiosities?"

"As something humans habitually do, yes. As a constant; part of a fascinating social phenomenon."

"So not just as functioning psychomantiums," Connie Peake said. "You want the range of possibility behind them."

Now Paul and I did exchange looks. *Where did you find this woman*? mine said. *I had no idea*! said Paul's.

Again, I barely hesitated. Connie was surprising me, changing the preconceptions I had of her. "Exactly. It's the infinite regress that's the common factor, and Janss has created it here using a hexagon, what I consider the classic form. The reflections in the angling of two facing mirrors have to be as old as reflective surfaces: the first virtual reality. It must have always been profound, something people just naturally hooked things onto. The French have the perfect term for it—*mise-en-abîme*: plunged into the abyss."

We gazed into that abyss now, the endless rush of corridors taking the three of us off to infinity, doing it in long curves, sending us to the left in one mirror wall, to the right in the next, back to the left, and so on. The ceiling light had seemed kind at first, pleasantly free of glare. Now my eyes had adjusted, and it lent a hard, almost clinical quality to the unending rooms and hallways, making me think of the oppressive cubicles in George Tooker's *The Waiting Room*. I couldn't prevent it.

"Have you seen many?" Connie asked, almost in a whisper. The faux cathedral space seemed to demand it.

"Not dedicated ones like this. Mostly you get full-length mirrors set opposite each other in drawing rooms and parlors that give the regression effect, or batwing dressing tables with adjustable side mirrors set a certain way. Sometimes it's hard proving they were intended as psychomantiums at all.

There are a lot of hoaxes; descendants staging the effect for tourism purposes, claiming all sorts of things. Paul and I are looking for prime naturals, dedicated setups like this, with no trumped-up back-story to work through."

"And you've been lucky?"

"We've seen most of the famous ones," Paul said. "But it's the newer kind, the local ones, we're after. I've found four naturals, none as fine as this. Andy's located five, including a dodecagonal room—twelve mirror walls marked out according to the hours of the clock—a splendid octagonal, and two rather poor hexagonals."

"Using candlelight?" Connie indicated the candle stand.

"Almost always," Paul said. "It gives the most powerful—and traditional—effects."

"The most suggestive, I imagine. The most scary."

"No, powerful," I said, interrupting. "Look for yourself. This present lighting is effective. Janss knew to use a low-wattage, yellowish bulb, but it's like you get on mirror-wall escalators in malls and old department stores. It's not optimal, hence the candle stand. He wanted a controlled effect. So far as we can tell, all the naturals originally involved candles."

"Janss let his burn down," Connie said.

"And that's what we'll do," I said, letting Paul know that it was all right for Connie to know more. He'd accept the decision. "We'll sit here and let ours burn down."

"Turn about," Paul said.

"Turn about," I confirmed.

"You'll do it alone?" Connie actually gave a shudder. "It reminds me of that old skipping song we sang at school."

"I'm sorry. The what?" Paul asked.

"A skipping song." She gave an odd smile, part self-consciousness, part excitement, and recited it in the singsong rhythm of the schoolyard.

> *One thing about the night,*
> *One thing about the day,*
> *You turn around and meet yourself*
> *And go the other way.*

She gave another little smile. "The rope would be going really fast, and everyone kept singing it over and over till you had the nerve to turn around. If the rope was long enough, you'd either move back to where you started and duck out, or you'd keep changing directions on the word 'way' until you were out. The one who turned the most times won." She gazed off into the regress. "I guess Janss did his sittings mostly at night."

Now she had me. "Why do you say that? The room is completely sealed. It shouldn't make a difference."

"I think it completes the effect. He's got infinite night in here, but the sense of corridors leading off would be completed at night."

"It's less virtual."

"That's it." Connie checked her watch, but instead of reminding us she had to go, she surprised me again. "Can I stay for part of this? I won't intrude. I'd just like to . . . well, know more."

"We'll consider it, Connie," I said, the best refusal I could manage after a long flight and having been awake for twenty hours.

"You hope to find Janss."

"We're doing this irrespective of Janss," I said too quickly, too harshly. "Excuse me."

"Can you explain that?" she asked. "Before I go?" Connie Peake was proving to be a master at this, and her enthusiasm was infectious.

Paul came to my aid. "Janss left no journals, no papers, doesn't seem to have had a computer. We probably won't ever know what he was really doing. We'll have to go by what he made here."

"It's like archaeology," Connie said and turned to me again. "That other word you said about using mirrors. Catop—catop—something."

"Catoptromancy. Catoptrics is the branch of optics concerned with reflection, with forming images using mirrors. Catoptromancy is scrying by mirrors. A catoptromantium is an arrangement, sometimes a room, for doing this."

I hoped my tone would warn her off, remind her that I

wanted to examine the room with Paul. She did begin to move to the door.

"So you can't know for certain if a room was meant as a psychomantium or not?"

"No, the distinction has been lost." My tone was even cooler. *Please go, Connie, go.* "It's more dramatic to talk of contacting the dead. It gets the media attention." Why was I encouraging her?

"I bet. And I guess you have lots of models at home. Miniature rooms made of mirror tiles."

She'd done it again. I had to laugh. "Yes, I do. It's a hobby."

"It's more than that," she said. "You're trying to know something. Look, Andy, can I see you? Can we go for a coffee or a meal?" She was so direct it stunned me. It was as if Paul wasn't even standing there.

"Connie, ask me another time. I've just arrived. I'm jet-lagged and there's a lot to do."

"Of course. But another time. Please."

"Another time," I said, and we saw her out, to discover that the weather had turned. Rain squalls blew in across the river and the park, keeping farewells to a minimum. We watched Connie drive off, then hurried inside. Paul locked the back door behind us.

"Sorry, Andy. She was more high-maintenance than I expected."

"But valuable, Paul. We don't have a pedigree for this one, and the chances of demolition are considerable. It's all we can do."

Another time, we'd have postponed our first session, allowing for my jet lag, or Paul would have done a solo sitting. But we really didn't know how long we'd have, and we'd been at so few sites together that we wanted to make a start, to log the room's properties and just enjoy being there. Tomorrow we'd alternate solo sittings, overlapping a half hour or so to share information, then try another joint sitting later in the week, if we had that long.

Paul brought in a chair from Janss's makeshift bedroom out back and we sat with our camcorders and Pentaxes, taking footage and snapping dozens of shots, first by the overhead light, then using the new candle fitted in the stand.

It didn't matter that it was windy and rainy outside. In Janss's mirror room, it was lit as if for night. There were no windows for the rain to beat against, just blind brick. In a real sense, time had ceased to matter. We could have been anywhere, and in day or night for all the difference it made.

Though Connie had been right. It did make a difference. Of course it did. Doing this at night would complete something when the candle burned away. When darkness was restored.

We measured the room's dimensions next—smiling as we always did at the play on words—dividing the space into a clock face for easy reference. The door in its mirror wall was at six o'clock; that wall's juncture with the next, going clockwise, was seven; the center of that face eight; the next juncture nine, and so on. Twelve o'clock was directly opposite the door; the concealed light switch was at eleven, a tiny, cunningly hidden press button, virtually invisible unless you knew where to look.

We didn't move the bentwood chair, of course. Its position to the left of the candle was as Janss had last had it, his back not to six o'clock but facing the full mirror wall at two, with the eight-o'clock mirror wall behind. It had to be significant.

Paul and I were enjoying ourselves. His long-suffering wife, Cindy, had sent along a "care package," as she called it: chicken sandwiches, blueberry muffins, and a thermos of coffee, complete with a note: *Don't stay up too late.*

When we were finally settled in our chairs, we shared a modest candlelit meal with our myriad selves out along the ever-dwindling boulevards, remarking on whatever details of construction or effect caught our attention, even beginning to work out a timetable for the next day. Paul would do a four-hour morning watch before going in to the office. I'd do the late afternoon and evening, and he'd pick me up around nine.

Connie was right. I wanted to be there at night. Night did make a difference.

Inevitably we fell silent, looking off into the regress. As in other dedicated mirror rooms we'd logged, all the familiar things were there: the certainty of valid distance and genuine form, the sense of being watched, the uncanny stillness in which the smallest actions—gestures, sudden turns of head or body—sent immediate and startling motion across the lines, set crowds of ourselves gesturing, mimicking, almost urging stillness again by their manic imitation.

Paul and I knew the routine; nothing had to be said. We became utterly still, gazing into the deep, horizontal domains as Janss must have. In our sweaters and slacks, we made a dark knot at the heart of each chamber; faces and hands glowing in the candlelight like countless studies for Rembrandt's "Nightwatch." The corridors and mirror rooms took that calm as far as the eye could see, into the impossibility of dimensions that couldn't exist, yet did: space wrested from illusion, imposed on perception, demanding to be real.

We managed nearly two hours before jet-lag torpor made me call it quits. We hadn't let the candle burn away yet, but my journey across the world was already worth it. If Janss turned up right now, even if the police arrived and evicted us, we'd been in the Janss room at 67 Ferry Street. We were smiling as we went out into the rainy night and drove home.

I slept late, lulled by rain on the roof and wind around the eaves, and never saw Paul leave for his early sitting. An old friend of Cindy's dropped by and I didn't get to Ferry Street until after five. The rain had continued. The harsh autumn wind gusted in the trees, and the park and the river were reduced to so many inkwash veils in the chill afternoon.

I was glad to lock the back door behind me, to place my bag in the laundry and enter the mirror room again. Paul had left the ceiling light on, with a precisely measured candle in the stand so I could do a burn-down. It would take two hours. My mobile was off. My checklist and clipboard were on my lap, my tai-chi chime ball in my pocket. There was a penlight in case it was needed; my main torch, camcorder, and camera were on the floor at my feet. Everything was ready.

At six sharp, I lit the candle, switched off the overhead light and returned to the chair, sitting with my eyes closed for maybe a minute so they could adjust. Finally, I opened them on the miracle of the mirror world.

I sat at the hub of an amazing wheel. Stretching away on all sides were corridors that existed only as reflection, arching off into replicated chambers of stars where other solitary watchers sat, eternally together, eternally alone. Each separate wall of the hexagon led into another hexagonal mirror room in which I was turned away, which then led into another where I was angled back, on and on, this way, that way, off to infinity, but with curves and archings according to counter-reflection and the imperfections and anomalies of the mirrors themselves.

In the ten-o'clock wall, lines of Andy Galt made an infinite corridor to the right. In the nine-o'clock wall, he arced to the left, then right, then left again in those puzzling alternations no one could satisfactorily explain. If I looked near where two mirrors joined, there was a boulevard, the sense of a shadowed avenue between infinite lines of Andy.

Mesmerizing didn't cover it. It was compelling, arresting, powerfully entrancing. I'd focus on a corridor, find myself staring at it, down it, across it, along all those curving lines of myself made into a string of honey-colored moons, party lanterns strung out forever along drained midnight canals and antique avenues. Yes, I was at the center of a universe. No other term came close. Janss had made himself a universe here, an orrery of realms in an arrangement few ever got to see, had brought endlessness into a red (and gray)-brick suburban home, put eternity into grains of sand and silvered glass.

I logged the usual tricks when they came, the catoptric anomalies triggered in brains not intended to face things like infinite regress: the twelfth or seventeenth figure out behaving differently, the conviction of a light source not my own, the sense of rippling or of movements delayed or prefigured somewhere among the myriad forms, the constant game of "Simon Says" you played until you were sure one doppelganger was truly, even purposely, out of sync.

Complex mirror reflections like this had no precedent in nature, hadn't existed for the eye and brain to adapt to in the evolution equation. Perhaps mirrors were the most profound, the most dangerous, the very worst human invention. They suborned the integrity of the mind, couldn't do otherwise. We were never meant to have mirrors more elaborate than calm pools, clear ice walls, lightning-fused sandglass, and sandstorm-scoured sheets of metal of mica, dishes of water, blocks of obsidian, screens of iron pyrites, or oddities like Dr. Dee's lump of polished coal.

In the second hour, torpor took its toll, had me nodding off until—using the old Thomas Edison trick—I dropped the chime ball I was holding in my left hand and woke myself.

That was the cycle until 7:52, when the candle was barely a finger's width above the cup. The rooms were dimming on every side, readying themselves for night. It seemed as bright as ever, but that was an illusion. My eyes had adjusted to what light there was, had made an Indian-summer noon out of a generous twilight. It was like the heat death of the universe out there, all that warmth and life being drawn away in subtle shifts, like some pattern of entropy replicated in an insect's eye. Janss had seen this, had been in *this* chair, seeing *these* gradations of night come.

Absurdly, I recalled the title of a Giacometti sculpture: "The Palace at 4 A.M." It felt like that dead hour now.

Connie's song was there, too, surprising me, the old schoolyard refrain about meeting yourself. That's what I'd been doing. Cued by the words, I turned, swung round in my chair. There I was on every side: flickering, faltering selves out in what was left of the vast, fading starwheel.

They trapped my eye, drew me image by image out into the regress. They were holding me there, fading, darkening. *Be easy now, easy. Be with us. Let it come.*

I felt a rush of dread, sudden and utter panic. The chime

ball clanged against the floor; my clipboard clattered as I rushed for the switch, fumbled with it, brought up warm yellow light, saved us all.

Not tonight. No darkness tonight. I couldn't bear it. It was the jet lag, whatever. I'd do a burn-down at some other sitting. *We* would.

When Paul arrived at 8:53, he found me under the porch outside the bricked-up front door, sheltering from the rain.

Neither of us had managed a burn-down, it turned out. Perhaps it had to do with the room itself, the circumstances of Janss's disappearance, the unseasonal weather, even Connie's song. We agreed that it might be something best done together.

I did a nine-till-noon sitting the next day, taking dozens of photos and more video footage, this time using a tripod and automatic timer for PR shots, and adding a sporadic commentary, anything to keep me from pondering why I hadn't let the candle burn away. It had been a crazy thing last night; it was irrational now, but I couldn't help it.

When Paul arrived for his five-hour afternoon session, he brought a lunch invitation from Connie. There was a twinkle in his eye as he handed me the car keys and gave me directions. He knew how on-again, off-again my relationship with Pamela was back home. This would get me out of the loop, he said. It was good for me.

I felt trapped but pleased. I didn't try to consider motives. I'd keep it easy, light and professional, and with luck, get more of Connie's enthusiasm.

We met at a café in a rainy village court in Putney. Connie had her hair out and wore a shiny black raincoat too blatant to be calculated.

"I looked up the mancy words," she said as I sat across from her. Her smile utterly transformed her face.

"The what? Oh, the mancy words. Right."

"I never realized people took it so seriously. Lithomancy: scrying by the reflection of candlelight off precious stones.

Macharomancy, for heaven's sake: reading swords, daggers, and knives. Imagine specializing in that. Clouds: nephelomancy. Things accidentally heard: transataumancy." She pronounced the word so carefully, as if relishing it. "It's like people made them up for the fun of it. Came up with wacky names like those collective nouns you get: a murder of crows, a parliament of owls."

"A loony of researchers!" I said. I wanted to see her laugh.

We ordered the lasagne with salad and coffee, then sat watching cars go by in the rain. I let Connie bring us back to it.

"Andy, if it's a natural like you say, Janss had probably never heard of catoptromancy. Never knew the word, never knew any variants."

"So the room is a psychomantium, and all he was trying to do was reach his family. Maybe voices told him to do it; maybe he went quietly nuts."

"Surrounded by ordinary households and normal lives," she said. "Sat there while candles burned down. Did it again and again. Then probably sat in darkness, for who knows how long, without the reflections."

I couldn't help myself; I'd had a bad scare the night before. "Without reflections, but with the sense of all those rooms *still* there, those avenues filled with night. You can't help it."

Connie gave a shudder. "That's a chilling thought."

"It's part of the effect. Both Paul and I have let candles burn away." Not this time, I didn't add, and wondered why I didn't, why it mattered. "You feel the . . . pressure . . . of the rooms still out there, going on and on. You know there's nothing there, that reflections need light—"

"But the brain registers images for so long it can't give them up," she said, going to the heart of it. "A retinal afterimage thing. Like a ghost arm effect."

"And you can restore it all so easily. The little switch is right there, and your torch and your Bic lighter and matches. But the feeling is that they're still there."

"That's creepy, Andy. You're the master of all those rooms. They exist because of you."

"And the mirrors."

"No, you. It's *your* perception. *Your* conviction that they're still there. *You're* the activating factor."

The food arrived, but we let it sit a moment. "It gets stranger, Connie. Paul and I have confirmed it. When the candle finally does go out and you're in total darkness, it's as if your reflections, all the mirror versions you've been watching for hours, are pressing up against the glass. You even think you hear them moving in."

"That has to be hyperaesthesia. Anomalous perception. That's—"

"A mind thing, I know. It's exactly what it is. But it *feels* real."

We began eating, looking through the big window, again watching the cars in the rain.

"What if it's sciamancy?" she said between mouthfuls.

"It's what?"

"Sciamancy. What if it's a sciamantium: a place for making shadows, for reading shadows?"

I must have grinned in wonder, for she smiled back. "Andy, what?"

"You've been busy."

"I mean it. What if Janss made a shadow place? Not to contact spirits or read reflections—"

"To scry the darkness." It was so close to my own catoptromancy fixations that I felt alarm, genuine delight, true fascination. It was so good to share this. "Connie, maybe it is a . . . sciamantium."

"Night has to be psychoactive for us, doesn't it? You reach a point where a perception, even a misperception, triggers something in the psyche. You haunt yourselves. Janss, Paul, all of us. Everyone who tries it."

"I hope so. I hope that's what it is." All it is, I didn't add, didn't need to.

We finished eating. The plates were cleared and second coffees brought.

"It does have to do with light, doesn't it?" she said.

"Darkness."

"You know what I mean."

"It's an important distinction. Light running out, darkness being restored, what you were saying. We've always feared night, responded to it dynamically. We made use of that fear, and did pretty well, considering, but the primal response was to endure it, wait it out, worship and appease it."

"But mostly separate ourselves from it in sleep."

"Right. When we developed enough tribally, socially, to sleep safely. Then we modified the relationship over centuries, generations. Gas and electric light changed it, let night become romantic, a time for leisure and shift-work."

"The brain does learn."

"It has to. But only to a point. It's a dual thing: the adjustment *and* the remembering. My relationship with darkness was probably determined by how it was presented to me as a kid. Maybe Janss sussed it out, was taking the appropriate next step of embracing the night for *all* it is, revisiting it as a conditioned mind liberated from fearing it."

"The throwback fear thing hardwired in, but the framing culture telling us it's okay. Maybe the energy behind that fear *can* be directed differently. We don't do an ordinary lunch do we, Andy?"

"We didn't want one."

Connie smiled. "So Janss is a creature of his time, one more solitary watcher responding to what night has become for us. What *else* it has become. Something to inhabit and colonize, something to avoid. Have you ever tried infrared cameras?"

There she was, blindsiding me again. "What, and night-vision goggles?"

"Why not? It might give something."

"We've never been set up that way. We're more your boutique operation." Then it came out. "Connie, we haven't let candles burn down in the Janss room yet. Neither of us has."

There was kindness, instant understanding in her eyes. "So it might be sciamancy. The room could be a place for reading the form and nature of shadows, for creating intricate shadows, and both you and Paul sensed it."

It occurred to me then that if Connie was a natural, too, I should let her be one. "Make an argument."

"What?"

"Make an argument. It's a sciamantium. Convince me."

"All right. It's what we said. Janss was calling up the night. Humans have that ancient . . . an atavistic connection with darkness, *and* with the subtleties."

Subtleties. One word glossed it all. "He was creating an *effect* of night," I said, daring to believe it again.

"An *effect* of shadows and night that only the mirrors bring."

"Trying to reach his wife and son."

"You don't believe that any more than I do. It was accentuation. No, intensification. It mightn't even be related to the deaths."

"Go on."

I expected her to say that she should accompany me.

"That's all. I just know that you have to be alone in there, Andy, like Janss was. It won't work with the two of you. It can't work. If it's psychoactive, it has to be just the individual enabling what happens with the mirrors, *your* mind reacting to the shadows. And keep Paul out of there. You should keep him out. He has a family."

"I'll do a burn-down tonight."

Despite what she'd said about being alone, I truly expected her to ask if she could be there. Part of me hoped.

"Just be careful," was all she said, and we returned to watching cars in the rain.

I napped from three till five. After enduring Cindy's jibes about going on a date with Connie, I relieved Paul just after five. We sat in the warm calm of the Janss room for a half hour or so, discussing everything but what Connie had suggested about sciamancy. One of us had to stay unbiased, and he didn't need to be burdened with additional labels and characteristics yet. That's what I told myself.

He finally left me to my evening shift, hurried out to the car and drove off through the bleak, wet evening. This time we'd agreed to leave our mobiles on. We didn't need to say why.

I filmed, I photographed, I did more commentary into the pocket recorder. I reached 7.00 P.M. without dropping my chime ball once. Everything was the same. Everything was different. Just the names: sciamantium and sciamancy took it from a familiar candlelight vigil to something new and unsettling: a night watch for shadowforms out in the marshes, the shadowlands, a warding off of unproven enemies in the backwaters of forever.

By 8:10 P.M. I was exhausted, ready to call it quits. It was all too still, too constant, too laden with immanence. No, not constant, I kept reminding myself. Now and then the hot blade of the candle did stir, perhaps from something as simple and immediate as my breathing or a microzephyr sneaking around the cracks and doorsills, finding a way in, and the lines of flames trembled, wavered, shook their points of light as if to catch my attention, as if to test me. *Did you notice? Did you notice?*

But mostly it was still, *we* were still, all of us in our articulated, nautilus chambers, our adjoining rooms.

The notion of a sciamantium kept me there, kept me resolved as the candle burned away, knowing that Janss had done this again and again, sat beside solitary flames made legion, watching himself parceled off into mirror chambers that gradually sank into night. He hadn't just been alone in a bricked-up suburban house, not merely in a fabulous mirror world, but at the focus of rooms destined for darkness. He'd made waiting rooms, filled them with light, then watched them empty out.

Waiting rooms, yes, where you waited for darkness to come, infinite, replicated darkness, growing, settling across all these real, unreal spaces. There could be no reflection, no possibility of rooms and boulevards when the flame died and the nautilus rooms emptied and slowly ceased to exist. Yet what if the opposite *was* true—if only in the mind? It was the old question of whether a tree falling in a forest made a sound if there was no one to hear it.

I kept wondering about defaults in the brain. How was mine dealing with the idea of all those darkening rooms out there, the prospect of what might use those boulevards when the light was snatched away? What was it devising even now to protect. Andy Galt from inconceivable, unprecedented threat?

Minutes felt like hours. I'd look at my watch to find the hands had barely moved. It was like being on detention at school, time cruelly stretched and distended. The thought sent Connie's schoolyard rhyme running through my mind. But I'd already turned, faced where I'd been, met as much of myself as I could, my selves, going this way, that way, mocking me, taunting shadowforms in the infinite regress. The song's words were an incantation, a maddening litany. What had Janss been doing?

Then something caught my attention.

Did I imagine it, or was there a shadowing off in the distance—the false distance at two o'clock, where the images blurred into uncertainty? I blinked, took off my glasses and rubbed my eyes. There did seem to be something, a dimming, a shadowing out there.

I quickly looked about me. Behind and to the sides, the infinite rooms were as bright as ever, star chambers arcing off like settings for outdoor recitals. Carols by candlelight. Madrigals by Mirrorlight. A Cappella, in the Waiting Rooms. Nothing had changed. It was only ahead, in the mirror wall at two, that there seemed to be a darkening, like a storm at the edge of the world, spilling a little to the sides, but only a little, and way out in those real, unreal, never-real distances.

It was impossible, of course. Physically impossible. Any shadowing had to be replicated, shared, made part of all the reflection corridors and boulevards on every side. It was basic catoptrics.

Or selective self-delusion. Something served up by fatigue and an over-stimulated mind.

My adrenaline rush was real. I went into automatic observer routines, questioning everything. If the candle flame had been down at the rim, close to guttering, I'd have accepted it more easily, but two centimeters of candle stood well clear of the cup.

It was me. It had to be. Some optical trickery, some effect

of jet lag. I'd been sitting and staring too long. My bored brain was entertaining itself. Finding things. Making things.

Or it was the room!

I reminded myself that the imperfections of an average wall mirror enlarged to the size of the Gulf of Mexico became waves twenty meters high. Could it be the mirrors? Part of Janss's intended effect?

He had to have seen this, had to have been in this exact situation. That was why the chair was angled so. Checking the anomaly at two o'clock.

And he hadn't survived it.

Or he had simply gone away, seen something that drove him off.

Again I removed my glasses, rubbed my eyes. Again I checked the image field. It was there, definitely there, something was, something like swelling, burgeoning night, or perceptual trickery in the glass or in the vision centers of the brain. Defaults, yes, that was the word. What were the defaults set there?

Enough. I'd give it up for tonight.

As a way of withdrawing, anchoring myself in the reality of 67 Ferry Street once more, I located the tiniest black dot of the light switch where it sat in the join at eleven o'clock, looked over my right shoulder to confirm the barest hairline of the door in the mirror wall at six.

One more glimpse, one more try, I decided, as Janss must have.

The shadowing was there—the spreading "darklands," whatever they were. I smiled at the fancy, a hopeless victim of autosuggestion now. It was crazy. Too much peering off into distances, making eyes track vistas rarely, if ever, seen in nature, never meant for eyes with a such a highly developed, reactive brain behind them. I simply wasn't sure what I was seeing.

I had my mobile. Now was the time to call Paul, to have him join me and verify what was happening.

Connie's words stopped me. I had to be alone with this, had to allow that the eye-brain link was overwhelmed, set to doing the only thing it could: imposing order, treating this as something real, even as crisis, but rigorously dealing with it. Of course there were shadows, optical tricks. Of course there was fear, feelings of disquiet and alarm. What we'd said about the night related to eyes and mirrors, too. Just as we were completing our connection with night, so too we were changing what eyes, what brains, needed to do.

The darklands seemed to be growing, pushing from the two-o'clock focus into the mirror rooms at one and three. Behind, everything remained as bright and steady as ever. It was in that two-o'clock spread that it was happening.

"Let it come!" I spoke the words to hear myself say them, aware of what an ominous line they would make on the audio track. I took more video footage, more photographs. I filled the time with deeds, filled with the dying of the light.

The flame sank closer to the rim.

My mobile rang. Thank God! Paul offering a reprieve!

But it was Connie.

"Andy, do you know what sciamachy is?"

Not now, not now, I wanted to tell her, but the word held me.

"Say again, Connie. What what is?"

"*Sciamachy*. Not mancy, machy!"

"Not offhand. Something to do with shadows."

"Fighting shadows, Andy. The act of fighting shadows. Imagined enemies."

"Okay. Look, I'm nearly done—"

"Andy, what if it's a sciamachium?"

"Hey, look, thanks." I wanted her to go. I didn't want her to go. "Connie?"

"Yes?"

"Thanks. I mean it. I'm doing it. Alone. I'm doing it."

"I know. I know, Andy. But a sciamachium. Just call me when you're done, okay?"

"Promise."

She had known, I realized as I put the phone away. She was a natural and she had known.

The shadowing beckoned, teased at two, flexed dark fingers. *Look at me, look at me!* Everywhere else the rooms were bright and constant, seemed to be. I sat watching the darklands, wondering how they could exist, finally convinced myself that they spread only when I glanced away. It was using my mind, my eyes, to build itself.

I held the darkness with my eyes, daring it to slip into new rooms, consume new Andys. With all the bright rooms at my back, I held it at bay with my eyes and Connie's words, Connie's skipping song running through my mind.

Urging me. Connie the natural urging me to turn around.

I did so, looked over my shoulder at the eight-o'clock wall.

And there was dead-black night filling the glass, night the hunter pressed to it like a face at a window. The shadowing at two had been the bait.

I tipped forward in shock, slammed hard against the floor, reached for the first thing I could find—the candle stand—meaning to angle it up, to fling it at the dead-black wall of glass.

But stopped in time. Barely managed. Do that and I'd be in darkness when it shattered. Night would be everywhere, flowing out.

I scrambled to the eleven-o'clock corner, reached for the tiny button.

Yellow light filled the rooms. Most of the rooms. The black wall held at eight like onyx, obsidian, a membrane about to burst. The darklands shadowed off at two, but just the lure, just the distraction.

Now I flung the candle stand. Now it struck the glass, crazed and shattered the wall. The pieces clashed down, left dead-gray Besser brick beyond. At two o'clock, the darklands were no more.

When Paul arrived fifteen minutes later, Connie was with him. They found me standing by the front gate in the wind and rain, cold and shivering.

"Janss didn't know he had to turn around," I told them as I climbed into the back seat. "He never turned around."

Peace on Suburbia

M. Rickert

M. Rickert lives in Saratoga Springs, New York, where she works as a nanny and writes. She had only three stories published prior to 2003. However, she appeared almost every month in 2003 in Fantasy & Science Fiction, with a number of different and excellent stories, including "The Chambered Fruit," "The Super Hero Saves the World," and "Bread and Bombs," work good enough to make her the hot new writer of the year in our opinion. She says that her love of mythology is reflected in the fact that many of her stories are retellings of myths as a lens on our current world.

"Peace on Suburbia" is from Fantasy & Science Fiction, and is a vaguely contemporary urban fantasy about a suburban mom caught in a web of interlocking narratives, with hardly time to think. Her father is dying, a war may be starting, and meanwhile something strange and annoyingly distracting is happening involving her son. It is a story with a really chilling twist.

The children come home from school, spinning off the bus, screaming nonsense, waving at glowering strangers in their warm cars, then running into the house, shedding coats, dropping book bags with heavy thuds, and racing up the stairs to open the refrigerator and stare at its cheesy, milky, brown lettuce contents and moan about hunger and homework. You say, "Close the refrigerator. Choose something healthy. How about an apple?" and your son looks up at you with those blue eyes that have recently become hooded by eleven-year-old lids that do not reveal the clear wide beauty you remember and says, "I think I'm going to be one of those kids who die young."

"What?"

He shrugs. Turns away. "So it doesn't matter what I eat."

You don't know what to say. He wanders out of the room and you stand there, your mouth hanging open, and wonder if he is right, which sends a shiver down your spine that causes you to lose your mind, evidenced by your daughter standing there talking and you have no idea what she's saying. She spins away, like a nutcracker snowflake or a Sufi dervish.

You are worn out from the weekend spent with your parents. Your mother will not admit that your father is dying, though the hospice workers said, well, not that word, but that they were there to "help with the final stages of life," and your father, his eyes closed, his breath heavy, but sitting in his favorite chair and only a minute before talking to you, must have heard them, though he gave no sign and your mother nodded as though she understood but later, after he had gone to bed and you had called home to make sure everything was fine she sighed and said, "Don't change your plans for Christmas. This could go on for years."

"I want the ones I circled most and the ones with stars I

want a lot and the ones with stars and circles I also want."
Your daughter hands you the Target insert from Sunday's
newspaper. You flip through the pages and see that almost
everything is starred or circled or starred and circled. She
even starred a box of tampons, which, actually, are on sale
at a very good price. You stare at it until you feel like crying
and then you set it on the kitchen counter, carefully, as
though you will peruse it closely later to discern out of all
those circles or stars and circles-and-stars what is the right
combination to give your daughter a perfect Christmas.

The thing is, you might not need a box of tampons that
large. Things are changing, you notice, your emotions especially seem so strange lately, as though they weren't yours at
all, the way they used to feel like they came from you, but
rather, they seem to be happening to you, like a train
wreck. Mostly the emotion that keeps happening to you is
the feeling that there isn't enough. Enough what, you
couldn't say.

"Hey Mom, come look at this," your son calls from his
bedroom where you find him lying on the floor. "I can
shoot darts laying down." He does. The plastic dart with
the dull tip sails through the air in a perfect arc and hits the
dartboard with a small thwack. "Pretty cool, huh? I don't
even gotta stand up."

"Is your homework done?"

"We had a substitute."

"Again? Was Mr. Festler out again?"

"She yelled at us because we were doing stuff RIGHT."

"What are you talking about?"

"Mr. Festler says he wants us to share our work and help
each other but Mrs. Buttface yelled at us and said we were
cheaters."

"What's her real name?"

"Butta, Battaf. I don't know."

"Do your homework."

"What's the point?"

"I want you to stop talking that way right now, do you
hear me?"

He looks at you as if he fully knows he is going to grow

up and write a bestselling book about his recovery from your abuse which will make him a very rich man whom no one will begrudge because look what you put him through and says, "Well, why should I do it when she ain't even gonna be there tomorrow and we'll have some other teacher who won't even look at it?"

You turn and walk out of the room. You finally learned not to answer these questions that unwind only more questions and put off the inevitable task the questions seek to avoid. You wonder what he is muttering but you just keep walking to the kitchen where your daughter sits at the table bent with serious expression over her homework. She looks up at you and smiles.

"That's quite a lot of stuff you circled and starred," you say.

She shrugs. "I just thought I could show Santa everything I want, but I don't expect all of it."

You nod, slowly. It's a hard game, this. What does she know? What does she believe? Doesn't it seem strange to circle things in the Target catalog for Santa Claus to bring? After all, she's eight years old. Certainly she can't be so gullible? Certainly she knows the truth?

The phone rings. You answer it.

"Did you hear?"

You hate it when he calls from the cell phone. His voice crackles like a fire or an old man's voice and he isn't old. Or burning.

"Mr. Fensletter was out again. Don't you think this is getting a little strange?"

"They declared war. Turn on CNN."

You don't even get to say good-bye. You stand there saying his name over and over again but you've lost the connection and it's only a coincidence that it's happened at this time which makes it seem so apocalyptic. You hang up the phone. It has begun to snow. You stare at the falling snow.

"It's snowing!" your daughter shouts. Your son comes out of his room, a pencil tucked behind his ear. He blinks rapidly, and his eyes widen, he grins at you and says maybe tomorrow will be a snow day.

You ruin it by saying no, the weather report says it'll be just an inch and then you hug him which he allows for a full thirty seconds before he pulls away and walks into his room as though things are vastly safer in there.

The snow swirls big beautiful flakes that fall and fall without a sound.

You go downstairs into the cold family room of your split-level ranch. You like this room in the summer and hate it in the winter. You lift cushions and blankets and pillows and shoes until, in exasperation, you stand in the middle of the room and feel your chest expand, your breath fill with anger and then you see it in the damnedest of places, right where it belongs, on top of the television. You pick up the remote control and aim it at the TV. You walk to the couch and sit at the edge of it as you press through the channels, which almost all feature someone beautiful in an open collar revealing a young throat, you press through to CNN and then sit and look at the blue screen dotted by spots of light that blink bright and dim while someone's voice says things you only vaguely hear like "explosions" and "missiles" and "Mom?"

You point and press the power button.

She stands before you with her hair pulled back in an undone braid, her eyes clear and bright, she looks at you as if she knows something so immense you could never understand it and you wonder where she got that expression from.

"Oprah," you say.

She nods but smirks as she does, so you think she knows you weren't watching Oprah at all. How long had she been standing there?

"They want a talk to you."

"Who?"

"The men. At the door."

You open your mouth and close it. Haven't you told her a million times not to answer the door without you? You walk up the stairs and find three men standing politely on the front porch, in the snow, the door wide open. You look at your daughter. She looks at the bearded strangers, only curious, with no idea that she just risked all your lives. How to make her understand danger? You turn to the men who all smile and actually sort of bow. "We've come for your son," the tallest one says.

"What?"

The tall man steps forward slightly. "We have gifts."

You notice that all three men carry packages wrapped in brown paper tied with string.

"There seems to be some mistake," you say, beginning to inch the door shut.

You hear him coming down the hall, the pad of his feet against the carpet. You press the door shut faster but not fast enough and for a moment their eyes meet; your son, and the strangers whose eyes widen when they see him. You push the door shut and lock it.

"Who were they?"

"Salesmen." You turn to your daughter. "Didn't I tell you never to open the door to strangers?"

"I think they're still out there."

You make sure the door is locked and then you tell your children, in a calm voice, to get back to their homework. They ignore you but don't follow as you go through the house making sure all the doors are locked.

"They're going!" your son calls. "Hey, they left us presents!"

"Don't touch that door."

"But they left us presents."

"Go do your homework."

He mutters. Again you do not ask him what he's saying. Your daughter stands there, watching you. "Homework," you order.

"Why?"

"Why what?"

She shrugs and walks away slowly, as if weary and old.

You look out the window. The packages, simply wrapped, sit in the snow. What if it's anthrax? Smallpox? A bomb? Oh Jesus, what if they are bombs? You run to the telephone, dial 911. All in a rush you tell the operator about the three strangers, the packages, the possibilities you've imagined.

"Well, did you try shaking them?"

"What? Are you kidding?"

"Maybe it's just chocolate or something."

"Who are you? What are you doing answering this phone? Don't you know they've declared war? Don't you know we're in real danger here?"

"You don't have to be so hysterical. I'll send someone over. The fire department, how's that? But you should know you're not in any danger."

"How would you know that? Hello? Hello?"

You try calling your husband but you only get a recording saying that the cell phone customer is out of reach at this time. The fire engine comes wailing down the street and pulls into your driveway. Your children come running into the living room to look out the large picture window that overlooks the porch and driveway. The fire engine has a green wreath attached to the front with a paper menorah in the center. The firemen jump out of the truck and then they just stand there talking to the one with the fanciest hat. Your children narrate everything that's happening in excited voices. "They're standing around talking. The light is still going. Oh look, now he's coming on the porch." They both squeal away from the window heading toward the stairs until you command them back. They groan but run back to the window, giggling. "He's shaking them! Now he's smelling them! He's ringing—"

The doorbell rings. The children scream.

"Calm down," you yell. "Stay right there." They stare at you like wounded animals, perfectly still. You walk down the stairs. Open the door. You hear the children behind you, at the top of the stairs.

The fireman has a face like chiseled rock, and kind eyes. He holds, in his big hands, the presents wrapped in simple brown paper with string for bows. "I don't think you got anything to worry about here."

"Please. Just take them away."

He looks over your shoulder and smiles. "How you doing?" he says.

"Good." Your son answers as if they know each other.

"I just think, well, you know, under the circumstances, just some admirers probably left these."

"Admirers?"

Behind him the other firemen are all creeping closer to the porch, pointing and whispering.

"Just take them away," you say again.

"Sure." The fireman smiles but he is not smiling at you. You turn to follow the direction of his gaze. Your son smiles down at him. You move to block the exchange.

"Well, all right then," the fireman says. He turns. You close the door.

"What was that all about?"

Your son shrugs.

"Do you know him?"

He shrugs again.

The phone rings. You walk upstairs to answer it. The children stand at the window waving as the fire engine backs out of your driveway. Several firemen wave back. You don't see faces, just hands, waving through the falling snow.

Your mother is on the phone. She is crying. At first you think it is about the war but then your realize it is about your father. Oh yes, she's saying, he's gone completely nuts now. He says he sees angels. She cries and you try to comfort her. "We'll come up," you say, "we'll leave after dinner." What are you talking about, she says. Aren't the kids still in school? "But he's dying," you say. For a moment there is only silence and then she says, "Not yet he ain't. He's sitting right here eating goulash. You want a talk to him?" You hear her saying, "Your daughter thinks you're dying" and then his voice, the one you remember from before he got sick, "How's my girl? How's my girl?"

You feel like crying for that old voice. "Dad?" you say, and your own voice cracks as if he is already a ghost.

"Don't you go burying me yet, little girl. I'm feeling great. Just great."

You can hear your mother in the background, your father's muffled reply. "Dad?"

"Your mother says to tell you about the angels."

"Angels?"

"Yeah. But I don't think she believes me. You do, don't you?"

"So you're seeing angels?"

"If I only knowed, you know?" he says all earnest. "I tried to be a good father."

"You were, Dad."

"So the angels tell me our grandson's going to be some kind a hero."

"He is?"

"Don't that make you proud? What's that? Your mother says to tell you how the angels look, you want a hear?"

"Yeah, sure, but also, what's this about him being a hero?"

"First they is real small like fairies, you know?"

"Fairies?"

"Yeah, tiny like snowflakes. Hell, first time they came I thought it was snowing right in my bed. Jesus Christ, I thought I was losing my mind."

"But you weren't?"

"Heh, heh. Good one. But then they sort of grow and it's just what you expect, a lot of light, wings, you know, angels." He lowers his voice. "Listen I want a talk to you about your mother. I think maybe she's got the oldzheimers she's—" Suddenly his voice booms through the receiver, "So? Is that right?"

"Dad, what do you mean a hero?"

"Well, you know," he says and then your mother is back on the phone.

"Fairies," she says. "Snowflakes that turn into angels."

"It's snowing here," you say.

"Not you too?"

"No. Snow. You know, flakes. Outside. Mom? What's he talking about?"

"Who knows? Nothing makes sense."

"Have you talked to his doctor? Called the hospice?"

"The doctor's too busy to talk to me. The hospice work-ers all wanta come and take over the house but they don't know nothing. You know what one of them says to me?"

"What?"

"She says, well maybe he really does see angels."

"What did you say?"

"I said nothing. I got one person to talk nonsense with all day. I don't need another."

"Mom? Did you hear the news? About the war?"

"War? That ain't news. War happens every day. Did I tell you about Hilda Mealene's daughter? You remember Tanya, don't you? She went to school with you?"

"Listen, Mom. I gotta go. Can I call you later? Tonight?"

She says good-bye and you stand there listening to the dial tone. That's how things have always been with your mother. You hurt her feelings all the time though you don't mean to, not since you were a teenager. You hang up the phone. Walk down the hall. Your son lies on his bed doing his homework.

"Honey, do you ever see, you know, angels?"

As soon as you say it you know you are doomed. He will remember this question, this absurd question and it will rend him from you forever. He will enter his teen years re-membering that you asked him such a thing and he will de-scribe you and know you always by this single mistake. It will define you and your relationship and it's happened and you can't take it back. You turn away.

"Sometimes," he says. "Just the usual."

You stop and consider this fantastic reply. You can't think of anything to say. You walk down the hall and find your daughter standing at the window, watching the snow fall. Sometimes you catch her like this, in a dreamy state, she turns and looks at you with a beatific smile.

"Honey, do you see angels?"

She walks over to you and lays one small warm hand with purple painted fingernails on your thigh. She looks up at you but suddenly you feel small. She doesn't answer your question, she just stands there smiling and touching you as if she is sainted. As if you are forgiven.

You watch the snow fall. Your daughter wanders out of the room. Across the street, the Smythe's Christmas lights glow primary colors against the white and down the road several more houses are lit with color and white, a deer made out of light and a moose.

Suddenly one of those feelings comes to you, the way that's been happening lately. Standing there, in the dim December living room, you see flakes of falling light and for just a moment you are part of this light and its silence. This is temporary, but it is enough.

Across the street shepherds gather and point at your house. No, they must be school children, carolers, a large family from a foreign country. In the distance you hear the voices of your own children. You don't know what they're saying but by the pitch you can tell they're fighting. You walk to the window and press your fingers against the cold glass. The shepherds kneel in the snow. You watch them for a moment, then you pull the drapes shut.

Moonblind

Tanith Lee

Tanith Lee [www.tanithlee.com] lives in the south of England in a house with a name, and its name is Vespertilio. Her fantasy and horror fiction have put her in the forefront of both genres in recent decades. She began publishing in 1968, and her first novel, The Birthgrave, *was published in 1975. Among her most famous works is the series of fantasy stories of Flat Earth, collected in* Night's Master *(1978),* Death's Master *(1979),* Delusion's Master *(1981),* Delirium's Mistress *(1986), and* Night's Sorceries *(1987). She has published more than seventy books, and continues to publish a steady stream of impressive short stories.*

"Moonblind" was published in Realms of Fantasy. *It is a story that shows not only Lee's seemingly effortless use and transformations of standard fantasy images, but also her ability to reimagine them and make them new. The men in the Hunt are tough and brutal, carry weapons and dressed in cool outfits. They hunt and kill the fierce wolves. As a boy Kevariz wants nothing more than to join the hunt, and at eighteen he does, and takes one of the Master of the Hunt's daughters as his wife. He thinks he is happy until he finds a love that changes him.*

Yet once more, from an Idea by John Kaiine

His mother kept the inn, and he was a child when he saw it first, the Hunt. Evading his chores, he had escaped into a high loft, from where he found it easy enough to climb out on the roof. He lay along the thatch, looking down into the stony yard before the inn-house. Sunset had begun, the sky that night red from end to end. As the riders and the dogs assembled, all redness fell and caught on them, as if they had been doused in a shower of freshest blood.

There were 30 men, 30 horses, and 60 dogs.

The inn-maids went round with the cups of drink, finest silver cups, somewhat dented, that the inn kept solely for those 12 nights. Even on the roof, the child could smell the strong wine, and the pungency of spice and herbs stirred in.

He noted the powerful horses, and especially the dogs. These hounds were white and gray, long-haired, long-nosed, and bone-slim on long legs. All the men seemed loud and laughing, cracking jokes. Respected and revered, still they would boast of their participation in a Hunt. Already the child had heard how such men, wherever they went, whatever their birth or station in life, were treated like lords.

Next the red sky changed to a clear plum darkness, and the moon came up over the woods, round and white, with freckles on her surface. The Hunt saluted the moon, standing in their stirrups.

Then they slung the drained cups away, as if worthless, ringing on the stones, and turning their horses' heads, at a sudden gallop raced from the yard, among a streaming torrent of dogs.

It was as they left the light and shadow of the inn that the moonlight instead caught them. What had flashed and dripped scarlet at sunfall now blazed up like a bonfire of molten silver. On the roof, the boy was dazzled, eyes and brain. Ten years later, dazzled still, he presented himself to the Hunt Master in the Big House on the hill.

"You'd be happier—and far more safe—staying on in your family's inn."

"So I've heard, but here I am."

"What of your poor mother? Don't you care how she'll fear for you? How will she manage if you're killed?"

"She'll manage. And I don't care a jot."

Perhaps approving his impudence, the Hunt Master called his servant. He had the boy sent at once to undergo the proper tests. They were difficult and terrible, and he passed them all. By the time he was 18, Kevariz, the inn-woman's son, was himself a member of the Hunt.

Kevariz sat drinking at the inn.

He was 29 years old, and it was the night before Full Moon, and Tyana expected him home. However, his mother had said she wished to see him. Now, if he came to see his mother, it was always a visit, an occasion. He had brought her a rose-plant in a pot, and a little silver luck charm to hang on the rafters. She could brag that her son, who rode with the Hunt, had given it to the inn-house—but he doubted she would.

After the third tankard, he went up the cranky stair to her room above.

Of course he had been up here since his youth, but the room seemed every time more alien to him. Perhaps, even as a boy of nine or ten, it had been so—and all of the inn the same. He had thought himself made for another destiny.

"Mother. You're looking well."

"Yes, you prefer me to be well. It lessens your guilt in leaving me." He put down the rose and the talisman beside it. She nodded. "Thank you," she said, stiff and cold.

"You sent your boy for me."

"I've had a Dream."

Kevariz waited. His mother, when she reported this, meant only a single sort of dream; one which was prophetic. She had had them now and then, and her Dreams were always of something bad, and usually they came true. She had Dreamed, for example, of the wolf which killed Kevariz's father, on his journey back from the south. Three days after she Dreamed it, men carried the body, what was left—not much—home to her.

Kevariz met her eyes steadily now. She was a gray-haired matron, well-off and proud. She had never liked his leaving her, let alone leaving her for a Hunt. On days and nights he had come back from his training to help her at the inn, she treated him with scorn. Always she carped and chided, but never once had she said she did not *want* him to go, to please, *please* not abandon her and throw himself in the way of such danger. As a girl, she had elected to perform her Town Service in the silver mine, alongside the young men. Girls were never forced to do this, and few volunteered; they liked the softer work better, sorting the ore, or helping in the metal shops. But it showed her character.

He thought now, *She'll tell me she's Dreamed I'm going to die tomorrow.*

What if she did? It could make no difference. No man could resign from a Hunt, once he had joined it. Any who deserted before his 50th year was thrown in the jail to rot. It was like that everywhere.

"Well, mother," he said.

"I Dreamed," said Kevariz's mother, "that you had a son. No, don't interrupt me. He wasn't what you'd care for. He was a wolf."

"God's Silence, mother!"

She had at last managed to shock him.

Not since she had beaten him first, when he was five years old, had she knocked him back like this.

"Sit down," she said.

He sat, and she put one of the best pottery cups in his hand. It had brandy in it—she had kept it ready.

Kevariz drained the brandy.

She added nothing. It was her moment of triumph after all, 12 years waiting to pay him back, one year for every one of a year's Hunt Nights. It must feel as good as the strap had in her hand, when it rang on his shoulders.

"It was a true Dream, you'd say?"

"Yes."

She stood by the mantelpiece, and he sat turning the pottery cup.

In the end he said, "I suppose you think Tyana's betrayed me with some—with someone who has the strain."

"She's your woman. What do you think?"

"Four years, we've taken care—we've no children. That suits me fine, and her too. So far as I know, she's never strayed from my bed."

"Better be sure," said his mother.

"All right." He spoke shortly. He got up. "Thanks for your warning. I must be going, tomorrow is—"

"I know what tomorrow is, Kevar. Haven't I watched you ride off at every tomorrow of Full Moon, in your silver, and on your horse and with your dogs?"

He would not look at her; he could hear the mockery and rage in her voice clearly enough. He thought, *Is it that she didn't want to lose me, or that she wishes she could take my place?*

She was a hard woman, his mother.

Tyana was not like that, but wild and fey and loving, passionate and all for him. Or so he had thought.

When he climbed up the hill to his house, the lamp burned its yellow welcome in the window. Tyana was there, laying out the supper plates. Her hair was the color of copper, a fiery veil as she bent above the candles or the fire.

She came at once to greet him, shoving the two great dogs away so she could kiss him first.

Tyana seemed just the same. Her scent of warm flesh, cinnamon and mint, her hungry mouth, unchanged and solely his.

As they ate the food, he said, "Sergan's woman's in the

family way again." And when Tyana agreed, he added, "You're not missing that, perhaps?"

Tyana laughed. "I? No. I want only you."

"But a child, 'Yana—"

"I've no fondness for children." She frowned, apparently uneasy. "Is it you that wants me to have children? I will," she said, "if I must, to please you. But I can care for you better if it's just the two of us."

After all, he saw the stubborn streak in her then. Of course, if he had insisted, by law she must obey and allow herself to conceive. She had taken up with a Huntsman, and knew the rules. But oh, he could tell, in that case he would have been made less comfortable. She would make sure of that.

But well, then, she was not presumably pregnant by some other, or she would have jumped at this excuse. Nor, he thought, would her reluctance let her get herself so.

"Why all this about children?" she asked.

Kevariz said, "I thought, sometimes, those times I'm away with another Hunt—you might like the companionship."

"No, because you leave the dogs with me then, and they're companions enough."

"You're too attached to the dogs. Dogs get slaughtered every Full Moon, somewhere or other."

Heartless despite her smile, Tyana said, "Then the Master would give you another pair."

We grow unfeeling, Kevariz thought later, as he lay beside a Tyana relaxed and sleeping after sexual love. *Heartless. Yes, I'm like that, too.* He was. He knew it. Though he *made* love with Tyana, he did not love her. Nor had he ever loved his mother. Neither did he love his comrades, nor, as some men did, his dogs or his horse, though he would groom them so carefully. *Do I like anything?*

Yes, he thought, *I like the Hunt, God help me. That's what I like and love.*

As for his mother's Dream—it could have been a lie— just her malice. She was getting old, nearly 50 herself. She was a woman.

He turned on his side and shut his eyes and for a moment was in the black-green forest, not riding but running, and there was fur on him, and he had four feet. Waking with a start, he lay an instant in suspended horror. Then it passed. They all dreamed things like that, once in a while. Had the Master not told him, told them all in the beginning, "You'll become partly what you Hunt, and *they* are also partly like you. But remember, they're of the earth, and you are of the world. That's what keeps you separate."

Kvariz the Huntsman was dressing for the Hunt, with the help of his woman, the excited dogs leaping about in the room below, barking, till he shouted for them to be quiet.

Tyana, very skilled after four years, laced him into the linen and leathers, helped push on his boots. She plaited his hair, added as she did so the silver ribbons that must mingle with the braids. She had scrubbed his back in the iron bath, and shaved his jaw and cheeks with care. There must not be a nick on his face, nor any open cut anywhere on his body—if any were found, the wound must be cauterized with a hot metal rod and sealed by wax. She was adept at all of that, Tyana. But really, all the women on the hill were adept. They had had their training, too.

After the dressing and hair-braiding, Tyana opened the chest and undid the box. She performed this duty with ceremony, as Kevariz sat like a prince in his chair.

The box was of black-lacquered wood, inset with palest mother-of-pearl in a design of leaves and crossed knives. When she undid it, the low sun splashed up again from what lay there. The box was full of silver, and piece by piece, with the correct attention and reverence, Tyana brought the pieces out and laid them before him, and then, as he selected, she put them on his body.

Through the piercings in his ears and nostrils and chin went the silver studs and rings. Around his neck and wrists, and over the ankles of his boots, were clasped the larger rings. Into the lacings of his garments silver chains were threaded, and done up with silver locks. Silver buttons were attached to his coat, not by thread, but with silver claws. On to his fingers slid 10 silver coins set in silver. Then he stood up, and raised his arms, and around his waist was cinched the great belt of silver plates, each with its hammered crescent moon, but the buckle was shaped like the sun. Penultimate from the box, out from under a velvet cloth, the woman drew a pistol of white bone chased with silver, a silver-handled knife, and long, incised, silver-hilted dagger.

"There," she said. "We're almost done."

And finally then, almost slyly, like a secret treat put by for a child, she drew from the bottom of the box the velvet bag and handed it to him. Kevariz himself loosed its drawstrings. He shook into his palm the cache of silver bullets.

"How beautiful you look," Tyana said. Her eyes glowed, catching the glimmer of the silver. "As if the moon had rained white fire on you."

She always said similar things. She wanted sex then against the wall. This frequently occurred at that hour, and not only with them, but among other couples on the hill. He gave her what she wanted, it took little enough out of him, because at such times she was quick as any man.

Downstairs, the dogs were already dressed. He had seen to it as always, when earlier he groomed them. They, too, had their earrings and studs of silver, their collars. Their legs had thin silver rings, their claws were painted thick with silver, and silver wires were fastened in the long hair of their backs.

Out of the door they walked, he and they, along the hill, to the Big House.

The houses of Huntsmen clustered the hill, each with its grove, its little orchard, vineyard, kitchen-garden, which the servants and women tended. No one went without any good thing here. There was always plenty of food, and sufficient drink, women, fine clothing, even books if desired.

In the late afternoon light, dense and rich as amber honey, the trees were dark, and where the workers stood to watch, they clapped their hands and waved the men on.

All the Hunt was pouring up toward the Big House. Fifty

men this season, and a hundred dogs. From the stables on the hilltop the horses, readied like the dogs that morning, neighed and stamped, calling and eager to be off.

As the Huntsmen greeted each other, at first sober, brief, and businesslike, the grooms began to lead their horses out.

Kevariz saw his gelding appear, black as any night, and with a moon-white mane and tail—a classic horse he had bargained with the Master for, three years ago, after the original horse was eviscerated in the woods. The gelding also had silver through its ears, silver bells plaited in its mane, silver embroidery on the saddle-cloth, and flat studs fixed through the saddle. While over stirrups and the iron hoofs, silver was newly plated. This was common with all the horses.

He took the bridle from the groom. Among a crowd of men who did the same, he stroked the face of his horse, the long arch of neck, and the bells shook and made their faint sound. Up into the saddle Kevariz sprang, and the two tall dogs pranced around the horse, as all the dogs did—well-behaved now, used to the mounts, and to each other since they had kenneled together in their puppyhood, and run out together ever after. Only if sent to some other Hunt Meet must a man leave his own hounds behind. He must take loan of the wolfhounds of the Hunt that required him, to save the dogs quarreling. Kevariz had never minded this, providing the loaned animals were healthy and well got-up.

Golden light played on silver. Kevariz recalled how he had seen it first, all that metal blazing in the moonshine. Dazzled, still dazzled. It had been easy, in a way, to be brave and single-minded, and to forego almost every other thing.

Just then the door of the Big House opened and the Master came out in his blood-red brocaded coat and antique silver adornments passed, father to son, for 16 generations.

The men cheered the Master. They always did. He bowed to them, as always too, and the servants and grooms clapped again.

"It's a fine night," called the Master, "a clear moon white as starch. We've heard, haven't we, there's one main pack this month, down by the river road. It's those we'll take. And any stragglers. Not too unworthy a job of work."

The first cups went round. These were made of black bronze, and the wine had accordingly a bronze tang. Sergan said, joking, "It'll taste better at the inn."

Kevariz considered his mother a moment, when they were in the inn yard. He puzzled, did she truly spy on him, unseen, from a window?

Why had she told him that stupid fool's rigamarole?

Probably because it could haunt him forever, if he let it. For there were other women he had and could sleep with, and any one might announce she was to give him a son.

One day—one *night*—they would have wiped the strain, this strain of Hell, out. Scoured it off the face of the earth. So they always swore.

He put his mother and her Dream from his mind.

It was the earliest training, to be able to clear the brain on a Full Moon Night.

The sun sank into the land. The inn wine had been consumed. They saluted the rising moon. They flung away the silver cups, symbol of their own recklessness in the matter of their own lives, rode for the woods and the forest, flying now, the hounds, horses, and men. This was what Kevariz knew best; this fearful time, strangely, was when he felt the most secure.

The dogs started the first one down by the old mill-pond.

As they tore around the tarn, with its water-wheel standing obsolete now, in a moonlit verdigris of moss, across the clearing there loped something thin and white.

The hounds were belling, yowking. The men shouted excitedly. The moon-blaze of silver was all around, and through it, as if through an iridescent fog, Kevariz made out the shape of the wolf as it sped away, threading itself like an ivory needle back into the trees.

But the dogs were hot on its heels.

The Master yelled. They broke across the clearing and pelted down the ancient overgrown road beyond the ruined mill. Ten years since that mill had been in use. One night, the mill folk had died, all of them, murdered and eaten. There was barely enough left lying about for the town to identify. But this was what wolves did, a wolf-pack, and usually they were in packs. This individual, running in front of the hounds, though solitary, would be making for the familial lair.

Now the creature ahead, wanting more speed, dropped to its four feet—that was, what passed for feet. It bounded, ungainly, appalling, *swift*, leaping across obstacles along the road, the upthrust paving, the tussocks of weeds and bramble clumps.

Kevariz had seen every action it made before, and countless times. He kicked at his horse's sides, howling like the dogs, longing to catch up to their quarry and have it down.

But as usually happened, the dogs got there first, catching the wolf in the second it swerved and tried to head off again into the deeper forest, away now from where the river was and the lair.

It had made no sound until then, as the dogs sprang on it. When the biting fangs and silvered claws sank in, it began to emit the noises of its fury and agony—a horrible and filthy gutteral screeching and growling.

The dogs swarmed over their captive. Huntsmen rode forward into the melee. It was strong, the wolf, as always. One dog was flung up and over, just like the silver cups in the yard—spinning, dented, and silent—broken. One of Kollia's pair, Kevariz vaguely thought, his gelding stamping forward shaking its head. The bugle yapped, calling the dogs away. As they let go, sprawling down, the guns were out, and their voices barked in turn.

The bullets spat forward in stinging silver jets. Kevariz saw his own shot go home, deep into the shaggy face of the thing writhing now, bloody, wrecked, and refusing to die, there on the forest floor.

Kevariz found himself out of the saddle. He ran in. Into his hand, almost before he expected it, came the great coarse ruff. He pulled the head upward, and felt the claws of the beast scrape at him, sliding on leather, burnt by silver, gouging the flesh between. "*Good night, shitspawn.*" Kevariz plunged the long silver-hilted dagger in at the side of the neck, through fur and skin, flesh and skeleton. He heard the spine crack, felt it, saw the knife reappear on the neck's other side. The beast sagged. Its eyes, black as the darkness, each holding a miniature of the moon, stared into his. They looked blind, blind as his own.

The thing was dead.

Kevariz stood off. Hands clapped him on the back, and a flask arrived. He swallowed brandy, as in his mother's room. Then they were all up in the saddles again, the living joyous dogs, bearded with blood, yipping for more, and the bugle summoning them on, for the rest.

Where the river opened up the forest, in places the banks were steep and full of holes and caves. Frequently this was where they chose, the wolf-packs, to lair. As the Hunt had been told, tonight it was the same.

Two males came bounding out, one nearly pure white and one much browner. They leapt at the horses, straight up, and Kevariz saw Zivender's mare fall shrieking, even as Ziv seized the monster's hair and stuck in his knife. Then they were lost in a kaleidoscope of limbs and weapons.

A female came out next, after the males were down. They had heard this pack comprised four or five members, which meant, when the dogs had also got the female down, and the Master himself had ridden over to dispatch her, that one more beast might still be inside the cave.

Presently, as the shouts and shots died away, and the bubbling growling was silenced, they heard the final wolf, there inside the bank. It had begun howling, enraged, or frantic, but it did not come out.

The hounds were fierce, their blood was up, and the same for the men. The Master pointed. Sergan, and Ziv, who had struggled off his dying horse unharmed, but weeping with sorrow and anger, scrambled up the bank, their four dogs moving belly-down beside them, like snakes. They all vanished in at the maw of the cave.

Utter quiet was maintained outside. The Huntsmen there waited, guns positioned, their well-trained horses rock-still, so even the bells made no noise, the dogs crouched ready yet motionless.

The interior hubbub of battle was brief. The last wolf was one against six. Though these things had the strength of devils, seldom could even the larger packs of 10 or more do much against the amalgamated might of a Hunt, protected by its silver—for which any town's youth were prepared to die in the mines—armed and organized like warriors for war.

After a few minutes the disturbance in the cave stopped, Zivender and Sergan's dogs instead bayed in triumph. They alone, having entered the lair, would be allowed the hearts and livers, the rest of the hounds must make do with a chop or two. The Master had done excellently, selecting Sergan for the honor, and Ziv, who had loved his horse as much as his woman, and would mourn her for months.

He was not the first to enter the cave. The Hunt Master had called to Kevariz, and embraced him for his bold kill of the previous wolf. Possibly, when they all dined that night in the hall of the Big House, the Master would publicly title Kevariz "son." They were related that way, because Kevariz lived with Tyana, one of the Master's own daughters, but it was always "son" not "son-by-law" that the Master titled Kevariz when he had been particularly effective in a Hunt.

The brandy had gone round once more. Next they would quarter the woods hereabouts, to be sure. But the reliable reports had only been of this one pack. As a rule there was at least one wolf to be dealt with every month. No sooner had a Hunt burned out a nest, than more of the creatures slipped into the area, often inadvertently driven in from other spots, by other Hunts. Only twice, in all the years Kevariz had been a Huntsman, had they ridden all night without a single kill.

It was Zivender who asked Kevariz to go into the cave.

"I've lost my pocket-watch, damn my carelessness. No, it's not on poor Sdina." Sdina was the dead mare. "It must have dropped out of my coat in the lair. It's silver—"

"I know," said Kevariz.

"My father gave it to me for my first Hunt. I'd go back in but I've got Sdina to see to, can't just leave her lying."

"I'll be glad to have a look for the watch. Do what you have to here."

And so Kevariz climbed up to the cave.

The moon was going over by now, toward the west, and shone diagonally through the trees below, and across the inky water stretched a pointing finger of bleached fire.

So beautiful, the moon, that stirred up so much stinking dirt.

Kevariz had seen and entered other lairs. They were generally similar. Bones lay about, reeking and foul, though wolves, unless very old or sick, would empty their bladders and bowels elsewhere. There were always possessions in the lairs—sometimes a new Huntsman was unnerved to find a hairbrush or a doll. They had furniture too, many of them. Not the rough wooden stools and mattresses stuffed with dried grass that were normally found, but wonderful things that perhaps had come from great houses—a carved chest, or decorated ebony chair. However fine, no man coveted them. The lair would be fired and burned out, and anything like that with it.

There was some furniture in this cave, but only of the crudely made sort. The bed, though, had a raised wooden frame, and he discovered the dogs and men had killed the last wolf on it. It was another female, and initially he thought the copious bloodstains were only from the slaughter.

Ziv's silver watch was nowhere Kevariz could see, despite spending a while turning over the stuff in the lair, even picking about in the cold fireplace. In the end, Kevariz bent down to look under the bed-frame, for during the skirmish the watch could have rolled there.

Something had.

When he saw the glint of light, he took it for silver, and reached out and only snatched back his fingers in time. Under the bed, where the female must have thrust it when the Hunt approached, was a wolf-cub, not two days old.

Kevariz stared in at it. It was too young yet, for much to happen with it on a Full Moon. To the unaccustomed eye, it looked only like a baby, rather thick-haired and downy, with wide, gleaming eyes. Even the dogs had overlooked it, its small scent hidden by the odor of the lair, the blood, and entrails.

"God's Silence." Kevariz stood up. He had heard of, but never before had to contend with, such an eventuality. To butcher the full-grown ones, even if he had been told to do it at other times of a month, when they appeared nearly human, would have been seen to without a qualm, once he was sure. He had witnessed this once, a female wolf in her woman shape, hanged in the market by a silver rope, her feet weighted by iron. He cheered with everyone else when the rope pulled off her head. But this—this cub—this *child*—

Kevariz stepped back, knelt down, peered again in under the bedframe. It was crying now, the—the cub. So tiny and feeble, it made scarcely any sound, as he had sometimes found with sickly human infants when so young.

It was female.

"Devil's turd" Kevariz said to it. "*Werewolf*," he said, giving it for once its full title. He hated it. He pushed his hatred in at it, like a blade.

The baby only lay crying under the bed, under the mattress and the corpse of its mother, whose heart, liver, and lights had already been removed and thrown to the hounds of Zivender and Sergan.

"God," said Kevariz.

He stood up again, again stepped backward, and trod with a crunch on the face of Ziv's silver watch, lying unseen among the general mess.

Kevariz sat drinking at the Master's table.

It was the Hunt Dinner, and Tyana would not expect him home much before the third hour of morning. None of the women were present. The Dinners at Full Moon, especially after such a successful Hunt, were often rowdy.

The men recounted what they had done, over and over—
the audience, which had already seen most of it, was not
bored. They told how Zivender and Sergan had gone into
the cave, how Kevar had wrenched back the first wolf's
head and sliced its spine, they told the courage of the dogs,
the rewarding offal. They admired the claw-scorings on Kevariz's arm, which Tyana had already attended to.

"You see, son," the Hunt Master said to Kevariz, putting
an arm about his shoulders, "when I was your age, I was the
same. Riding through, getting a grip. That second when the
knife *bites*—God and Hell, there's nothing like it. Not even
sex."

Kevariz nodded. "It's like true love," he said.

"Yes—you're right. *Love*. We *love* the brutes, don't we, we
love them and we kill them. Can't do the one without the
other."

They laughed. The fortified wines by then were passing
round, purple in color, heavy and fiery, after the meats and
sweets.

The welter of blood had not put any of them off the food.

When they staggered back to their houses on the hill,
most of the Huntsmen would be busy with their women.

But *Better than sex*—

"Did you ever kill a cub?" Kevariz asked, as if curious.
His face was happy, flushed with wine and good-will.

"It was my luck, just the once. They look like real babies,
even on Full Moon. Mostly."

"I heard of a man once," Kevariz said, "my mother told
me about it at the inn—it made him ill to do that, though he
was a terror with the grown ones, male or female, they
could hardly hold him off from them."

"Your mother? She was trying to put you off," said the
Master.

"Yes, I believe she was," Kevariz nodded.

"If ever you come across a wolf-cub and you're squeam-
ish, son, you call for me. I'll see you through."

"I—," said Kevariz. His voice was weak suddenly, with
recollection. But the Master never noticed, as he had not

suspected the lie of Kevariz's mother's tale. Instead the Master was getting to his feet, calling out another toast for the night, and the victory in one more battle.

Play-fighting, some of the Huntsmen crashed onto the table, and the remains of food, cutlery, and some wine spilled on the ground. The Master only laughed again. He valued his men. He was a good sort.

Tyana sat up from his body, and gazed down at her by-law husband. She was surprised and disappointed.

"I'm sorry," he said. "I drank too much at dinner in the Big House."

"You drank too much—that's happened before on Hunt Nights. It makes no odds. You still want me."

"I want you. But I'm unable."

She sighed. He saw now she could be petulant, as well as stubborn. Her attractions, even her glory of hair, tonight grated on him like the stinging salves she had applied to the scratches the wolf had made as he killed it.

Soon she gave up on him. She lay down, sullen, and turned her back. "You don't love me so well as you did."

I never loved you, said the voice in his heart. He had only fancied her body, and needed a woman to keep his house better than a servant, and the Master anyway had said to him, playfully, "My 'Yana looks at you a lot." The Master had 13 daughters by various of his women, but no sons. He must get sons, therefore, through liaisons between his Huntsmen and his daughters. Was Tyana the loveliest daughter? Was Kevariz likely to be the one the Master chose to follow him in the Master's role? On other nights, when he called Kevariz "son," Kevariz had thought it might be so.

Kevariz said, "I love you like the spring, Tyana. Now close your eyes and go to sleep."

"How can I sleep without—?"

Kevariz felt himself heave out of the bed, landing on his feet on the night-frigid floor. "Be quiet!" he bellowed at her.

Then he saw her looking up at him in fright, afraid of a blow that would spoil her looks. Kevariz shook himself. He sat down leadenly in the chair by the hearth.

"Listen, 'Yana, tonight I had to kill—I had to kill a cub."

"A wolf-cub?"

"Yes, what else would I mean? God's Curse, it was bad for me. It looked just like a human baby. And—it cried so."

Her face was all incomprehension. Well, she had said she had no feeling for children. But the face of any one of his comrades would be the same. *It* had not *been* a human baby. It was a *wolf's* child. Left to live, it would grow, swiftly as any actual beast, to adulthood—and then the murder of the real children would begin, and it would rejoice as it ate their meat.

These lands were rife with wolves. Indeed, it *was* a war. And though a child in an ordinary war might be spared, *not* a child that, less than two years on, would wield the powers and blood-lust of a full-grown, supernatural enemy.

"Oh, I know," Kevariz said. "Oh, 'Yana, I won't hurt you. Stop cowering and lie down. Go to sleep. I'll take a walk along the hill. Clear my head. The dawn's coming and the moon's down. It's safe enough."

Did he realize, as he walked along the slope? Maybe he did. All the lights were out in the houses, save for the lamps left here and there in a porch. The windows of the Big House glistened only with the dim return of morning, and the sky was hollow. The grass was wet with dew. Kevariz walked on, toward the woods, the forest.

He knew, and had known. Of course he had known. He had come out of the lair and coined at once his beginning lie. "Ziv—look—I found it like this on the floor—you or Sergan must have trodden on it as you slaughtered that thing on the bed." And Zivender's long face, not just his beloved mare dead, but now his family keepsake smashed.

On another night, Kevariz would have told him the facts. That *he* had inadvertently trodden on the watch. He would have paid in the town for a repair, which anyway very likely would be done free for any Huntsman. But Kevariz lied, to practice.

Then, Kevariz had strolled off a way into the trees, mentioning he needed to relieve himself. No one was suspicious, why should they be?

He thought it might have smothered, bundled there inside his coat, and the silver button-claws scorching it. It was so little, not one of the others had taken it for anything more than the pack of cloth he held in there, to a nonexistent wound. Nor did it cry anymore, frozen by its contact with this otherness—Kevariz—which had dragged it from beneath the bed-frame, parceled it into the cloth kept for staunching blood, clutched it between a coat and an inimically silvered body that, to the cub, must scratch, scald, and *smell* so very wrong, a human man whose odor was not of wolf, but of wolf-killing.

The dogs still did not nose it either. Even his two, when they came bouncing at him—but to them he smelled properly of butchery, and besides, he threw them the chops that were their lot. That was what interested them.

Down in among the trees, out of sight, he had found a bush of wild eucalypt, removed the baby and rolled the cloth in the bush. Then he put the baby back into the perfumed cloth, and stowed it in one of 50 craters in the tree trunks, well off the ground, higher than his own head would be, when he rode a horse.

He thought he was giving it, the cub, a chance. But later, after they had ridden through the woods and no one had discovered the child, or even wondered if anything was in a tree, Kevariz grasped the thorny idea that really he had only given it a slow, painful death—instead of a painful death that was fast.

Again and again that night, he cut himself on this idea, while thrusting it from his mind. For always it came back.

Now *he* was going back, back to the cratered tree, around the tumble of the river bank.

He knew what he would find, and found it. Light by then was coming through the wood like rosy smoke. In the soft rays, as he lifted the cub from the tree, a human baby lay in his hands, watching him with clear and fully focussed eyes that were like two blue moons.

Kevariz carried her down to the river, and washed her gently in the water. By this he demonstrated to himself he knew also she was far more than human. No human child so young could have stood the water's dawn cold—but she did not mind. He too was now clean of the tang of blood. He fed her the milk he had stolen from his own cupboard in the house, the home the Master gave him, that was no longer his. The wolf-child drank the milk. She was far more couth and coordinated than the human baby she seemed to be. She could already help hold the crock. Tomorrow, he must find a cow on the edge of the town, where they went out to pasture after Full Moon. But soon she could be weaned to easier stuff.

Kevariz tucked the baby in his arms, sitting under the tree, as sunlight bloomed in a giant flower of flame, and altered the forest from shadowed savagery to innocence.

It was as if he had been waiting for this hour.

Kevariz felt no compunction. As he had not when he left the inn, as he had not ever when he slew a wolf. He was pitiless, even in compassion, Kevariz.

The baby slept. Idly he rocked her, as he had seen women do.

For now—for a year and a half, at most, two—she would be his child, the child he had never wanted, and now did. Then she would be grown, like all her kind, into a young woman of about 17 years—Tyana's age, when he courted her. As in a pack it happened, they would thereafter be different with each other, the wolf-girl and Kevariz the Huntsman.

Except, he would never Hunt in that way again.

He would have to become one with her, live as she did, always potentially concealed, canny; if located then pursued. With Kevariz and his Huntsman's education to help her, she—and he—could perhaps survive a great while. But, if he considered sensibly, in fact they would not last long at all.

Already he had removed his silver, dropped it under the

hill. The dogs, sleeping by the fire, had glanced up. He had nodded, and gone out of the door.

He recalled now the Master's words, "You'll become partly what you Hunt, as *they* are also partly like you." They were of the earth, the Master said, but men were of the world—this was not honest. Kevariz did not believe it finally. Men too were of the earth, men too were wolves, or how else, in the case of *her* kind, could they ever be both at once?

Startling him, despite everything, the child spoke her first word to him at that moment. "Da," she said, "Da—."

"Yes, baby, I'm your da."

And in two years, he thought and knew, he would be her husband, by the oldest law there was. She was very fair, blonde and pale. Once a month, she would be one of the pure white ones.

Soon he got up, and walked them deeper into the forest, into those areas he had come across in the past, the wolf-places. For now, secure enough.

They would think, at the Big House, on the hill, he had lost his nerve and become a coward, as sometimes Huntsmen did, after which they ran away. They would search for him in the town, and in other towns—never in the woods. They understood Kevariz, the Huntsman, was too wise to hide there from jail, where the wolves might get him.

How many others, through the years, had done as he did?

It had been waiting for him, oh, yes. He who had never loved or liked, not mother or wife, not child, not even friend, not even loyal horse and hound. And when he killed the wolves, *loving* it—it had been *fear* of love, not *love* at all, that had made him brave and mad. Protesting too much, he had blinded himself, as at the start the silver ornaments had blinded him, in the moonlight. Now, he saw. He had seen the instant he had looked at her, beneath the bed.

Like his mother, however, Kevariz had discovered he possessed the prophetic streak. His Dream was a waking one, as he walked away into the wolf-heart of the forest, beyond the lairs of men.

He saw it all before him. The way she would grow, his

adopted daughter. He saw the way, at each Full Moon, she changed, coated in fur, running now upright, now on taloned hands and feet, her back raised impossibly, her face all eyes and fangs. He saw it did not count anymore, the numbers of her kind he had killed, nor the countless numbers of his kind, killed by hers. He saw that she would never, even as a beast, hurt a hair on his head. While he, to save her, would die.

He beheld them living in caves, the boles of dead trees, or running fleetly from a shouting pack of silver-clad men. He beheld them lovers, and their own first, and only, child—a boy, who, naturally, would inherit her blood, not his. His son that, as Kevariz's mother had foretold, would be a wolf. Somewhere too he watched them slain together, all three of them—but yet there was so much before that to come, so much of *life*, a living life Kevariz had never known. Surely it was worth the price.

The baby slept. This deep in the forest, even by day, the world grew darker and more profound. Since he had prophesied like his mother, and because of her foretelling of his fate, he decided he would call the child in his arms by his mother's name, Sosfiya.

Professor Berkowitz Stands on the Threshold

Theodora Goss

Theodora Goss [people.bu.edu/tgoss] lives in Brighton, Massachusetts. Her first child has just been born and will be nearly four months old when this book is published. She graduated Harvard Law School ("If you have ever dreamed, as I often do, of walking down the streets of a strange city at night, knowing that you are lost and vaguely fearing that something—you know not what—may be following behind, you have known what law school is, for a writer.") and worked as an attorney ("Then came the brief nightmare of working as an international corporate attorney—in New York City, on the forty-second floor of the Metropolitan Life building above Grand Central Station, where the elevators always seemed, somehow, to be descending—even when going up"). She is getting a Ph.D. in English now, and is better. She began publishing fiction only three years ago and has published five stories. More are forthcoming in semiprozines—Polyphony, Alchemy, and Lady Churchill's Rosebud Wristlet.

"Professor Berkowitz Stands on the Threshold" was published in the genre-bending original anthology, Polyphony 2. It is a procvocative inversion of the It Was All a Dream trope which comes down on the side of real fantasy, and has a special poignancy for all past or present English majors. It is also an interesting comparison and contrast to the Gene Wolfe story later in this book.

⟶ I. The Sun Rises in an Ecstasy of Brightness

When the sun rose, Alistair Berkowitz realized that he was standing on a beach. His slippers were covered with sand, and cold water was seeping up the bottoms of his pajamas. He could smell the sea, and as the mist began to dissipate he could see it, a line of gray motion closer than he had imagined. He stood beside a tidal pool, which was probably responsible for the uncomfortable feeling of wet fabric around his ankles. In it, iridescent snails crawled over a rock. In the distance, he heard the scream of a gull. He shivered. The wind off the water was cold.

Then the sun shone on the water, creating a gold pathway, and he said without thinking,

the sun rises in an ecstasy of brightness,
like a lion shaking its mane, like a chrysanthemum
discovering itself

"Ah, you speak English."

Berkowitz turned so quickly that he lost a slipper and had to find it again in the sand. The man behind him was dressed in a suit of purple velvet. Dark hair hung over his eyes. It looked as though he had combed it with his fingers.

"Myself, I speak English also. My mother, when she was sober, told me my father was an English duke. When she was drunk, she told me he was a Russian sailor. Unfortunately I speak no Russian."

Berkowitz stared at him, then looked down at his slippers and shifted his feet. Why was he wearing pajamas? He rubbed his hands in an effort to warm them. "I'm assuming," he said, "that this is a dream. Sorry to imply that you're a figment of my imagination."

"*Pas du tout,*" said the man in the purple suit, smiling. His teeth were crooked, which gave his smile the charm of imperfection. "Although as for that, perhaps you are a— how you say? Figment of my imagination. Perhaps I am lying with my head on the table of a café in Montmartre, and Céline is drawing a mustache over my mouth with charcoal, while that scoundrel Baudelaire is laughing into his absinthe. Perhaps all of this," he extended his arms in a gesture that took in the rocks behind them, and the sand stretching down to the water, and the sun that was rising and covering the gray sky with a wash of gold, "is all in my head. Including you, *mon ami*. Although why I should dream of an Englishman . . ."

"American," said Berkowitz. "I'm American. From Vermont." Then, putting his hands in his pajama pockets, he said, "I'm a professor. At a university."

"Ah," said the man in the purple suit. "If my father were an English duke, I might have traveled to the land of Edgar Poe. It is a difficult question. Did my mother lie when she was drunk, or when she was sober?"

"I mean," Berkowitz continued, annoyed at the interruption. It was what he habitually said when students interrupted his lectures with ringing cell phones. "I mean, I'm not an art historian. But Baudelaire. *'Le Visage Vert,'* about the death of the painter Eugène Valentin, poisoned by his mistress Céline la Creole. At a café in Montmartre. It makes sense for a professor of comparative literature to dream of Eugène Valentin. Not the other way around."

Valentin looked up at the sky. "Citron, with blanc de chine and strips of gris payne. Ah, Céline. Did you love me enough to poison me?"

Berkowitz shifted his feet again, trying to knock sand off his slippers. A gull flew over them, its wings flashing black and silver in the sunlight. How much longer would he remain a professor of comparative literature? Next week was his tenure evaluation. The department chairman had never believed in his research, never recognized the importance of Marie de la Roche. No wonder he was talking to a man in a purple suit, on a beach, in pajamas.

"And is she a figment of your imagination as well?" asked Valentin.

A woman was walking toward them, along the edge of the water. Her skin had the sheen of metal, and she was entirely hairless, from her bald head to her bare genitals. She had no breasts. Berkowitz would have assumed she was a boy, except that she lacked the usual masculine accoutrements.

Berkowitz stared at her and rubbed the bridge of his nose.

"If I imagined a female form," Valentin added, "it would look like Venus, not Ganymede."

The woman stopped a few feet away from them and, without speaking, turned and looked at the water. The two men turned as well. Between the sky and the sea, both of which were rapidly beginning to turn blue, a black speck was moving toward them.

"What is it?" he asked Valentin. He really should get glasses.

Valentin brushed his hair back from his eyes. "A ship. At last, I believe something is beginning to happen."

⌐ II. Seashells, Whose Curves are as Intricate as Madness

The harbor was built of stone blocks, so large that Berkowitz wondered how they had been moved. Like those statues on Easter Island. He looked over the side of the ship, at the waves below. If he were in someone else's dream, he would disappear when the dreamer woke up. What did that remind him of? Humpty Dumpty, he thought, and realized that he had answered in Helen's voice. Once, they had gone to Nantucket together. He remembered her sitting on the beach under a straw hat, taking notes for her article on the feminist implications of the Oz books. He wondered how she liked Princeton, and tenure.

He stumbled as the ship pitched and rolled.

Valentin opened his eyes. "You have kicked my elbow." He had been asleep for the last hour, with his head on a coil of rope.

"Sorry," said Berkowitz. The metallic woman was sitting on the other side of the deck, legs crossed and eyes closed.

She seemed to be meditating. About noon, Berkowitz had decided to call her Metallica.

Valentin sat up and combed his fingers through his hair. "Have you considered that perhaps are are dead? If, as you say, I am poisoned . . ."

Berkowitz looked around the deck and up at the sails. "This isn't exactly my idea of death."

"Ah," said Valentin. "Are they still dancing, *les petits grotesques?*"

They were not dancing, exactly. But they moved over the deck and among the rigging, women with the calves of soccer players below gossamer tunics, like the workings of an intricate machine.

Berkowitz said, "At first I thought they were wearing masks."

One had the head of a cat as blue as a robin's egg, with fins for ears. Another, the head of a parrot covered with scales, the green and yellow and orange of an angelfish. Another, a pig's head with the beak of a toucan. This one had taken Berkowitz's hand and said in a hoarse voice, as though just getting over the flu, "The Luminous Vessel. The Endless Sea." Then he had realized they were not wearing masks after all. Now, they seemed to be taking down the sails.

"You know," he said to Valentin, "I think we've arrived."

Metallica rose and walked to their part of the ship. She looked over the side, at the harbor and the water below.

Berkowitz whispered, "I wonder if she's a robot?"

"Look at their legs," said Valentin, rising. "So firm. I wonder . . ."

The path from the harbor was covered with stone chips. Berkowitz felt them through his slippers, edged and uncomfortable. They walked through a thicket of bushes with small white flowers.

Ahead of him, Valentin was trying to put his arm around Catwoman's waist. Berkowitz touched him on the shoulder. "Feathers," he said. "Not flowers. See, on the bushes. They're growing feathers."

"Yes?" Valentin asked. "I have made a discovery also, *mon ami*." Catwoman took the opportunity to walk ahead. "She is a flirt, that one. But look, you see our silver-plated friend?" Ahead of them, Metallica and Pigwoman walked together. They were gesturing rapidly to one another.

"Are they playing a game?" asked Berkowitz.

"I think," said Valentin, "it is a conversation."

They emerged from the bushes. Ahead of them was a castle. At least, thought Berkowitz, it looks more like a castle than anything else. It was built of the same stone blocks as the harbor, but on one side it seemed to have grown spines. On the other, metal beams extended like a spider's legs. Towers rose, narrowing as they spiraled upward. What did they remind him of? Something from under the sea— probably seashells. He suddenly understood why Marie de la Roche had compared seashells to madness. The castle glittered in the sunlight, as though carved from sugar.

They passed through a courtyard carpeted with moss and randomly studded with rocks, like a Zen landscape. They passed under a doorway shaped, thought Berkowitz, like the jawbone of a whale. He felt as though he were being swallowed.

The room they entered seemed to confirm that impression. It was large, with a ceiling ribbed like a whale's skeleton. Pale light filled the room, from windows with panes like layers of milk glass. Valentin's footsteps echoed. He could even hear the shuffle of his slippers reverberating.

At the other end of the room, he saw robed figures, huddled together. They looked like professors in academic robes. In the moment it took for his eyes to adjust to the light, he imagined they were discussing his tenure evaluation. But when they turned, he clutched Valentin's arm. They were not wearing masks either. One had the head of a stag, its horns tipped with inquisitive eyes. Another was a boar, with bristles like butterfly wings. Another seemed to be a serpent with spotted fur. Their robes were a random patchwork of satin, burlap, and what looked like plastic bags, held together with gold thread and bits of straw.

They moved apart to reveal an ordinary kitchen chair,

painted a chipped and fading green. On it was sitting a girl in a white dress, sewn at the sleeves and hem with bleached twigs, coral beads, pieces of bone. Her hair was held back by a gold net. She looked like she had been dressed for a school play.

Pigwoman curtsied. "The Endless Sea," she said. "The August Visitors."

The girl rose from her chair. "*Bienvenu, Monsieur Valentin*. Welcome, Professor Berkowitz." She turned toward Metallica and bowed. Metallica answered with a movement of her fingers.

"I understand you have been communicating in English," she continued. "I shall do the same. Aeiou, of course, requires no verbal interpretation."

The collection of vowels, Berkowitz assumed, was Metallica's name. He stared at the girl. What had Helen told him? "Look at Alice, and Ozma. Literature, at least imaginative literature, is ruled by adolescent girls." Then she had leaned across the library table, with her elbows on a biography of Verlaine, and asked him on their first date.

"Of course you have already learned one another's qualifications?" She looked at them, as though expecting confirmation. "No? Well then. Eugène Valentin, perhaps most celebrated for your *Narcisse à l'Enfer*. Although *L'Orchidée Noire*, your painting of the dancer Céline la Creole, is equally magnificent, *Monsieur*. Professor Alistair Berkowitz, translator of the fragmentary poems of Marie de la Roche. I am, of course, addressing you chronologically. Aeiou, follower of Vasarana, the goddess of wisdom, once temple singer for the goddess." She turned to Valentin and Berkowitz. "Her name, as you may have guessed, is a chanted prayer. I have not pronounced it correctly. Her vocal cords were surgically removed during incarceration, to prevent her from spreading the teachings of her sect. Professor, I believe you have heard of American Sign Language? She has asked me to tell you that she wishes you the blessings of wisdom."

She looked at them, as though waiting for a response.

They looked at each other. Valentin shrugged. Then, simultaneously, Valentin said, "We are pleased to make her acquaintance," and Berkowitz blurted, "I don't understand. Who are you? Where are we? What kind of dream is this, anyway?"

She raised her eyebrows. "I am the Questioner. Haven't you discussed this at all among yourselves? Surely you must have realized that you have come to the Threshold."

⏤ III. The Sea is as Deep as Death, and as Filled With Whispers

Valentin and Berkowitz stared at the mossy courtyard.

"This garden was planted to represent the known world," said the Questioner. "The mosses, of course, represent the Endless Sea, with darker varieties for the depths, lighter for the relative shallows. And there," she pointed to a central area where rocks were clustered, "are the Inner Islands. That gray one is your island."

"I still don't understand," Berkowitz whispered to Valentin.

Valentin looked back at the doorway, where Pigwoman stood as though on guard. "I wonder if she is so firm everywhere, *mon ami*?" he whispered.

Berkowitz edged away from him. Did he have to share his dream with a lecherous Frenchman?

"Around the Inner Islands lies the Endless Sea," said the Questioner, "unnavigable except in the Luminous Vessel. Anyone sailing to the Outer Islands must stop here, at the Threshold."

She turned to them and smiled as though she had explained everything.

"I still don't understand," he said.

The Questioner frowned. She looked, thought Berkowitz, as though she were trying to solve an algebra problem. "Professor Berkowitz, I have tried to suit my explanation to your understanding. But you are a man of the space age. Perhaps if I call those central rocks the Inner Planets, and the mosses an Endless Space, and tell you that you can only reach the Outer Planets in the Luminous Rocketship. To a tribesman I might speak of the Inner Huts. Aeiou, who needs no explanation, understands them as representations of Inner Consciousness. The result is the same. Tomorrow I will ask you the Question, and based on your answer you will either return to the Inner Islands, or proceed onward."

"But I still don't . . ." said Berkowitz.

"Excellent," said Valentin. "Look, *mon ami*. We are from there." He pointed to the central cluster of rocks. "But we have qualifications, as she said. You have your book, I have my paintings, and our companion of the vowels has evidently been singing. If we answer her question correctly, we will be allowed to go on."

"But to where?" asked Berkowitz, with exasperation. He was coming to the uncomfortable conviction that, rather than dreaming, he was probably going mad. Perhaps he was at that moment being strapped into a straitjacket.

"Out, out!" said Valentin. "Have you never wanted to go out and away?"

He suddenly remembered a story he had told Helen, when they had been together for almost a year. One morning in high school, the captain of the wrestling team had locked him into the boy's bathroom, shouting, "Man, if my name were Alistair, I would have drowned myself at birth!"

He had wanted, more than anything, to go out and away. Away from the small town in New Jersey, away from his father, a small town lawyer who could not understand why he had wanted to study something as useless as literature. Helen had smiled at him across the scrambled eggs and said, "Lucky for me you had a lousy childhood."

Perhaps that was why he had become interested in Marie de la Roche. She had wanted to go out and away. Away from her parent's olive trees, away from the convent. He imagined her, on her cliff beside the sea, in a hut made of driftwood lashed together with rope. Each morning she climbed down its nearly perpendicular face to gather seaweed and whatever the sea had left in tidal pools: crabs, mussels, snails. Fishermen claimed her broth could revive drowned men. Each afternoon she sat on her cliff and wrote, on driftwood with sharp rocks, on scraps of her habit with cuttlefish ink, and sent the fragments flying. Fishermen believed they brought a good catch. He thought of the year he had spent studying her fragments, now in a case at the Musée National. How many had been lost, buried by sand or floating out to sea? She had found her way out, through madness and suicide. Fishermen had built a church in her honor, and in certain parts of Brittany she was still considered a saint. Was that what had fascinated him, her willingness to toss everything—her poems, herself—over a cliff?

Valentin and the Questioner were staring at him. How long had he been standing there, lost in thought?

"Perhaps," said the Questioner, "if I showed you the Repository?"

It looked like a museum. Where the walls were not covered with shelves, they were covered with tapestries, paintings, photographs. Metal staircases twisted upward to balconies, containing more shelves. They were filled with books and scrolls, disappearing upward into the shadows of the ceiling. Toward the center of the room were glass cases filled with manuscripts, small statues, things he did not recognize. One looked like a collection of sea sponges. They passed a sculpture that looked suspiciously like the *Nike of Samothrace*, and the skeleton of a rhinoceros painted blue. "Not bad, that," said Valentin, examining it with admiration.

"By those who have come to the Threshold," said the Questioner. "I believe my collection is fairly complete." At the end of the room was a fireplace. Over it hung Van Gogh's *Irises*. She walked to a long table that looked like it belonged in a public school library. "Ah," she said, "the collected works of Keats. I wondered where I had left it." She opened a box on the table, which began to play music, low and melancholy, that Berkowitz faintly recognized. "Lady Day," she said. "And of course Elihu's *Lamia*." She tapped her index finger on one of the glass cases. A green glow levitated and stretched elegant tendrils toward her, like an art nouveau octopus. "So simple, yet so satisfying."

"My *Narcisse*, is it here?" asked Valentin.

"I will show it to you," said the Questioner. "But I believe Professor Berkowitz would like to see this." She opened a glass case and took out a scrap of fabric. "When Marie de la Roche leaped into the sea, she held this in her hand. It was the last piece of her habit. She gave it to me, when she passed through the Threshold."

Berkowitz took the linen, which looked fresh although worn, as though it had never touched sea water. He recognized her angled writing. Mentally, he translated into rough iambs and anapests:

the sea is as deep as death, and as filled with whispers of the past

She had been here. She had walked through the Threshold. He wondered what sort of question he would be asked, and whether he would pass the test.

⌐ *IV. My Mind Crawls, Like a Snail, Around One Thought*

Berkowitz drank through a course of tangerine fish and fish-shaped tangerines, through a course of translucent jellies. The liquid in his glass was the color of amber, and shards of gold leaf floated in it. It tasted like peaches and burned his throat going down. Every once in a while he had to peel gold leaf from his teeth.

He looked down the table and felt a throbbing start in his left temple. A woman with what looked like a flamingo on her head winked at him. The flamingo winked as well. Too much fur, too many wings, and not a single nose was the correct shape or size. The Abominable Snowman jogged his elbow.

He stared at his soup, which tasted like celery.

The Questioner leaned over to him and said, "Aeiou is a neighbor of yours. She comes from Connecticut."

"Oh," said Berkowitz. She smiled encouragingly, as though waiting for him to respond with something clever. He said, "Connecticut isn't really that close to Vermont."

He tried to laugh and knocked over his bowl, which looked like a sea urchin. Soup spilled over the table.

She turned to Stagman, who was sitting on her other side.

Damn, thought Berkowitz. I've already failed. Who made up the rules of this game anyway?

The Questioner rose. "I believe it's time for a quadrille. Are the musicians ready?"

They evidently were, because the music began.

The Questioner led with Stagman. Valentin, who was learning the steps as he went along, capered behind Pigwoman.

Berkowitz drank, and despised them all. He despised the musicians, playing citoles, lyres, pipes that curled like the necks of swans, and what looked like the lid of a trash can. He despised the dancers, gliding or shuffling or hopping in complicated figures he could not understand. He despised Aeiou, weaving through them in a dance of her own, and Valentin, who kept treading on Pigwoman's toes. He despised himself, which had never been difficult for him. The department would never give him tenure. The chairman had told him that Marie de la Roche was marginal. Hell, how much more marginal could you get than an insane nun living on a cliff? He should have written a book on Baudelaire. He should have stayed in New Jersey and become a lawyer. By the time he began to despise Marie de la Roche, on her damn rock, with her damn poetry, the room was beginning to look distinctly lopsided.

"Enough," said the Questioner. The music, which had been drifting from a waltz to cacophony, ceased. Valentin stopped abruptly and would have fallen, except that his arm was wrapped around Pigwoman's waist. "It is time for your questions."

Already? thought Berkowitz. I didn't even have a chance to study.

"Tomorrow morning, as you know, I will ask each of you the Question that will determine whether you step through the Threshold." There she went again with her "as you know." As though they knew anything. "Tonight, however, you may each ask me a question of your own."

Stagman brought her green chair, and she sat in the middle of the room. Light flickered from candles and oil lamps and fluorescent bulbs. That explained why the room was beginning to blur. Berkowitz pinched the bridge of his nose. Helen had been right—he should get glasses.

Valentin, who had been trying to kiss Pigwoman's neck, stumbled and kissed the air. He must be drunk, thought Berkowitz.

"Aeiou will begin," said the Questioner. Aeiou gestured. The pain spread to Berkowitz's right temple. God, he needed an aspirin.

She smiled and nodded. "Your songs will be sung for a thousand years, until the factories and prisons of the Imperium return to dust, and pomegranates grow on Manhattan Island."

Aeiou bowed her head, and metallic tears ran down her cheeks. The audience clapped.

Damn, thought Berkowitz. This must be part of the test. The Questioner looked at him. Not me, he thought. Not yet. I need time to think.

"Monsieur Valentin," she said. "What would you like to ask me?"

Valentin looked down at the floor, then said, "Did she poison me? Céline."

The Questioner looked amused. "Yes, in the absinthe. If you choose not to return, she will wear black orchids in your memory." The audience clapped. The Abominable Snowman giggled, and Catwoman nudged whoever was standing beside her.

What a stupid question, thought Berkowitz. That won't get him any brownie points. He tried to think of something profound.

The Questioner said, "And finally, Professor Berkowitz."

Profound. What was the most profound question he could think of? He needed a hundred aspirins. She was leaning toward him, waiting for his question. Berkowitz said, "Is there a God?"

She leaned back in her chair. She seemed disappointed, or perhaps just tired. "Yes," she said. "Once, she would visit

our island. We would work in the garden together, tying
back the roses. But she has grown old, and sleeps a great
deal now. I do not know what will happen when—but that
wasn't your question."

There was a moment of silence. Then the audience
clapped, without enthusiasm. A thousand aspirins, that's
what he needed. Berkowitz took another drink and despised the universe.

Later, lying in bed and trying to keep the room from
spinning, he thought about the test. Clearly, he had already
failed. All the failures of his life gathered around him. Failing to make the soccer team because he couldn't kick
worth a damn. Failing calculus. Failing to get into Yale.
Failing with Helen, who had waited for him in the kitchen,
under a lightbulb he had forgotten to replace, with the letter from Princeton in her hand. "Tell me," she had said.
"How am I supposed to compete with a dead nun?" Failing his tenure evaluation, because he already knew he
would fail.

Marie de la Roche had not failed. She had succeeded at
going mad, at committing suicide, at becoming a saint. She
had stepped through the Threshold.

The question. His mind crawled around it like a snail.

Valentin would get through, because the Questioner
liked him. Look at the way she had answered him tonight.
She didn't like Berkowitz. The question. His mind crawled
around and around it, in the darkness.

～ V. Faith, Like a Seagull Hanging in Mid-Air

Berkowitz woke with the sun shining on his face and a
headache that made him long for swift decapitation. Seeing
no sign of breakfast, he walked to the moss garden.
Valentin was standing with his hands in his pockets, staring
at the central rocks.

"Sleep well?" said Berkowitz. His voice sounded unnatu-
rally loud, and his tongue was a piece of lead covered with
felt.

"No," said Valentin. "That is, I did not sleep. She was very firm, the *petit cochon.*" He smiled to himself.

"What do you think the question will be?" asked Berkowitz. He had no desire to learn the details of Pig-woman's anatomy.

Valentin shrugged and touched a rock with the tip of his shoe. "A little gray stone. Just what one would expect, no?"

Stagman walked into the courtyard. He looked at Valentin and said, "The Ambiguous Threshold."

"My turn," said Valentin. "The one of the vowels has already gone."

"Good luck," said Berkowitz.

"*Mon ami,*" said Valentin, "I suspect luck has nothing to do with it."

When Valentin had gone, Berkowitz walked around the garden, looking at the Outer Islands. Rocks, no different than the ones in the central cluster. Rocks scattered across a carpet of moss.

He looked down at his pajamas. They were badly wrinkled, and one sleeve was spotted with soup. Didn't that prove this was a dream? Showing up for an exam in pajamas. One of the classic scenarios. Lucky he wasn't naked. He wondered if Marie de la Roche had been.

"The Ambiguous Threshold." Stagman was waiting for him. Berkowitz felt a sudden impulse to shake him by the shoulders and beg him to say something, anything, else—to get one real answer in this place. His stomach gave a queasy rumble. They could at least have fed him breakfast.

Instead, he followed Stagman into the garden. They passed between rosebushes that seemed to whisper as he walked by. Berkowitz looked closely and realized, with distaste, that the petals on the roses were pink tongues. They passed a fountain, in which waterlilies croaked like frogs. In alcoves on either side of the path, ornamental cherries were weeping on the heads of stone nymphs that were evidently turning into foxes, owls, rabbits—or all of them at once. He brushed against a poppy, which fluttered sepals that looked like lashes.

Beyond the fountain was a hedge of Featherbushes, with

an opening cut into it, like an arch. Berkowitz followed Stagman through the archway.

The hedge grew in a circle, its only opening the one they had passed through. Grass grew over the ground, so soft under his slippers that Berkowitz wanted to take them off and walk barefoot. He had often gone barefoot as a child, but he could not remember what it felt like, walking on grass. The grass was spotted with daisies that were, for once, actually daisies.

At the center of the circle was a stone arch, shaped like the arch in the hedge, but built of the same blocks as the harbor and the castle. Its top and sides were irregular, and broken blocks lay scattered on the grass beside it, as though it were the final remnant of some monumental architecture. Sitting on one of those blocks was the Questioner.

"Good morning, Professor," she said. Today she was wearing a blue dress decorated with bits of glass. Her hair hung in two braids tied with blue ribbons.

"Good morning," said Berkowitz, trying to put as much irony into his voice as he could with a felted tongue. The silence in the circle made him uncomfortable. Even the sound of the fountain was muted.

The Questioner rose and said, "Are you ready for the Question?"

"I guess," he said. He looked at Stagman, waiting with his hands folded together, like the Dalai Lama. This had to be a dream.

"Would you like to step through the Threshold?"

"What," said Berkowitz, "you mean now?"

"That is the Question, Professor. The only Question there is. Would you like to step through the Threshold?"

Berkowitz stared at her, and then at the arch. "You mean that thing?" Through it he could see the hedge, and grass spotted with daisies.

The Questioner sighed. "That thing is the Threshold. Everything you see around you, including myself, is what you might call an emanation of it. If you step through it, you will proceed to the Outer Islands."

"So that's the whole test?"

"There is no test," said the Questioner. "There is only the Question. Would you like to step through the Threshold?"

"What if I don't?" asked Berkowitz.

"You will, of course, return to the Inner Islands."

"You mean I'll be back at the university?"

"Yes," said the Questioner. "You will return to your life, as though you had never left it. You will forget that you once stood on the Threshold, or you will think of it as a dream whose details you can never quite remember."

"And if I do?"

The Questioner tugged at one of her braids. For the first time, she looked like an impatient child. "You will, of course, proceed to the Outer Islands." She added, slowly and with emphasis, "As I have previously explained."

"What about the university?"

"You will appear to have died. Probably of a heart attack. Your diet, Professor, is particularly conducive." She gave him a lopsided smile, which looked almost sympathetic. "Unless you would prefer suicide?"

"Died?" said Berkowitz. "No one said anything about dying. If I go back to the Inner Islands, whatever they are, will I ever come here again?"

"No one gets more than one chance to stand on the Threshold."

"Why?" asked Berkowitz. "Look, here are the things I want to know. What exactly are the Outer Islands? What will I be if I go there? Will I be me or something else, like a chicken man with daisies growing out of my head?"

"Enough," said the Questioner. She was no longer smiling. "I am a questioner, not an answerer. When Marie de la Roche stepped through the Threshold, she said,

la foi, une mouette suspendu
au milieu de l'air

Professor Berkowitz, will you step through the Threshold?"

Berkowitz looked at her, standing beside the archway. He looked at the arch itself, and through it at the hedge. A breeze ruffled the feathers on the bushes.

He thought of returning to the house they had rented, without Helen. Without the smell of her vegetarian lasagna, without her voice, which would suddenly, even while reading the newspaper, begin reciting "Jabberwocky." To his bookshelves, now relatively bare. He thought of gray rocks scattered across a moss courtyard. Of the collected works of Keats, a woman with a flamingo on her head, roses whispering as he walked by. Of the university, and his students with their ringing cell phones. Perhaps Helen would call. He did not think so.

Then he looked at Stagman, who was rubbing the side of one furred cheek. This was a dream, and next week was his tenure evaluation.

"No," he said. The Questioner nodded with finality. He looked at her for an excruciating moment, then put his hands over his eyes. He waited to wake up.

Louder Echo

〜〜〜

Brendan Duffy

*Brendan Duffy [www.critters.org/bios/duffy_brendan.html]
lives in Melbourne, Australia. He did his Ph.D. on the mo-
lecular evolution of mammalian sex chromosomes. He is a
strong new genre writer, with only a few stories yet published, and those exclusively in Australia until now. He attended the first Clarion South writing workshop in Brisbane,
Australia, in 2004. He's one of the younger Australians
about to break out into the rest of the fantasy world.*

*"Louder Echo" was published in the original anthology
of new Australian genre writing, Agog! Terrific Tales, edited by Cat Sparks, in the second volume of the series. It is
currently the showcase anthology series for new Australian
genre writers, and often features stories that mix or combine genres. This energetic tale of the scientific supernatural
is situated somewhere in Tim Powers steampunk territory,
but with the fierceness and themes of Ted Chaing's "72
Letters."*

*The intelligence which can reproduce the lost claw of
a crayfish can reproduce the entire animal.*
NICOLAAS HARTSOEKER, 1722

My enraptured throng of Lesser Animalia had finally formed
their sections and were warming up under the chair. Crickets and beetles, moths and frogs, all rehearsing scales,
practicing squawks and squeals, creaks and croaks; a brilliant pre-operatic cacophony abuzz with acoustic anticipation. I tapped the baton to the lectern, and the hubbub
gradually quietened as compound and complex eyes turned
to focus on me. Finally there was silence. I threw to the
string section and opened my favorite Opera, *Il Barbiere
La Seviglia*.

I commanded the chirping woodwind with decisive fervor, lifted the percussive beating of wings to punctuate the
tempo, and introduced the toad's croaking baritone.
Through my baton the cicadas and crickets of the string
section hinted at more complex motifs to come.

I conducted this magnificent orchestra with a poignant
aplomb, and built the piece to its aria, "Largo al Facto-
tum," where Figaro sings his famous solo. Of course, I was
Figaro. It was ecstatic and I found myself singing the aria,
modified to accommodate my ultra falsetto, with a passionate gusto. I had just thrown across to the big bugs of the
brass when I was prized from my reverie.

Something new: a smell. A new smell. My Master had
just bought some strange kind of food. It was fresh and
richly aromatic, hypnotic, reaching even this deep into the
cellars to find me. Wrenched from my solo I ditched the
philharmonic and scampered across cold flagstones in dark
workshops. I rushed upstairs, crept past the kitchen and

larders, ran through empty halls with closed doors, then stole into the parlor.

There was no one to be seen, but the room was warm: a welcoming fire crackled in the hearth. My Master had left this wondrous thing up on the table, so I climbed arm over arm up the table leg, then hauled myself over onto the table top. Before me was a sight I had never before beheld, but I had my suspicions. I guessed it was a gigantic cob of bread, because I'd heard tell of such things. The giant loaf, still steaming from the baker's oven, rested on a wooden cutting board.

My mouth watered. I looked about; shadows danced across the walls, urging me to eat. Little grains embedded in the crust stared seductively; they winked at me in the flickering light. Mesmerized, I couldn't break their gaze. I staggered toward the awesome boulder of bread and embraced it, hugged a warm wall of food!

I was so hungry and it begged me to eat it, so I quietly chewed a window through the crust, then burrowed into the fluffy interior. By the time I was sated I had eaten my way to the center of the loaf and lay in a cozy hollowed den. It was soft, warm, and dreamy. Feeling tired from my repast I belched, rubbed my swollen purple tummy, then curled up with a soft lump of fluffy and slept.

I awoke to the sound of My Master's voice and another more authoritative tone—a resonant voice used to unquestioning respect. It spoke thus:

"Lazzaro, the Church's views on generation are founded on the teachings of Aristotle and the Ancients. All this talk of Preformation is dangerous! I don't like the unrest and division it's causing. Tell me of your investigations. Do you think it's true, or is it just some new Protestant blasphemy?"

"I have long suspected the truth in Preformation," spoke My Careful Master. "The works of all of the Church's great scientists actually imply this axiom, if you look carefully."

"Continue."

"All animals of all species that would ever walk God's

earth were formed *ab origine mundi* by the Almighty Creator's loving hand during the six days of Creation, and tenderly placed inside each other, within the first of each respective kind, preordained to unfold down the generations to come. The Preformation was a work done at a single stroke by His Adorable Will."

"Ah, a beautiful theory."

"It's more than a theory. I have made some interesting observations using careful modifications to Leeuwenhoek's microscope and methodologies."

"The Protestants are saying that semen contains little animals. Tell me, have you seen these Eels of Man?"

"I have seen them. But they are not eels; they're animalcules, spermatick vermiculi. Worms."

This subject was My Master's passion, but his enthusiasm was dampened by an impatient, patronizing tone. It meant he was speaking to someone who didn't agree with him. Sometimes he called them "People Who Don't Use Proper Scientific Methodology." Other times he called them "Priests."

He despised the clergy for their blind heavy handedness: proposing interpretations of the Bible and calling all else heresy. My Master had rigorously taught me Proper Scientific Methodology, and I wondered if I should likewise educate this Priest. "Make exhaustive observations of different sides of the argument, then interpret them by the shining light of the Bible so you aren't executed by ignorant zealots."

My Master and I had spent many an evening in the laboratory, examining diagrams drawn by Europe's finest scientists and worst blasphemers, poring over secret texts by alchemists and investigators. My Master had performed experiments on generation many times, and had documented what he called "The Empirical Proof." Together we'd repeated the experiments of Buffon and Needham, My Master precisely determining where they went wrong, and carefully demonstrating it to me, he often cursing and swearing, me often joining in, once I learned how.

My Master told me that I was his Magnum Opus.

I practiced my sourest condescending expression while this obviously foolish Priest continued to dispute with My Master:

"It's just as Aristotle says! And Buffon!" exclaimed the Priest. "When higher animals die they decompose and spontaneously revert back into the lesser animals from which they arose: worms and flies! Vermiparous generation, all life springs forth from worms!"

"No, not like Aristotle. Well, a little," spoke My Master. "There is no spontaneous generation. Meat left protected in a mesh enclosure does not spontaneously sprout worms and flies upon decomposing, and infusions of broth enclosed in glass bulbs do not spontaneously ferment. Aristotle is wrong! Something cannot spring from nothing, thus the theory of Preformation must be correct. Just as the caterpillar contains the chrysalis, which contains the butterfly, and the tadpole unfolds to become the frog, these spermatick worms are human worms that generate humans—the head of each spermatick worm contains a little Preformed manikin waiting to be born. In woman they find nurture to become Man. I have seen it."

"You have seen the Little Man!"

"Yes! As have others. Dalenpatius documents that he has even seen spermatick vermiculi throw off their skins to reveal complete miniature men dancing! In fact, I have examined the testes of many animals and have seen smaller animals of their type within their spermatick worms. But I have also examined the ovaries of many animals. They also appear to contain small animals. I need a better lens. Preformation is true. The only question remaining is whom God chose to bear this burden. Man or woman? Animalcule or ovary? Adam was the first man, but we are all born of woman, like a great unfolding."

"Bah! It's obvious! The race of Man is not called Woman. A woman's role is to bear a man's children. If Preformation is true it must be through the male."

"But to provide conclusive proof of Animalculist Preformation I must also disprove Ovist Preformation. Ovism must be fully investigated to be refuted, just to be sure."

"That is not necessary. Ovism cannot be true. You've seen the Little Man! You said so yourself! Why would God choose sinful woman to be the bearer of body and soul? Six thousand years ago God created Adam in Eden. Adam was the first man, Eve was made from him, as are all God's children. Preformed in Adam's testes was the body and soul of every person that would ever walk God's world, down through the male lineage, through all of God's children until judgment day."

He coughed wetly before continuing. "Lazzaro, I don't much care for science, but those cursed Protestants are investigating Preformation. Garden has made progress documenting the Eels of Man! He's a Bishop in the Church of England! We cannot let the Protestants feather their caps with scientific innovation. Catholic superiority must be vigorously maintained and demonstrated. What notes have you made?"

"These are diagrams of my observations."

I peered through my crusty window at the decrepit Priest as he flipped through one of My Wonderful Master's notebooks: secret drawings of dissected animals, ovaries and testes, the microscopic secrets of semen.

"Lazzaro, isn't the collection of semen a sin against God?"

"Normally yes, but when it's for science God doesn't mind."

The old Priest frowned and turned to the well-thumbed *Essai de Dioptrique* by Nicolaas Hartsoeker, an early Animalculist, with the renowned drawing of the Little Man curled up in the head of a spermatick worm. The first picture of me! He fixed My Master a worried stare, and then saw the forbidden recipe by Paracelsus the alchemist.

"The Generation of Homunculi," he gasped. "This recipe is from a banned book!"

"Yes. But I have proof of Animalculist Preformation. I have made an homunculus!"

"What! Is it dangerous? Is it an abomination in the name of Our Lord?"

"No, but I made it from spermatick worms that have never touched a woman."

"Then this is all we need!" hissed the Priest. "We've beaten the Protestants at their own game: the ultimate proof of Animalculist Preformation. The body and soul carried within man alone!"

"I'm not so sure. I don't think it has a soul."

My ears pricked up. What was My Master saying?

"But it must have a soul," said the Priest, "if Animalculist Preformation is true."

"It failed the Turing Test," answered My Master. So that was what all those questions were—a test to see if I had a soul! The Priest looked at the notes.

"Some of this writing is Arabic! Imagine if the Moors could do this! Or worse, the Protestants! Are we likely to face an army of homunculi marching in the name of the heathen? I want to see the homunculus!"

I crawled out of the loaf and picked up the breadknife. I marched across the table toward the Priest, singing a reveille and spinning the knife in my hands like a halberdier on parade. He stared in astonishment.

"Shalom Allah!" I said, and stood to attention before the Priest, saluting.

"Oh the Lord and Holy Land, it marches for Islam!" He crossed himself and staggered backward. I dropped the knife and poked out my tongue, making faces and waving my hands at my ears.

"By God, it has no genitalia! Why all the purple birthmarks? It looks like a tiny adult baby—one that should have been knocked on the head!"

He was very rude so I did a little dance, turned around and poked my bottom out at him, wagging it about, pointing at it.

"Wicked little monkey!" The Priest whipped out a wooden staff and smashed it down on the table exactly where I was, but I had dashed back into the loaf. I hid deep inside and buried my head in the warm fluffy, shaking from this violent outburst. That bad Priest had tried to get me!

"Ecce! Behave yourself. Come out and apologize," said My Master.

I slowly peeked out, then rushed to My Benevolent Master,

quaking with fear, hiding from the bad Priest behind My Master's huge fleshy hand. My Master patted my head until I was smiling. The Priest stared.

"Can the homunculus see the future?" he asked. "Does it summon demons?"

"No, no. It has knowledge of math and speaks many languages. It has much innate knowledge."

"It could scour the earth with pestilence and hellfire! It's happened before!"

"Signore," I said with a bow to My Master, then addressed the Priest. "The homunculus apologizes, Your Grace, and wishes to report that it cannot see the future, and nor does it summon demons." I held my hand out to the Priest. "Je m'appelle Ecce Homo." We shook, and he snatched his hand back.

"I'm feeling sick! It must be working its magicks on me!" He searched his hand for magick marks. "It's an abomination with no parents."

"And how many parents do you have, Your Grace?" I asked from the security of My Master's loving hand.

"Two, of course!" he spat, insulted and uncomfortable.

"And how many grandparents?"

"Four."

"How many ancestors from ten generations ago?"

"Umm," he paused, looked at the ceiling and counted fingers off.

"One thousand and twenty four," I answered for him. Shortly he nodded, quiet now. "And how many ancestors did you have at the time of Adam and Eve?"

He looked at me blankly.

"According to the Archbishop James Ussher of Armargh the world was created at noon on the twenty-third of October, four thousand and four, BC." The Priest looked nonplussed. "Say, two hundred and thirty generations ago," I reminded. He flashed me an annoyed glance then resumed staring at the ceiling, petitioning Our Lord for mathematical assistance in His loyal servant's moment of need.

While the Priest was searching the ceiling My Bemused Master looked at me, smiled, and quietly shook his head;

the Priest, My Master's Patrone, was a fool. I could tell My Master appreciated me. He loved me. I did this for him.

I gazed back at My Beautiful Master and he scratched behind my ear, then down my neck. It was really good, so good I stretched my head up into the air. My Master obliged, scratching under my chin. My foot started tapping up and down, in time with the scratching, then he hit the sweet spot and I suddenly snapped and bit his forefinger, not hard though. I just softly brushed my teeth on the giant finger. Just enough to let him know without breaking the skin. He laughed and patted my head.

"That's enough," he whispered, indicating the still counting Priest.

I approached the Priest.

"How big was Eden? Bigger than Zanzibar?" I laughed. "Standing room only! No room to move! But where did all those people go?"

The Priest looked at me with scorn, then turned back to his fingers, determined. I did a little dance behind his back. I'd put him out of his misery soon. I readied the sword for the mercy blow.

"At some stage the number of ancestors you have is larger than the number of people alive on God's earth."

"True!" He turned and looked from me to My Master. "But how could that be so?"

"Ancestors traced down one line are also ancestors traced down others, so they're multiply represented."

"Oh, I see," he nodded, then looked confused again. "But how can that be?"

I held him there for a moment, then brought the blade down.

"They were all having sexual congress with each other!"

The Priest's mouth fell open.

"Holy Lord, it is a Protestant!" He crossed himself again. "Oh my, this is complicated! Tomorrow I'll give it a Catholic baptism. Him, him, give him. And get it into a confessional! He talks like The Devil himself!" The Priest stood and hurried to the door, shaking his head. "We must beat Garden! Animalculist Preformation is true, so it must have a soul. Make it sit the Turing Test again." He looked back. "And Lazzaro, my son, if it fails the test, it is not one of God's Preformed, therefore it is an abomination and you are a blaspheming alchemist, and I am an alchemist's ex-chequer, and we're all in trouble. I will have a new Venetian lens ground to your specifications. Use it to further science wisely.

"As for you, little Ecce, it was very crowded in Eden. Every one of God's children was there. Even you!"

With a toothy smile I scampered across the cold flagstones to where My Glorious Master worked. The workshop floor was strewn with straw and sawdust, offcuts from his con-traption. I crept up behind My Master's towering form. He was hunched over some blueprints at his bench, cursing Leeuwenhoek for a buffoon. He sat amongst a confusing system of calipers and vices, wires and cord, all strung about a wooden framework of dials and pulleys. A great many lenses of specially ground Venetian glass hung in the web, sparkling like morning dew. The largest, the new Great Lens, was like a smooth aquamarine from a king's crown, as large as an eyeball.

This would be funny, and My Master would think me very smart. It should help him see the ridiculous nature of Ovism. I could barely contain my mirth as I carried the huge doll in my purple arms. The anticipation was too much; a snigger escaped my thick red lips and I froze, hand on mouth, almost dropping the wooden doll. Fortunately, My Master didn't hear because just at that moment he fussed with the microscope settings. The sound of my glee was covered by the clatter and creak of cords and pulleys as My Clever Master lowered one of his new lenses into the microscope.

I almost burst out laughing from my joke. My Master would love it! All would be forgiven and he would pro-nounce me of soul. He turned away from his workbench to face whence I had come. I crept behind his towering form, snuck under the workbench and saw a weird knot of wood protruding from the chair leg. It smelt like some strange animal: exotic and hairy. Distracted, I put the doll down and rubbed my head back and forth against the knot. I closed my eyes and got stuck into an itchy bit behind my ear. It was so exhilarating I found myself singing Figaro's aria from where I'd previously left off with the philharmonic. Somehow my *sotto voce* must have become *grosso*, and My Master looked about.

"Ecce! Ecce!" My Master called, deep and rumbling. I grabbed the doll and climbed up the bookcase, shelf by shelf, finally lugging the heavy doll out onto the bench top. Exhausted, I leaned on the doll while catching my breath. My Master had his back to me, facing the door.

"Ecce!" he called, "Ecce. Come help align the lenses!"

Oh, My Master was a genius! The greatest thinker in Europe, patronized by royalty and the Church. Beneath the microscope a doe lay on blocks of packed snow, limbs bound. Her sleek fur was brown with small white spots. Etherized to insensibility, she lay with her side flayed open, layers of skin and muscle pinned back to reveal her internal workings, God's secrets. And an ovary, the subject of My Master's study.

"Master, what have you found?" I called, trying to obscure the doll with my body.

"Eh?" He spun about to face me. "Oh, there you are. I think it is as I suspected, Ecce. Something is carried by the female line in the ovary." He noticed I was hiding something. "What have you got there?"

I was biting my lips, trying not to laugh. "Oh, Master, I have a present for you!" I hoisted the Russian babushka doll in my arms and carried it across the workbench to him. He took it in a great fleshy hand and examined it while I burst out laughing and danced with glee.

"Did you make this doll, Ecce?"

"Si. Si, Maestro! Per voi!"

My Master wore his full winter costume, and puffed little white clouds into the air. He turned the doll over in his great hands, admiring the craftsmanship. I had painted it to resemble an English maid. I sang a crazy song, hopping from one foot to the other, waving my gangly arms in the air. Soon he'd get the joke. But I had to try to control myself; this was serious. I tried to concentrate. The doll should keep him occupied for a while.

While My Master examined the doll I slunk across the workbench to the semiconscious deer. It was twitching and would shortly awaken. I tipped some surgeon's ether onto a rag and held it to the deer's nose. It relaxed and I examined My Master's apparatus. The fog of My Master's breath usually condensed on the lenses as he worked, and he needed me to polish them clean. The cold didn't bother me, and my breath didn't fog, so I often worked with him and was familiar with the operation of his tools and subject. Indeed, I was a product of them.

I looked down the microscope eyepiece and fiddled with the fine focus dials as I had seen My Master do. Set on medium magnification I saw the doe's ovary in amazing detail: great swirling images of a hidden world. I swung another lens into place and focussed. Inside the doe's ovary were little animals, like in My Master's drawings of spermatick vermiculi. They were pretty little deer, exact and precise, though not yet fully unfolded: not yet born. About the size of rice grains, they appeared as though formed of a translucent primordium. I could see their gelid insides as though each had been laid open to cross section by My Master. Eight miniature deer stood in two rows on the ovarian scaffold, presenting their innards for inspection.

So it was true, something of God's Preformed was carried down the female lineage, too. Behind me My Master opened the doll to reveal another inside, exactly the same but smaller. He laughed, but I ignored him. I had to know more.

I looked at these miniature deer, little does and bucks. I focussed onto the ovary of a miniature doe. I grimaced and increased the magnification, engaging the Great Lens. Within the gelid ovary of the miniature doe was another ovarian scaffold, and seven more deer stood upon that scaffold, tiny, awaiting their eventual birth. Deer within deer within deer, all Preformed, through the female lineage. I stared down through three generations, as far as I could see into the future.

But what of Animalculist Preformation? I swapped back to the lenses of lesser magnification and scanned across the ovarian scaffold to a miniature buck. I saw the confusing vesicles in its testes, just like the drawings from My Master's vivisection notebooks. I swung the Great Lens into place and saw turmoil. The spermatick worms were moving too fast, but I found some sleeping ones and focussed on their heads. It was hard to be sure, but inside one I glimpsed odd swirling shapes: legs kicking, a tail twitching. Was that a deer's head? I saw antlers!

I played the fine focus and there it was, a perfect little buck, hale and robust. Eager to be off, it stamped its foot and brandished its antlers, then leapt away. It vanished! There was nothing discernible left inside: no little buck staring back at me, nothing. I gave chase, hunting the deer in other spermatick worm heads, but it was gone, like a ghost, an echo. I kept searching but found nothing. Just mushy lumps at a dead end in the chain of life. It seemed that Ovism was correct, Animalculism was not.

I beheld God's great plan with my own eyes. It didn't include me.

My vision swam, I pulled the focus back; pretty little deer danced on their scaffolds, so miniature and perfect. I looked up at the ceiling timbers until my vision cleared. My Master laughed with delight as he opened more dolls to reveal yet more dolls.

"Ecce. You've even painted them to look like English maids!"

"Yes, Master. It's an English Russian doll!" I walked across the bench top to My Master. "You could have it delivered to Garden in England! As a present to his pregnant wife, Master. From you! From Lazzaro Spallanzani. The Ovist."

My Master bellowed, but I wasn't laughing. I rubbed my head in my leathery hands. The Animalculist investigators were wrong. Garden the Protestant Bishop was wrong.

Males were dead ends. Dear God, the Ovists were correct. My Master would soon prove his new theory true and demonstrate it to everyone.

"Yes! It could be Garden's wife! And a daughter. Bravo, Ecce!" He held my gaze with a quizzical expression. "You're a clever one!"

"Yes, Master, yes! Very clever! Let me sit the Turing Test again!"

"Ecce." My Master chided. "We've been through this before. You failed."

"But Master, remember what the Priest said! Give me a second chance!" I fell to my knees before My Master, hands clasped together in supplication.

"Ecce. Second chances don't come into it. You're either conscious or you aren't. I administered the Turing Test and caught you cheating. You had answers written all over your arms!"

"But Master, I'm conscious! And I'm smart and can make you laugh."

"Ecce, you're not conscious. The natural beauty of flowers can inspire rapture in a man, but it doesn't mean they're conscious and have a soul. Ecce, you are as wood, live, but with no soul." My Master placed the Russian doll before me. It leered at me with its garish, painted face.

"No, Master! I want to sit the test again!"

"No, Ecce. It doesn't matter now. I'm currently proving that the body and soul are in the ovaries, not the spermatick worms. So you can't possibly be conscious!"

"But Master, maybe the body is in the ovary and the soul is with the spermatick worm!"

"Ecce, you have no soul. I'm sorry." My Master meant that I wasn't human. I was a monster, an abomination. "I called you Ecce Homo because I was sure that Animalculist Preformation was correct. I thought you would grow to be a man, and that your innate knowledge heralded the person God had ordained you to become. I thought you were the future, but I was wrong. I'm renaming you Echo Homo, for your knowledge is merely a reiteration of the past; you are simply a lesser version of your template, the man whence the seed was collected and you were made. A travelling musician, a vagabond, now dead."

My Master walked to the door. He called back over his shoulder.

"I'm going to make a new homunculus, this time from ova. I want you to mix the reagents."

I scowled and spun away from him, to look straight into the eyes of the garish Russian doll, still leering at me, mocking my hopes. This joke wasn't funny anymore. I slapped it off the table and simmered.

Not the future, just a reflection of the past. My Master would replace me with something better.

And he wanted me to help.

The Priest administered my Catholic Baptism in a private vestibule, but it didn't make me feel any more human or closer to God's Glory. I just felt like an awkward initiate to some esoteric venerable fraternity—a soulless impostor.

Afterward I sang Handel's baroque oratorios in my perfect ultra falsetto, higher than any castrato. Notes hung in the chamber like pure crystal spheres, and the Priest closed his eyes and wept passionately. Later he was quite jovial and we made jokes in Latin; then I prompted the discussion toward the intrigue of Church politics. He told me that he didn't really care about scientific theory, just the advantages that could be secured through it. Everything has its uses, he'd said. Except Ovists and Protestants.

My Manic Master wouldn't let me repeat the Turing Test. He rushed about, ignoring my petitions. He was too busy now and had driven me out of his life so that he could concentrate on The Important Things. I read through his old notebooks and followed after him, clutching his early drawings of me: the Little Man in the head of the spermatick worm. He wasn't interested anymore.

I kept out of his way, quietly trailing behind, collecting his flotsam. I occasionally observed him from my lurk in the rafters or espied him through some ratty hole. Late one night while skulking in the corridor I heard a curious noise behind the oaken door to My Master's chambers. I lifted back the escutcheon and peered into the keyhole-shaped light.

I gazed upon My Master entertaining a lady friend in his boudoir. They were talking and laughing. Deep into the wee hours I spied them through that tarnished, brassy hole, and the things I saw: hurried whalebone fumbling, riotous shrieking, the slap of quivering, pink flesh. Oh, My Lascivious Master! He beguiled her into quaffing copious amounts of absinth, then sniffing from his bottle of surgeon's ether. She fainted and he quickly had her up on the table where he had his way with her.

How I watched My Wicked Master do unspeakable things! I guess the collection of ova isn't a sin against God, either, when it's for science. There would be trouble with the Church if My Suicidal Master continued these dangerous investigations into Ovist Preformation. When I could watch no more I closed my eyes and saw bundles of kindling being bound with twine by cackling, toothless hags.

The next morning My Master hurried about the hallways with notes and a quill. He found me moping about near the larders. He wanted me to mix a new range of liquors, some of which I'd never heard of. He'd even made a list. I knew he wanted me to mix these reagents to generate a new homunculus. What would it be like playing second fiddle to some Ovist homunculus? My Mistaken Master already had a perfectly good homunculus and didn't need another. He sensed my reluctance.

"Ecce, if you make these reagents, we'll repeat the Turing Test!"

"Really! And then will I have a soul?"

"We'll see."

"But what of this new homunculus you wish to make?"

"No, I've changed my mind. I'm not making another. It's too dangerous in the current political climate," said My Surprising Master. "I've given up on Ovist Preformation and stopped all my mistaken investigations. I was wrong."

"Really? N'est pas? Pourquoi?" I followed after him.

The workroom seemed different. I climbed up onto the

workbench. He had packed most of his equipment away! Only his precious microscope remained. Maybe it was true! A sheaf of papers lay neatly on his workbench, designs for a large glass bottle, some kind of complex fermentation tank for brewing.

"We're going to continue our early investigations cataloguing microscopic life." He gathered the diagrams and left.

I explored his bookshelves with renewed vigor, scanning through standard church issue—safe, recommended reading—but also scientific texts. Among the recipe books were some interesting works: seminal texts by the Ancients on spontaneous and vermiparous generation, experimental investigations by fringe alchemists, how to generate different dog breeds, how to spawn monsters, create golems, summon demons! I saw some works on Animalculist Preformation, and Paracelsus' recipe: The Generation of Homunculi.

I found recipes for vital fluids and prolific liquors and collected the things I'd need from the materials cabinets: solids, powders and liquids, mixtures and compounds, although I'd also need some more arcane ingredients. My Master kept human specimens and essences in a special cabinet. I took the key from his desk drawer and unlocked the cabinet to reveal a glass jar atop a notebook and a formidable old leather-bound tome with brass fittings.

I picked up the jar and a chill passed through me. I was looking at three gelid babies, the size of rice grains. Preformed fetuses extracted from the ovarian scaffold of that shrieking harlot.

I opened My Master's notebook and surveyed the evidence of his recent investigations: detailed drawings of rabbit and mouse vivisection, exposed ovaries. My Master had drawn the fully laden ovarian scaffold of a doe—three generations deep, just as I had seen.

I examined the old tome. The gilt title read *De Generatione*. The solid cover was engraved with a picture: Jove holding an open egg, from which sprang forth many different types of animals. Underneath was written the Latin inscription, *Ex Ova Omnia*, "from the egg, everything." The incriminating book was penned by William Harvey, a blasphemous Protestant Englander. It was the legendary first work on Ovist Preformation and was banned by the church soon after its release. I leafed through the pages; it discussed oviparous and viviparous generation and set the theoretical foundation that led to Ovism. My Meticulous Master's dirty bookmarks were all through the section detailing the manner in which an Ovist homunculus might be made.

In a glass fermentation tank.

I couldn't believe my eyes. My Deceitful Master had lied to me. He hadn't stopped his investigations into Ovism, he'd finished them and was now moving on to their more practical application—not brewing ferment for microscopy but brewing my replacement. My Lying Bastard Master was an Ovist scoundrel. He'd never give me the Turing Test and I'd never be pronounced of soul. He didn't care, he just wanted me slaving away on his potions so he could generate his Ovist Homunculus.

The Priest would be interested to know of this! There would be trouble.

I'd see to it.

I wandered about the deeper sections of the cellars, feeling betrayed and desperately alone, while My Master busied himself upstairs with his new glass fermentation tank. I crept between stacks of discarded notebooks and explored the piles of abandoned glassware that lay strewn about. I recognized equipment from My Master's now forgotten past—experiments I had helped with.

It was damp and cold, and I was hungry. I chewed at the bottom of my candle as it burned, but it provided grim succor. The prey I stalked was behind a heap of old microscope pieces. I heard the tinkle of glassware and doubled back, then saw it: a hideous monster twice my size! No, just an ordinary bug magnified behind a glass bulb: a tasty meal.

My prey scuttled from the glassware. I froze: a statue, David—the perfect man. Two fingers on my right hand twitched, testing the air like antennae. The bug halted, then carefully responded, and an antenna dance ensued. I played it with my lure, enticing it closer with all the right promises. Mesmerized by my lying semaphore my prey courted its treacherous mate, and slowly climbed up onto my outstretched statue arm. I sprang, ripped its head off and scoffed it down, holding its body like a tankard of juice with six twitching legs.

Sated, I leisurely sipped at the tangy juices while searching among the piles of junk. I heard a desperate tapping and found a pile of sealed jars, each containing a prisoner—victims of My Cruel Master's experimentation in regeneration. I couldn't prize the lids off so I smashed each jar in turn and liberated the hungry, motley crew, naming each after one of My Master's rivals. I freed a tailless skink, a one-clawed crab, a three-legged salamander, a one-eared rat, a one-eyed mole, a snail missing its entire head, and a mouse with a human ear on its back.

They were happy to be freed and vowed to help me. We danced in circles around smoky chemical fires, cheering and making merry. Feeling heady from the bug juice I summoned my throng of Lesser Animalia and assembled the philharmonic orchestra. My New Chums gladly joined its ranks. We spent the evening discussing generation and feasting to song, the philharmonic supplying all our needs, although the arias were getting pretty thin with the decimation of the string section.

Amidst the revelry I fixed a candle onto one of My Master's notebooks and lit it. My shadow, big and impressive, almost a man's, fell onto the wall before me. Laughing, I danced to the music and watched my shadow dance. I scattered handfuls of sulfur and saltpeter across My Master's open notebooks and waved my arms over intricate diagrams of animalcules and ovaries, dissected beasts, ink pentagrams, sigils and magick numbers, singing my favorite operatic excerpts.

I danced before a mirrored glass, making faces. I turned

around and wagged my ass in the mirror. Looking back, I saw it wasn't my ass but an ugly assface. I spun around to check my ass but I couldn't see it properly; I had to run in circles to catch up. When I caught it I saw that it was just my ass, and the mirror was just the mirror. With a shrug I eased my way back into the dancing—and saw assface in the mirror again.

"Ciao! Ciao!" it said. I spun about but it was gone. I poked my ass in the mirror again. "Ciao amico! Si parle Italiano?"

"Si, si," I said.

"Echo Homo, reflection of man!" It laughfarted in an old Calabrese dialect.

"No, no. Ecce Homo! Behold the man!"

"Echo, you don't have a soul! Do you want one?" asked my asshole.

"No, I already have one! A Priest said I do!"

"A Priest said! Ha! He's playing you like a pawn! You don't have a soul and you know it! Now pick up that chalk and draw! Left, left, now straight ahead . . ."

Under its rude direction I chalked a pentagram onto the flagstones and arranged five candles. Upon lighting the last there was a great sulfurous explosion. A slopping wet pile of offal fell out of the air and filled the pentagram. Atop the pile of putrefying entrails and scabrous bat wing was a stinking-furred goat head. My eyes watered from the stench. Its flesh pulsed, glistening with heat sheen, and motion stirred its evil eye. The philharmonic dashed for cover. It appeared that Those Stupid Priests were correct about some things.

"Ciao, bello!" I said in my oldest Italian.

Laughing, it metamorphosed into an extremely handsome youth wearing the gilt and bejewelled dress of an impeccable Calabrese noble, exquisite and ostentatious.

"Hail Caesar! Cicco Ghibbeline," he said in Italian older still. He held his immaculately manicured hand forward and we shook. "Your Master, Lazzaro Spallanzani, is doing interesting work."

"He's a great Catholic scientist, a devout and learned

man, once a Jesuit Priest! I'm going to get him in trouble with the Church. Maybe banished or burned at the stake!"

"Get him excommunicated and you will be in my favor." Cicco examined his fingernails and smiled with indulgent pearly-white beattitude. His halo brightened—a band of bright antiworlds orbited his head: colored souls slowly tumbling through the air like tiny glowing babies, each softly screaming distant, high pitched Latin woes.

I stared at them. "Oh, I want a soul!"

"Hmm . . . No." Cicco shook his head and the little souls jangled in my face. "That won't be possible."

"What would it take?" I begged.

"What have you got to offer? Nothing. Forget it. You would have to summon hellfire for me to pronounce you of soul." He was a seasoned horse trader—diabolically cock-sure. My asshole was right—as far as pronouncing me of soul, My Master didn't, the Priest couldn't, and Cicco wouldn't.

"Then I want a microscope to see further into the ovaries than My Master can."

Cicco made a play of patting down his pockets. "Unfortunately, I didn't bring a microscope with me . . ."

"A Great Lens, then. Better than My Master's!"

Cicco waved his hand. "Only what I have on me. Anyway, why a lens? Do you think that will make him like you again?"

"No. I already know how to make him like me," I laughed. "Give me a Great Lens, and I will get him excommunicated."

"Hmm," Cicco raised an eyebrow, then nodded. "So be it!" He surreptitiously looked about then opened his pantaloons. He held his perfect penis in his immaculately manicured hands and winced in red-faced pain as he strained and pushed. A huge lump slowly, agonizingly, moved down the length of his distended member. He grimaced and gasped as blood dripped from his urethral opening. With a final demonic bellow Cicco peeled back his foreskin and passed the gigantic kidney stone into his hand, buffed and polished from its tight journey. He wiped the blood away.

"Whew!" Cicco dabbed the sweat from his brow with a gilt embroidered pocket kerchief. "To excommunication!"

He vanished, leaving me holding the shiny, clear lens.

I was the apprentice, but it was time for me to become the Master. I knew how to make My Fickle Master like me—I'd continue his work and generate my own homunculus in my new laboratory underground. I'd show him how clever I was! I explored every corner of the dark catacombs, collecting bits and pieces, the legions of my philharmonic dragging them back to the new lab we created at the bottom of the staircase. I located much of My Master's original equipment and re-created his early workplace, the beakers, bulbs, and burners, all arranged according to his diagrams—candles and condensers, burettes and pipettes, droppers and stoppers. We reconstructed a microscope and fitted the Great Demonic Lens.

The philharmonic played my favorite pieces while we worked. We ground solids to Albinoni's harpsichord concertos and mixed liquids to Mozart. I made My Master's potions, his prolific liquors and vital fluids, and when the passion seized me I conducted the philharmonic with one hand, while directing manufacture with the other, as my industrious insects carried weighed portions of powders to mortar and pestles, measured ounces and drams, and stirred and simmered, while vapors flowed through the condenser to form precious essences.

The vapors cascaded through my head as I commanded the philharmonic to perform *Don Giovanni*, a disturbing piece about a lusty, deceitful scoundrel blinded by pride. With a stroke of my baton a bevy of bugs placed the crystal birthing dish before me. I brandished the baton as though smiting foes as the Lascivious Don slew and seduced his way through the men and women of Seville, and was finally confronted by the statue of a man he murdered. I laughed hysterically as he fearlessly invited it to dinner!

With each ominous parry and riposte the orchestra conjured minor chords of sinister portent. I conducted with oblivious fury as bottles oozed oily fluids into a swirling puddle in the dish. With the baton in one hand and a dropper of human essence in the other I built to the moment when the colossal statue arrived for dinner. As it dragged the Unrepentant Don down to the fiery pits of Hell I let the drop of human essence fall into the pearly puddle.

It splashed into the greasy swirling rainbow and the liquids changed and congealed. By flickering candlelight I glimpsed anatomy, a gathering nativity. Form condensed in scintillating colors: hands, a face, then were gone. I sprang back and resumed conducting the piece with added fervor, pouring my energy into it, barking commands at the philharmonic.

Something took shape in the liquid! A head. Eyes staring straight at me, lips smiling savagely. He slowly rose from the rainbow liquor as new anatomy congealed: shoulders, chest, hands already on hips—a little man, just like me! I laughed. He laughed, too, as his legs formed and he rose further from the liquid in the dish. He looked like me, but smaller. His skin was pinkish-gray with purple birthmarks, just like mine. He stood before me, whole, glistening, dripping from his spawning. He looked at his body, flexed his arms, and stepped from the birthing dish.

"Grazie, Maestro, grazie," he said. I administered the Turing Test.

"Are you Homo sapiens?"

He flexed his little muscles, "I am an echo of Man, an echo of the man I am!"

"God made Man in His image, but you're an echo of Man made more in mine."

"Then I am an echo of an image of God, made more in the image of an echo of Man!

"I name you Piccolo Eco, the Little Echo of the man you are."

"Grazie, Mio Buono Maestro." Piccolo bowed to me. We held hands and danced in a circle, singing while the philharmonic played faster.

"I'm an echo of the man I was!"

"And I'm an echo of the man I am!"

* * *

"Quiet everyone," I yelled. "Quiet!" The hordes of chattering homunculi quietened, and I looked upon Friedrich, the little man who had just arisen from the birthing dish. At two centimeters tall he was the smallest yet, a tiny echo of a man not yet born. The deeper we delved into the scaffold for our samples the smaller were the homunculi we made, and the quieter they spoke—but the more bizarre their stories became. Generation seven spoke of the strangest wonders. We hushed as he told of the entire world at war. Again.

"Oppenheimer, Julius Robert, born in 1904."

"And what did he invent?" I asked.

"The first atomic bomb."

"And what is that?"

"A piece of the sun."

"Hmm," I'd heard this chilling story a few times now. "And your brother?"

"He designed the fuel injection for the Messerschmitt 262 jet engine."

"So this was your youngest brother, Hans, born in 1909?"

"Yes."

The gelid fetus I had stolen from My Absent Master's locked cabinet now lay beneath my microscope, submerged in a preserving buffer. My microscope, equipped with the Great Demonic Lens, was trained onto its ovarian scaffold, focussed seven generations deep into the future: the Guenther family scaffold.

I looked down the eyepiece.

"A gauche, a gauche, a gauche . . ." A horde of our smallest homunculi carefully adjusted the fine scrolling of the stage, scanning across from Friedrich, past siblings, to his youngest brother, the last male on the Guenther scaffold.

"Halt!" I was looking at Hans Guenther. I gave the command. My Miniature Technicians began the process of delicately extracting spermatick worms from this fetus. We'd find a manikin in his spermatick worms and in a few hours his echo would be arguing with the others about future history. Together they may remember enough to draw up plans for a flying machine.

I joined Piccolo and examined our map of the ovarian scaffold. We'd made homunculi from each generation and asked them about their family, the world, and anything they could remember. Piccolo was a meticulous bookkeeper, penning in names and professions as we explored this expanding family tree, cataloguing them for later reference. He also recorded a detailed history of the future they described.

We never made Ovist homunculi because My Master might be right. If Ovist Preformation was true, they would be real people born too early. It would alter the timing of God's divine plan, and He may send an avenging angel to correct things. We would have to replace this fetus soon, so it could bear its fruit.

We only made Animalculist homunculi, soulless echoes of the future, copies, using spermatick vermiculi samples taken from the testes of the male fetuses on the scaffold. We were always careful not to injure or harm the fetuses, as they were yet to fulfil their destiny. One day Hans Guenther would be born, ignorant of the echoes made from him 130 years prior.

We heard noises. People were descending the stairs. Pandemonium erupted as everyone ran and hid. I stood there, dumbfounded, looking at books, recipes, chemicals, scales, measuring cylinders, pipettes, bubbling vials—every stage of the process accounted for. I'd even automated the process by rigging pipes and taps straight to the birthing dish. It was an homunculus manufactory, and looked like one.

The squeaking and tittering died down and all was quiet. A small pool of ink spread across the table. Tiny ink footprints across an open page recorded the first homunculus stampede. I turned the page.

The Priest stepped forward into the light. "Ahh! Here he is!"

"Your Grace." I bowed deeply.

"Dear Ecce! The proof of Animalculist Preformation!" The Priest patted my head. "How wise I was to fund this research. The Papacy shows me favor. Although, imagine what would have happened if I'd been caught funding research into Ovist Preformation!"

We both laughed. My Shadowy Master huffed and stepped into the flickering light, shaking his head.

"You shouldn't discount Ovism too soon!" he said. I heard that impatient, patronizing tone taint his voice; he would unthinkingly reiterate the tired empirical rhetoric. He waved his forefinger. "Other options should be investigated before being discounted. Rigorously apply proper scientific methodologies: make exhaustive observations of all aspects of the argument, then interpret the results making the least assumptions."

"You proved Animalculist Preformation," said the Priest.

"You proved Animalculist Preformation," I echoed. "So say I have a soul!"

My Master scowled at me so I backed behind the Priest's hand.

"But what of truth?" My Master asked the Priest.

"Animalculist Preformation makes the most sense," said the Priest. "It combines the beauty of Preformation with a theory already endorsed by the Church: Aristotle's vermiparous generation."

"Ha! Worms! Ridiculous! There is only oviparous and viviparous generation," My Master scoffed, "and I think that even viviparous animals actually use a form of oviparity. Ex Ova Omnia!"

"That is a dangerous catch-cry, Lazzaro."

"But what about maternal inheritance of traits like polydactyly? It is well documented and supports the theory of Ovist Preformation! Also, there is parthenogenesis in many aphid and skink species! No male is needed for generation!"

"So now you're comparing us to insects and lizards, Lazzaro?"

"But I have seen the ovarian scaffold!"

"You've seen an optical illusion caused by refraction!

Lazzaro, I paid you to revive Animalculism and refute this growing Ovism! God would not have chosen woman. It's against the Church! We are the moral guardians of the flock. They are incapable of making correct choices without our guidance. A place for everything, and everything in its place, Lazzaro, or we'll have women as priests and scientists! And where would that get us?"

"Your Grace," I said, "he possesses many arcane tomes! The intricately described works of schismatic dissidents and deluded alchemists! Blasphemers! I've seen *The Second Book of Natural Magick* by Giambattista della Porta. It contains the recipes, "How to generate preti little dogs to plae withe," and "How living creatures of divers kinds may be mingled and coupled together." It's a treatise on how to warp God's creatures. He wants to create life himself! Abominations! Monsters, golems, and demons!"

The Priest looked to My Wayward Master.

"It's nothing," said My Master. "I never made any of them."

"But you do not deny this?" said the Priest, more an accusation.

"No. It was an early work that contributed to the formulation of Animalculist Preformation theory. I had to read it to do the study you asked for! It has the original recipe for vital fluid."

"He has a book," I said, "called *De Generatione*, it is an Ovist tome dedicated to making Ovist homunculi!"

"It's just another old book." My Master shrugged.

"It's a dangerous work of blasphemy by an enemy of the church," I said.

"So was *The Generation of Homunculi*, but you don't seem to care about that!"

"*De Generatione* was banned by the church," I said. "Penned by an Englishman! A Protestant!"

"What!" said the Priest.

"It's in a locked cabinet in his workroom, along with samples of ova he removed from a harlot he drugged one night and operated on! Here is the key."

"Lies!" My Master made to grab it, but the old Priest held him back with a wave of his hand.

The Priest took the key. "Continue, Ecce."

"He is growing an Ovist homunculus in a glass tank in his workroom!"

"Lazzaro! After all the help I've given you, this is how you repay me?"

"He means to use it to prove Ovist Preformation theory and bring you down!"

"This is outrageous!" said the Priest.

"No, no, it's not true!" said My Lying Master. "Ecce! Why are you doing this?"

It was time to play for checkmate. My Foolish Master's Ovist days were over.

"Your Grace," I said. "The Ovist homunculus—My Master is trying to generate a pure person, untainted by desire and sin, the physical act."

"Yes," the Priest was fuming. "What of it?"

"Derived from woman only."

"Yes . . ."

"With no father. When else has this happened? Immaculate conception!"

The Priest's mouth fell. "The Messiah! He's trying to resurrect Jesus Christ!"

"It's a Protestant conspiracy!" I said. The Priest staggered and leaned on his staff, wide eyed. I played him with my lure. "A soulless Antichrist summoning demons, hellfire, and pestilence!"

He choked and spluttered, clutched at his chest, then crossed himself with the cabinet key. "This has gone too far! I will not protect you now, Lazzaro! I'm calling for an inquisition! You will be investigated!" He hurried up the stairs, calling for his escort. "Excommunicated!" He bellowed. I smiled.

The look of death simmered in My Murderous Master's eyes. I ran for cover. I saw an old box and crawled inside. Piccolo and the others were cowering in the corner. I cowered, too.

"Ecce! What is the meaning of this? Come out! I'll get you!"

My Master's great arm reached into the hole and patted about inside, feeling its way around the rubbish. A team of us slid a large nail from the wood as the hand approached. I charged the hand and stabbed it in the forefinger, yielding a resounding yelp. The hand ducked around wildly and grabbed Piccolo. He screamed and flailed about helplessly as it dragged him from the box. I rushed to his aid too late, and was left peeking from the hole.

My Evil Master clutched Piccolo tightly around the torso. Piccolo struggled but couldn't escape; his arms and legs were trapped. Only his head and shoulders protruded from the top of My Seething Master's fleshy hand, and his little purple feet kicked back and forth underneath. He held Piccolo at eye level and stared, more furious than I had ever seen.

"After all I've done for you! Why are you doing this? You've wrecked everything!"

"Let me go! Let me go!" Piccolo screamed and struggled in his grip.

"Ecce! How could you do this! I made you!"

I walked from the box, across the bench top to confront My Ignorant Master. "No, I made him."

My Confused Master looked from Piccolo to me and back again, stunned, then surveyed the lab, noting the equipment.

"You've made another!" He suddenly snatched me up, too, clutching me in his other fleshy fist. I screamed and pummeled his hand with all my might but to no avail.

"Which one of you is Ecce?" He scowled at us in turn as we both struggled in his clenched fists. I conjured my throng of Lesser Animalia. They swarmed around us like a plague, and My Rationalist Master saw spontaneous generation occur before his astounded eyes.

"Attack!" I screamed. Wasps stung his head as he ducked about, spitting them from his mouth. Bugs and ants crawled among his clothes and over his skin. Then I summoned my

Greater Animalia, "Malphigi, Maupertuis! Allez! Allez! Attendez-moi!"

All My New Chums ran to the rescue. Malphigi Mouse snuck into his sleeve while Maupertuis Mole disappeared up his cavernous pants leg. My Ex Master jumped from foot to foot, then Cruikshank Crab scuttled up his collar and pinched him on the earlobe while Reamur Rat sunk incisors into his big toe. Leeuwenhoek Lizard and Swammerdam Salamander rushed into his robes.

Lazzaro hopped about, swearing and bumping into chairs, crab swinging from his ear, rat hanging from his toe, snarling homunculus in each hand. Swarming with insects, he wailed:

"Ecce! How could you? I treated you like a son!"

"The son you didn't want!"

"But I gave you life! I made you!"

"And then I made you!" I said. "In my image!"

Lazzaro followed my gaze to the homunculus in his other hand.

"Don't you recognize me?" Piccolo laughed. ". . . Papa!"

Lazzaro's eyes widened. His blotchy, insect bitten face paled as he stared into Piccolo's blotchy homunculus face and saw an echo of his own. We tittered.

"I know what you're thinking!" said Piccolo, then bit him on the thumb, hard. Lazzaro yelped and dropped us.

We ran.

"And how many brothers and sisters did Olge have?"

"There were three older sisters, then Olge, then a younger brother and sister."

He gave us their names. Piccolo looked up and nodded. It was the right family.

"What region of Wurttemberg was this?"

"Neustadt."

"And what was her mother's name? Think, think!"

"I can't remember, I was too young when she died! Umm . . . Helscha? Helschen?"

We were making a generation map that led to the man

called Robert Oppenheimer. We had traced his family tree from the future back to the current generation, the one alive now. Somewhere in Europe his great-great-great-great-grandmother was living her life with him packed seven generations deep inside her ovaries. Helscha of Neustadt? We would find her.

Piccolo penciled in the last step of the generation map.

"I wonder what it's like in the Alps this time of year," I said.

Piccolo looked up thoughtfully, "He feels cold and unhappy. You know, we should mail him that English Russian doll as a memento."

It sat on the desk, leering at the both of us with its wooden glare.

We tittered.

I closed my eyes and beheld the future: cinders—cities scoured with searing atomic hellfire, and Cicco with my bright and shining soul.

The Raptures of the Deep

Rosaleen Love

*Rosaleen Love [users.bigpond.net.au/RosaleenLove] lives in Australia. She has taught for twenty-five years, first at Melbourne University, then Swinburne University, in the history of philosophy of science, then most recently at Victoria University, in professional writing. She is currently Senior Research Associate at Monash University in the School of Literary, Visual and Performance Studies, and is writing and researching full-time. She began writing fiction in the early 1980s, and published two collections of science fiction with the Women's Press, London—*The Total Devotion Machine *(1989) and* Evolution Annie *(1993), both distinctly feminist in tone, and edited an anthology of Australian science writing,* If Atoms Could Talk *(1987). Her most recent nonfiction book is* Reefscape: Reflections on the Great Barrier Reef *(2001).*

"The Raptures of the Deep" was published, like the Gahan Wilson story earlier in this book, in Gathering the Bones. *It is a small masterpiece of cosmic horror in the tradition of H. P. Lovecraft, which fuses the Lovecraftian with the biological weirdness of undersea hot vent ecologies. It begins: "How I used to enjoy the shimmer of light on water. Now I look out and know it is from there that the terrors that beset us have come." The tone, characterization, and paranoid atmosphere are perfectly controlled.*

How I used to enjoy the shimmer of light on water. Now I look out and know it is from there that the terrors that beset us have come. Worms walk on the land and blind white crabs skittle and skuttle and munch and slide under doorways and ride elevators to penthouse suites and adapt to underground tunnels and eat and eat and eat everything that they find.

Crustal plates collide. The earth quakes and people have cell phones and call from the fallen house, the village deserted and all around them fled.

The giant squid came from a trawl a thousand meters down the Manus Trench. They showed it on TV, flopped off the edge of the dissection slab, eyes glazed, tentacles akimbo. An intelligent species, they said, its neural system intricate and mysterious.

Tasted good, stir-fried with garlic and ginger, at least the parts that didn't turn to mush on the haul up from the pressures of the deep. Curious pads on the tentacular tips. The camera zoomed to close-up. Pads too tough for stir-fry.

The sea crept farther up onto the land. Worms islandhopped, crossing species from fish to pigs to human, the way these things do, from Manus to the islands strung out along the coast, one by one, until they reached Moresby, Brisbane, London, Paris, Rome.

It was my job to fit stuff like this together into a pattern. I look at things you won't find in the formal systems of zoology. If I say Bigfoot, you get the lunatic end of the spectrum, but giant squid, oarfish that bask on the surface of the water, monster turtles that walk up onto the beaches, that was my scene. Cryptozoology.

That was how I found myself in the submersible a couple of k's under the sea down the Manus Trench.

Scott drove. I observed. Worked with Scott before, down

the Pual Ridge, with the NASA nuclear program. Bad news, that. Dump radioactive waste down a hydrothermal vent, see where it gets you.

I had been with Scott enough times to cope with fear of the submersible, fear of being crushed to death in the deep. I had faith in the vehicle and the equipment. What if it failed? Death would come swiftly. The prospect of a swift death if things go wrong, I could handle that. I was not afraid of my own personal death. But I discovered there are things worse than the death of the individual, and it was on that dive I began to know it.

After Pual, Scott took off and went to work for Tristar. Mined deep under the sea, two kilometers near the hydrothermal vents. Brought up gold, copper and silver. Other stuff as well, squid, fish, worms, mussels, crabs, stuff that exploded on the way to the surface, so that gold came mixed with the shredded flesh of rare and wondrous deepsea creatures.

There'd been trouble at Tristar. As we sank under the sea, Scott filled me in. "That squid on TV? Get this. That squid was only the beginning. The TV crew came on board. They wanted a squid and we got them a squid."

I looked out into the dark around us. "Nobody goes to all this trouble for a squid." I shivered. We were padded against the cold, but still it seeped through, getting colder and colder as we descended. Our headlights poked through gloom.

I caught glimpses through thick glass, and readings on the sonar, of creatures that came and went, registering as shadows in the glass, on the screens of the panel of instruments.

"The trawl gear went down and the squid came up from a thousand meters, right? That's only halfway to the bottom. Halfway down to the vents on the ocean floor."

At the vents, liquid rock and superheated steam surge from the earth's core. There's a smell that bubbles to the surface round the Tristar mining ships, part bad eggs, part rotting fish.

In my line of business, you soon develop peculiar tastes,

at least they seem weird to others. Bella didn't like the person I became when I started work on the trawls. She soon took off. I didn't notice the slide from good to bad. I descended into weirdness without knowing it and others couldn't or wouldn't get used to the weirdness that entered into me, that wouldn't let me go back to whoever I once was, that bright-eyed boy straight out of ecology school, ready to take on the world and change it for the better.

Down deep in the vents, life takes a sulfurous path. Sulfur feeds microbes; microbes form mats; worms grow in the mats; fish eat worms; blind white crabs eat everything. Dark ecosystems exist, with dark thoughts, dark motives, dark desires.

"More to come," said Scott. "Got some black smokers down there, you'd love them. Beauties. Name of Satanic Mills. Roman Ruins." Black smokers form where black steam feeds the red-fronded tubeworms, and crabs claw their way across smoking fumaroles.

"Okay, the trawl goes ahead. We get the squid and bring it up, but the net is weird, full of large holes. The net is tough stuff, monofilament sure, but thick. It just can't break. But it can burn."

First I'd heard of it.

"Tore holes the size of houses, looks like the mother of Jaws got there before us. Get this. They found stones tangled in the nets. The rocks shouldn't have been there. Ocean floor's a thousand meters farther down. What're they doing, halfway to the surface? And they were hot, burning hot to touch."

My field, as I said, is cryptozoology. I study the rare and wondrous, the animals of folklore and personal testimony, not yet the creatures of formal classification in zoology. I study the creatures of the deep that have washed up onto land, here a half-rotten carcass, or the distant sighting of a monster by a sailor exhausted by the night watch, deeply untrusting of the testimony of his senses. They call me when they do not know what it is they are encountering and it becomes necessary that they know in order to do the work of the day.

I never knew about hot rocks until they hit me.

They hit and the submersible juddered to one side with a series of huge jolts to the metal shell. They came like asteroids pounding a spaceship.

Scott moved fast. He kept his eyes on the sonar and dodged through breaks in the blips. He guided the sub like a spacer.

I watched. I listened. I felt.

The noise was deafening. Before, the sea had seemed empty, with few things out there to watch us watching them. Now, caught in the wildly swinging headlights, I could see what was hitting us. Rocks like the rocks Scott talked about, but these rocks were covered in wildlife. Large red tubeworms, giant mussels, white crabs skittering. The rocks hit the glass, and I could see the worms squelch up against the glass and disintegrate. I sensed the power of ancient forms of life that followed the path not taken by life that, long ago, had crawled up from the sea to colonize the land.

I looked again at the sonar screen. It wasn't a random pattern of rocks on the screen. The rocks were on the move, but in the same direction.

Scott saw it too and swiftly steered us to one side, out of the tumbling rocks.

Looked like the rocks were heading south. "There's been a bit of action in that direction, down on the ocean floor. New vent opening." Scott pointed to the map.

Rocks on the move? Worms moving south? I could hardly believe what he was saying, nor accept what I was seeing. A vent opens in the cold depths of the ocean. Soon red-fringed worms appear, and giant clams. New life arrives, mysteriously, across the cold dark sea. Life that loves heat travels through deep cold.

"How's it going?" I asked Scott. He was checking out the instruments. "Want out of this?"

"Still looking good," said Scott. Scott was skipper. "We'll keep going."

The sub dived and the rock belt vanished off the screen.

Red eyes glinted at us, red eyes floating in the sea. Millions of tiny red eyes. Mussels and worms floated free in the water, huge worms writhing around the submersible, pressing against the glass, looking in. Worms don't have eyes. Red-eyed shrimps clustered in red fronds, navigator shrimps, shrimps with a sense of direction, showing worms where to go, what camera to slither over, what hatch to prize open, what human to head for, what gut to infect, what . . .

I caught myself falling into panic and pulled back.

Scott sat at the controls, frozen. I shook him.

Worms don't have eyes, but they have worked out ways to see. There's something stirring out there.

Scott was out to it. His eyes were open, but he did not move.

We continued to sink, as if weighted by heavy stone.

Scott passed out. He slumped over the control panel.

I yelled at him, and punched him, and pushed him away from the controls, his eyes closed, his breathing shallow.

If I was in an auto on the highway I'd reach over, try to take the wheel, try to pull the keys out, screech to a stop, anything to stop the vehicle moving.

I did not know how to drive the sub.

They have hit the oxygen supply, I thought, the rocks, the worms. They have done something to our air and soon I shall pass out, like Scott, and never wake up. I am caught in the raptures of the deep. I am narced, like a diver where bubbles in blood and brain bring on a swift descent into drunkenness. I am going deeper and deeper into unknown places. The cold of the sea has entered my bones and the spirit of these dark places has entered my blood and I am enraptured.

From the lofty plateaus of my bubbling thoughts I felt deep pity for Scott. His mind had caved in to the darkness of unknowing. I sought out the other minds out there, minds that were open to me, and I heard their call. I had the desire to go deeper, that exhilaration that cuts in sharply and rides the diver with a madness of the spirit, in which is entwined the intellectual desire to know, to go deeper, and deeper, forever. I must know the raptures of the deep, even if that knowledge kills.

I looked out at the waving fronds of life and knew they were showing us what they could do. They were showing the way the human world will end.

We will come to our natural end, just as the dinosaurs and the woolly mammoths.

The submersible bobbed to the surface, rescued by the dead man's clutch. We came aloft and they said I had bad dreams down there, with the lack of air and the damage to the controls.

I wait, here in my chalet high in the Alps, and look at the world and see the links between this and that, here the rise of the sea level, there an infestation of intestinal worms.

Weird life is coming on land, like it's migrating. It's coming to change our world. Change, when it happens, will be sharp and swift.

What did I see? I saw a whole lot of wildlife where it shouldn't have been, doing things it shouldn't have known how to do, sulfurous life with a kind of instinct, a talent for survival. All life has it. Witness the worms.

The thoughts I have are dark and formless.

They are on the march and they're bringing their environment with them.

The first colonists they send out will die, just as with the first Pacific voyagers who sailed out from their homes to distant lands. Some made it to New Zealand; many others died along the way. They're bringing their home environment with them, as once the New Zealanders brought their trees, their dogs, their pigs.

The dark world brings warm stones, clouds of sulfurous bacteria, shoals of mutating worms.

That which is under the sea is coming out onto land. Life that glows with the sulfurous flame will rise up to terraform the earth. They will bring the earth back to where it once was, just as once oxygen-based life took over from those that preferred an atmosphere of methane. Once more the red fronds of the giant tubeworms will waft in bubbles of volcanic gases, at Yellowstone and Rotorua, and the mats of sulfur-munching bacteria spread outward from mud springs to slide over and smother the green plants of the land.

I came back from below knowing too much. Once we were fearful that spaceships would come from the sky, with aliens. But now I know that yes, they are sending their ships to earth, but theirs are the ships that rise up from beneath. We were wrong to think they would come from the skies.

They are all carnivores down there.

Fable from a Cage

Tim Pratt

Tim Pratt [www.sff.net/people/timpratt] lives in Oakland, California, where he works as an assistant editor and book reviewer for Locus. *He also edits* Star*Line, *the Journal of the Science Fiction Poetry Association. He has only been publishing for a few years, starting in 1999 in the small press and online, but is building an impressive body of short fantasy fiction. He published eleven stories in 2002, and fifteen in 2003. He is the co-author of two chapbooks,* Floodwater *and* Living Together in Mythic Times, *and his first collection,* Little Gods, *appeared in 2003. He has rapidly become one of the most promising young fantasy writers.*

"A Fable from a Cage" was published in Realms of Fantasy. *It is a complex and clever story about a thief, captured and caged by one of the fair folk, and charged with retrieving for the queen a jewel stolen by a mortal. It has magic, irony, and stories within a story.*

Let me tell you a little fable, a story I crafted while sitting inside this dangled cage, where the rooks shit on me and steal my bread all day, and the smoke from your town fires stings my eyes all night.

Did you know the owls feed me? They bring me rats, mice, squirrels, and I eat them. That's why I haven't died yet. I'll never die, not here, wait all you like.

Once there was a thief who wandered in this country, passing from valley to valley in the night, loosening the ropes on cows and leading them away to sell in another town. He lifted bags of fruit from wagons, he picked up things that others put down. He was not a brigand, understand—he did not knock down defenseless women, he did not swagger with a looted sword on his hip, he did not terrorize the roads; indeed, he traveled *between* the roads more than on them. His crimes were all crimes of opportunity, but for an observant man, there are many opportunities for crime.

Not a brigand, no, but also nothing so grand as a burglar or a master thief. For there are men who can be like artists of the criminal trades, and this thief had known such men, but he did not compare to them. His was a lonely life, always running from one village to another, and he wondered sometimes how he had come to live in such a way—he, who had been born in the city.

Oh, yes, the city, you greedy little shits, look how your eyes widen and the drool falls from your lips. This thief had been born in the city, son of a banker, and he might have had a nice life there if he hadn't dallied with the daughter of a ship's captain . . . but that is a different story, and not a fable at all—not a moral tale, in any sense, my young ones.

So this thief—who had a fine, black beard, his one vanity,

a beard as fine as mine was before this month without trimming—had fallen on hard times. He was down to his last coins, and his fine clothes (lifted from a tailor's shop, and almost exactly the right size) were stained from trying to steal a pig the night before, an act below even his usual flexible standards.

He was musing on what to do next, for he had decided that three years traveling this way was more than enough, but he felt too old to apprentice himself to a trade. Indeed, he knew himself well enough to know that the moment his master smith or cooper turned his back, he would feel compelled to snatch up his tools and run away, as much from boredom as from habit.

Walking through the forest that day in a dour mood, he caught his foot on a root and went sprawling. The fall knocked the wind from him, and he lay gasping on the forest floor. Because he could not do otherwise, he stared before him . . . and noticed a large, golden bracelet in the dirt.

The thief sat up, smiling, for here was the perfect crime of opportunity, a bit of jewelry dropped by some passerby, which would not be missed, and which would enrich him. He reached down, wrapped his fingers around the gold, and tried to pick it up.

It moved a little, but something held it fast. The thief brushed the dirt away around the ring and found half of it sealed in black metal. He brushed away more dirt, curious now, and cleared a square of metal three feet to a side. The ring was no bracelet, but a handle for this trapdoor. The handle wasn't really gold, either—just brass.

The thief hesitated. He'd heard the stories, of course, of brigands with secret treasure troves in the forest, where they kept their choicest things. Had he found such a place? And if so, did someone keep guard and watch over it?

Ah, but the opportunity. How could he walk away from such a rich possibility?

The thief wrapped his fingers tight around the ring and pulled. The door moved with surprising ease, without so much as a squeal of hinges. A great cloud of dust rose up with the trapdoor, and the thief turned his face away and coughed, his eyes watering. He let the trapdoor fall back, revealing a black square of darkness.

The thief got down on his knees and peered in, wishing for a lantern. There was no ladder and no steps—did the brigand king lower himself down with ropes suspended from the treetops?

Something shoved him from behind. The thief screamed as he fell—the brigand king had come upon him, and now he would die, sealed in with the dusty old treasures!

He hit the ground quickly, far sooner than he'd expected—and it wasn't ground at all, but a pile of soft fabric, furs and silks. A bit dusty, but more than enough to break his fall. Should he pretend to be dead? He turned over slowly, reasoning that since he'd been unable to see the bottom of the shaft from above, whoever had pushed him would be similarly blind. He peered up at the square of sky and branches, and saw no one. He sat up gingerly, but found no injuries or pains.

He sat waiting for a few moments, expecting a face to appear above, or a voice to call out, or—worst of all—for the trapdoor to swing shut, sealing him in irrevocably, leaving his spirit to guard this pile of fabrics and whatever other treasures lay in the darkness.

Something hissed, like a spitting cat, and the thief shrieked.

Then he saw light. The hiss had been the sound of an oil-soaked wick igniting.

Someone was down here with him.

He could see the lantern, a glass-sided, intricate thing, fit for a rich man's house. It sat on a marble pedestal, like the hacked-off base of a column. He saw no one near the lantern.

"I saw the trapdoor," he began. "I found it by accident, and, well—just natural curiosity, you understand—I wanted to see what was underneath. I mean no harm—"

"You're a thief," a low, neutral voice said. It came from a place in the cavern far from the lamplight.

The thief turned his head that way, startled. "Oh, no, I'm just a journeyman carpenter and—"

"A thief, and a liar." There was satisfaction in the voice now. The only ones who ever sounded satisfied about finding a thief were people who planned to kill or beat that thief very badly.

"I have need of a thief," the voice said, and then a figure stepped into the lantern light.

It was a woman.

Stop your tittering, snot-noses. This isn't a bawdy tale; you'll have to lurk under the tavern windows to hear one of those. No, she wasn't a beautiful woman. She looked like all your mothers, I'd wager, gray in her hair, lines in her face, a good sturdy build. Not a beauty. Not like that ship captain's daughter who got our thief in so much trouble. Not at all.

The woman was dressed incongruously in a fine fur coat. "You must be hungry," she said. "Would you like something to eat? I have some meat roasting."

"I didn't mean to—to fall into your . . . home," the thief said. "If you'll show me a way out, I'll be going."

"It's not a home, thief. It's a burial chamber, like the men in the desert are reputed to build—that's the joke, I think. A cavern filled with all the things I'd need to live well, after death. Fine dishes, fine silks, lanterns, pots, tools. All I've lacked is servants." She smiled. "At least, until you arrived. And you want to leave? If I'd wanted you to get out, thief, why would I have shoved you *in*?" Her eyes were no particular color, it seemed to him, perhaps the gray of dirty washwater, but she stared at him, not smiling at all now.

"Ah," he said. "You pushed me, you say."

"You opened the door to my prison, thief. I wanted to thank you properly, and I couldn't do that with you up there." She held up her arms, her sleeves falling away to reveal her forearms, which were covered with scars. "I have hands of air and fire. I can touch things far away."

The thief's obsession with opportunity extended to his

words as well. He never knew when to keep silent, and he said, "It seems to me that if you could push me *into* the hole from down here, you could have lifted that trapdoor yourself, and there'd be no need for thanks. Not that I don't appreciate your hospitality."

"It seems to *me* that a prison with a door that opens from the inside is no prison at all."

"Prisons are usually more secure than that," the thief agreed. He had some experience in such matters. "But they don't usually open for the casual passerby, either."

"You are not a casual passerby. You are the thief I've been waiting for. No one else would even have seen the door, but you . . . you were meant to find me."

"I'm sure I don't—"

"Shut up," she said sharply, and then took a deep breath. "I offered you food, before. You smell like pigshit, but not roast pork, so I assume you had a wrestling match with dinner and dinner won. Eat with me, thief."

As he was hungry, and trapped anyway, he nodded. "I'd be most pleased."

"You have odd manners for a thief." She turned, reaching into the darkness, doing things with her hands that the thief could not see.

"I have not always claimed that occupation. There was a time when I supped at tables, not in caverns underground."

She shoved a platter toward him. Several large, green leaves sat in the center, covering something. "What's this?" he said, lifting a leaf away.

The glassy eyes of a dead owl stared up at him, and the thief turned his head away in disgust. The bird's head was twisted completely around, its neck broken. "Good Lord, woman, are you mad?"

"You'd better hope I'm not mad," she said, her voice low again, and serious. "Because if I'm mad, you're going to eat that owl—beak, feathers, and all—on a madwoman's whim, and have nothing to show for it but stomach cramps and shit that cuts you."

She was serious, the thief could tell. "And if you're not mad?"

"Then after you eat that owl we'll get out of this hole, thief, and we will steal something grand."

"I can't," he said, looking at the dead bird. It was *huge*—even plucked and beheaded and cooked he couldn't have eaten it all. "I'm sorry, I don't know why you ask this of me, but I can't."

Something tightened around his throat, like blunt, flat fingers, cutting off his air. He choked and clawed at his throat, but his fingers touched only his own skin.

"Eat it, or die," she said.

He gasped his agreement—he had little choice. The invisible fingers loosened, and the thief rubbed his throat. "Can I have a knife at least?" he asked, dismayed by the roughness of his voice.

"Of course," she said, and tossed a blade onto the furs beside him. He'd expected a jeweled dagger, but this was a working man's knife, serrated on one side, sharp on the other, with a stained leather grip. He looked at the owl, at the knife, at the woman. "Aren't you afraid I could kill you with this, faster than you could stop me, hands of air or not?"

"Not at all," she said.

He winced, nodded, and looked at the owl.

"It's fresh," she said, her voice surprisingly kind. "As fresh as it can be. I caught it before I was trapped here, a long time ago, intending to use it myself. I've spent considerable effort to preserve it. You don't have to eat the entrails. They'd make you sick, and anyway, I have other uses for them. And you can have lots of water, while you eat." She passed him a fine porcelain pitcher, and he dipped his fingers in to feel cold water. "We're not barbarians here."

Yes, he ate the owl, the whole thing—eyes, claws, beak, feathers. She let him grind up the talons with a stone and mix them in with water because he feared they'd cut his throat going down, otherwise. He didn't vomit, because she told him that if he did, he would have to eat what he threw up, every foul speck.

Oh, you boys love this one, don't you? You'll be telling it to your friends for months. The more disgusting it becomes, the more horrible, the more you'll eat it up. You shits.

Be gladdened, then. It gets worse.

She refilled the pitcher from the spring twice, and he drank it all. His stomach clenched, and it took all his concentration not to vomit. He'd never tasted anything so foul, never endured anything so horrible.

The woman spread the owl's gray, flecked entrails on a square silver tray. She prodded them, smiling and nodding as the thief fought his urge to gag.

"Eat a dead owl for breakfast," the woman said, laughing softly, "and nothing worse will happen to you all day."

"Now will you show me the way out?" the thief asked through clenched teeth, arms wrapped around his belly.

"No, dear. Now you'll sleep, and then *you'll* show *me* the way out."

The thief did not believe he'd ever be able to sleep, not with that pain in his belly, but the woman offered him a cup, and he drank something sweet and heady from it, and fell into sleep.

He dreamed of flying, and swooping down from the night, and listening. The world was a teeming place of flitting movements; small sounds fraught with significance, strange odors. Eating was everything. Blood was everything. Flying was not the way humans imagined it, a consuming thrill of freedom, a transcendent experience

Flying was just the fastest way to get to the blood.

The thief woke, opening his eyes to sunlight and trees. No furs beneath him—only soil, and a root digging into the small of his back. He would have believed it all a dream, if not for the rough, thick taste of feathers still on his tongue. Not even two pitchers of water had been enough to wash that away.

"You see, you *did* show me the way out," the woman said. "You flew, and took me with you."

He turned his head slowly. His stomach didn't hurt so much now, but his limbs felt stretched, and his head hurt. The woman sat crosslegged in the dirt, her sleeves pushed back, the scars on her arms horribly white in the sun.

"We're free," he said.

"I'm free, my darling," she said. "You belong to me for a while yet. But I'll make it worth your while. You used to be the lowest of the low, but soon you'll be a master thief." She touched his forehead, and he flinched away at first, but her fingers seemed to soothe the pounding in his skull, so he let her go on.

When she drew her hand away, he saw her scars again. "What happened to your arms?" he asked, and then regretted it instantly. What madness, to remind a woman—a creature!—like this of an old injury, and old pain!

She didn't get angry. She just said, "A knife happened," and stood up. "Let's go, thief."

"You call me thief. It's a good enough name. But what do I call you?"

"Call me Mistress, call me wench, I don't care. Come *on*."

He got to his feet. "What really happened? How did we get out?"

"You consumed the owl, and partook of its spirit. Part of its power became yours, and you flew from the pit. You carried me with you."

"That's unbelievable. I've heard stories, but . . ."

"I'm what the stories are made of," she said. She set off into the forest, walking with long strides.

"I guess the owl energy is all used up now," he said, a bit wistfully, following her.

She laughed. "It's not like a skin of wine. It's the creature's *soul*, and you consumed it. Its power is in you forever, for as long as your own soul endures." She glanced at him over her shoulder. "That doesn't mean you know how to use it, though. You took on the properties of the beast and then you fainted. I'll expect better than that when we get where we're going."

"Which is where?"

She said the name of the thief's home city.

He stopped short. "I can't go there! I've been exiled from that place!"

"Some say Fate can be bargained with, when the wind is right. But I'm not Fate, and you won't change my mind."

"We won't make it before the snow," he protested.

"Not by walking," she agreed. "That's why we'll have to fly part of the way."

She didn't demand that they fly right away, just that they walk.

He squatted behind a rock about noon, but saw no feathers in his shit.

He tried to make conversation. "How did you wind up in that hole?"

"I thought there was something inside it that I wanted. So I went in after it, and then someone shut the door on me."

"What were you trying to find?"

"The same thing we're going to steal, thief, so you'll know soon enough."

They reached a village just before dusk. She led him through the rutted streets to a thatched building, an inn. The sign read "Goats and Compasses" and depicted a ram's head and a compass rose. The woman nodded toward the building. "You should eat, and I should get used to people again. Let's go inside."

"I'm almost out of money," he said. "I can't afford a night in an inn."

"I suppose you didn't notice that you were in a cavern of *treasures* last night, did you? I have coins. Old coins, from kingdoms long gone, but they'll still recognize silver, I wager."

She started for the door, then paused, looking above the lintel. "Oh, what's this?"

The thief peered upward. "Just a horseshoe nailed over the door. For good luck."

She laughed. "What good do they think that will do? Did you know that, in the olden days, a king passing judgment would make the petitioner pass through an iron gate, to prove he wasn't enchanted, or one of the Fair Folk? People believed that a fairy creature would scream and burn at the mere proximity of iron, and they hung up horseshoes over their doors to keep such creatures from passing freely." She smiled at the thief, looking not at all motherly. "It's good to see that human foolishness endures." She strode through the door.

The thief followed, shaken. He'd been denying the obvious, trying to convince himself the woman was just a witch or a madwoman touched by the gods, but now he began to wonder if she was human at all, or actually something from the twilight realms. *He'd* believed that the Fair Folk would recoil from the sight of iron, if such creatures existed at all. Apparently they were sturdier than he'd supposed.

He wondered at the scars on her arms, though. A knife, she'd said, but what kind of a knife could harm the likes of her, with her hands of air and fire? One with an iron blade? Perhaps the presence of iron alone couldn't harm one of the Fair Folk . . . but it could be that their bodies were vulnerable to iron's touch.

He would have to keep that possibility in mind.

What's that, snot-nose? Your father's a smith, and he told you that devils and monsters and Fair Folk flee from the sight of iron?

Well, that's as may be. This is a fable, not a true history, and fables have all manner of fantastic things in them, don't they?

And you, what is it? Oh. You thought fables all had talking animals. Well, mayhap the owl spoke before our thief ate it, hmm? Could well be.

Do you care to hear about their evening in the inn, and the music they heard, and the strange way the

woman had of laughing at people and the way they
dressed? Or do you wish to move ahead, on to some-
thing bloodier?

I thought so. I know boys. I used to be one.

They shared a room. The thief took the bed gratefully,
though he suspected the woman was not being kind—she
would not sleep at all, he supposed. She sat on the floor
with a lantern by her knees, shaking bits of bone and brass
onto a cloth and studying the patterns they made. Sometimes she frowned. Sometimes—and this was worse—she
giggled.

After what felt like only a few moments of sleep, the thief
awoke to a great pounding on the door, and someone shouting. "This is the innkeeper! Open the door!"

The woman stood by the window, her mouth turned
down. The thief looked at her. "Should we go out the window?" he said, knowing the sound of trouble when he
heard it.

"No. I'm curious to see what he wants. Open the door."

The thief pulled his shirt on. The door shuddered in its
frame. The innkeeper was hitting it with something heavier
than his fist. "Don't knock your own door down!" the thief
yelled. "I'm coming."

He unhooked the lock and pulled the door open. The
innkeeper stood in the doorway, his face red with fury or
exertion, and he held an iron-headed cudgel in one hand.

"What is it, my good man?" the thief asked.

"This money," he said, and flung a handful of coins at
the thief's chest. "It's nothing but painted bits of wood! I
don't know how my wife mistook it for the real thing in the
first place, but I'm not so easily fooled. You owe—"

"Painted *wood*?" the woman said sharply. "It's not
real?"

The thief stood aside, more than willing to let her take
over. She went to the door. "I'm . . . sorry for the mistake.
Here . . ." She opened her coin pouch and shook the contents into her palm. She looked down at the coins in her
hand and made a small sound of dismay.

"More painted wood," the innkeeper said. "That's won't buy you much, I'm afraid, not even mercy. *You* can leave, old woman. But I'm going to have your son lashed with a horsewhip. It's been a while since the mayor worked his arm."

"I have money," the thief said, reluctant to part with his few coins—which wouldn't cover the room and their meals anyway—but even more eager to avoid a flogging.

"That bastard," the woman said, still looking at the coins, oblivious. "It wasn't even a real treasure trove, just enchanted junk. I wonder what I was *really* resting on all those years, that I thought was a pile of furs?"

"Don't talk about enchantment," the innkeeper said, fear showing beneath his anger. He lifted his cudgel. "I won't have talk of witchery here."

"You may not forbid me anything," she said, looking into his face. "Stand aside, and we'll be on our way."

He slapped the head of the cudgel into his hand. The thief saw how her gaze followed the movement. She feared the weapon.

"Stand aside, or you'll be a puddle of blood in a moment."

He laughed aloud. "You should be whipped, too, woman. I'll see to it."

"Oh, will you?"

His arm, the one holding the cudgel, bent backward. He cried out and then his forearm bent sharply in an impossible direction, and the bone cracked. The cudgel fell from his hand, and the woman jumped back when it hit the floor.

The man opened his mouth as if to scream, but no sound emerged. His other arm jerked, and then his left leg, and he fell to the floor. The woman's hands of air and fire were at work again.

The thief stood with his money pouch in hand, afraid to move. The woman glanced at him. "Come on, thief. Follow your calling. See if he has a purse. We're not as well off as I'd supposed before. We'd best replenish our coffers."

The thief did as he was told, though he found the man's silent thrashing pitiful and disturbing. He fumbled at the man's belt and found a small purse that jingled. He snatched it away, breaking the leather thong.

The man slid into the room on his face, dragged by invisible hands. The door swung partway shut, but the cudgel was in the way, and held the door ajar. "Move that club!" the woman said. "Now!"

The thief did so, nudging it out of the way with his foot. The door slammed shut. He looked down at the weapon. Perhaps the old stories had a grain of truth to them after all. Perhaps the Fair Folk *couldn't* touch iron—at least, not with their hands of air and fire. They could move doors, beds, people, but nothing made of iron.

The trapdoor over the cavern had been made of iron, he recalled. And probably the walls of the cave were full of it as well. Whoever had imprisoned this woman had done his work well, until the thief came along and ruined it.

He heard a horrible, wet noise from behind him. He didn't look. "What are you doing?" he asked.

"Turning him into a puddle of blood, like I promised," she said. She did not sound angry, or pleased, just . . . intent. She was a woman doing a difficult job well.

The thief kept his face turned to the wall.

Long minutes later, she said, "I don't suppose it's worthwhile to eat him. His spirit can't have much of use. Stupidity and miserliness and little else."

"Can we go now?" the thief asked, shuddering. He would not eat human flesh. Never that, no matter what she said, no matter if it gave him the strength of a giant or the mind of a scholar or the power of a king. Never that.

"We can go if you're ready to fly. I'd prefer if you did it without fainting this time."

"All right. I'll try."

They slipped out of the inn quietly, going down the back stairs. To avoid exiting through the front, they went into the kitchen. They could escape through the back door.

A little boy, shirtless, no more than 10, stood by a long table, munching on a piece of bread. The thief and the woman stopped short. The boy swallowed silently, then narrowed his eyes. When his expression soured, it became obvious that he was the innkeeper's son—their features were nearly identical. "Father!" he shouted, startling the thief. "Father, people's in the kitchen, trying to leave without paying!"

"Shut up, boy," the woman said, and stepped forward, raising her scarred hands.

"No!" the thief said. "Let's just go, we'll fly, come on! He's only a boy."

The woman glared at the boy and hissed. The boy's head rocked as if he'd been slapped.

The thief grabbed the woman's arm—it felt like flesh, ordinary flesh, but what did he know?—and pulled her toward the door.

They emerged into the wide space between the inn and the stables. "We need open air," the woman said. "Too many eaves here." She started toward the back of the inn, and the thief followed. In the open space out back, the woman turned on him. "Now fly, you bastard. South."

"I—I don't know how—"

"You know," she said. "You remember it in your bones and in your bowels. What's flying? Why do you fly?"

He struggled to put the concept into words. "To get to the blood," he said, remembering his dream, remembering the strange experience of viewing the world through an owl's senses. "I fly to get to the blood."

"You *remember*," she said, "you *imagine*, and that is but one short step from the act itself."

"Yes." He stared past her, into the sky. Sky above, blood below. Yes.

He heard footsteps and a shout. Dimly, with a bird's disinterest for things scurrying on the ground, he saw the innkeeper's son, still holding his chunk of bread. The boy yelled something the thief couldn't understand.

The thief wondered if the boy was blood, and decided not. Too big.

Since there was nothing to eat here, the thief flew away.

He felt something—a presence next to him, or on him, or beside him—but that seemed only right and natural, and he thought of it no more.

He flew south, toward blood.

After a long time, the thief stood swaying in a field, the taste of something nasty in his mouth. He spat out bits of fur.

The woman stood beside him. She patted him on the back. "You swooped down and snatched up a mouse. Sorry. I couldn't stop you."

He spat again, and gagged.

"Oh, stop that. You ate a whole dead owl, surely you can stand the taste of one little mouse. The essence might help you be stealthier, too."

"I wish I'd never fallen down your god-rotted hole," he said, spitting again.

"That's only because you haven't found untold wealth yet. Come, we're near the city of your disgrace. It's been a long time since I've been there. I wonder how it's changed?" She glanced at him. "Do you want to see your parents or . . . anything? You humans have strange ideas about such things. You've been good, I'm willing to indulge you." She walked through the moonlit pasture, beckoning him to follow.

He didn't look at her. This was the first time she'd openly admitted that she wasn't human. "No. They . . . they agreed with the judgment passed down by the mayor. They agreed that I should be exiled. They're very strict, very traditional. They forget what it's like to be young and hot-blooded . . ."

"Young and hot-blooded." She shook her head. "Your kind mystify me. I've always been as old as I am now."

He sighed. "Can't you even pretend to be a normal woman?"

"Once we're inside the city walls, certainly. If that proves advantageous. But here, between us . . . what's the point?"

"What's going to become of me, when all this is done?"

Humans never got the good end of a bargain with the Fair Folk in the stories, and he hadn't even struck a bargain with this one, just been coerced along.

"I think I'll keep you for a while. You are a useful set of hands, and you have some spine, though it's buried deeply. We've had a rough time of it these past two days, I know, but things will get better, once I take care of this little errand." She shook her head. "I left the Isle of my people a very long time ago, to fetch this item. I never imagined it would take so long. It's even possible that my Queen grows impatient, and her patience is like that of a mountain."

"What are we stealing? Why do you insist on keeping it secret?"

"Just contrariness. Why do you want to know so badly?"

"If I'm supposed to *steal* something, it would be helpful to know what it is, so that I can make plans!"

"You never make plans anyway," she said, waving his objections away. "You wait for a clear opportunity, and you seize it. In this case, I'm going to prepare the opportunity for you. All you have to do is grab what I tell you to grab and then follow me."

The thief was unhappy with that, but he could do little about it. So he followed the woman as they neared the city of his birth, a walled city on the coast. As they neared the gates (which were just opening as dawn approached), the thief noticed something strange. Several wooden crosspieces had been erected outside the wall, and a metal cage hung from each beam. "What are those for?" the thief asked.

"I don't know. It's your city."

"They didn't have these last time I was here."

A man sat in one of the cages, his legs crossed beneath him. The bottom of the cage hung at roughly eye level. The cage was floored with wood, and the prisoner sat staring blankly toward the city.

"What's this?" the thief called to him. "What's the meaning of this cage?" The man looked at him for a moment, then turned his face away and wept.

"Imprisoned in an iron cage," the woman said, horrified. "I wonder if he's only meant to hang there for a short time, or if they'll leave him until he dies."

The thief only shook his head.

"You humans. Your ingenuity never fails to amaze me."

You look like you're about to piss yourself, smith's son. What is it?

Yes, I know every town you've ever heard of has punishment cages, like this cursed one I'm inside, like the ones the thief saw, yes. What of it?

He'd never seen one before because this fable takes place in the past, in a time before any of you were born, when your parents, if they lived at all, were mere children themselves. The cages were a new thing, then.

Ask your mothers and fathers if you don't believe me, or your grand-parents. I wager they'll tell you they used to live in pleasanter times, that people haven't always been so treacherous and cruel, and that there was no need for these cages, long ago.

They're wrong, though, my boys. People have always been as they are now, throughout all time.

I know, you're impatient. We're almost done. I'll pass by their arrival, the way they came through the gates unnoticed, the thief surprised and a little dismayed to find that his exile was of so little importance that the guards didn't even recognize him. He knew there were those in the city who would know his face, though, even with his black beard, and so he walked with his head down. The woman walked the streets with great assurance, and the thief's heart sank as it became clear that she intended to begin this grand theft of hers right now, in daylight.

And then they reached the destination, and it was a house the thief knew.

"No," the thief said, stopping short on the cobbles. "Not that house."

"None other," the woman said. "Do you know it? Is it the home of a childhood friend, perhaps?" She half smiled, and the thief wondered how much she knew about him, wondered if she could see his dreams, or hear his memories and thoughts.

"It is the captain's house. The house of the man who had me exiled."

"Well," the woman said, pleased. "I told you it was destiny, didn't I? You're familiar with his house, then, the arrangement of rooms?"

"Yes," the thief said, because she would know if he lied. "Yes, I've been inside many times. What can he have that you want?"

"Something his father stole . . . or his father's father, or perhaps the one before that. Who knows? I can't keep up with your teeming generations, thief. Some ancestor of his landed on the Isle of my homeland and, through blind luck and stupid audacity, made off with something that belongs to my Queen. When I came to steal it back . . . I found that I could not do so alone, that I needed a human agent. Before I could get help, I was tricked into the prison where you found me."

"How did you wind up in a place so distant from here?"

"That's a long story," she said darkly. "And one I have little interest in telling you. I imagine the one who holds that treasure now will be less cautious, less resourceful, than his forefather."

The thief knew the captain, and he doubted her assessment. The captain was a formidable man. "How do you know he even has the treasure? Fortunes change over generations."

"It's in the house," she said. "The owl's guts told me that much."

"Ah. What do we do now?"

"We break in, and murder everyone in the house, and you scoop up the treasure when I point it out to you. Easy enough, yes?"

The thief stared at her. "Murder?"

"Yes," she said placidly. "I am to kill the thief—or his

descendent, as that's the best I can do—and all who serve him, and all who dwell in his house."

"But . . . his daughter . . ."

"Ah, yes. The root of your exile. You'd best hope she's married, and living in another man's house, hadn't you?" She raised her eyebrow. "But I suppose her value as a wife might have been . . . diminished . . . by the cause of your exile? Unless human customs have changed greatly while I've been underground."

"I won't help you if you kill her," the thief said.

"We'll see," she said.

They proceeded up the walk to the captain's front door. The woman pounded on the wood with her fist, then frowned. "Look, the doorknob's made of iron," she said. She peered at the door jamb. "And there's iron hammered onto the frame, here. That wasn't here the first time I arrived. It appears I taught the old man caution, though as usual they misunderstand the relationship my kind has with iron."

"I knew a man once," the thief said slowly, "who couldn't eat shrimp or lobster. If he did, his skin puffed up and turned red and split. Is it something like that, that iron does to you?"

Before she could answer, the door opened. The thief tensed, expecting to see the captain's face, expecting to be shouted at and struck.

Instead, it was the captain's daughter, a bit older of course but still lovely, her hair falling in fine curls around her face. Seeing her brought forth a welter of emotions—shame at what he'd done to her life, wistfulness for those sweet, exciting days with her, sadness at what had become of his life, resentment of her as the fundamental cause of his current situation.

"Yes?" she said. "Can I—" Her eyes widened as she recognized the thief. "You," she said, and for a moment he thought *she* would strike him—he'd chosen exile over marriage to her, which certainly gave her cause for anger. But she only said, "You have to go! What if my father sees you?"

"My nephew has come to beg your father's forgiveness," the woman said.

The thief stared at her—fortunately, the captain's daughter did, too, and so she didn't notice his expression. "What? I don't—"

"He's my grand-nephew, in truth, and after his . . . unfortunate experiences here . . . he came to live with me. He has made quite a life for himself, down the coast, and he has always regretted what happened. He'd like to speak to your father, to offer his apologies, and—if possible—find out what he has to do to make things right." Then, as if the question had just occurred to her, the woman said, "Have you married, child?"

The captain's daughter looked at her, then at the thief, and shook her head. "No. I never have."

"Then we've come in time," the woman said. "May we come in?"

The captain's daughter stepped aside. The woman glanced at the thief, grinning with her eyes, and stepped through the door. The thief followed.

The daughter led them down the hall, glancing over her shoulder at the thief all the while, worry and confusion showing in her face. The thief avoided her gaze, glad the woman hadn't killed her straight out, but troubled by this pretense. There could be no neat way out of this. There would be a theft here, at the very least, and if he knew this woman at all, there would also be blood.

Perhaps I can intercede to save her life, he thought, looking at the curls falling down her back.

But that was a foolish thought. To avoid thinking, the thief looked around the house. It hadn't changed much. The walls were hung with brass nautical implements and lined with shelves and cabinets, which held strange curios from other lands—figurines, bits of statuary, slivers of petrified wood, crystal formations.

The daughter led them to a sitting room. "Father is in his

office. I'll . . . I suppose I'll go and get him. You can wait here."

After she left, the woman said, "Do they have servants?"

The thief jumped. "N-no, they didn't, anyway. A woman came in the evenings to cook for them, but that was all. The mother and daughter kept the house in order otherwise."

"So just the parents and the girl to contend with. Good."

"Why did you tell her all of that, about my coming to make things right?"

"I was going to twist her head off, thief, but I decided to honor your wishes, for the time being, at least. I told you you'd been good. I'm feeling indulgent."

"You don't—"

Someone shouted elsewhere in the house, and something crashed, like furniture falling over. Boots pounded down the hall.

"I think Papa's coming," the woman said.

The captain entered the room, stopping just inside the door. He ignored the woman entirely, staring at the thief. "You," he said. "I didn't believe her. I didn't think you were *this* sort of a fool." Daintier footsteps followed, and the daughter and her mother appeared behind the captain, each laying a restraining hand on his arm. He shook them off and stalked into the room. He was not a big man, but strong, his muscles standing out like ropes.

The woman raised her arms, and the captain stopped in mid-stride, his eyes bulging.

"Now that you've calmed down, perhaps we can talk," the woman said. The daughter and the captain's wife stood unmoving, too, their eyes wide. "You have something that belongs to my mistress—a jewel, a green jewel. One of your grand-sires stole it, and I've come to take it back." She stood and approached the captain. She brushed back her sleeve and turned her arm, showing him the scars. "That old thief cut me, too, and trapped me. You look very much like him, and if you don't cooperate, I might forget the distinction between you and your ancestor. We wouldn't want *that*."

The captain twitched a little around the mouth. The

woman stepped close to him and touched her finger to his chin. His mouth dropped open. He made a low, moaning sound.

"You don't want that old jewel anyway, do you?" she asked softly.

"No."

"So where is it?"

"My office."

She turned and looked at the thief. "Let's go fetch it, then."

The thief nodded, queasy. He'd thought he hated the captain, but seeing him like this, afraid and paralyzed, made him sick, not satisfied.

"This is a good opportunity for you," the woman said. "We've got him right where we want him. You can make any . . . demands . . . that you like. I'll see that he agrees." She looked, pointedly, at the captain's daughter.

The thief looked at her, the woman he'd loved once, or believed he'd loved. At her body, still beautiful, which had once moved under him and still moved in his dreams. He could have her, he knew. Take her with him. The woman could even make her . . . love him. If he wanted that.

But he hadn't wanted her enough to stay and marry her the first time, had he? And he shouldn't do so now. She deserved better.

Slowly, the thief shook his head. "I want nothing from this house."

The woman curled her lip. "You think you're being noble, I suppose. She might have had a pleasant life, with you. I could have made her forget this nonsense." She clapped her hands together, as if brushing off dust. "Very well. Let's go." She lifted her hand, and the daughter and her mother fell, to lie stiffly on the carpet like tumbled statues. The thief winced, but he could do nothing to help them. He'd done all he could.

They went to the captain's office. The woman stepped inside, assessed the room—shelves of books, a large desk, lamps, chairs—and walked straight to a glassed-in case. "There," she said. "The jewel."

The thief looked into the case, and saw no jewel. Only a large dark sphere of . . .

Ah. It was an intricate, spherical metal cage, a thing of curves and layers. A journeyman smith's useless piece of finery, perhaps. An iron ball of filigree, as big as two fists held together, with a tiny green jewel set deep in the center.

"You can't even touch it," the thief said.

"Why else do you think I brought you?"

The thief nodded. He took a heavy piece of quartz from the captain's desk and shattered the glass, then reached inside and grasped the iron cage. "It's cold!" he gasped.

"I imagine," the woman said. "Though it would burn me. That jewel is from my Queen's crown, and it carries a little bit of her royalty still—like a scent that lingers on a pillow. To have even the Queen's decoration trapped in a cage of iron . . ." She shook her head. "The antipathy is strong, and it makes the iron cold."

"What do we do now?" the thief asked, his fingers growing numb. "Where . . . where do we go?" For he was thinking of the far Isle of the Fair Folk, and of the wonders and horrors he would see there, of the madness and forgetfulness that would surely overcome him on those shores.

"Back to the hole in the ground," she said. "There are smith's tools there, among all the other things. And as iron cannot be enchanted, I know those tools are real, and not bits of wood or offal made to look like coins and furs."

"You want me to break this cage, and free the jewel," he said. "I've never used smith's tools."

"If you can't figure it out, my thief, we'll just find a blacksmith and let you eat him whole, hands and ankles, heart and eyeballs. Then you'll know how to wield a hammer. Do you prefer that course?"

"I . . . think I can learn enough on my own to break this cage."

"Acts of destruction *are* the easiest to learn, aren't they, thief?"

They went down the hall.

"What will become of the captain and his family?" the thief asked. "Will you spare them?"

"Would you like to consume the daughter, eat every bit of her, and keep a little of her with you always in that fashion?"

"Gods! No, monster, I would not!"

"Very well. Then her soul will be consigned to wherever such things go. I'm going to kill them all, thief."

"You horrible—"

"Clutch that ball tightly, my dear," she said. "And go to *sleep*."

The thief did.

He woke, groggy, lying on a pile of musty furs.

"My sleepy thief. I hit you with that enchantment hard. I'm sorry."

He sat up in the dimness and screamed as every part of his body exploded into pins and needles as his sleeping limbs woke.

Only his hands, still clasping the metal ball, were awake. The proximity to the iron had kept her enchantment from making his hands fall asleep.

"That's right, move around," the woman said. "Work out the stiffness."

"We're back?" he croaked, his throat dry. "Under-ground?"

"You walked the whole way, though it's a jerky, stiff-legged walk, and it tired me out to drive you and that way. I thought you'd wake up sooner, but I was a little . . . an-noyed . . . when I put you under. You really shouldn't speak to me harshly, thief. I had you drag away the old metal trapdoor and build a wooden one to replace it, and there's a ladder now. Otherwise, yes, this is our familiar abode."

"The girl, the captain's daughter—"

"A puddle," she said, waving her hand. "A pool of noth-ing much. When your arms are well awake, the smith's tools are there, and I've got a fire going. We'll figure out how to break that ball."

"Why did you kill them?" The thief squeezed the cold iron ball.

"Because of the hurt their ancestor gave me. He was beyond my reach, so I contented myself with the descendents."

"You're inhuman."

"You state the obvious."

"I need water," he said suddenly.

"I imagine."

"The pitcher is . . . ?"

"Over there," she said, and stretched out her arm to point.

The thief saw his opportunity. He hurled the ball as hard as he could toward her midsection.

She grunted as the ball struck her, then screamed. Smoke rose from her dress as it caught fire. In the dimness, the thief could hardly see what had happened, but it seemed that the iron ball had buried itself into her stomach.

"You shit-eating bastard," she shrieked. She reached down as if to pull the ball away, but screamed and pulled her hands back when she touched it.

Insubstantial hands gripped the thief's throat, and he grunted and started toward the fire and the smith's tools. The hands fluttered, faded, returned. She'd been tired anyway, she said, and now she was grievously wounded. Her hands of air and fire were tired. Still, his vision dimmed and he fell to his knees near the anvil. He reached out and gripped a pair of iron pincers. He struggled to lift the heavy tool, but managed to press it to his throat.

The woman screamed anew, and the invisible hands withdrew.

The thief laboriously gained his feet and stepped toward her. The ball of iron was almost invisible now, burning its way deeply into her guts.

"We could have had such fun," she said, coughing up smoke. "You would have lived forever, if you'd just agreed to serve me."

"I think I might have figured out a way to do that anyway," the thief said. He struck her in the face with the iron pincers.

* * *

It took him almost a full week to eat her body. She had no organs or bones, just soft, spongy meat throughout, which both relieved and disturbed him. Her flesh tasted like nothing at all, but it still repulsed him to cut and consume her.

The stories said that the Fair Folk had no souls, and so he wondered whether eating her would have any effect—what good was ingesting the spirit of a soulless thing?

But the night he finished her, he had strange dreams. And when he climbed the ladder and emerged into the dark forest, he discovered that he had hands of air and fire, and could move things with a thought, and feel them from far away.

As the years passed, he found that he did not age as men did, nor did he take wounds.

And so he felt satisfied, at last, that he was a master thief.

That's my story, boys. And now the sun's near gone, and you should go home, yes?

Ah, the questions, the questions. What became of the thief? Well. Long after he ate the woman who was not a woman, after many years of wandering, he began to ponder his weakness. Because you see, along with his hands of air and fire and his long life, he'd also acquired the woman's weakness. He could no longer touch iron—the metal grew cold if he even put his hand near it, and he knew it would burn him if he touched it.

But he thought to himself, Am I not, at bottom, a man? Could I not, perhaps, overcome this weakness, if I only had the right meal?

The thief thought back to the woman's suggestion that he could eat a smith to gain familiarity with tools. And the thief thought, Yes—perhaps I'll eat a smith, and gain his ease with iron, and the metal will vex me no more. For it is amazing how many things in this world are made of iron, boys, not least of all this cage. The thief had never eaten a man—he'd kept that vow all those years, because the woman did not count as a human, you see—but he thought the time had come to forget silly vows, just as he'd forgotten the face of the captain's daughter.

So the thief came to a village, and took a room in an inn, which had a ram's head on its sign, as many of them do. And the next day he went to the smith's. He was uncomfortable around the horseshoes and the anvil and the hammers but managed to put on a peaceful face. He hailed the smith, intending to inquire after a bit of work and then kill him and spirit his body away for a leisurely meal.

The smith looked familiar, and from the way his eyes went wide, the thief knew he recognized him, too.

Ah, boys—your own eyes are wide. Is this a familiar story?

The smith looked just like the old keeper of the inn, the one the woman had killed that first night the thief traveled with her. Casting back, far back in his memory, the thief thought that this, perhaps, was that same village, grown a little larger, but still the same. He realized the smith was the innkeeper's son all grown up, that with his father dead he'd had to apprentice to a trade other than inn-keeping.

The son recognized the thief, and in his face it was clear that he remembered the witchery, remembered the murder and seeing the thief fly away.

The thief threw out his hands of air and fire, but the smith had iron all around him, and a hammer in his hand, and the invisible hands rebounded from those things.

The smith struck our thief with a hammer, and knocked him down, and the thief woke in a cage— yes, like this one, very like—with a grievous burn on his face from the hammer's iron. The thief tried to escape, but he could not open the cage himself, because his hands could not touch the iron bars, neither his real hands nor his other ones.

And now, my boys—the moral.

I fear I have misled you. There is no moral. Because a moral comes at the end of the tale. If I stayed in this cage, and died, there might be some lesson to be learned from my long life. But my life hasn't ended yet, and so it's a poor time for accounting, before the ledger's even closed.

Because I can still grab you, brats, despite this metal all around. I can reach my hands of air and fire through these bars and grasp you lightly by the necks, as I've done now. And you, smith's son . . . you'll go, and take—and steal—your father's smallest hammer and chisel, and come back here in the dark, and break this cage open. If you don't, I'll squeeze your friends until they're blue, and then black. And if you serve me . . . perhaps I'll teach you secrets, and show you wonders.

You only look afraid, now, but you'll learn to look happy, and hopeful, and bright, in time.

And after you release me, perhaps we can find something good to eat, yes?

A Quartet of Mini-Fantasies

Arthur Porges

Arthur Porges [Fan site: www.fortunecity.co.uk/jodrellbank/ gargoyle/7] lives in Pacific Grove, California. The tribute website contains an extensive essay on his life and career. His first story, "The Rats" (1950), is a minor classic of horrific SF. Subsequent stories have appeared frequently in Fantasy & Science Fiction (he says he learned much about writing with the help of editor Anthony Boucher), Fantastic, Alfred Hitchcock's Mystery Magazine, and Ellery Queen's Mystery Magazine, especially in the fifties and sixties. He taught mathematics at the college level before retiring to be a full-time writer in 1957. Then he stopped publishing SF or fantasy with any frequency after 1966, moving nearly entirely into the mystery markets. He never published a science fiction or fantasy novel, and so although fairly widely anthologized from the 1950s through the 1970s, his name is no longer widely known to this audience. His first collection of SF & fantasy, The Mirror and Other Strange Reflections, appeared in 2002.

"Four," a quartet of mini-fantasies, first published in Fantasy & Science Fiction, is an assemblage of four short short stories, or vignettes, compressed to their most effective elements and images. We are reminded that C. S. Lewis, in his Experiment in Criticism, said that there is a basic type of story (he called them myths) that yields its full power regardless of the manner or length of the telling. These four are full power, lyrical, and elegant.

～ One

There was nothing whatever jolly about this dwarfish Santa. He neither spoke nor laughed, but showed a faint sneer as he repeatedly pointed to the big placard hung about his neck. In large black letters it read:

Please Help!
Deadly Anthrax!

Curious, I moved closer to see who sponsored such a graceless oddball, and wondering, too, about the grayish powder, presumably raw sugar, he sprinkled on each cookie he was handing out to those who put money in his cup. Then my stomach contracted like a clenched fist. Between the two giant phrases, in very tiny print, was one more word: SPREAD.

～ Two

There are very few Shadowsmiths left. Theirs is an arcane craft, the mastery of our only two-dimensional entity, soundless, weightless, intangible, eerily supple, capricious, and willful, able to bend smoothly over a curb, or scale a high wall. Cast by Sun, Moon, oil-lamp, candle, or light-bulb on black loam, blue water, purple snow, or yellow sand, fixed, or capering wildly, each shadow is unique.

With his long, prehensile fingers, oddly adhesive at their tips, a Master Shadowsmith, by tugging cunningly at its edges, will make you an elegant new shadow, your very own Dark Other.

314

⌒ *Three*

I never wanted to become a vampire. Born in this town long plagued by the vile aberrations, I put garlic everywhere, and always wore a cross. That kept me safe for years, but last night He materialized in my bedroom, and when I thrust out the crucifix, the handsome devil said pleasantly, "That has no power over me, young lady. In life I was Rabbi Israel Horowitz." Too late I realized my fatal mistake, and am now one of the undead. I should have used pork-links instead of garlic, and worn a Star of David!

⌒ *Four*

I was greatly intrigued by Harry's wife right from the start. An odd match. She was pretty, elegant, but somehow different, with opalescent eyes that never seemed to blink. And she was too young for my portly business partner, who was pushing fifty. Her strange watchfulness was almost reptilian, suggesting a lizard in the sun waiting for an unwary insect.

This morning his car broke down, so I came to pick him up, and as I poured some coffee at the mirrored sideboard, I saw something in the glass which they didn't realize I'd seen, what with my back to them. A squirt of grapefruit juice had struck her left eye, and amazed I saw her tongue slide out of her red lips to wipe the eyeball clean.

Señor Volto

Lucius Shepard

Lucius Shepard lives in Vancouver, Washington. He's a poet and rock musician who began to write SF and fantasy fiction in the early 1980s, and became prominent with his first book, Green Eyes, *one of the six Ace Special first novels in 1984—the series that included first novels by Kim Stanley Robinson, William Gibson, and Michael Swanwick. His stories, many of them novellas (the length he most often prefers) have been the basis of his high reputation since, with such impressive pieces as "The Man who Painted the Dragon Griaule," "R&R" (which became his second novel,* Life During Wartime), *"Barnacle Bill the Spacer," and "Radiant Green Star." His collections include* The Jaguar Hunter *(1987) and* The Ends of the Earth *(1991). The year 2003 featured a burst of novellas and stories by Shepard, fourteen or fifteen of them, both SF and fantasy, many of them longer than this one.*

"Señor Volto" was published at SciFiction, and this is perhaps its first printing. The Volto of the title is a Carnival entertainer in Central America, the location of many of Shepard's earlier heart-of-darkness stories, who here claims to have amazing powers from electricity, including the ability to bestow powers on others. Aurelio Ucles, the central character, is goaded into taking a fairground challenge to shake hands with Volto, and does indeed gain some disturbing powers. And then the trouble really starts.

Ladies and gentlemen! I have come to your beautiful village tonight . . . and I offer this compliment without irony, with no hint of ridicule, for your village is, indeed, beautiful. Far more beautiful than even you who dwell here know. I have come tonight to give you a jolt from the electric truth of my existence. It is my belief that among you there is an individual with an irresistible affinity for that truth, someone whose drab mental sphere I intend to illumine as though it were a bubble filled with lightning, so they may continue the grand traditions of my kind. I know, I know! Doubtless you are saying, "This fool must think us unsophisticated. Every carnival that travels the length and breadth of Honduras carries with it a man who calls himself Señor Volto. A man who straps a car battery to his chest and attaches paddles to his hands in order to transmit shocks to whoever grasps them. None of them offer illumination, only the chance to measure one's resistance to pain." But I am not those other men, my friends. I am the one and only Señor Volto, and to prove the point, before I provide you with the opportunity to test yourselves, I will tell you my story.

My name is Aurelio Ucles and I was born in Trujillo on the north coast. When I was twenty-two, my father died and left me the deed to the Hotel Christopher Columbus, a blue-green rectangle of concrete block that occupied a choice section of beach property, with a pool and a mahogany-paneled bar that opened onto a deck. Few tourists came to Trujillo, put off by the high incidence of violent crime and drug trafficking in the region, yet I managed the hotel successfully for the next twelve years. The larger part of my clientele consisted of officials and guards who worked at the state prison located near the center of town, an edifice hidden behind a high yellow wall. They used the hotel as a place where they could bring their women and after a time they took me into their confidence and allowed me to assist in dispersing the cocaine they stole from imprisoned traffickers and laundering the money they received in return. I was never their friend, merely a useful associate. The fact is, I feared them. They carried pistols and cattle prods and treated me with contempt. Though I prospered, though my wife, Marta, bore me two healthy sons, I yearned for respect, both that of the prison guards and of the common people of the town, many of whom repudiated me for my criminal activities. This lack of respect, I believed, was all that kept me from contentment; but I have since concluded that my discontent was less associational than intrinsic. I was an unhappy child and had grown into an unhappy man. No ordinary sinecure, however honorable and profitable, would have sufficed to placate my inner demons. It may be I was looking for a judgment to complete my life. We tend to hide such desires from ourselves, to dress them in more reasonable cloth, knowing we will never be able to satisfy the standards against which we seek to be measured.

If such was the case, then judgment came to me in the form of a mechanic. It would be nearly as accurate to claim it was a woman, but I am appalled by clichés, even those attendant upon my nature, and since it was the mechanic who contrived the shape of the judgment rendered, I am inclined to give him credit. The woman, Sadra Rosales, was only a conduit, though perhaps I do her a disservice by this dismissal. Unlike most of the women who patronized the bar in my hotel, she held a position of some respect—editor of an English language newspaper. Yet like those other women she had a history of drugs and romantic mistakes, and was always on the look-out for a fresh mistake, one that would temporarily present an impersonation of hope. She was thirtyish, with a broad Mayan face, a little thick in the waist: on the scale of Honduran beauty, she was no more than attractive, but she had a buoyant energy that lent her the gloss of beauty and though I did not love her, I was in no mood to resist her. She suited the moment, she pleased my heart, she excited my body, and she was grounds for divorce. The problem of what I might tell my wife and of how divorce would affect my children, all the accompanying karmic issues . . . these questions troubled me, but I was never able to confront them because Sadra's problems pushed my own into the background. It was one thing after another. An assistant was sabotaging her at work; the father of her child was suing for sole custody; her best friend, Flavia, was telling lies about her sexual practices. The latest and most pressing problem concerned her pride and joy, a gray Toyota whose dented grille expressed the automotive approximation of weary disillusionment. She had taken it to a mechanic, a friend named Tito Obregon, for a brake alignment and claimed he had stolen the new engine, replaced it with an inferior one. Now the car wheezed, stalled, and smoked. The police would do nothing—Tito was the lieutenant's closest friend. Sadra was considering a lawsuit.

I went with Sadra one afternoon to see Tito at his shop on the outskirts of town, a low yellow building of concrete block with an enormous blue Aguazul logo painted on its side, like the flag of a proud nation. It stood at the center of an acre of ochre dirt and was hedged in back by the lip of the jungle. Weeds, banana trees, palms. A group of ragged kids was playing soccer out front and two teenage boys were leaning against Tito's tow truck, smoking and looking bored. Sadra insisted I stay in the car. She said she didn't want to involve me, but of course she had already done so by bringing me along. As they talked just inside the door, or—more precisely—as Sadra talked to him, Tito stared in my direction the entire time. Had Sadra, I wondered, trusted her car to a jilted ex-lover to fix? Such a stupidity would be in keeping with her character: a stew of feminism, manipulative pettiness, and a kind of sprained innocence.

It grew ovenlike inside the car. The soccer ball bounced out onto the highway and a tiny kid in red shorts ran to retrieve it, darting across the path of a bus that never slowed and missed him by a fraction. A smoky gray mist began folding itself over the crests of the hills behind the shop and

Tito came to lean in the doorway, wiping his hands on an oily rag. He was skinny and vulpine, with prematurely gray hair and a heavy beard shadow, wearing chinos and a Hard Rock Cafe tank top. I looked away from his stare. Beyond the weedy vacant lot on the opposite side of the road, a wedge of the bay was visible, slate blue water armored with an unyielding glitter. Soon Sadra returned, threw herself behind the wheel, and slammed the door. "Puto! He says he doesn't care what I do." She swerved out into traffic, telling me everything Tito had said, interpreting his perfidy, initiating a monologue that continued long into the night over shots of vodka and a quantity of excellent cocaine.

Over the course of the following week I felt marooned in the midst of my life and saw no sign of salvation on the horizon. More often than not I found myself sitting at the bar, gazing glumly across the deck at the untroubled waters of the bay and the desolate point of land that, enclosing it, formed the Cape of Honduras. It was just off the Cape that Christopher Columbus had anchored during his final voyage; he had been gravely ill and never set foot on the shore himself, thereby, I conjectured, establishing the pattern that governed our trickling tourist trade. A group of Americans returning from the Miskitia jungle booked rooms on Wednesday morning, bringing an uncommon and not altogether pleasing energy to the hotel, splashing and shouting in the pool, spilling drinks at dinner, and staying up until all hours playing cards. On Friday some prison guards installed several women from La Ceiba in the third floor suite. The women never ventured into the bar, and the guards—those not occupied with the women—would sit at a table on the edge of the deck and drink. They were of a set, these men. Swarthy, thick-waisted, with oily hair and froglike faces, dressed in slacks and short-sleeved shirts. Their wrists and hands heavied with gold rings and watches looted and extorted from prisoners. While most of them took their turns visiting with the women, the senior guard, Jorge Espinal, the widest and shortest among them, only strayed from the table to walk down to the beach and relieve himself. On occasion he would summon me and ask for more beer and snacks. He refused to place orders with my bartender, preferring to treat me as a menial. Whenever I came over, he would greet me with false effusiveness and wink at the others as if sharing a private joke, then laugh uproariously when I walked away. Furious, humiliated, I left the hotel early that evening, a couple of hours before I was to meet Sadra, and went striding along the beach and up through town without a thought for destination, imagining the violent humiliations I would visit upon Espinal if he were me and I him.

Across from the old graveyard in Trujillo, a weedy ruin hemmed in by a crumbling stone wall and an arched gateway with no gate, situated on a red dirt road that angled uphill and west from the center of town, lay a flea market: a row of ramshackle wooden stalls in which were displayed T-shirts, soccer jerseys, aprons; toys and dolls; kitchenware, cutlery and other household items; key chains, switchblades, barrettes, cassette tapes. All manner of cheapness. White and blue and yellow plastic banners advertising Nacional Beer were strung above the stalls and behind them was a grassy area where beer was sold from a metal cart. At the rear of this area was a little hand-cranked carousel suitable for toddlers, a circular platform no more than six feet wide that supported four tiny seats. A handful of women stood watching their children go round and round. Two of the kids were wailing and I nourished the embittered notion that they were becoming aware that this tight repetitive circle was all the ride they might expect from life. A dozen or so working-class men were drinking and talking in a group. I bought a beer and leaned against the cart. The sky was hazy, a few blurred stars showing in that muddled darkness, and the air was thick and warm, infused with the scents of roast chicken and ordure emanating from shanties tucked in among palms and banana trees beyond the carousel. Radio music contended with the crying of the children. Gradually I grew calm. I bought a second beer and debated the idea of buying a present for Sadra. Something funny to take her mind off Tito and the Toyota.

I suppose it was chance that led me to the market, but on

turning from the beer cart and seeing Tito Obregon barely an arm's length away, dressed as Señor Volto in a straw hat and a farmer's rough clothing, battery strapped to his chest, braced in a harness of leather and steel that resembled some perverse sexual accessory, the cables running back to an alternator resting on the ground, a control box clipped to his belt, and narrow black paddles extending from his hands . . . when I saw him, I was afflicted by a frisson and had, albeit fleetingly, a more complicated understanding of the operations of chance, recognizing that coincidence and fate were likely partnered in the moment. I nodded to Tito, said, "Good evening," and started toward the street; but Tito's voice, amplified and lent a buzzing inflection, brought me up short:

"IS AURELIO UCLES AFRAID OF EVERYTHING? MUST HE ALWAYS HIDE BEHIND A WOMAN'S SKIRTS . . . OR DOES HE DARE TEST HIMSELF AGAINST SEÑOR VOLTO?"

One of the teenage boys who had been leaning against Tito's tow truck was holding a microphone to his mouth— Tito himself could not grasp it, thanks to the paddles strapped to his hands. The boy smirked at me and Tito said, "PERHAPS OUR AURELIO IS NOT A MAN AT ALL. PERHAPS WHAT SADRA ROSALES SAYS ABOUT HIM IS THE TRUTH."

Though it was customary for Señor Volto to offer such challenges, the anger in Tito's face was that of a scorned and possibly demented lover, and it occurred to me that Sadra was not so important that I cared to risk my well-being in a dispute concerning her. Since the battery was being powered by an alternator, it had no inhibitor and thus Tito was capable of transmitting a fatal shock. I was certain he knew that if he were to kill me, the prison guards would be more than a little upset with him over the loss of someone who served them as financial conduit and host for their debauches. Nonetheless, I balked at the thought of grasping the paddles. The working men had broken off their conversation and were drifting toward us, nudging one another and grinning.

"PERHAPS IT'S TRUE," Tito went on, "WHAT SADRA TELLS ALL HER FRIENDS AT THE NEWSPAPER—THAT THE HEAD OF AURELIO UCLES' PRICK WOULD FIT INSIDE A THIMBLE."

The working men thought this a grand joke and offered commentary. My anger building, I told Tito to fuck his mother, I wasn't going to be playing his game.

"EVEN A BOY'S GAME IS TOO MUCH FOR AURELIO!" Tito nodded at his assistant. The boy took a stand in front of him and gripped the paddles. Tito twitched the controls. Voltage sizzled. The boy stiffened, but did not release the paddles, not even when Tito turned the voltage considerably higher. At last he broke contact, smiled and displayed his reddened palms to the men who had gathered round—they voiced a murmurous approval.

"DO YOU SEE? EVEN THIS BOY IS MORE OF A MAN THAN AURELIO UCLES!"

I can't recall who it was that said everything is explicable in terms of a small child's behavior—I believe the comment was offered pertaining to the functioning of the cosmos, not merely the actions of human beings, but it was certainly applicable at that moment. A petulant rage possessed me and I thrust out my hands, intending to seize the paddles; but the boy stepped between Tito and me and demanded five lempira.

My rage was such that having to pay for the privilege of experiencing a shock did not deter me. I fumbled out some bills, flung them at the boy, then shoved him aside and confronted Tito. Daunted by his appearance, I hesitated. With his face shadowed beneath the straw hat, the battery mounted in its brace of leather and metal, cables running off beneath his arms, and those featureless black paddles lashed to his wrists, he looked the embodiment of an arcane peril. The group of men encircled us, lending a ritual symmetry to the scene, and more people were filtering between the stalls, made curious, I imagine, by the pointedness of Tito's insults. Among them I recognized the jefe of the prison, an elderly white-haired version of the squat unprepossessing men who were at that very moment carousing on my deck. The old man's contempt for me was especially poisonous, and I could not bring myself to back down from Tito's challenge with him looking on.

I remember taking hold of the paddles, hearing the faint hum and buzz of the voltage as the prickling crawl of electricity in my palms evolved into pain; and I remember also how, as the pain grew intense, my vision reddened and my focus narrowed to encompass the lower half of Tito's face, his teeth bared in a snarl as if the pain were flowing out of his flesh into mine. This notion, that pain—or some unknown agency of which pain was a by-product—was leaving Tito's body and entering my own, was reinforced by the fact that his expression became increasingly one of relief and surprise—it seemed he, too, was aware of a sea change. Soon the only sound I could hear was the reedy whine of my nervous system, like a desperate insect trapped inside my ear. Shattering vibrations flowed along my arms. My heart bucked and stuttered. My hands were on fire and that fire darted into my chest, snagged in my bones. I wanted to let go of the paddles, I intended to let go, and there came a moment when I was certain I would let go. What inhibited this impulse, I cannot say. Stubbornness was part of it. Stubbornness and the fear of greater humiliation. Yet, another element was involved in my resistance and in the midst of pain a bubble of clarity briefly enveloped me, allowing me to consider what this element might be. I had the sense of being guarded, protected in some fashion, and I also had the impression of having bonded with that protective force and thus being sealed away from the possibility of mortal harm. Then clarity evaporated. My head shook violently; my eyes felt dry and rattling in their sockets. Fumes of smoke wisped up between my fingers and the comprehension that my flesh had begun to scorch was the last thing I remember.

Permit me, ladies and gentlemen, to put forward a thesis, to suggest that it was not electricity that changed me, and there is no doubt that I had changed, for upon waking in the hospital, my burned palms bandaged, my fingers red as tomatoes and covered with salve, I was not, as might be expected, possessed by shame and rage over what had transpired at the flea market, but rather evidenced an unreasonable calm and a pragmatic appreciation of both the event and my resultant injuries . . . so permit me to suggest rather that electricity opened me to change, that the precise amount of voltage transmitted through Tito's paddles caused me to become accessible to an entity, perhaps a devil, or perhaps one of those numinous creatures that dogs and drug addicts see when they lift their heads from the stuporous contemplation of a roach or a stain upon the floorboards to a corner of the ceiling and thereafter track the invisible-to-others progress of some impalpable curiosity across the room. It's possible, of course, that my unnatural steadiness of mind was a consequence of madness or physical damage, but I have come to believe that the apprehension of bonding I experienced while gripping the paddles was evidence of a symbiotic attachment or possession, because when I left the hospital shortly before midnight and strolled through the town, though I was thoroughly familiar with the potholed streets and the little stores and the ragged crescent of the beach lined with shanty bars, they seemed at the same time new to me, and when I came in sight of my hotel, its shape as simple as a child's block, when I entered and saw the mahogany sweep of the bar with the rectangular portal in the wall behind it through which I commonly viewed the bay and the deck where Espinal and his cronies still sat and drank, I found the whole of it diverting and strange, as if another soul were sharing my eyes, a soul with a unique passion for life, greedy to observe every detail of this familiar—yet unfamiliar—scene.

The strongest proof of my thesis was yet to come. I went behind the bar, poured myself a vodka, and while I was scooping up ice cubes, Espinal pushed back his chair and walked past me without a word. He stood, I tell you, and yet he did not move from the chair. It appeared he had divided into two Espinals, one of whom headed along the corridor toward the apartment where I dwelled with my

family. Though puzzled by the phenomenon, I took it more-
or-less in stride and followed him, noticing that this figure
was somewhat dimmer and gauzier than the one who remained seated, a colored shadow of sorts. The shadow Espinal tapped on the door of my apartment (the tapping
made no sound) and was immediately admitted by my wife,
wearing a flimsy peignoir that must have been a recent purchase—she had never worn it for me. I was unclear as to
what I was witnessing, uncertain both of what it signified
and whether it was real or a by-product of my disorienting
encounter with Señor Volto. I refused to accept the obvious,
that Espinal and Marta were having an affair. After a
minute, I opened the door and crept toward the master bedroom. On the bed were two Martas, one asleep on her side
and the other—a somewhat less substantial and entirely
naked female form—mounted atop Espinal, riding the sluggish thrusts of his hips, eyes closed and fondling her own
breasts. For all their passion, there was no sound of breath
or fleshly contact, but the sight of Marta thus engaged,
even if she were only a phantom, tore at my spirit. I was
convinced that this was at the least a shade of infidelity, the
reflection of an actual event.

It was not my love for Marta that kindled violence in my
heart; rather, it was violence, the allure of it, that opened
me to love. Aboil with hatred and confusion, I closed my
eyes; when I opened them, I saw only the sleeping Marta.
Espinal and the second Marta had vanished. Watching her
stir beneath the sheet, my desire to hurt Espinal was married to a recognition of how little I had valued her, how utterly I had neglected her. I stepped forward, intending to
make some show of affection and forgiveness, and spotted
something under the edge of the bed: Espinal's cattle prod.
A shiny black cylinder with a button trigger that he usually
carried hitched to his belt. He had been here, I realized. Inside my wife. The carelessness of the man, the lack of respect implicit in his carelessness, it assailed me, as did the
phallic shape of the prod—I wondered if he had left it there
to goad me. I picked it up, and my anger seemed to course
into it, to assume the form of that cold black stick. Ignoring

the pain in my hands, I gripped the handle hard and visualized myself jamming the tip into Espinal's fat neck, triggering off charge after charge. How could Marta have made love to such a toad? Recalling her abandon caused my anger to spike, and, eager to demonstrate that no man could treat me so, I hurried from the room.

Anger was free in me as never before, ungoverned by its normal restraints, but upon entering the bar I was stalled in my vengeful progress by what I saw on the deck. Illuminated by the pool lights, five guards, Espinal among them, were seated around a table, talking easily, laughing, and those same five guards, or rather their colored shadows, were moving away from the table in various directions, vanishing around corners and through doors. Like bright ghosts standing up from their bodies and going off on spectral errands. At the instant these phantasmal shapes would disappear, other identical shadows stood and went off in directions different from the ones they previously had chosen. Almost the same scene repeating itself over and over, as if the seated guards were generating a flow of afterimages . . . and not just afterimages, I told myself. Fore-images as well. Images of what might come to pass. This was not mere speculation, for as I watched, one shadow got to its feet, extracted his car keys from a trouser pocket, saluted his companions, and went through the gate by the pool leading to the parking area, and another passed out, slumped in his chair, mouth agape, chest rising and falling regularly. Yet the first shadow I had seen, Espinal's, had been the shadow of an action taken in the past. The cattle prod was proof of that. A third guard jumped up in apparent alarm and swung a beer bottle in a forceful arc through mid-air as if showing the others how he had subdued a dangerous criminal. It seemed I was witnessing a mingling of the past and possibility. Did this indicate that the past embodied the condition of possibility, that it, too, was mutable? Before I could explore this question, anger overwhelmed me once again. I approached the table, holding the prod behind my back. Espinal glanced up. Amusement deepened the lines at the corners of his eyes. He spoke to his colleagues, words I

failed to hear, and they laughed. As was my habit when exposed to such ridicule, I offered a pleasant smile, pretending to accept their laughter as expressive of a mood of good
fellowship; but my smile was not its usual strained self,
supported in this instance by a foundation of joyful and
vengeful intent. Espinal didn't bother to look at me as I
drew near; he only said, "Bring us another round of beers,
Aurelio."

"Perhaps you'd care for some chips and salsa?" I asked,
and jabbed him in the neck with the prod.

The shock elicited a grunt from Espinal and lifted him up
from his chair to fall across the table. His arms swept
empty bottles onto the floor. I jabbed him in the side and his
torso spasmed, his head jittered against the tabletop. His
mouth gaped, his eyes bulged, his limbs trembled. Pleased
by his aghast expression, by the quivering of his muscles, I
prepared to deliver a third charge, but then I sensed movement behind me and turned to see another guard swing a
beer bottle at my head, the same act I had witnessed him
performing moments before.

Armed with that foreknowledge, I anticipated the arc of
the blow and so was able to dodge it. I jabbed the cattle
prod into the guard's chest and he fell twitching onto the
floor. My anger was supplanted by the eerie calm that had
possessed me at the hospital. As the remaining guards came
to their feet, I snatched Espinal's sidearm from its holster
and told them to put their weapons on the table. Once this
had been done, I ordered them to dive into the pool. They
cursed and threatened, but obeyed. Seeing them so helpless,
with only their heads clear, staring balefully at me, water
dripping from their hair, I gave thought to shooting them.
How satisfying it would be to watch them flounder as I
picked them off one by one! Though this desire was fueled
by a residue of anger, it was not a fierce impulse—I was already beginning to regret my intemperate actions, wondering if it might be possible to rectify the situation. I would
have to hide out for a while, there was no doubt of that. Perhaps Marta's cousins in the Bay Islands would be of help.
Then something struck the back of my head, sending white

lights spearing into my eyes. Dazed, my skull throbbing, I realized I had fallen. Marta was standing over me, still in her nightdress, holding a beer bottle. She said something in a contemptuous tone, but the words were muted, unintelligible, as if she were speaking from behind thick glass. I heard other voices, equally muted. The guards. They gathered around me and as they began to beat me, it seemed they were multiplying infinitely, producing hundreds upon hundreds of shadow selves that separated from their bodies and hurried off to accomplish innumerable missions, moving more rapidly than humanly possible, as if God had speeded up the film of the world in order to show me everything that might then happen, the variety of my potential fates, none of which I understood.

The cell in which I waked was empty of furnishings. No cot, no toilet; only a drainage hole at the center of a slightly concave floor. The walls were not much farther apart than my outspread arms could reach and were painted canary yellow, a color that seemed to amplify a reek of stale urine. A rich golden light, the light of late afternoon, slanted through a slit window that was set too high to afford a view of anything other than a rectangle of cloudless sky. Every part of my body ached. Dried blood was crusted on my lips. Now and then a guard would pass by the barred door of the cell, trailed and preceded by his shadowlike variants. The effect, I observed, had diminished—the shadows were scarcely more than gauzy flutterings. Moving gingerly, I propped myself up against the wall and sat with my head hung down, weighted by a recognition that I was finished. The best I could hope for was torture followed by a term of prison. Knowing Espinal's coarse sensibilities, having listened to countless stories relating to the brutal autonomy he wielded within the wall of the prison, I doubted I could hope for even that. I thought of Marta with bitterness and longing, and of my two sons. I thought, too, of my hotel. I had perceived it as a prison that defined and delimited me, but now, held within an official confine, that blue-green cube with the ocean stretching out before it appeared to embody the very essence of freedom. Tears started from my eyes. I could blame no one except myself. If I had treated Marta with respect and love, she would never have betrayed me. Such thoughts accumulated in my head like a soggy mess, a wad of misery and self-abnegation, and I lapsed into a fugue, aware of intermittent voices, of men passing in the corridor, of the light dimming. I stood up once to urinate into the hole. For the remainder of the day, I sat without moving, empty and humiliated, more a relic than a man.

It was after dark when Espinal came along the corridor to my cell. He leaned against the gate, peering through the bars, his face neutral. Expressionless as a frog, you might have said. Yet even a frog's face is colored by a kind of gloating simplicity, and though Espinal bore some resemblance to that creature, neither gloating nor triumph nor emotion of any sort surfaced from his depths, as if only his bloated body were present and his soul had flown elsewhere, perhaps attached to one of the flimsy shadows that proceeded from him. He said nothing and the silence seemed to hollow out a vast space around us, to create a universe populated by a single torturer and his victim. He was dressed as for an evening out. Dark, neatly ironed slacks and a sports shirt bearing a batik pattern. A gold chain cinched his swarthy neck. The cattle prod was hitched to his belt.

My instinct was to plead with him, to reason. Where, I wanted to ask, would he find a more efficient conduit for his drugs? Now that I was in his thrall, I would prove a thoroughly malleable host. Any room he wished, any number of rooms, might be his at any hour of the day. But the silence pressed against my chest, my Adam's apple, choking me, and I could not speak. Oddly enough, I felt a measure of anticipation for what was to come, and when Espinal opened the gate, rather than cowering, I sat up alertly like a child expecting a treat.

Espinal did not bother to shut the gate behind him. He unhitched the cattle prod and showed it to me, letting the light play over the shiny black cylinder. A smile hitched up a corner of his mouth. "You truly are a stupid piece of crap, Aurelio," he said.

Though these words offered no promise of mercy, that he had acknowledged me in any way generated an ounce of hope. I marshaled my arguments, ordering them into a logical progression, but before I could state my desire to please him, Espinal stuck the cattle prod into the pit of my stomach and triggered off a charge. My memories of the next hours are fragmentary. I recall Espinal standing above my prone body, spitting into my face, cracking me with his fists, cursing me, his puffy cheeks mottled with rage. At several points he broke from his exertions, and on one such occasion, sitting with his back against the wall, smoking a cigarette, he informed me of his plans to marry Marta and thus gain ownership of the hotel.

"She's a terrific fuck," he said, "but the world is full of terrific fucks. I would never tie myself down to her if not for the hotel. You didn't understand how to make full use of either your hotel or your woman, Aurelio."

He paused, blew a smoke ring and watched it dissipate. "Women," he said musingly. "They have their subtleties, their eccentricities. But at heart they only want to be secure. Perhaps if you had been stronger, if you had been a fortress for Marta, and not a little house of straw . . . perhaps she would not have sought me out."

I must have made a noise of some kind, for he patted my shoulder and said, "Don't try to speak. You'll merely exhaust yourself, and we have so much farther to travel, you and I." He stubbed out his cigarette on the floor and voiced a sigh of—I thought—satisfaction. "I intended to have you disappeared, but your fit of temper makes things so much the easier. No one will initiate an inquiry if something happens to you now."

In the course of his abuse, Espinal frequently employed the cattle prod, and despite the excruciating pain, the spasms, the bile rising in my throat, and the trembling of my limbs, instead of growing weaker and more mentally disorganized, I grew stronger, centered in my outrage, as if some portion of my being were receiving a positive charge, becoming further enlivened by each and every jolt. The colored shadows that prior to Espinal's appearance in my cell had all but vanished now proceeded from him in a continuous flow, clearly visible, giving me a preview of the torments he might soon visit upon me, and so it was that when, after another cigarette break, he bent down to retie his shoelace, I had already watched his shadow self perform this act and was able therefore to avail myself of the opportunity, lashing out with my right leg and catching him flush on the chin. He fell onto his back, moaning, still conscious. Denying the pain that attended my least movement, I scrambled up, seized the cattle prod and jabbed it into his chest, jolting him again and again, hoping to explode his flabby heart. His eyes rolled back. Thick strings of drool eeled between his lips. His belly heaved and jiggled. Yet he refused to die.

So frustrated was I by Espinal's persistence, I wrangled out his sidearm, intending to shoot him, but footsteps in the corridor awakened my desire for self-preservation. A young guard with a wispy mustache was ambling toward the cell. As he drew near, I stepped forth and ordered him to unlock the other cells, an order with which he did not hesitate to comply. Seven bleary, dispirited prisoners tottered out into the corridor, staring at me with fear and bewilderment. I bound and gagged the guard and sat him down beside Espinal. Then, turning to the prisoners, I told them that salvation was at hand.

Atop the green mountain that rises behind the town of Trujillo, hidden most of the days by mist, enclosed within a cyclone fence, stood a powerhouse and an antenna belonging to Cablevision, the cable company that serviced the region, and a tin-roofed cabin of unpainted boards where lived the caretakers, Antonio Oubre and his wife Suyapa, family friends of many years' duration. It was there I headed after negotiating my escape, which was not so difficult a feat as one might imagine. Having been complicit with Espinal for over a decade, I knew he had protected himself by giving into his lawyer's custody evidence against his various associates that was to be made public in the event of his untimely death. Two of my fellow escapees dragged Espinal along, I held the gun to his head, and we were passed through the main gate of the prison without significant delay by men who could not afford to let us murder him. We crammed into Espinal's SUV and I drove west toward La Ceiba. Three miles outside of town I stopped the car, handed the keys to a cocaine dealer with bloody broken teeth, and, stuffing the gun in my belt, carrying Espinal's cattle prod, I began hiking through the jungle toward the mountaintop. I had no illusions as to Espinal's future now that I had abandoned him to the mercies of those he had brutalized. They would keep him alive for a time in order to guarantee their safety, but judging by the hateful relish with which they stared at him, I knew they would ultimately seek retribution. I hoped they would be deliberate, that they would, as he had done, fully explore the dreadful potentials of the human nervous system . . . though necessity dictated that they not be too thorough in their vengeance. They would not survive him for long. Sooner or later, the car would be spotted, and since escaped prisoners were rarely afforded an opportunity to surrender, the chances were good that they would not live to report on my whereabouts.

Although they were drug traffickers and deserved no sympathy, I experienced guilt over my manipulation of these men. Such a cynical disregard for life, even for misbegotten lives such as theirs, was not part of my character; but from the moment Espinal began to use his cattle prod on me, it seemed I had not been myself, that my usual tendencies were overthrown and my weaknesses bulwarked by a calm single-mindedness that had grown increasingly dominant with every jolt. As I labored up the trail, however, my composure frayed and I came to feel every twinge accumulating from Espinal's torture. Mist obscured the moon and stars. The darkness, the delicate night sounds, the imminence of jaguars and wild boars, these things played with my nerves. By the time I reached the summit, after four hours on the trail, the sky had paled and I was spent.

It had rained on the mountaintop. The air was thick with

a chill dampness. Puddles lay everywhere, and the ground was mucky, furrowed with tire tracks. Towering into the mist above the Cablevision compound, the antenna looked to have acquired a magical aspect, resembling a four-sided steel ladder ascending into an unstable dimension of swirling gray. Beneath it, the powerhouse—a green lozenge of concrete block—chugged and hummed. No smoke issued from the cabin chimney, Antonio's venerable Hyundai pickup was not in evidence, and I assumed that he and Suyapa had driven into town for the early market. As empty of hope and energy as I had been while in my cell, I sat down on a rock just outside the cyclone fence, at the summit's edge, and gazed out across a sea of mist. I made out peculiar shapes moving therein, attributing them to a perceptual impairment caused by my enervated condition; but as the sun climbed higher and the mist burned away, revealing the slope of the mountain, the town laid out along the crescent of the bay, and, closer to the horizon, the narrow point of land that formed the Cape of Honduras, those ephemeral shapes became more substantial, though as yet poorly defined, hundreds upon hundreds of them, drifting through the air, transparent in the way of jellyfish. I suspected they might be akin to the shadows I had seen emanating from the corporeal bodies of Espinal and the other guards, and thus might offer some clue as to what was happening to me; and I was then led to consider the fact that each time I received a jolt of electricity, the shadows had grown clearer. I wondered if another jolt would make them clearer yet.

The prospect of using Espinal's cattle prod on myself in order to test this hypothesis did not set easily, but neither did it seem a complete absurdity. From the inception of the idea I felt the same upwelling of anticipation that I had when Espinal entered my cell, as if something inside me desired it, and that feeling came to outweigh all my reservations. I pulled up my trouser leg, placed the tip of the prod against the flesh of my calf, and, after a moment's hesitation, triggered off a charge. When I recovered—and my period of recovery was much shorter than it theretofore had been—what I saw caused me to reevaluate not only my understanding of all that had happened to me, but as well my basic assumptions concerning the nature of the world.

We live, ladies and gentlemen, at the bottom of an ocean of the air. It is a tired metaphor, yet nonetheless true. We inhabit a depth, scuttling crablike along the bottom, our vision limited to the straight-ahead, unaware of the myriad swimmers above and around us, believing we are alone. Had I been sitting on the summit prior to my confrontation with Tito Obregon, I would have seen nothing more than blue sky and white clouds building on the horizon, the glittering sea, the town, the palms and fig trees and other vegetation figuring the mountain slope, whereas now I saw those myriad swimmers, countless thousands of them. Drifting, darting, sailing. They maintained their transparency, yet were of every hue—shadings of red, blue, yellow, green—and posed a veritable circus of forms, like a fever dream from the mind of a Bosch or a Brueghel. Predominant among them were slightly curved, roughly circular creatures fringed with cilia, a pale mottled brown in color, six to eight inches in diameter and thin as tortillas, which I took to calling melchiors because of their resemblance to the liver-spotted scalp of my maternal uncle, Melchior Varela; but many other species were visible. Some were serpentine, others like partially deflated balloons, others skatelike . . . There were far too many to catalogue. I have since recorded and studied several hundred species, and that is but a fraction, I believe, of those that exist. They occupied every level of the sky, but clustered so thickly above the town that all but a handful of roofs were obscured. Behind me, the antenna and the powerhouse were covered by a bobbing, eddying sheath of such creatures, like sponges moved by a current. I conjectured that they might be attracted to the electricity, but if this were so, why then did they congregate so heavily above the town, many sections of which had no power?

After half an hour or thereabouts, the creatures began to fade, growing increasingly transparent, and I was forced to use the cattle prod on myself once again so as to restore them to brightness. It may seem unreasonable that I would undergo such pain, but the way they moved, both separately and in schools, like the dance of sea creatures along a reef, and the thought that Trujillo was, indeed, a reef of sorts, a habitat where they could flourish, and the quirky complexity of their bodies, all equipped with inflatable sacs that, I assumed, enabled them to float upon the air, and with cilia and with other anatomical features whose purposes I could not fathom, curiously configured tubes and slits and spindly structures . . . I was fascinated by them, compelled to observance. I noticed that each time I used the prod, various of the creatures would flock toward me, this supporting my suspicion that they were attracted to electricity, and once, while I lay recovering from a shock, a swizzle stick (this the name I gave to a type of serpentine creature, because they reminded me of the plastic appurtenances with which cocktails are stirred) approximately ten inches in length—its body rippled, almost serrated in aspect, tinted a watery green—eeled close to me and, before I could recoil from its touch, nudged my forehead with a blind, mouthless snout. I felt a tingling—not in the least unpleasant—beneath the skin of my forehead, as if the snout had penetrated a centimeter or two, and this was followed by a stronger tingling that emanated from deeper within my skull, and an accompanying flash of irascibility. The swizzle stick zipped off into the upper air, losing itself among a school of pinkish half-deflated-balloon creatures (I called them bizcochos after the little cakes with pink icing that my mother made for my birthday). Thereafter I felt another tingling in my skull, softer and less agitated, conveying a soothing effect, as of something settling back after a moment of alarm. I recalled the impression I'd had while grasping Señor Volto's paddles that something was passing out of Tito's body and into mine. The idea that one of the swizzle sticks—or some similar creature—might be coiled in my brain, feasting on its trickling output of electricity, revolted me, and I jumped to my feet; but almost instantly a fresh infusion of calm flooded my mind and I was unable to sustain revulsion, as if the unknown thing I believed to be inside my head were responding to my stress and acting to placate me.

The sun was nearly at the meridian and I was still engaged in watching the surreal spectacle unfolding in the sky when Antonio's battered red pickup came jouncing up the potholed road from town and stopped inside the fence. Suyapa, a sturdy, honey-skinned woman perhaps twenty years his junior, climbed from the cab and went into the cabin, trailed by a procession of shadow selves; and Antonio, a stocky, elderly man with a dark, leathery face and straws of gray hair protruding from beneath a New York Yankees baseball cap, stepped off to the side of the cabin and urinated onto a patch of grass, an act mirrored by a succession of shadows who, having done their business, flowed away in different directions. On seeing me, he called out, "Aurelio?" He zipped up and came over to the fence and gave me a puzzled look. "Your hair . . . What happened?"

I touched my hair, found it as ever.

"It's like mine," Antonio said. "All gray."

He guided me into the cabin, two tiny rooms whose plank walls were decorated with dozens of pages torn from religious magazines—photographic images of the Pope, statues of the Madonna, depictions of Christ. In a scrap of clouded mirror affixed to the door, I saw that my hair had been leached of black and now had the hue of cigarette ash. My face was haggard, its lines deeply etched—I might have aged ten years in a single night. I sat down by a little table against the wall, reeling from this latest shock.

"You are in desperate trouble, my friend," Antonio said, joining me at the table. "Everyone in town is talking about the prison break."

He asked how I reached this pass and I related the events of the previous day. I told him that no matter what fate awaited me, at least I could derive some satisfaction from having avenged myself upon Espinal, and Antonio said, "Espinal is not dead."

This revelation left me speechless.

"The other prisoners were apprehended in Puerto Castillo

while stealing a boat," he went on, and Suyapa added, "They tried to use Espinal as a hostage, but the police shot them before they could do him injury."

She set a plate of chicken and rice before me, but I was too upset to eat. Saying that I needed to think, I went outside and sat on the ground, shielding my eyes so I would not be distracted by the cartoonlike creatures that populated the air. Until I discovered Marta's affair with Espinal, I had never hated anyone. I had feared and resented, but my mental soil had proved unsuitable for the cultivation of strong emotion. Even my love for Marta had been an indifferent thing. Knowing Espinal was alive, however, and not just alive, but free to be with Marta, whom I now loved with uncharacteristic intensity, that knowledge inflamed me. Hate became a star exploding in my interior sky and I was consumed by the desire to kill him. I have since come to recognize that the creature that possessed me, a creature whose identity I will not know until the moment it vacates my body, a moment that is, I believe, nearly at hand ... I recognize that it was responsible for this amplification of emotion. The relationship between us was not that of parasite and prey, but of symbiotes. I provided it with a nice warm skull and a steady diet of electrical energy; in return, it maximized me, made me more of who I essentially am. I understood none of this at the time. My thoughts were directly solely toward Espinal. I could not wait to kill him.

I remained sitting outside the cabin for many hours, less thinking of than focusing upon Espinal. I conceived no plan, but I knew I needed to get closer to my enemy, and I believed that my altered appearance, my gray hair and deeply lined face, would permit such an approach. At one point during the afternoon, Suyapa came out of the cabin and told me apologetically that I was welcome to stay in the compound for a day or two, but no longer. Though we had not been close since the death of my father, for whom they had worked as cook and caretaker, sooner or later someone was bound to recall the connection between us. As much as they considered themselves friends, she and Antonio had to look to their own survival.

I was a child during the days when Suyapa and her husband worked for my family, and though I had borne them a modicum of affection, I neither loved them nor appreciated them as I did that afternoon. It seemed I was now able to perceive their essentials, the core of devout simplicity that was both their strength and their weakness, the quality that invests the Honduran soul with its capacity to endure the outrages of Honduran fate. I informed her I would be leaving later that evening and said that if I could borrow some of Antonio's old clothes and catch a ride into town, I would be grateful.

"You will be killed," she said solemnly. "It would be safer if you let Antonio take you inland . . . or perhaps north into the Picos Bonitos."

My response was a despondent statement whose brighter meaning I had yet to comprehend. "I am dead already," I told her.

So it was, ladies and gentlemen, that I came to Trujillo at twilight on that same day, dressed as an old beggar in a patched suit coat and grimy trousers, a frayed straw hat with a wide brim shadowing my face, sweating profusely in the thick heat and carrying a sapling trunk that I had cut for a walking stick. I hobbled in from the outskirts of town, where Antonio had dropped me, and made my way along the airport road until I reached the turn-off that led toward the beach and the Hotel Christopher Columbus. I had not used the cattle prod on myself in several hours—the prod and Espinal's pistol were stuck into my waistband—yet my ability to see the creatures who flocked overhead, almost completely obscuring the indigo sky, was undiminished. I believed I must have passed some electric threshold, perhaps accumulating a sufficient charge so as to empower this facet of my vision. The shadow effect, however, had diminished. Though I could still make them out, streaming from the bodies of passersby, they were barely perceptible, and remembering that I had not seen the shadows directly after my confrontation with Tito in the flea market, I understood that my sharp perception of them was likely only a stage in the process of my transformation . . . and I did feel transformed. Clear as never before. So much of my life had been spent—as is much of every life—in attempting to elude the judgment of fate, and now I embraced that judgment without trepidation.

The aerials (my generic name for the creatures occupying the air) were, indeed, feeding on the citizens of Trujillo. For the most part this feeding appeared to do no harm. An aerial would drift or dart close to someone's head; a charge of pale electricity would spray upward into the body of the aerial from the top of the head, and thereafter that person would continue on with whatever he or she had been doing, displaying no ill effects whatsoever. But as I made my way along the access road toward the beach, passing a group of schoolboys in white short-sleeved shirts and dark blue trousers, I noticed among the melchiors, the swizzle sticks, the bizcochos, and the other varieties of aerial swarming overhead, a smattering of bloated forms with stubby tubes protruding from their underbellies, all a purplish black in hue, roughly corresponding in size and shape to that of a human heart (blackhearts, I called them). One of these creatures settled upon the head of a skinny schoolboy who was swinging his backpack about, swatting playfully with it at his fellows. Almost immediately after the blackheart had come to rest, the boy ceased his energetic activity and walked stiffly, slowly, for several paces, his face devoid of expression, and even when the blackheart floated away, he did not regain his good spirits at once, but moved dazedly, falling far behind his classmates. I had not planned how I would kill Espinal, but the realization that certain of the aerials had a deleterious effect upon the body inspired me to think that exposing him to the ravages of the blackhearts, luring them to him in some way and watching them drain him of energy, that would be a most fitting end for the man.

It grew dark as I hobbled along the beach, presenting the image of a doddering old man who had gotten lost and strayed toward the tourist end of town. The young men standing outside the beachside bars taunted me and laughed. I had behaved with a similar lack of respect when I was young, hurled similar taunts, and now, consumed by an unfocused hatred that was in no small part self-loathing, I extended my left hand to them and begged for a lempira, for whatever they could spare, keeping my right near the grip of Espinal's gun, speculating that it might not be so important to kill Espinal, tempted to believe that exterminating any of these cruel shapes would serve my purpose. Set adjacent to my hotel was Gringos, an establishment of bamboo and thatch above a concrete deck and open to the air—a tourist bar that, since there were no tourist, catered chiefly to expatriates and young Honduran women. As I passed I glanced inside, and there, sitting at a table beneath a bobbling cluster of melchiors and bizcochos and panuelos (flimsy yellowish raglike creatures that had the look of unwashed handkerchiefs), Sadra Rosales was nursing a margarita, talking to her best friend, Flavia, a slightly overweight and overly made-up woman with dyed red hair. Sadra's manner struck me as being inappropriately blithe for someone who had lost her lover, and curious about her, I entered the place. The bartender tried to shoo me out, assuming me to be penniless, but I showed him my money, ordered a whiskey, and chose a table adjoining Sadra's, sitting with my back to her, no more than a foot away.

". . . so confusing," Sadra was saying. "I never thought Aurelio had it in him . . . that kind of passion. Especially where Marta was concerned."

"That sow!" Flavia said. "She goes around acting like a princess, yet everyone knows she's a complete slut."

"God, yes! She must have fucked the entire staff at the prison."

"Why don't you do something to her?"

"What do you suggest?"

"I don't know. You'll think of something. Maybe you can write something about her for the paper."

"Oh, I don't care that much about her. I just miss Aurelio."

"Liar!" Flavia said. "You were only using him to get Tito back."

"That's not true! I liked Aurelio." A giggle. "Well, maybe I was using him a little."

Both women laughed, and then Sadra said, "I simply don't understand what happened with Tito."

"What's there to understand? He's a man. He's probably gone off with another woman."

"But to leave the shop like that . . . to just up and vanish. It's not like him. He's always been so responsible about his business." A pause. "Then, he has been acting strangely for most of this year. He's been so distant! That's why I pretended to break up with him. I . . ."

Flavia made an amused noise. "So you were pretending, were you?"

"You know. I thought he was losing interest, and I decided he might get interested again if he thought he was losing me."

"Maybe Aurelio threatened him, and that's why he left in such a hurry. You said they had some sort of run-in."

"Yes, but he didn't seem concerned. It was like his mind had gone off somewhere else. Like he was . . . he wasn't himself."

"Didn't he say where he was going in the letter?"

"The mountains. That's all he said. He said he had to go to the mountains, and then he rambled on about finding God for a couple of pages."

"God!" Flavia snorted in disdain. "It's another woman, for sure. Men only tell that kind of lie when it's about sex."

Sadra gave a dramatic sigh. "It's so depressing, losing two men almost at once."

"Don't worry! There are plenty of men left in Trujillo . . . though not many as rich as Aurelio."

"And none with as big a prick as Tito. My God, it was enormous!"

They laughed again, and the conversation turned to a party that was to be held later that night in Barrio Cristales.

I drank my whiskey in a single gulp and went out onto

the beach and flung myself down on the sand close to the tidal margin and contemplated how thoroughly betrayal had been woven through the fabric of my life. Of course I understood that I deserved no less—I had been living my fate all the while—and this understanding, at such odds with my usual tendency toward self-pity, caused me to become aware that although I regretted a great deal, I was not overwhelmed with regret. I thought of what Sadra had said, that Tito had grown distant—that word was as good as any to describe how I felt about Sadra and much else. I could sustain no bitterness toward her. Whatever role she had played with me was no less false than the one she was playing now, and whatever she had actually felt for me, however true, was nothing more than a by-product of the insanity between men and women. The only portion of the past that roused my emotions was the affair between Espinal and Marta, and even that passion seemed to have acquired a formal gloss. Not that my desire to kill Espinal had abated, but it seemed now more a consequence of human office, as if hatred were a contractual concession made between the soul and the mind to allow their coexistence. I wondered if Tito's prematurely gray hair could be taken as a proof that he had been possessed by the thing I believed to be living inside me. If so, what did its absence mean to him? Why had this provoked his sudden exit?

Little waves delicately edged with foam rolled in to film across the sand. Lightning strobed in the darkness beyond the cape, and a wind tousled the palm tops, a storm blowing in from the Caribbean. I smelled ozone on the air and noticed that the aerials were massing together and moving toward the hills in a stately migration of cartoonish forms, perhaps giving evidence that a big electrical storm was dangerous for them. Strung out along the shore, the lights of the bars and shanties looked to be spelling out a curving sentence of bright blurs and dots. I felt stranded in the place and moment, utterly alone. Red lightning cracked the sky, followed by a peal of thunder that had the sound of an immense fake, as if a giant had struck a vast sheet of flexible metal.

A disco beat became audible over the gusting wind, and I glanced toward the hotel. Several dozen people, silhouetted against hot lights, crowded together under the roofed portion of the deck. Espinal's welcome home party, I imagined. A stairway of nine steps led up from the beach to the deck—I gave it a wide berth, keeping close to the water, and headed for a spot some fifty feet farther along, a narrow inlet shadowed by a group of corosal palms, beneath which a fallen palm trunk still attached to its stump provided a makeshift bench. There I sat while the party raged and the storm gathered. A rain squall, outlying the storm, came to dimple the water of the inlet, and the thunder grew more frequent. The majority of the aerials had passed off inland, but hundreds yet remained, hovering above the beach, most of them blackhearts. The fronds of the surrounding palms lashed and slithered together. Burning stick men jabbed and dazzled on the horizon, seeming to reflect the lightning of my thoughts, strokes of hatred illuminating a dark matter.

I had entertained a vague notion of waiting until the party ended, then sneaking into my apartment and catching Espinal with Marta, but as things turned out I needed no plan. Soon a torrential rain, driven slantwise by the wind, sent the partygoers scurrying from the deck and into the hotel. The sea tossed and billowed, heavy waves piling in upon the sand. The roiling clouds were illuminated by lightning strokes, and the thunder grumbled constantly, with now and again a powerful detonation that gave me a start. None of this appeared to disturb the remaining aerials—buffeted by the wind, sent bobbling this way and that, they nonetheless maintained their relative positions along the shore—and neither did the weather appear to disturb the drunken, thick-bodied man who was making a wobbly descent of the stairs, reeling sideways as he set foot in the mucky sand. In a lightning flash I saw him. Espinal. The gold chain winking at his neck. He ploughed forward against the wind and took a stand at the water's edge, his head thrown back, as if daring the storm to do its worst. That, I suspected, was precisely his state of mind. That was the character of his arrogance. Having survived my attack, a kidnapping, and being taken hostage, he believed, or half-believed, he was indomitable, himself a force of nature. Wind, waves, lightning. What were they when compared to the mighty Espinal? After a moment, he unzipped his trousers and urinated into the wind. A few splatters of piss on his trousers—what did this matter? Nothing could blight his potent aspect. I doubted he would have felt so invincible had he been able to see the blackhearts massing above him, gathered into an eddying cloud that seemed in miniature a representation of the storm clouds overhead. I expected them to drop down upon him, that my idea concerning their role in his demise would prove to have been a presentiment; but instead they drifted apart. Lightning struck close by, a stroke that speared the sand several hundred feet farther along the beach, the blue-white flash blinding me for an instant. The blast did not bother Espinal. Once more he adopted a defiant stance and gazed out across the toiling waters of the bay.

I cannot say exactly when it was I began to sense a new electric presence in the air, but I believe it was a subtle stimulus deriving from this presence that encouraged me to act; and I am certain that I experienced a surge of that curiously disassociative anticipation such as I had first felt in my prison cell. Espinal, still daring the sky to kill him, did not notice me emerge from the palm shadow. The storm was reaching a crescendo. A barrage of lightning struck offshore, deafening bluish-white explosions that shed a hellish illumination, and for the duration of those flashes the sea looked to be aboil, waves leaping, plying in every direction; the hotel and the bars and the shanties that ranged the shore appeared to flicker in and out of existence. Thunder came full-throated with the roaring light, and the wind, unheard in all that concatenation, peeled up the tin roofs from shanties and bent young palms horizontal. I could have fired off a cannon and no one would have known, but I wanted Espinal to understand that I was responsible for his sorry end. I moved to within six feet of him before he caught sight of me. He was very drunk and did not recognize me, even after the wind blew off my hat; but he saw the gun, and his slack features tightened with alarm. Only when I pulled out the cattle prod did recognition dawn. He shouted at me, the words taken by the wind. Then, as I thought how best to prolong his torment, formulating insults I might express as he lay dying, Espinal threw himself at me and knocked the gun from my hand.

The rumbling that filled the world seemed a result of our rolling about on the wet sand, as if the beach were a drum skin against which we beat an ungainly rhythm. Heavier than I and stronger, Espinal succeeded in turning me onto my back. His breath was sour as a beast's. My arms were wrapped around his neck, but he managed to hump up and down, his sloppy weight driving the air from my lungs. He started to come astride my chest, trying to pin me with his knees; but in his drunkenness he overbalanced, and as he righted himself, I jabbed him with the cattle prod. He toppled onto his side. I triggered off a second charge into his stomach, a third into his chest, and came to my knees above him. A fourth and fifth jolt, both delivered to his neck, rendered him unconscious. I intended to finish him then and there, but as I cast about for the gun I saw that several blackhearts had descended from the upper air and were drifting near. Unnerved, I scrambled to my feet and retreated toward the water.

Rain was still pelting down, but the worst of the storm was passing inland, the lightning and thunder concentrated above the mountain behind the town, and though the wind still howled, the world seemed silent by contrast to the chaos that had ruled minutes before. In the dim, flickering light, the blackhearts, their ugly opaque forms trembling as if in a state of excitation, had a freakish, evil look, and as they drifted closer to Espinal, despite my hatred, I felt a twinge of sympathy for the man. I knew his fate was at hand, and knew this not by process of reason but by virtue of the thing inside me, by the way the knowledge welled up in my brain, spreading like dye through water, slow and pervasive, qualities that characterized all messages from my symbiote. I retreated farther from Espinal and watched as one of the blackhearts came to hover inches above his face. I thought it would settle atop his head as had the one I had earlier seen, but it did not—it settled instead upon his up-turned face and merged with him, disappearing into his head, somehow occupying the same volume of space. I was horrified to see this, suspecting that the creature inside me might not be benevolent, as I had begun to believe, but was draining me of life, for Espinal's reaction to possession was considerably different from my own. Rather than gradually returning to consciousness, he sat straight up from his supine pose, clutching the sides of his head, his expression reflecting pain and terror. He spotted me, staggered erect, his eyes wide and staring. He took a step toward me, then appeared to notice the other two blackhearts hovering at waist level to his right. Backing away from them, he stumbled and fell heavily. He regained his feet and lurched toward me, his hair hanging into his eyes, rain streaming down his face. I held out the cattle prod, halting his advance. He clutched his head again and dropped to his knees.

"What . . ." He shook his head wildly, as if trying to dislodge some awful restraint. "What is it?"

I had achieved a kind of remote distaste for Espinal. I had nothing to say to him. The rain slanted in from the sea, trickling cold down my neck; the wind prowled the shore, ripping the fronds, scattering palm litter across the sand, sounding a long despondent vowel.

Espinal struggled unsuccessfully to come to his feet. Judging by his clumsiness, his flailing efforts, I thought that the blackheart must be impairing his motor control.

"Aurelio!" he shouted. "Help me!"

His pleading was offensive, an indignity, and hardened me against him.

"Aurelio!" He screamed my name, called to God and continued struggling to rise, growing sluggish in his movements. Then his eyes rolled up to the heavens and he froze. The hundreds of blackhearts that had not joined the migration of aerials inland were stacked above him, arranged into an arrow-straight column rising toward the clouds, an unnatural order that seemed redolent of conscious purpose, as if they were marking Espinal's location. He renewed his struggles, calling to me again, promising rewards, offering apology. I paid him no heed, for I was listening to an inner voice that stained all my thoughts, and obeying its wordless instruction, I turned my eyes toward the mountain.

I have said that I had apprehended some new electric presence in the air—now that apprehension, previously subtle and peripheral, grew intense and specific, causing my symbiote to produce in me feelings of devotion and awe. Against logic, the central chaos of the storm was moving back toward the shore, contrary to the direction of the wind, an immense cloud lit from within by branches of lightning resembling traceries of nerves firing in darkly translucent flesh. It approached with the grand, ponderous slowness of a floating kingdom, and I observed that it differed in some details from ordinary clouds. Although its underbelly was contoured with bumps and declivities like that of a cloud, those contours neither roiled nor shifted, but—though somewhat fluid, pulsing a little—sustained a basic terrain; and rather than appearing to boil across the sky, it looked to be of one piece, a semisolid form towarding at a slight downward angle, presenting a view of its mountainous, tumbled height. I was too awestruck to know fear, too adulatory in my awe, but I knew the open area of the beach was not safe, and I hurried away from Espinal and the motionless column of blackhearts. I stopped beneath the cluster of corosal palms beside the inlet and looked back. At that distance, some forty feet, I could not read Espinal's face, nor could I tell much from his body language—whether in the grip of emotion or compelled to quiet by the blackheart nesting in his skull, he had ceased his struggles. I did not doubt, however, that he was afraid, that fear was a blazing shape that fit exactly into his skin, filling every crevice, all his mind focused on the cloud. It was bigger than I had thought. Big as a country. Even when its edges loomed overhead, its body kept on sliding past the crest of the mountain. Flocking beneath its belly were thousands upon thousands of aerials, acolytes to their god . . . and such was my feeling, ladies and gentlemen, for as I came to understand, to accept, that it was no cloud but an aerial itself, one impossibly huge, a vast presence hidden mostly from our sight, capable of lightnings, a creature in whose image other creatures had been made, I realized it conformed—albeit monstrously so—to my conception of God. Gazing up into its smoky flesh, past the madly agitated swarms of aerials that celebrated its passage, past the traceries of lightning, I saw a darker structure in its depths shaped like a great Aleph, the seat of its divinity, and persuading me of its godhood more than anything I saw was the aura of power and invincibility it projected. The air bristled with ozone and was heavied by a pressure that stoppered my ears, muffling every sound. Here was a beast for whom there could be no predator. What better definition of God is there than that?

As the stormdweller (so I have named it) stabilized above the beach, its body—by my estimate—no more than a hundred feet from the sand and extending to the visible horizon in all directions, I remembered Espinal. The column of blackhearts no longer stood above him—I supposed they had joined the swarms of their fellows above—but his posture was unchanged. Sitting back on his haunches. A man awaiting judgment. It occurred to me how like a ritual sacrifice this unearthly scene had played. The signal column of blackhearts, the processional of the cloud with its attendants, and the victim waiting alone, a victim prepared for the ritual by my actions. Perhaps I, too, had been prepared for my role, and what I understood of things was only an inkling of the complex intertwining between our lives and those of the aerials. I knew to a certainty this was true, knew it with the same intuitive certainty attaching to my conviction that Espinal was about to die.

The wind had subsided, as if quailed by the presence of the stormdweller, and the thunder was reduced to a grumbling that did not seem so much actual thunder as the record of some gross and gigantic internal process. The lightnings within the creature pulsed rapidly, decorating it with patterns that effloresced and faded too quickly for memory to fix upon, but conveyed by their mosaic structures the idea of symbol, of language. I wondered if Espinal had passed beyond fear and gained some appreciation of this momentous display. He was staring up into the lightning as if entranced. It might be, I thought, that finding himself at the mercy of a monster so much more potent than he, his own monstrous soul was satisfied and he perceived the rightness of his fate, and, peaceful, accepting, he was now reviewing his life. Whatever the case, I know he must have seen death coming, for I, who had a less perfect view, saw it come myself. Deep within the stormdweller a speck of infernal brightness bloomed. It took so long to reach the sand—at least ten seconds, I would guess—I had ample time to speculate on its nature, thinking it must not be lightning, for if it were it must have been generated at a point countless miles above, and, consequently, my estimation of the stormdweller's size was far too low. Of course it was lightning. God's traditional weapon. An enormous stalk of white-gold that sizzled from the belly of the stormdweller, searing the air and stabbing the beach, enveloping Espinal in electric fire. He vanished from sight, reappearing briefly as the incandescence flickered and danced about him, a solarized shadow. Then he was gone. Incinerated, vaporized, and perhaps absorbed into the massive engine of his destruction. Not a scrap left, though afterimages of his dying have prevailed in my mind ever since. I felt nothing for him. Our business was finished.

I hoped that as the stormdweller departed I would be able to gauge its size more accurately, but instead of sliding off to the south or out to sea, it lifted straight up, elevating into the sky until I could no longer distinguish it from the imaginary forms of night. With its departure, the storm dissipated, as if it had been the unifying force that commanded the elements to fury. Once it had disappeared, I was at a loss. Now that Espinal was no longer a factor, it was conceivable I might be able to reclaim my life. Bribes could be paid, relationships patched. But looking at the hotel, that blue-green prison where my soul had been stunted, and at the town, a seat of perfidy and hypocrisy, it seemed that all connection with my old life had been severed. Rather than devising a plan to regain my offices as businessman, father, and husband, I found myself thinking of bizcochos, blackhearts, melchiors and swizzle sticks, of the unknowable creature coiled within my skull, of the mystery these creatures posed, the exotic universal potentials their existence suggested, potentials most clearly expressed by the storm-dweller. Had it been a singular entity or was every tropical depression merely symptomatic of such a creature's passage near to the earth? And what larger mysteries did those passages portend? I wanted to know them, to understand the purposes of that unseen world and how they affected our own, and I wanted this with a passion such as I had never before experienced. I believed that Tito Obregon may well have felt this selfsame passion and had gone ahead of me in his search for absolute truth.

I had salted away funds against the day when I might decide to dissolve my marriage, thus I would have no difficulty in surviving, and though Marta had been less than an ideal wife, she was a good mother and would have enough from the sale of the hotel to get by. My sons, distant from me already, would not grieve deeply and would grow more distant. There was no compelling reason for me to stay. I took a last look at the deck, where the partygoers had begun to reassemble, some to dance, unmindful of the strangeness of the night, and tried to pick out Marta from among the dancers. I was certain she would be dancing, though perhaps she was growing a little impatient as regarded the whereabouts of her lover. The wind kicked up again as I went along the beach, heading for the Cablevision compound, where I planned to ask Antonio to drive me inland, away from those who might seek to confine me. It was not a harsh storm wind, but one that swept up from the south, bringing with it the cool freshness of the high places, and buoyed by it, reckoning it for a harbinger of my future, with every step I took, I felt easier in my skin and more confident of my course.

There you have it, ladies and gentlemen. My story . . . though not the whole of it. During the next few years, I traveled across the country, stopping in villages, everywhere inquiring about Tito Obregon, for I came to believe that his pilgrimage was my own, that his path was the one I was bound to follow; but I had no word of him, and I have since concluded that while our fates may be similar, our paths are divergent. I discovered that my symbiote occasionally required stronger doses of electricity than my brain could provide, and these I supplied by stripping lamp cords and applying the bare wires to my skin, until one night in Puerto Cortez I fell in with carnival folk and upon learning that they had no Señor Volto in their company, I suggested myself for the position, thereby becoming the electric personage you see before you tonight. Easy access to electricity was the motive underlying this career choice, but there was another purpose of which I was then unaware.

Over the years, I have learned a great deal about myself and about the creature who shares my body. I have learned, for example, to distinguish between my own thoughts and feelings and those it generates in me, and yet there is no longer much distinction between us. While our goals may differ in the specific, they were forged in the same lightnings. For my part, I am seeking God. Not the storm-dweller. I have witnessed it or its like many times since that night on the beach and I know now it is merely God's messenger on earth, whereas God Itself is a creature enclosing all of space and time, Its vastness too great to be contemplated. But despite Its vastness, It is no less a creature. I sense Its imminence and am led to believe It may be approached from a point high in the mountains, these same mountains in which your village lies. I further believe that I have been prepared by my symbiote for such an approach. God delights in such rituals—that is another thing I have learned. From what I have observed of the aerials and their interactions with our kind, I understand that much of human history is but a ritual orchestrated by the aerials in the service of their deity. Perhaps I am, like Espinal, a sacrifice, a tasty treat steeped for long years in the electric juices of the symbiote. Perhaps I will serve a more significant function. Whichever of these destinies eventuates, I am complete in my acceptance of it.

My symbiote, you see, is an evangel. It manifests to us, prepares us, and once its task is finished, moves on to another host. Tonight, having prepared me for the final stage of my journey, having formerly prepared Tito Obregon, it will slip from my body and traveling along the path of voltage, enter one of yours. That person will see, as I see now, the aerials massed above your village—a glorious profusion of bizcochos and swizzle sticks and more—and will begin a journey that mirrors mine, leading ultimately to a union with God . . . but I perceive that you doubt me, ladies and gentlemen. Some of you think I am mad. Others among you whisper that my story is a clever variation on the customary taunts offered by other Señor Voltos and is designed to provide an extra measure of fear that will make the act of grasping my paddles seem all the more courageous and thereafter will induce a delicious shudder in the young ladies who gaze into your eyes, searching for something out of the ordinary in their prospective lovers. Very well. I will not attempt to persuade you further of my truth, but rather invite you to experience it. Conquer your fears! Embrace your fate! The price is cheap. A mere five lempira. Come one, come all! Test yourself if you dare.

Shen's Daughter

~~~~~~

Mary Soon Lee

Mary Soon Lee [www-2.cs.cmu.edu/~mslee/hp.html] grew up in London, got an M.A. in mathematics, and later an M.S. in astronautics and space engineering. "I have since lived in cleaner, safer, quieter cities," she says, "but London is the one that I miss." She moved to Cambridge, Massachusetts in 1990, and then to Pittsburgh, Pennsylvania, where she divides her time between writing short stories and acting as a computer consultant to an artificial intelligence company. She has published more than thirty stories. She also runs a local writing workshop, the Pittsburgh Worldwrights. She has two collections in print: a science fiction collection, Ebb Tides and Other Tales, and a fantasy collection, Winter Shadows and Other Tales.

"Shen's Daughter" was published in Sword & Sorceress XX, the original fantasy fiction anthology, twentieth in the annual series originated by editor Marion Zimmer Bradley. In an oriental setting, a plain young girl sacrifices her future to pay for her mother's needs in old age and to help gain peace between warring kingdoms. She changes bodies with a princess and marries a beast. He's a real beast, not a shape-shifter, so how could she possibly live happily ever after? It's also an interesting comparison to the use and transformation of fairy tale motifs in the Pat Murphy story that appears earlier in this book.

This story came down the river with the rice boats, eighteen years ago. It began with the shape of a stranger sitting in the lotus position in the front of Eldest Uncle's boat.

Because of the way the stranger sat and because he wore a black robe despite the noonday heat, I took him for a monk. But he was the oddest looking monk I'd ever seen. His limbs were scrawny as a starving dog's, and he had thick white eyebrows that ran together. Strangest of all, he had two daggers strapped to his waist, one in a curved scabbard, one in a straight scabbard, both with plain iron hilts. The monks of the Long Way school study self defense, but they shun weapons and fight only with their bare hands.

I was so caught up by this mystery that I let slip the reed basket I was weaving.

"Eyes down, Wai Suan!" hissed my mother.

Ashamed, I looked down at my lap. My sister always behaved properly and dressed immaculately. I spoke when I was meant to be silent. No matter how tightly I coiled it, my hair wriggled free. My sarong and my shoes seemed to be magnets that called to any stray mud.

My sister had made a very favorable marriage at the last spring equinox. I was two years older than she, and so should have married first, but no family had ever inquired about my dowry. Even if I had been twice as decorous, twice as neat as my sister, it wouldn't have helped. My right heel turned inward so that I limped. Not even the poorest family wants a daughter-in-law like that.

I heard the men laughing as they approached the jetty, just a dozen yards away from where my mother and I sat beneath a willow. The water splashed noisily against the wood as the boats drew up.

"Who is the man in black?" I asked quietly.

"That doesn't concern you," said my mother.

"Will he be at the feast tonight?"

"Shush," said my mother, and then, softening, "I expect so."

Intriguing noises came from the jetty: men running back and forth, packages being loaded and unloaded. I worked at my reed basket, but bit by bit my head crept upward until I could see part of the jetty. The stranger was coming toward us! "Mother!"

"Shush!" said my mother, but I saw her look sideways to see who was approaching.

The man gave a deep bow to my mother. "Do I have the honor of addressing the widow of Mr. Shen?"

"I am his widow," said my mother.

"I knew your husband many years ago, may his soul eat the ghosts of his enemies."

What a strange thing to say! I wondered how he had known my father, who died when I was nine years old. I remembered playing Go with my father every night, how he would ruffle my hair before we started, how he treated our games as seriously as those he played against Eldest Uncle. I remembered the deep bass sound as he chanted the morning invocations, and how he loved the sweet dumplings my mother made. But I didn't know what my father had done outside our home. Once I had questioned my mother about him, but she grew so sad I never asked again.

"And you must be Shen's daughter." The man in black dipped his head to me. "There is a matter I need to discuss with you both."

The boatmen had paused in their work to stare at the three of us under the willow. The stranger moved his left hand in a curious gesture and the boatmen returned to their work. Had that gesture been a prearranged signal, or something more? Maybe the man wasn't a monk: maybe he was a sorcerer, or a demon, or—

"I am one of the emperor's advisors," said the stranger. He sat down on the ground facing us. "The war in the Eastlands is proving very costly for both sides. Last month the enemy sent a delegation proposing a new treaty, and the emperor, may his descendants be many and wise, agreed.

The treaty will be sealed by the marriage of the emperor's second daughter to an enemy prince."

"Poor girl," I said before I thought. My mother glared at me. One does not interrupt an advisor to the emperor, even if the advisor has just told you that an imperial princess is to marry a monster. Because although the advisor discreetly called them the enemy, even rice growers on the far side of the empire knew that vile beasts with horns and claws and scabrous skin inhabited the Eastlands.

"The second princess is spoiled." A hint of disapproval entered the advisor's voice. "The princess said she would sooner live in a pigpen than agree to the marriage. And the emperor, whose wisdom is without question, though at times his reasoning is obscure to one such as myself, promised his daughter she need not proceed with the marriage."

My mother covered her mouth with one hand. If the emperor had already agreed to the treaty and the marriage, how could he go back on his word without dishonor?

"There is a way to redeem the situation, though regrettably it requires both deception and sacrifice," said the advisor. He held my gaze as he spoke. "I have some skill in the Art Magic. I could exchange the princess' soul with someone else's, transferring their essences into each other's bodies. The two would then live out their lives in each other's place. The emperor has consented to this proposal, and has left me to find a suitable subject. Wai Suan, daughter of Shen, will you exchange your soul with the princess'?"

For an endless moment the world held stationary, the sun stopped in the sky, the breath stopped in my chest. I waited, waited for the moment to pass, for time to come back. And then the pulse throbbed in the old man's temple. A breeze sang through the willow leaves. And I, Wai Suan, the cripple-girl who had never been more than four leagues from my village, I found myself with something altogether unexpected: a choice. Not a small everyday choice, not a matter of which sarong to wear, or which dipping sauce to taste. But a choice that would alter the balance of my life.

If I said yes, I would no longer be Wai Suan of the village, but an imperial princess. My clothes would be made of silk and satin. I would live in a great castle. And my right foot would be whole—I could walk without a limp, could jump, leap, run.

If I said yes, I would have to marry a monster vile and ugly. His rancid breath would mark my days, his claws would mark my nights.

And I might never see my mother again. When she grew too old to support herself, she would have to live at her son-in-law's, dependent on his generosity, always taking second place to his own mother. "Will the emperor punish my family if I refuse?" I asked.

"No," said the advisor.

Perhaps I should have agreed out of loyalty to the emperor, but though our village was close enough to the imperial capital for me to fear the emperor, it was not close enough for me to love him. So I held my head up high, and said no.

My mother said nothing, but her hand stole across the gap between us and squeezed my fingers gently.

"A pity," said the advisor. "I needed someone trustworthy, someone who would keep this matter secret."

"Neither Wai Suan nor I will tell anyone else," said my mother.

"I know," said the advisor. He turned to me again. "Is there anything I can offer that would change your mind?"

I almost said no immediately, but the steady way the advisor looked at me reminded me of my father. *Don't rush*, my father had told me when we played Go. *A move that initially appears unpromising may hold merit when given careful consideration.* So I sat in silence for a while, thinking, before I said, "Gold. Enough gold to make my mother wealthy, arranged to seem like an inheritance from a distant relative. And your promise that my mother and I can write to each other as often as we wish."

"The gold is simple. The letter-writing poses a challenge. Why would a princess write to Shen's widow?" He paused, then nodded. "Difficult, but not insoluble. So let it be."

He held out both hands, palm up, and I laid my hands down on his to show my agreement.

"Be ready tomorrow morning an hour after dawn." The advisor stood up, bowed to each of us in turn, then walked away toward the village.

My mother folded me in her arms. Neither of us spoke. Even in the shade of the willow it was hot, hotter still when we clasped each other, and the boatmen on the jetty were watching us again, but we clung to each other for a long time.

I had thought the advisor meant to take me away on a boat the next morning, but instead he cast the spell within my mother's house. The distance between the palace and the village, he said, was much less than the distance between the princess' soul and mine. I limped across a white chalk mark on the bedroom floor, through a sheet of cold and dark, and out into the princess' bedroom.

Let us pass quickly over my stay in the imperial palace. Though the princess' aide, who knew about the spell, coached me in how to behave, still I found it difficult to play my part. True, the princess was so spoiled that I didn't have to feign demure politeness. But I had to learn names and faces and the layout of the palace, how to scold the servants, how to titter instead of laughing properly, how to pick at my food like a sparrow though it tasted so delicious I could have emptied the table. Hardest of all, I had to treat the emperor himself as if he were my father, as if I loved him.

The monsters insisted that the wedding take place at the height of the monsoon season. Rain filled the streets of the capital, drenched the crowds who gathered outside the Imperial Temple. I marched up the broad stone steps of the temple behind the emperor. A canopy stretched above us, but rain dripped through, spattering my silk wedding jacket.

Inside, the reek of the monsters overpowered the incense. The beasts smelled like putrefying meat. They squatted on the left side of the temple, dark lumbering shapes somewhere between oxen and giant dogs, but uglier than either, and with clawed hands in addition to four hoofed feet. As I walked toward the altar, the monsters clicked their claws together as if preparing to gut their prey.

I knelt on the mat before the altar, pressing my hands together to stop them shaking. The beast I was to marry squatted beside me, but I did not, could not look at him. Instead I stared at the red tassels bordering the mat while the priest chanted above us. *My marriage will end a war*, I told myself, but the cold heaviness in my stomach remained. *My marriage will bring my mother wealth*, I told myself, and for a moment I felt better.

The silvery chime of cymbals sounded the end of the first part of the wedding rites. The priest lowered the gold marriage bowl onto a stand between myself and the beast. Calling me by the princess' name, he bid me place my hands on the bowl to mark my consent. I laid my hands on the gold bowl.

The priest called on the beast beside me to place his hands over mine. The beast knocked the bowl from its stand with a clawed swipe. Frozen, I clutched the empty space where the bowl had been. Metal clanged on tile. Roaring, the beast swung round toward the king of the monsters. Over the screams of the imperial guests, the beast shouted, "No! I will not marry this puny, puling, witless creature!"

Many times I had overheard people in the village refer to me as the cripple-girl or Lame Foot, but no one called me those names to my face. At the beast's words, the heaviness in my stomach lifted and a hot madness seized me. I stood up in front of the crowds, in front of the emperor and the monster king and the raging beast, and I said, "Witless? You are the one who is witless! If you didn't want to marry me, you should have said so months ago! Now your stupidity is likely to start the war all over again."

The monster king reared upright. "You dare call my son witless, you scentless offspring of a degenerate line of a degenerate race—"

The emperor's guards drew their swords. The imperial guests screamed as the monsters surged forward.

"Wait," said a calm voice, and the word, though softly spoken, carried throughout the temple. People and monsters alike stood still as an old man in a black robe walked over to the altar. I hadn't known the emperor's advisor was back in the city.

"This matter of wits or the lack thereof can be settled simply," said the old man. "True, our two peoples share a common history of war, and we could shed more blood here today to celebrate that. But we share other customs too, ones better suited to determining mental superiority. I propose a game of Go, called Wei-ch'i by the traditionalists, between these two young people."

He clapped his hands and a Go board and pieces appeared before me on the mat. He looked at my bridegroom. "You do, I take it, know the rules of Go."

"Of course," snarled the beast. He snatched a black stone, thereby claiming the advantage of the first move, and placed it near the center of the board.

I picked up a white stone and laid it on the board, and it was as if I were a child again, sitting on the floor playing Go with my father, nothing else in the world but the two of us and the game. Yes, I heard the monsters' rumbles, the whispers of the imperial guests, but they had no place in the patterns of black and white stones, in the battle of boundaries and the waiting expanses.

Once, midway through the game, a dry cough sounded above me. I glanced up to see the old advisor's thick white eyebrows drawn into a frown. I looked down at the board again, and saw that I was winning, so why did the old man frown? Ah, yes, belatedly I recalled the broader implications of this match: best to win, but not to win too easily.

So I beat the beast by three points. When the pieces were all cleared away, I looked up from the board. Night had fallen. Candles lit the temple.

"Well played," said the beast opposite me. He picked up the gold marriage bowl and set it back on its stand. "I will marry you."

I laid my hands on the gold bowl, and he placed his hands, clammy and rough, over mine, his claws sheathed.

* * *

Before I left for the Eastlands with my husband, I spoke to
the emperor's advisor. "It's lucky I know how to play Go."

"Luck had nothing to do with it," he said. "Your father
was a master of Go. Did you not know that?"

I shook my head. I knew my father beat the other villagers, but that was all.

"Shen wrote to me once," said the advisor, "and mentioned you showed promise at the game." He paused. "I am
sorry for manipulating you into this marriage. May it turn
out better than you expect."

And so it has. My husband is quick-tempered, moody,
and hideous to look at, but he is also fair-minded, even
kind. We have no children of our own, of course, but we
adopted two, one of my race and one of my husband's.
While the children were home they made the great castle
less lonely.

And every night of our marriage, my husband and I have
played Go together. Each time as he squats down by the
board, my husband announces, "Tonight I will win."

But he never has.

Basement Magic

Ellen Klages

Ellen Klages [www.exo.net/~ellenk/klages.html] recently moved to Cleveland Heights, Ohio, from San Francisco, California, where she worked for the Exploratorium and developed her talent for stand-up comedy (she performs improv comedy with the Second City Organization). She has written four books of hands-on science activities for children (with Pat Murphy et al.) for the Exploratorium. The second book in that series, The Science Explorer Out and About, *was honored with* Scientific American's *1997 Young Readers Book Award. She is a stalwart supporter of the James Tiptree, Jr. Awards (is on the Motherboard), and runs the infamous Tiptree benefit auction at SF conventions around the country, during which anything can happen. She currently divides her time between San Francisco and Cleveland. Since 1999 her short fiction has appeared in science fiction and fantasy anthologies and magazines, both online and in print.*

"Basement Magic" was published in Fantasy & Science Fiction. *It is a midwestern fairy tale, about a little girl, her wicked stepmother, and a fairy godmother figure who may be the most interesting character in the story. Louise, the little girl, reads fairy tales and so she knows what to do when the chips are down. The bones of the fairy tale are wonderfully fleshed out in believable characters who interact convincingly.*

Mary Louise Whittaker believes in magic. She knows that somewhere, somewhere else, there must be dragons and princes, wands and wishes. Especially wishes. And happily ever after. Ever after is not now.

Her mother died in a car accident when Mary Louise was still a toddler. She misses her mother fiercely but abstractly. Her memories are less a coherent portrait than a mosaic of disconnected details: soft skin that smelled of lavender; a bright voice singing "Sweet and Low" in the night darkness; bubbles at bath time; dark curls; zwieback.

Her childhood has been kneaded, but not shaped, by the series of well-meaning middle-aged women her father has hired to tend her. He is busy climbing the corporate ladder, and is absent even when he is at home. She does not miss him. He remarried when she was five, and they moved into a two-story Tudor in one of the better suburbs of Detroit. Kitty, the new Mrs. Ted Whittaker, is a former Miss Bloomfield Hills, a vain divorcée with a towering mass of blond curls in a shade not her own. In the wild, her kind is inclined to eat their young.

Kitty might have tolerated her new stepdaughter had she been sweet and cuddly, a slick-magazine cherub. But at six, Mary Louise is an odd, solitary child. She has unruly red hair the color of Fiestaware, the dishes that might have been radioactive, and small round pink glasses that make her blue eyes seem large and slightly distant. She did not walk until she was almost two, and propels herself with a quick shuffle-duckling gait that is both urgent and awkward.

One spring morning, Mary Louise is camped in one of her favorite spots, the window seat in the guest bedroom. It is a stage set of a room, one that no one else ever visits. She leans against the wall, a thick book with lush illustrations propped up on her bare knees. Bright sunlight, filtered through the leaves of the oak outside, is broken into geometric patterns by the mullioned windows, dappling the floral cushion in front of her.

The book is almost bigger than her lap, and she holds it open with one elbow, the other anchoring her Bankie, a square of pale blue flannel with pale blue satin edging that once swaddled her infant self, carried home from the hospital. It is raveled and graying, both tattered and beloved. The thumb of her blanket arm rests in her mouth in a comforting manner.

Mary Louise is studying a picture of a witch with purple robes and hair as black as midnight when she hears voices in the hall. The door to the guest room is open a crack, so she can hear clearly, but cannot see or be seen. One of the voices is Kitty's. She is explaining something about the linen closet, so it is probably a new cleaning lady. They have had six since they moved in.

Mary Louise sits very still and doesn't turn the page, because it is stiff paper and might make a noise. But the door opens anyway, and she hears Kitty say, "This is the guest room. Now unless we've got company—and I'll let you know—it just needs to be dusted and the linens aired once a week. It has an—oh, there you are," she says, coming in the doorway, as if she has been looking all over for Mary Louise, which she has not.

Kitty turns and says to the air behind her, "This is my husband's daughter, Mary Louise. She's not in school yet. She's small for her age, and her birthday is in December, so we decided to hold her back a year. She never does much, just sits and reads. I'm sure she won't be a bother. Will you?" She turns and looks at Mary Louise but does not wait for an answer. "And this is Ruby. She's going to take care of the house for us."

The woman who stands behind Kitty nods, but makes no move to enter the room. She is tall, taller than Kitty, with skin the color of gingerbread. Ruby wears a white uniform and a pair of white Keds. She is older, there are lines around her eyes and her mouth, but her hair is sleek and black, black as midnight.

Kitty looks at her small gold watch. "Oh, dear. I've got to get going or I'll be late for my hair appointment." She looks back at Mary Louise. "Your father and I are going out tonight, but Ruby will make you some dinner, and Mrs. Banks will be here about six." Mrs. Banks is one of the babysitters, an older woman in a dark dress who smells like dusty licorice and coos too much. "So be a good girl. And for god's sake get that thumb out of your mouth. Do you want your teeth to grow in crooked, too?"

Mary Louise says nothing, but withdraws her damp puckered thumb and folds both hands in her lap. She looks up at Kitty, her eyes expressionless, until her stepmother looks away. "Well, an-y-wa-y," Kitty says, drawing the word out to four syllables, "I've really got to be going." She turns and leaves the room, brushing by Ruby, who stands silently just outside the doorway.

Ruby watches Kitty go, and when the high heels have clattered onto the tiles at the bottom of the stairs, she turns and looks at Mary Louise. "You a quiet little mouse, ain't you?" she asks in a soft, low voice.

Mary Louise shrugs. She sits very still in the window seat and waits for Ruby to leave. She does not look down at her book, because it is rude to look away when a grownup might still be talking to you. But none of the cleaning ladies talk to her, except to ask her to move out of the way, as if she were furniture.

"Yes siree, a quiet little mouse," Ruby says again. "Well, Miss Mouse, I'm fixin to go downstairs and make me a grilled cheese sandwich for lunch. If you like, I can cook you up one too. I make a mighty fine grilled cheese sandwich."

Mary Louise is startled by the offer. Grilled cheese is one of her very favorite foods. She thinks for a minute, then closes her book and tucks Bankie securely under one arm. She slowly follows Ruby down the wide front stairs, her small green-socked feet making no sound at all on the thick beige carpet.

It is the best grilled cheese sandwich Mary Louise has ever eaten. The outside is golden brown and so crisp it crackles under her teeth. The cheese is melted so that it soaks into the bread on the inside, just a little. There are no burnt spots at all. Mary Louise thanks Ruby and returns to her book.

The house is large, and Mary Louise knows all the best hiding places. She does not like being where Kitty can find her, where their paths might cross. Before Ruby came, Mary Louise didn't go down to the basement very much. Not by herself. It is an old house, and the basement is damp and musty, with heavy stone walls and banished, battered furniture. It is not a comfortable place, nor a safe one. There is the furnace, roaring fire, and the cans of paint and bleach and other frightful potions. Poisons. Years of soap flakes, lint, and furnace soot coat the walls like household lichen.

The basement is a place between the worlds, within Kitty's domain, but beneath her notice. Now, in the daytime, it is Ruby's, and Mary Louise is happy there. Ruby is not like other grownups. Ruby talks to her in a regular voice, not a scold, nor the singsong Mrs. Banks uses, as if Mary Louise is a tiny baby. Ruby lets her sit and watch while she irons, or sorts the laundry, or runs the sheets through the mangle. She doesn't sigh when Mary Louise asks her questions.

On the rare occasions when Kitty and Ted are home in the evening, they have dinner in the dining room. Ruby cooks. She comes in late on those days, and then is very busy, and Mary Louise does not get to see her until dinnertime. But the two of them eat in the kitchen, in the breakfast nook. Ruby tells stories, but has to get up every few minutes when Kitty buzzes for her, to bring more water or another fork, or to clear away the salad plates. Ruby smiles when she is talking to Mary Louise, but when the buzzer sounds, her face changes. Not to a frown, but to a kind of blank Ruby mask.

One Tuesday night in early May, Kitty decrees that Mary Louise will eat dinner with them in the dining room, too. They sit at the wide mahogany table on stiff brocade chairs that pick at the backs of her legs. There are too many forks and even though she is very careful, it is hard to cut her meat, and once the heavy silverware skitters across the china with a sound that sets her teeth on edge. Kitty frowns at her.

The grownups talk to each other and Mary Louise just sits. The worst part is that when Ruby comes in and sets a plate down in front of her, there is no smile, just the Ruby mask.

"I don't know how you do it, Ruby," says her father when Ruby comes in to give him a second glass of water. "These pork chops are the best I've ever eaten. You've certainly got the magic touch."

"She does, doesn't she?" says Kitty. "You must tell me your secret."

"Just shake 'em up in flour, salt and pepper, then fry 'em in Crisco," Ruby says.

"That's all?"

"Yes, ma'am."

"Well, isn't that marvelous. I must try that. Thank you Ruby. You may go now."

"Yes, ma'am." Ruby turns and lets the swinging door between the kitchen and the dining room close behind her. A minute later Mary Louise hears the sound of running water, and the soft clunk of plates being slotted into the racks of the dishwasher.

"Mary Louise, don't put your peas into your mashed potatoes that way. It's not polite to play with your food," Kitty says.

Mary Louise sighs. There are too many rules in the dining room.

"Mary Louise, answer me when I speak to you."

"Muhff-mum," Mary Louise says through a mouthful of mashed potatoes.

"Oh, for god's sake. Don't talk with your mouth full. Don't you have any manners at all?"

Caught between two conflicting rules, Mary Louise merely shrugs.

"Is there any more gravy?" her father asks.

Kitty leans forward a little and Mary Louise hears the

slightly muffled sound of the buzzer in the kitchen. There is a little bump, about the size of an Oreo, under the carpet just beneath Kitty's chair that Kitty presses with her foot. Ruby appears a few seconds later and stands inside the doorway, holding a striped dishcloth in one hand.

"Mr. Whittaker would like some more gravy," says Kitty.

Ruby shakes her head. "Sorry, Miz Whittaker. I put all of it in the gravy boat. There's no more left."

"Oh." Kitty sounds disapproving. "We had plenty of gravy last time."

"Yes, ma'am. But that was a beef roast. Pork chops just don't make as much gravy," Ruby says.

"Oh. Of course. Well, thank you, Ruby."

"Yes ma'am." Ruby pulls the door shut behind her.

"I guess that's all the gravy, Ted," Kitty says, even though he is sitting at the other end of the table, and has heard Ruby himself.

"Tell her to make more next time," he says, frowning. "So what did you do today?" He turns his attention to Mary Louise for the first time since they sat down.

"Mostly I read my book," she says. "The fairy tales you gave me for Christmas."

"Well, that's fine," he says. "I need you to call the Taylors and cancel." Mary Louise realizes he is no longer talking to her, and eats the last of her mashed potatoes.

"Why?" Kitty raises an eyebrow. "I thought we were meeting them out at the club on Friday for cocktails."

"Can't. Got to fly down to Florida tomorrow. The space thing. We designed the guidance system for Shepard's capsule, and George wants me to go down with the engineers, talk to the press if the launch is a success."

"Are they really going to shoot a man into space?" Mary Louise asks.

"That's the plan, honey."

"Well, you don't give me much notice," Kitty says, smiling. "But I suppose I can pack a few summer dresses, and get anything else I need down there."

"Sorry, Kit. This trip is just business. No wives."

"No, only to Grand Rapids. Never to Florida," Kitty says, frowning. She takes a long sip of her drink. "So how long will you be gone?"

"Five days, maybe a week. If things go well, Jim and I are going to drive down to Palm Beach and get some golf in."

"I see. Just business." Kitty drums her lacquered fingernails on the tablecloth. "I guess that means I have to call Barb and Mitchell, too. Or had you forgotten my sister's birthday dinner next Tuesday?" Kitty scowls down the table at her husband, who shrugs and takes a bite of his chop.

Kitty drains her drink. The table is silent for a minute, and then she says, "Mary Louise! Don't put your dirty fork on the tablecloth. Put it on the edge of your plate if you're done. Would you like to be excused?"

"Yes ma'am," says Mary Louise.

As soon as she is excused, Mary Louise goes down to the basement to wait. When Ruby is working it smells like a cave full of soap and warm laundry.

A little after seven, Ruby comes down the stairs carrying a brown paper lunch sack. She puts it down on the ironing board. "Well, Miss Mouse. I thought I'd see you down here when I got done with the dishes."

"I don't like eating in the dining room," Mary Louise says. "I want to eat in the kitchen with you."

"I like that, too. But your stepmomma says she got to teach you some table manners, so when you grow up you can eat with nice folks."

Mary Louise makes a face, and Ruby laughs.

"They ain't such a bad thing, manners. Come in real handy someday, when you're eatin with folks you *want* to have like you."

"I guess so," says Mary Louise. "Will you tell me a story?"

"Not tonight, Miss Mouse. It's late, and I gotta get home and give my husband his supper. He got off work half an hour ago, and I told him I'd bring him a pork chop or two if there was any left over." She gestures to the paper bag. "He likes my pork chops even more than your daddy does."

"Not even a little story?" Mary Louise feels like she might cry. Her stomach hurts from having dinner with all the forks.

"Not tonight, sugar. Tomorrow, though, I'll tell you a long one, just to make up." Ruby takes off her white Keds and lines them up next to each other under the big galvanized sink. Then she takes off her apron, looks at a brown gravy stain on the front of it, and crumples it up and tosses it into the pink plastic basket of dirty laundry. She pulls a hanger from the line that stretches across the ceiling over the washer and begins to undo the white buttons on the front of her uniform.

"What's that?" Mary Louise asks. Ruby has rucked the top of her uniform down to her waist and is pulling it over her hips. There is a green string pinned to one bra strap. The end of it disappears into her left armpit.

"What's what? You seen my underwear before."

"Not that. That string."

Ruby looks down at her chest. "Oh. That. I had my auntie make me up a conjure hand."

"Can I see it?" Mary Louise climbs down out of the chair and walks over to where Ruby is standing.

Ruby looks hard at Mary Louise for a minute. "For it to work, it gotta stay a secret. But you good with secrets, so I guess you can take a look. Don't you touch it, though. Anybody but me touch it, all the conjure magic leak right out and it won't work no more." She reaches under her armpit and draws out a small green flannel bag, about the size of a walnut, and holds it in one hand.

Mary Louise stands with her hands clasped tight behind her back so she won't touch it even by accident and stares intently at the bag. It doesn't look like anything magic. Magic is gold rings and gowns spun of moonlight and silver, not a white cotton uniform and a little stained cloth bag. "Is it really magic? Really? What does it do?"

"Well, there's diff'rent kinds of magic. Some conjure

bags bring luck. Some protects you. This one, this one gonna bring me money. That's why it's green. Green's the money color. Inside there's a silver dime, so the money knows it belong here, a magnet—that attracts the money right to me—and some roots, wrapped up in a two-dollar bill. Every mornin I gives it a little drink, and after nine days, it gonna bring me my fortune." Ruby looks down at the little bag fondly, then tucks it back under her armpit.

Mary Louise looks up at Ruby and sees something she has never seen on a grownup's face before: Ruby believes. She believes in magic, even if it is armpit magic.

"Wow. How does—"

"Miss Mouse, I *got* to get home, give my husband his supper." Ruby steps out of her uniform, hangs it on a hanger, then puts on her blue skirt and a cotton blouse.

Mary Louise looks down at the floor. "Okay," she says.

"It's not the end of the world, sugar." Ruby pats Mary Louise on the back of the head, then sits down and puts on her flat black shoes. "I'll be back tomorrow. I got a big pile of laundry to do. You think you might come down here, keep me company? I think I can tell a story and sort the laundry at the same time." She puts on her outdoor coat, a nubby, burnt-orange wool with chipped gold buttons and big square pockets, and ties a scarf around her chin.

"Will you tell me a story about the magic bag?" Mary Louise asks. This time she looks at Ruby and smiles.

"I think I can do that. Gives us both somethin to look forward to. Now scoot on out of here. I gotta turn off the light." She picks up her brown paper sack and pulls the string that hangs down over the ironing board. The light bulb goes out, and the basement is dark except for the twilight filtering in through the high single window. Ruby opens the outside door to the concrete stairs that lead up to the driveway. The air is warmer than the basement.

"Nitey, nite, Miss Mouse," she says, and goes outside.

"G'night Ruby," says Mary Louise, and goes upstairs.

* * *

When Ruby goes to vacuum the rug in the guest bedroom on Thursday morning, she finds Mary Louise sitting in the window seat, staring out the window.

"Mornin, Miss Mouse. You didn't come down and say hello."

Mary Louise does not answer. She does not even turn around.

Ruby pushes the lever on the vacuum and stands it upright, dropping the gray fabric cord she has wrapped around her hand. She walks over to the silent child. "Miss Mouse? Somethin wrong?"

Mary Louise looks up. Her eyes are cold. "Last night I was in bed, reading. Kitty came home. She was in a really bad mood. She told me I read too much and I'll just ruin my eyes—more—reading in bed. She took my book and told me she was going to throw it in the 'cinerator and burn it up." She delivers the words in staccato anger, through clenched teeth.

"She just bein mean to you, sugar." Ruby shakes her head. "She tryin to scare you, but she won't really do that."

"But she *did!*" Mary Louise reaches behind her and holds up her fairy tale book. The picture on the cover is soot-stained, the shiny coating blistered. The gilded edges of the pages are charred and the corners are gone.

"Lord, child, where'd you find that?"

"In the 'cinerator, out back. Where she said. I can still read most of the stories, but it makes my hands all dirty." She holds up her hands, showing her sooty palms.

Ruby shakes her head again. She says, more to herself than to Mary Louise, "I burnt the trash after lunch yesterday. Must of just been coals, come last night."

Mary Louise looks at the ruined book in her lap, then up at Ruby. "It was my favorite book. Why'd she do that?" A tear runs down her cheek.

Ruby sits down on the window seat. "I don't know, Miss Mouse," she says. "I truly don't. Maybe she mad that your daddy gone down to Florida, leave her behind. Some folks, when they're mad, they just gotta whup on somebody, even

if it's a little bitty six-year-old child. They whup on somebody else, they forget their own hurts for a while."

"You're bigger than her," says Mary Louise, snuffling.
"You could—whup—*her* back. You could tell her that it
was bad and wrong what she did."

Ruby shakes her head. "I'm real sorry, Miss Mouse," she
says quietly, "But I can't do that."

"Why not?"

"'Cause she the boss in this house, and if I say anythin
crosswise to Miz Kitty, her own queen self, she gonna fire
me same as she fire all them other colored ladies used to
work for her. And I needs this job. My husband's just
workin part-time down to the Sunoco. He tryin to get work
in the Ford plant, but they ain't hirin right now. So my pay-
check here, that's what's puttin groceries on our table."

"But, but—" Mary Louise begins to cry without a sound.
Ruby is the only grownup person she trusts, and Ruby cannot help her.

Ruby looks down at her lap for a long time, then sighs. "I
can't say nothin to Miz Kitty. But her bein so mean to you,
that ain't right, neither." She puts her arm around the shaking child.

"What about your little bag?" Mary Louise wipes her
nose with the back of her hand, leaving a small streak of
soot on her cheek.

"What 'bout it?"

"You said some magic is for protecting, didn't you?"

"Some is," Ruby says slowly. "Some is. Now, my momma
used to say, 'an egg can't fight with a stone.' And that's the
truth. Miz Kitty got the power in this house. More'n you,
more'n me. Ain't nothin to do 'bout that. But conjurin—"
She thinks for a minute, then lets out a deep breath.

"I think we might could put some protection 'round you,
so Miz Kitty can't do you no more misery," Ruby says,
frowning a little. "But I ain't sure quite how. See, if it was
your house, I'd put a goopher right under the front door.
But it ain't. It's your daddy's house, and she married to him
legal, so ain't no way to keep her from comin in her own
house, even if she is nasty."

"What about my room?" asks Mary Louise.

"Your room? Hmm. Now, that's a different story. I think we can goopher it so she can't do you no harm in there."

Mary Louise wrinkles her nose. "What's a *goopher*?"

Ruby smiles. "Down South Carolina, where my family's from, that's just what they calls a spell, or a hex, a little bit of rootwork."

"Root—?"

Ruby shakes her head. "It don't make no never mind what you calls it, long as you does it right. Now if you done cryin, we got work to do. Can you go out to the garage, to your Daddy's toolbox, and get me nine nails? Big ones, all the same size, and bright and shiny as you can find. Can you count that many?"

Mary Louise snorts. "I can count up to *fifty*," she says.

"Good. Then you go get nine shiny nails, fast as you can, and meet me down the hall, by your room."

When Mary Louise gets back upstairs, nine shiny nails clutched tightly in one hand, Ruby is kneeling in front of the door of her bedroom, with a paper of pins from the sewing box, and a can of Drano. Mary Louise hands her the nails.

"These is just perfect," Ruby says. She pours a puddle of Drano into its upturned cap, and dips the tip of one of the nails into it, then pokes the nail under the edge of the hall carpet at the left side of Mary Louise's bedroom door, pushing it deep until not even its head shows.

"Why did you dip the nail in Drano?" Mary Louise asks. She didn't know any of the poison things under the kitchen sink could be magic.

"Don't you touch that, hear? It'll burn you bad, cause it's got lye in it. But lye the best thing for cleanin away any evil that's already been here. Ain't got no Red Devil like back home, but you got to use what you got. The nails and the pins, they made of iron, and keep any new evil away from your door." Ruby dips a pin in the Drano as she talks and repeats the poking, alternating nails and pins until she pushes the last pin in at the other edge of the door.

"That oughta do it," she says. She pours the few remaining drops of Drano back into the can and screws the lid on tight, then stands up. "Now all we needs to do is set the protectin charm. You know your prayers?" she asks Mary Louise.

"I know 'Now I lay me down to sleep.'"

"Good enough. You get into your room and you kneel down, facin the hall, and say that prayer to the doorway. Say it loud and as best you can. I'm goin to go down and get the sheets out of the dryer. Meet me in Miz Kitty's room when you done."

Mary Louise says her prayers in a loud, clear voice. She doesn't know how this kind of magic spell works, and she isn't sure if she is supposed to say the God Blesses, but she does. She leaves Kitty out and adds Ruby. "And help me to be a good girl, amen," she finishes, and hurries down to her father's room to see what other kinds of magic Ruby knows.

The king-size mattress is bare. Mary Louise lies down on it and rolls over and over three times before falling off the edge onto the carpet. She is just getting up, dusting off the knees of her blue cotton pants, when Ruby appears with an armful of clean sheets, which she dumps onto the bed. Mary Louise lays her face in the middle of the pile. It is still warm and smells like baked cotton. She takes a deep breath.

"You gonna lay there in the laundry all day or help me make this bed?" Ruby asks, laughing.

Mary Louise takes one side of the big flowered sheet and helps Ruby stretch it across the bed and pull the elastic parts over all four corners so it is smooth everywhere.

"Are we going to do a lot more magic?" Mary Louise asks. "I'm getting kind of hungry."

"One more bit, then we can have us some lunch. You want tomato soup?"

"Yes!" says Mary Louise.

"I thought so. Now fetch me a hair from Miz Kitty's hairbrush. See if you can find a nice long one with some dark at the end of it."

Mary Louise goes over to Kitty's dresser and peers at the heavy silver brush. She finds a darker line in the tangle of blond and carefully pulls it out. It is almost a foot long, and the last inch is definitely brown. She carries it over to Ruby, letting it trail through her fingers like the tail of a tiny invisible kite.

"That's good," Ruby says. She reaches into the pocket of her uniform and pulls out a scrap of red felt with three needles stuck into it lengthwise. She pulls the needles out one by one, makes a bundle of them, and wraps it round and round, first with the long strand of Kitty's hair, then with a piece of black thread.

"Hold out your hand," she says.

Mary Louise holds out her hand flat, and Ruby puts the little black-wrapped bundle into it.

"Now, you hold this until you get a picture in your head of Miz Kitty burnin up your pretty picture book. And when it nice and strong, you spit. Okay?"

Mary Louise nods. She scrunches up her eyes, remembering, then spits on the needles.

"You got the knack for this," Ruby says, smiling. "It's a gift."

Mary Louise beams. She does not get many compliments, and stores this one away in the most private part of her thoughts. She will visit it regularly over the next few days until its edges are indistinct and there is nothing left but a warm glow labeled RUBY.

"Now put it under this mattress, far as you can reach." Ruby lifts up the edge of the mattress and Mary Louise drops the bundle on the box spring.

"Do you want me to say my prayers again?"

"Not this time, Miss Mouse. Prayers is for protectin. This here is a sufferin hand, bring some of Miz Kitty's meanness back on her own self, and it need another kind of charm. I'll set this one myself." Ruby lowers her voice and begins to chant:

> *Before the night is over,*
> *Before the day is through.*
> *What you have done to someone else*
> *Will come right back on you.*

"There. That ought to do her just fine. Now we gotta make up this bed. Top sheet, blanket, bedspread all smooth and nice, pillows plumped up just so."

"Does that help the magic?" Mary Louise asks. She wants to do it right, and there are almost as many rules as eating in the dining room. But different.

"Not 'zactly. But it makes it look like it 'bout the most beautiful place to sleep Miz Kitty ever seen, make her want to crawl under them sheets and get her beauty rest. Now help me with that top sheet, okay?"

Mary Louise does, and when they have smoothed the last wrinkle out of the bedspread, Ruby looks at the clock. "Shoot. How'd it get to be after one o'clock? Only fifteen minutes before my story comes on. Let's go down and have ourselves some lunch."

In the kitchen, Ruby heats up a can of Campbell's tomato soup, with milk, not water, the way Mary Louise likes it best, then ladles it out into two yellow bowls. She puts them on a metal tray, adds some saltine crackers and a bottle of ginger ale for her, and a lunchbox bag of Fritos and a glass of milk for Mary Louise, and carries the whole tray into the den. Ruby turns on the TV and they sip and crunch their way through half an hour of *As the World Turns*.

During the commercials, Ruby tells Mary Louise who all the people are, and what they've done, which is mostly bad. When they are done with their soup, another story comes on, but they aren't people Ruby knows, so she turns off the TV and carries the dishes back to the kitchen.

"I gotta do the dustin and finish vacuumin, and ain't no way to talk over that kind of noise," Ruby says, handing Mary Louise a handful of Oreos. "So you go off and play by yourself now, and I'll get my chores done before Miz Kitty comes home."

Mary Louise goes up to her room. At 4:30 she hears Kitty come home, but she only changes into out-to-dinner clothes and leaves and doesn't get into bed. Ruby says good-bye when Mrs. Banks comes at 6:00, and Mary Louise eats dinner in the kitchen and goes upstairs at 8:00, when Mrs. Banks starts to watch *Dr. Kildare*.

On her dresser there is a picture of her mother. She is beautiful, with long curls and a silvery white dress. She looks like a queen, so Mary Louise thinks she might be a princess. She lives in a castle, imprisoned by her evil stepmother, the false queen. But now that there is magic, there will be a happy ending. She crawls under the covers and watches her doorway, wondering what will happen when Kitty tries to come into her room, if there will be flames.

Kitty begins to scream just before nine Friday morning. Clumps of her hair lie on her pillow like spilled wheat. What is left sprouts from her scalp in irregular clumps, like a crabgrass-infested lawn. Clusters of angry red blisters dot her exposed skin.

By the time Mary Louise runs up from the kitchen, where she is eating a bowl of Kix, Kitty is on the phone. She is talking to her beauty salon. She is shouting, "This is an emergency! An emergency!"

Kitty does not speak to Mary Louise. She leaves the house with a scarf wrapped around her head like a turban, in such a hurry that she does not even bother with lipstick. Mary Louise hears the tires of her T-bird squeal out of the driveway. A shower of gravel hits the side of the house, and then everything is quiet.

Ruby comes upstairs at ten, buttoning the last button on her uniform. Mary Louise is in the breakfast nook, eating a second bowl of Kix. The first one got soggy. She jumps up excitedly when she sees Ruby.

"Miz Kitty already gone?" Ruby asks, her hand on the coffeepot.

"It worked! It worked! Something *bad* happened to her hair. A lot of it fell out, and there are chicken pox where it was. She's at the beauty shop. I think she's going to be there a long time."

Ruby pours herself a cup of coffee. "That so?"

"Uh-huh." Mary Louise grins. "She looks like a *goopher.*"

"Well, well, well. That come back on her fast, didn't it?

Maybe now she think twice 'bout messin with somebody smaller'n her. But you, Miss Mouse," Ruby wiggles a semi-stern finger at Mary Louise, "Don't you go jumpin up and down shoutin 'bout goophers, hear? Magic ain't nothin to be foolin around with. It can bring sickness, bad luck, a whole heap of misery if it ain't done proper. You hear me?"

Mary Louise nods and runs her thumb and finger across her lips, as if she is locking them. But she is still grinning from ear to ear.

Kitty comes home from the beauty shop late that afternoon. She is in a very, very bad mood, and still has a scarf around her head. Mary Louise is behind the couch in the den, playing seven dwarfs. She is Snow White and is lying very still, waiting for the prince.

Kitty comes into the den and goes to the bar. She puts two ice cubes in a heavy squat crystal glass, then reaches up on her tiptoes and feels around on the bookshelf until she finds a small brass key. She unlocks the liquor cabinet and fills her glass with brown liquid. She goes to the phone and makes three phone calls, canceling cocktails, dinner, tennis on Saturday. "Sorry," Kitty says. "Under the weather. Raincheck?" When she is finished she refills her glass, replaces the key, and goes upstairs. Mary Louise does not see her again until Sunday.

Mary Louise stays in her room most of the weekend. It seems like a good idea, now that it is safe there. Saturday afternoon she tiptoes down to the kitchen and makes three peanut butter and honey sandwiches. She is not allowed to use the stove. She takes her sandwiches and some Fritos upstairs and touches one of the nails under the carpet, to make sure it is still there. She knows the magic is working, because Kitty doesn't even try to come in, not once.

At seven-thirty on Sunday night, she ventures downstairs again. Kitty's door is shut. The house is quiet. It is time for Disney. *Walt Disney's Wonderful World of Color*. It is her favorite program, the only one that is not black and white, except for *Bonanza*, which comes on after her bedtime.

Mary Louise turns on the big TV that is almost as tall as she is, and sits in the middle of the maroon leather couch in the den. Her feet stick out in front of her, and do not quite reach the edge. There is a commercial for Mr. Clean. He has no hair, like Kitty, and Mary Louise giggles, just a little. Then there are red and blue fireworks over the castle where Sleeping Beauty lives. Mary Louise's thumb wanders up to her mouth, and she rests her cheek on the soft nap of her Bankie.

The show is Cinderella, and when the wicked stepmother comes on, Mary Louise thinks of Kitty, but does not giggle. The story unfolds and Mary Louise is bewitched by the colors, by the magic of television. She does not hear the creaking of the stairs. She does not hear the door of the den open, or hear the rattle of ice cubes in an empty crystal glass. She does not see the shadow loom over her until it is too late.

It is a sunny Monday morning. Ruby comes in the basement door and changes into her uniform. She switches on the old brown table radio, waits for its tubes to warm up and begin to glow, then turns the yellowed plastic dial until she finds a station that is more music than static. The Marcels are singing "Blue Moon" as she sorts the laundry, and she dances a little on the concrete floor, swinging and swaying as she tosses white cotton panties into one basket and black nylon socks into another.

She fills the washer with a load of whites, adds a measuring cup of Dreft, and turns the dial to Delicate. The song on the radio changes to "Runaway" as she goes over to the wooden cage built into the wall, where the laundry that has been dumped down the upstairs chute gathers.

"As I walk along . . . ," Ruby sings as she opens the hinged door with its criss-cross of green painted slats. The plywood box inside is a cube about three feet on a side, filled with a mound of flowered sheets and white terry cloth towels. She pulls a handful of towels off the top of the mound and lets them tumble into the pink plastic basket waiting on the floor below. "An' I wonder. I wa-wa-wa-wawuh-un-der," she sings, and then stops when the pile moves on its own, and whimpers.

Ruby parts the sea of sheets to reveal a small head of carrot-red hair.

"Miss Mouse? What on God's green earth you doin in there? I like to bury you in all them sheets!"

A bit more of Mary Louise appears, her hair in tangles, her eyes red-rimmed from crying.

"Is Kitty gone?" she asks.

Ruby nods. "She at the beauty parlor again. What you *doin* in there? You hidin from Miz Kitty?"

"Uh-huh." Mary Louise sits up and a cascade of hand towels and washcloths tumbles out onto the floor.

"What she done this time?"

"She—she—" Mary Louise bursts into ragged sobs.

Ruby reaches in and puts her hands under Mary Louise's arms, lifting the weeping child out of the pile of laundry. She carries her over to the basement stairs and sits down, cradling her. The tiny child shakes and holds on tight to Ruby's neck, her tears soaking into the white cotton collar. When her tears subside into trembling, Ruby reaches into a pocket and proffers a pale yellow hankie.

"Blow hard," she says gently. Mary Louise does.

"Now scooch around front a little so you can sit in my lap." Mary Louise scooches without a word. Ruby strokes her curls for a minute. "Sugar? What she do this time?"

Mary Louise tries to speak, but her voice is still a rusty squeak. After a few seconds she just holds her tightly clenched fist out in front of her and slowly opens it. In her palm is a wrinkled scrap of pale blue flannel, about the size of a playing card, its edges jagged and irregular.

"Miz Kitty do that?"

"Uh-huh," Mary Louise finds her voice. "I was watching Disney and she came in to get another drink. She said Bankie was just a dirty old rag with germs and sucking thumbs was for babies—" Mary Louise pauses to take a breath. "She had scissors and she cut up all of Bankie on the floor. She said next time she'd get bigger scissors and cut off my thumbs! She threw my Bankie pieces in the toilet and flushed, three times. This one fell under the couch," Mary Louise says, looking at the small scrap, her voice breaking.

Ruby puts an arm around her shaking shoulders and kisses her forehead. "Hush now. Don't you fret. You just sit down here with me. Everything gonna be okay. You gotta—" A buzzing noise from the washer interrupts her. She looks into the laundry area, then down at Mary Louise and sighs. "You take a couple deep breaths. I gotta move the clothes in the washer so they're not all on one side. When I come back, I'm gonna tell you a story. Make you feel better, okay?"

"Okay," says Mary Louise in a small voice. She looks at her lap, not at Ruby, because nothing is really very okay at all.

Ruby comes back a few minutes later and sits down on the step next to Mary Louise. She pulls two small yellow rectangles out of her pocket and hands one to Mary Louise. "I like to set back and hear a story with a stick of Juicy Fruit in my mouth. Helps my ears open up or somethin. How about you?"

"I like Juicy Fruit," Mary Louise admits.

"I thought so. Save the foil. Fold it up and put it in your pocket."

"So I have someplace to put the gum when the flavor's all used up?"

"Maybe. Or maybe we got somethin else to do and that foil might could come in handy. You save it up neat and we'll see."

Mary Louise puts the gum in her mouth and puts the foil in the pocket of her corduroy pants, then folds her hands in her lap and waits.

"Well, now," says Ruby. "Seems that once, a long, long time ago, down South Carolina, there was a little mouse of a girl with red, red hair and big blue eyes."

"Like me?" asks Mary Louise.

"You know, I think she was just about 'zactly like you. Her momma died when she was just a little bit of a girl, and her daddy married hisself a new wife, who was very pretty, but she was mean and lazy. Now, this stepmomma, she didn't much like stayin home to take care of no child weren't really her own and she was awful cruel to that poor little girl. She never gave her enough to eat, and even when it was snowin outside, she just dress her up in thin cotton rags. That child was awful hungry and cold, come winter.

"But her real momma had made her a blanket, a soft blue blanket, and that was the girl's favorite thing in the whole wide world. If she wrapped it around herself and sat real quiet in a corner, she was warm enough, then.

"Now, her stepmomma, she didn't like seein that little girl happy. That little girl had power inside her, and it scared her stepmomma. Scared her so bad that one day she took that child's most favorite special blanket and cut it up into tiny pieces, so it wouldn't be no good for warmin her up at all."

"That was really mean of her," Mary Louise says quietly.

"Yes it was. Awful mean. But you know what that little girl did next? She went into the kitchen, and sat down right next to the cookstove, where it was a little bit warm. She sat there, holdin one of the little scraps from her blanket, and she cried, cause she missed havin her real momma. And when her tears hit the stove, they turned into steam, and she stayed warm as toast the rest of that day. Ain't nothin warmer than steam heat, no siree.

"But when her stepmomma saw her all smilin and warm again, what did that woman do but lock up the woodpile, out of pure spite. See, she ate out in fancy rest'rants all the time, and she never did cook, so it didn't matter to her if there was fire in the stove or not.

"So finally that child dragged her cold self down to the basement. It was mighty chilly down there, but she knew it was someplace her stepmomma wouldn't look for her, cause the basement's where work gets done, and her stepmomma never did do one lick of work.

"That child hid herself back of the old wringer washer, in a dark, dark corner. She was cold, and that little piece of blanket was only big enough to wrap a mouse in. She wished she was warm. She wished and wished and between her own power and that magic blanket, she found her mouse self. Turned right into a little gray mouse, she did. Then she wrapped that piece of soft blue blanket around her and hid herself away just as warm as if she was in a feather bed.

"But soon she heard somebody comin down the wood stairs into the basement, clomp, clomp, clomp. And she thought it was her mean old stepmomma comin to make her life a misery again, so she scampered quick like mice do, back into a little crack in the wall. 'Cept it weren't her stepmomma. It was the cleanin lady, comin down the stairs with a big basket of mendin."

"Is that you?" Mary Louise asks.

"I reckon it was someone pretty much like me," Ruby says, smiling. "And she saw that little mouse over in the corner with that scrap of blue blanket tight around her, and she said, ''Scuse me Miss Mouse, but I needs to patch me up this old raggy sweater, and that little piece of blanket is just the right size. Can I have it?'"

"Why would she talk to a mouse?" Mary Louise asks, puzzled.

"Well, now, the lady knew that it wasn't no regular mouse, 'cause she weren't no ordinary cleanin lady, she was a conjure woman too. She could see that magic girl spirit inside the mouse shape clear as day."

"Oh. Okay."

Ruby smiles. "Now, the little mouse-child had to think for a minute, because that piece of blue blanket was 'bout the only thing she loved left in the world. But the lady asked so nice, she gave over her last little scrap of blanket for the mendin and turned back into a little girl.

"Well sir, the spirit inside that blue blanket was powerful strong, even though the pieces got all cut up. So when the lady sewed that blue scrap onto that raggy old sweater, what do you know? It turned into a big warm magic coat, just the size of that little girl. And when she put on that magic coat, it kept her warm and safe, and her stepmomma never could hurt her no more."

"I wish there really was magic," says Mary Louise sadly. "Because she *did* hurt me again."

Ruby sighs. "Magic's there, sugar. It truly is. It just don't always work the way you think it will. That sufferin hand we put in Miz Kitty's bed, it work just fine. It scared her plenty. Trouble is, when she scared, she get mad, and then she get mean, and there ain't no end to it. No tellin what she might take it into her head to cut up next."

"My thumbs," says Mary Louise solemnly. She looks at them as if she is saying good-bye.

"That's what I'm afraid of. Somethin terrible bad. I been thinkin on this over the weekend, and yesterday night I call my Aunt Nancy down in Beaufort, where I'm from. She's the most powerful conjure woman I know, taught me when I was little. I ask her what she'd do, and she says, 'sounds like you all need a Peaceful Home hand, stop all the angry, make things right.'"

"Do we have to make the bed again?" asks Mary Louise.

"No, sugar. This is a wearin hand, like my money hand. 'Cept it's for you to wear. Got lots of special things in it."

"Like what?"

"Well, first we got to weave together a hair charm. A piece of yours, a piece of Miz Kitty's. Hers before the goopher, I think. And we need some dust from the house. And some rosemary from the kitchen. I can get all them when I clean today. The rest is stuff I bet you already got."

"I have magic things?"

"I b'lieve so. That piece of tinfoil from your Juicy Fruit? We need that. And somethin lucky. You got somethin real lucky?"

"I have a penny what got run over by a train," Mary Louise offers.

"Just so. Now the last thing. You know how my little bag's green flannel, 'cause it's a money hand?"

Mary Louise nods.

"Well, for a Peaceful Home hand, we need a square of light blue flannel. You know where I can find one of those?"

Mary Louise's eyes grow wide behind her glasses. "But it's the only piece I've got left."

"I know," Ruby says softly.

"It's like in the story, isn't it?"

"Just like."

"And like in the story, if I give it to you, Kitty can't hurt me ever again?"

"Just like."

Mary Louise opens her fist again and looks at the scrap of blue flannel for a long time. "Okay," she says finally, and gives it to Ruby.

"It'll be all right, Miss Mouse. I b'lieve everything will turn out just fine. Now I gotta finish this laundry and do me some housework. I'll meet you in the kitchen round one-thirty. We'll eat and I'll fix up your hand right after my story."

At two o'clock the last credits of *As the World Turns* disappear from the TV. Ruby and Mary Louise go down to the basement. They lay out all the ingredients on the padded gray surface of the ironing board. Ruby assembles the hand, muttering under her breath from time to time. Mary Louise can't hear the words. Ruby wraps everything in the blue flannel and snares the neck of the walnut-sized bundle with three twists of white string.

"Now all we gotta do is give it a little drink, then you can put it on," she tells Mary Louise.

"Drink of what?"

Ruby frowns. "I been thinkin on that. My Aunt Nancy said best thing is to get me some Peaceful oil. But I don't know no root doctors up here. Ain't been round Detroit long enough."

"We could look in the phone book."

"Ain't the kind of doctor you finds in the Yellow Pages. Got to know someone who knows someone. And I don't. I told Aunt Nancy that, and she says in that case, reg'lar whiskey'll do just fine. That's what I been givin my money hand. Little bit of my husband's whiskey every mornin for six days now. I don't drink, myself, 'cept maybe a cold beer on a hot summer night. But whiskey's strong magic, comes to conjurin. Problem is, I can't take your hand home with me to give it a drink, 'long with mine."

"Why not?"

" 'Cause once it goes round your neck, nobody else can

touch it, not even me, else the conjure magic leak right out." Ruby looks at Mary Louise thoughtfully. "What's the most powerful drink you ever had, Miss Mouse?"

Mary Louise hesitates for a second, then says, "Vernor's ginger ale. The bubbles are *very* strong. They go up my nose and make me sneeze."

Ruby laughs. "I think that just might do. Ain't as powerful as whiskey, but it fits, you bein just a child and all. And there's one last bottle up in the Frigidaire. You go on up now and fetch it."

Mary Louise brings down the yellow and green bottle. Ruby holds her thumb over the opening and sprinkles a little bit on the flannel bag, mumbling some more words that end with "father son and holy ghost amen." Then she ties the white yarn around Mary Louise's neck so that the bag lies under her left armpit, and the string doesn't show.

"This bag's gotta be a secret," she says. "Don't talk about it, and don't let nobody else see it. Can you do that?"

Mary Louise nods. "I dress myself in the morning, and I change into my jammies in the bathroom."

"That's good. Now the next three mornings, before you get dressed, you give your bag a little drink of this Vernor's, and say, 'Lord, bring an end to the evil in this house, amen.' Can you remember that?"

Mary Louise says she can. She hides the bottle of Vernor's behind the leg of her bed. Tuesday morning she sprinkles the bag with Vernor's before putting on her T-shirt. The bag is a little sticky.

But Mary Louise thinks the magic might be working. Kitty has bought a blond wig, a golden honey color. Mary Louise thinks it looks like a helmet, but doesn't say so. Kitty smiles in the mirror at herself and is in a better mood. She leaves Mary Louise alone.

Wednesday morning the bag is even stickier. It pulls at Mary Louise's armpit when she reaches for the box of Kix in the cupboard. Ruby says this is okay.

By Thursday, the Vernor's has been open for too long. It has gone flat and there are no bubbles at all. Mary Louise sprinkles her bag, but worries that it will lose its power. She is afraid the charm will not work, and that Kitty will come and get her. Her thumbs ache in anticipation.

When she goes downstairs Kitty is in her new wig and a green dress. She is going out to a luncheon. She tells Mary Louise that Ruby will not be there until noon, but she will stay to cook dinner. Mary Louise will eat in the dining room tonight, and until then she should be good and not to make a mess. After she is gone, Mary Louise eats some Kix and worries about her thumbs.

When her bowl is empty, she goes into the den, and stands on the desk chair so she can reach the tall books on the bookshelf. They are still over her head, and she cannot see, but her fingers reach. The dust on the tops makes her sneeze; she finds the key on a large black book called *Who's Who in Manufacturing 1960*. The key is brass and old-looking.

Mary Louise unlocks the liquor cabinet and looks at the bottles. Some are brown, some are green. One of the green ones has Toto dogs on it, a black one and a white one, and says SCOTCH WHISKEY. The bottle is half-full and heavy. She spills some on the floor, and her little bag is soaked more than sprinkled, but she thinks this will probably make up for the flat ginger ale.

She puts the green bottle back and carefully turns it so the Toto dogs face out, the way she found it. She climbs back up on the chair and puts the key back up on top of *Manufacturing*, then climbs down.

The little ball is cold and damp under her arm, and smells like medicine. She changes her shirt and feels safer. But she does not want to eat dinner alone with Kitty. That is not safe at all. She thinks for a minute, then smiles. Ruby has shown her how to make a *room* safe.

There are only five nails left in the jar in the garage. But she doesn't want to keep Kitty *out* of the dining room, just make it safe to eat dinner there. Five is probably fine. She takes the nails into the kitchen and opens the cupboard under the sink. She looks at the Drano. She is not allowed to touch it, not by Kitty's rules, not by babysitter rules, not by Ruby's rules. She looks at the pirate flag man on the side of the can. The poison man. He is bad, bad, bad, and she is scared. But she is more scared of Kitty.

She carries the can over to the doorway between the kitchen and the dining room and kneels down. When she looks close she sees dirt and salt and seeds and bits of things in the thin space between the linoleum and the carpet.

The can is very heavy, and she doesn't think she can pour any Drano into the cap. Not without spilling it. So she tips the can upside down three times, then opens it. There is milky Drano on the inside of the cap. She carefully dips in each nail and pushes them, one by one, under the edge of the dining room carpet. It is hard to push them all the way in, and the two in the middle go crooked and cross over each other a little.

"This is a protectin' hand," she says out loud to the nails. Now she needs a prayer, but not a bedtime prayer. A dining room prayer. She thinks hard for a minute, then says, "For what we are about to receive may we be truly thankful amen." Then she puts the Drano back under the sink and washes her hands three times with soap, just to make sure.

Ruby gets there at noon. She gives Mary Louise a quick hug and a smile, and then tells her to scoot until dinnertime, because she has to vacuum and do the kitchen floor and polish the silver. Mary Louise wants to ask Ruby about magic things, but she scoots.

Ruby is mashing potatoes in the kitchen when Kitty comes home. Mary Louise sits in the corner of the breakfast nook, looking at the comics in the paper, still waiting for Ruby to be less busy and come and talk to her. Kitty puts her purse down and goes into the den. Mary Louise hears the rattle of ice cubes. A minute later, Kitty comes into the kitchen. Her glass has an inch of brown liquid in it. Her eyes have an angry look.

"Mary Louise, go to your room. I need to speak to Ruby in private."

Mary Louise gets up without a word and goes into the

hall. But she does not go upstairs. She opens the basement door silently and pulls it almost shut behind her. She stands on the top step and listens.

"Ruby, I'm afraid I'm going to have to let you go," says Kitty. Mary Louise feels her armpits grow icy cold and her eyes begin to sting.

"Ma'am?"

"You've been drinking."

"No, ma'am. I ain't—"

"Don't try to deny it. I know you coloreds have a weakness for it. That's why Mr. Whittaker and I keep the cabinet in the den locked. For your own good. But when I went in there, just now, I found the cabinet door open. I cannot have servants in my house that I do not trust. Is that clear?"

"Yes, ma'am."

Mary Louise waits for Ruby to say something else, but there is silence.

"I will pay you through the end of the week, but I think it's best if you leave after dinner tonight." There is a rustling and the snap of Kitty's handbag opening. "There," she says. "I think I've been more than generous, but of course I cannot give you references."

"No, ma'am," says Ruby.

"Very well. Dinner at six. Set two places. Mary Louise will eat with me." Mary Louise hears the sound of Kitty's heels marching off, then the creak of the stairs going up. There is a moment of silence, and the basement door opens.

Ruby looks at Mary Louise and takes her hand. At the bottom of the stairs she sits, and gently pulls Mary Louise down beside her.

"Miss Mouse? You got somethin you want to tell me?"

Mary Louise hangs her head.

"You been in your Daddy's liquor?"

A tiny nod. "I didn't *drink* any. I just gave my bag a little. The Vernor's was flat and I was afraid the magic wouldn't work. I put the key back. I guess I forgot to lock the door."

"I guess you did."

"I'll tell Kitty it was me," Mary Louise says, her voice on the edge of panic. "You don't have to be fired. I'll tell her."

"Tell her what, Miss Mouse? Tell her you was puttin your daddy's whiskey on a conjure hand?" Ruby shakes her head. "Sugar, you listen to me. Miz Kitty thinks I been drinkin, she just fire me. But she find out I been teachin you black juju magic, she gonna call the po-lice. Better you keep quiet, hear?"

"But it's not fair!"

"Maybe it is, maybe it ain't." Ruby strokes Mary Louise's hair and smiles a sad smile, her eyes as gentle as her hands. "But, see, after she talk to me that way, ain't no way I'm gonna keep workin for Miz Kitty nohow. It be okay, though. My money hand gonna come through. I can feel it. Already startin to, maybe. The Ford plant's hirin again, and my husband's down there today, signin up. Maybe when I gets home, he's gonna tell me good news. May just be."

"You can't *leave* me!" Mary Louise cries.

"I got to. I got my own life."

"Take me with you."

"I can't, sugar." Ruby puts her arms around Mary Louise. "Poor Miss Mouse. You livin in this big old house with nice things all 'round you, 'cept nobody nice to you. But angels watchin out for you. I b'lieve that. Keep you safe till you big enough to make your own way, find your real kin."

"What's kin?"

"Fam'ly. Folks you belong to."

"Are you my kin?"

"Not by blood, sugar. Not hardly. But we're heart kin, maybe. 'Cause I love you in my heart, and I ain't never gonna forget you. That's a promise." Ruby kisses Mary Louise on the forehead and pulls her into a long hug. "Now since Miz Kitty already give me my pay, I 'spect I oughta go up, give her her dinner. I reckon you don't want to eat with her?"

"No."

"I didn't think so. I'll tell her you ain't feelin well, went on up to bed. But I'll come downstairs, say good-bye, 'fore I leave." Ruby stands up and looks fondly down at Mary Louise. "It'll be okay, Miss Mouse. There's miracles every day. Why, last Friday, they put a fella up in space. Imagine that? A man up in space? So ain't nothin impossible, not if you wish just hard as you can. Not if you believe." She rests her hand on Mary Louise's head for a moment, then walks slowly up the stairs and back into the kitchen.

Mary Louise sits on the steps and feels like the world is crumbling around her. This is not how the story is supposed to end. This is not happily ever after.

She cups her tiny hand around the damp, sticky bag under her arm and closes her eyes and thinks about everything that Ruby has told her. She wishes for the magic to be real.

And it is. There are no sparkles, no gold. This is basement magic, deep and cool. Power that has seeped and puddled, gathered slowly, beneath the notice of queens, like the dreams of small awkward girls. Mary Louise believes with all her heart, and finds the way to her mouse self.

Mouse sits on the bottom step for a minute, a tiny creature with a round pink tail and fur the color of new rust. She blinks her blue eyes, then scampers off the step and across the basement floor. She is quick and clever, scurrying along the baseboards, seeking familiar smells, a small ball of blue flannel trailing behind her.

When she comes to the burnt-orange coat hanging inches from the floor, she leaps. Her tiny claws find purchase in the nubby fabric, and she climbs up to the pocket, wriggles over and in. Mouse burrows into a pale cotton hankie that smells of girl tears and wraps herself tight around the flannel ball that holds her future. She puts her pink nose down on her small pink paws and waits for her true love to come.

* * *

Kitty sits alone at the wide mahogany table. The ice in her drink has melted. The kitchen is only a few feet away, but she does not get up. She presses the buzzer beneath her feet, to summon Ruby. The buzzer sounds in the kitchen. Kitty waits. Nothing happens. Impatient, she presses on the buzzer with all her weight. It shifts, just a fraction of an inch, and its wire presses against the two lye-tipped nails that have crossed it. The buzzer shorts out with a hiss. The current, diverted from its path to the kitchen, returns to Kitty. She begins to twitch, as if she were covered in stinging ants, and her eyes roll back in her head. In a gesture that is both urgent and awkward, she clutches at the table-cloth, pulling it and the dishes down around her. Kitty Whittaker, a former Miss Bloomfield Hills, falls to her knees and begins to howl wordlessly at the Moon.

Downstairs, Ruby hears the buzzer, then a crash of dishes. She starts to go upstairs, then shrugs. She takes off her white uniform for the last time. She puts on her green skirt and her cotton blouse, leaves the white Keds under the sink, puts on her flat black shoes. She looks in the clothes chute, behind the furnace, calls Mary Louise's name, but there is no answer. She calls again, then, with a sigh, puts on her nubby orange outdoor coat and pulls the light string. The basement is dark behind her as she opens the door and walks out into the soft spring evening.

The Tales of Zanthias

Robert Sheckley

Robert Sheckley [www.sheckley.com] lives in Portland, Oregon. A satirist even better known for his short stories than his novels, he has been writing since the early 1950s, and is one of the classic SF writers of the last five decades. His hundreds of wild, ironic, and stylistically graceful stories over the years tend to combine elements from a variety of genres: fantasy, science fiction, detective, and even conspiracy theory. He is known as a master of the plotted story, the kind that ends with a satisfying turn of events. He wrote "The Seventh Victim," which was the basis for the sixties' movie The Tenth Victim, *starring Marcello Mastroianni and Ursula Andress. Many of his stories are collected in* Citizen in Space, Can You Feel Anything When I Do This?, *and seven other books. He has written sixty-five books. His most recent stories have been appearing with some regularity in* Fantasy & Science Fiction *for the last few years.*

"The Tale of Zanthias" appeared in Weird Tales, *and is one of several Sheckley stories published in the last year or so using supernatural and fairy tale motifs. It takes place in a part of hell, and all the characters are therefore dead, including the werewolf.*

I knew I had to get down to the train station and meet the new people. They would probably arrive today, frightened, unsure of themselves, clumsy, some of them apathetic, others manic, apt to do themselves and others an injury. It's my job to calm them down, tell them what they need to know, welcome them to the village. Help them to find their own scenes.

But as strong as that inclination was in me, first I had to make a thorough search for my wife, Rosamund. When I woke up this morning, she was not in the bed with me. She was not in the house. I didn't know where she was.

I decided to seek out Tom the Cobbler, who always seemed up on the latest gossip. He wasn't at his cobbler's shop, so I looked for him at the livery stables, where I knew he frequently went to look for a horse, though what he needed one for I don't know. He wasn't at the stables, so I went to Ma Barker's Saloon & Luncheonette at the end of town, and sure enough, Tom was there, sitting in a booth in the back with three of his cronies.

They all greeted me pleasantly enough—"Ah, Zanthias, how good to see you today—" Greetings to which I nodded, since they needed no more acknowledgement than that. One of them was a zombie, and he quickly finished his beer and left almost at once. He must have known that it is improper for zombies to be in the village, though I have made no direct law against it. The other two men soon said they had errands to attend to, made their excuses and left.

"Tom," I said, once the others were gone, "Have you seen Rosamund this morning?"

He gave a guilty start. "No, Zanthias, I have not seen her for the last several days. Is she missing?"

"I believe she is," I said. "I need to find her as soon as possible. She is not well, you know."

"Really? I am sorry to hear that. A minor indisposition?"

Tom was making too much conversation now, and he knew, or should have known, that I am not one for idle chatter. If Tom did not know, or was unwilling to say, there was no sense wasting time asking anyone else. I would have to search in the places where she might be.

"Don't forget," Tom said, "the new people are supposed to arrive today."

"I remembered. But thank you."

The new people! Isn't that just the way life always goes in a village like ours? You drift along, nothing much happens, you do what you have to do . . . and suddenly your wife is missing and you have to get down to the train station to meet the new people. Your boring life has fallen apart and suddenly become unbearably crowded.

But that's how life goes in this village of ours. That it is a place of punishment seems to have been understood by everyone from the start. But wasn't that self-judgment on the villages' part? What terrible deeds had these villagers to atone for? Even I, Zanthias, the brightest among them, and, in a way, the most twisted, was a good person most of the time. The village can be called a place of punishment only in regard to self-viewed values, which take as punishment any state that is not actively pleasurable. What right-thinking person would use that as his or her standard for excellence? Of myself, at least I can say, I was not guilty of the sin of passivity.

But what about the unearthly creatures, you ask? The zombies, the calibans, the witches, the ghosts? I reply that we do not know what they are doing here, and it is not my intention to try to elucidate the cosmic scheme that placed them. I am only trying to deal in simple logic here. The village and its conditions by any standard are not so bad. Not for unearthly creatures, if that's what zombies and calibans are. Perhaps they are a sort of way station on their way to somewhere else, life by life, place by place. Is this the cosmic scheme? How would I know?

I told Tom to keep the new people at the station if they arrived before I got back. Then I went home, put on my stout hiking boots, took my walking stick, and set out to find Rosamund.

All this time I was wondering how she could have gotten out of bed and left the house without waking me up. I am normally a light sleeper, I always have an ear open for sounds of distress from the townspeople. I am always ready to get out and save them from what would usually be their own foolishness.

Now I walked down the road toward the communal cornfield. There was someone standing there. I saw it was the scarecrow.

When Rosamund came to our village, it had been winter. Snow lay on the ground and on the branches of the trees. There were icicles hanging from the eaves. Horses moved slowly, and you could see their breath. There was frost on the pumpkins.

Overhead, the skies were leaden gray, punctuated by dark clouds when storms swept in. Day and night, an icy wind blew in from the north.

Some days the skies would lighten, a hint of sun would appear, and the villagers would think that winter was over at last. But always, next day, the skies darkened again, the angry storm clouds returned, the north wind piped up, and winter was still here.

When Rosamund came, the change was evident the very next day. The skies lightened, patches of blue appeared. The north wind veered to the west. Little green plants began to thrust their way out of the snow cover, and the snow itself began to melt. Day after day the climate grew milder and fairer, and each day there was more sun.

Although Rosamund was a beautiful woman, she was much more than that. I saw from the start that she was something special. I spent time with her, I courted her in my fashion, which was neglectful but persistent. I provided for her comfort to the best of my abilities, and overwhelmed her with my attentions. Given what she found in the village, it is no wonder that she chose me, and that we were married.

Those were good days in the village. Life was, if not positively good, at least not entirely bad.

And now she had disappeared.

I came up to the scarecrow, set on his pole, his arms flapping in the breeze.

"Good morning, Edward," I said. "Have you seen Rosamund?"

He couldn't speak, of course. But he could indicate. One of his boneless arms, guided by a salient impulse from the quick West wind, pointed in the direction of the witches' house, over toward the Mountain.

"Thank you, Edward."

We are quite punctilious here in our speech. Although Edward was a scarecrow with no brains at all, he was also an indicator of recent events, and, when you spoke to him politely, he was willing to point the way. Just because he has no discernible personality was no reason to treat him as if he didn't exist.

I continued toward the witches' house, and I was thinking, not for the first time, that the region in which I live is a strange realm. There are mountains and marshes and moors, and all are haunted by something or some things. And you can't get away from here to some place different.

You can hike across the mountains, come down into a distant valley, and it's just the same as the one you left. Oh, there are minor differences—some regions have smaller mountains, some bigger. Some have more marsh than forest, and others have other differences. But they all have the essentials—the same regions, the same people, the same problems, the same deaths.

In these other towns, however, you don't have a person who corresponds to me and who fills my role. The other villages don't have leaders. I have visited five of them, and they all contain masterless men and women, with no leader or ruler to look out for them, to help them. And they don't help each other.

I could expand my rule, to these other towns. But why should I? This one village gives me enough trouble, and has the same potentiality for pleasure as the others.

What are we doing here? Most of the villagers are not what you'd call good people. They raven, they kill, they are merciless in their hungers. But what about me? Here I am, and I have appointed myself guardian over these people. But why did someone or something put me here in the first place? I am not one of the undead, I am not a ghoul, and I am not a victim. So what am I doing here?

The answer I get is not forthcoming. Any way I look at it, I am either here to punish or to be punished. Since I don't know the answer, sometimes I do the one and sometimes the other.

I went along the trail through the woods that led to the witches' house. Rosamund might have spent the night with the witch. There was no reason for it, but it was possible.

The faint trail through the woods led me through tall trees with intertwining branches, and twisted twigs that coiled around each other like dead men's fingers. The sun, coming out from behind clouds, and shining through the innumerable spider webs that covered the topmost layer of forest's branches, suffused the place with a sort of pearly opalescence. I didn't see any spiders, though. I've heard that some of the larger spiders hunt songbirds. I have no objection to that. The spiders belong here, too. Let nature do what it needs to do. We who are people know more than to guide ourselves by nature's practices.

I had to pass through the swamp on my way to the witches' house. The swamp lies all about the forest, and even coexists with a part of it. The waters of the swamp are gluey, and they have a stagnant smell. It is filled with the bodies of dead men. The crowns of their heads just break the surface of the water. With a little agility, you can step from head to head, and scarcely get your feet wet.

Occasionally a head will roll around and try to bite you on the foot. A swift kick takes care of that. You don't have to kick too hard—they get the idea at once, and anyhow, can feel no pain. Their vengeful volition must be checked, however, since it does themselves and others no good. That sort of behavior is not how I want to run my village.

Just before I reached the shore, a caliban came swimming up. He was shaking his head vehemently and pointing. The calibans, despite their urgent need to communicate, are unable to speak. They are the size of dwarves, physically indistinguishable from humans except that their tongues are too big for their mouths. Once I examined the body of one; his head was human-size, but his tongue could have belonged to a cow, and it was crammed too tightly in his mouth, impeding his breathing, which he didn't need to do anyhow, since breathing, like eating, is one of those affectations from a previous existence that we still preserve when we can. But the calibans suffer from a condition we cannot treat. I have often wondered at the cruelty of whoever sent such creatures here, to this place where we have no medical facilities and no tradition of doctoring.

You never know what these caliban creatures are referring to, but I went in the direction he indicated. Sure enough, he had been directing me to a young suicide, lying face down in the marshy mud, her long hair streaming. It was not Rosamund, however. I recognized this woman as one of the recent arrivals—a skinny little thing, with peculiar, simple ways—not pretty enough find a mate, not smart enough to set up as a witch, not skilled enough to do anything beyond simple chores. I used to give her food from time to time to let her know she wasn't alone; even though she was.

She'd had no friends, no children, no mate. . . . And she had finally come to this. Despair can drive even the most phlegmatic among us to this final deed. This death would probably be for keeps, because, as far as I knew, she would never be brought back, never resuscitated, never reborn, suicide seems to be final.

I went on. Soon I was back on firm land, and a little while after that I was standing on the little pavestone walk which led to the witches' house.

The house itself had been constructed on a craggy ledge just in front of the peak of the hill on which it sat. The house rose story by story into the mist-streaked sky, and its proportions were quaint, childlike, and sinister. Its narrow stories and excesses of gingerbread decoration as good as told you this place was unwholesome.

The witch came out on her third floor balcony.

"Rosamund? She was going to come by for a cup of tea and a chat. But she never came. Search the place if you like!"

I didn't bother. But I would need to find out later how Rosamund and the witch had become friends. We villagers don't associate with witches or any of the other supernatural and undead things that are also sent here. We pretend not to notice the demons and zombies, the dwarves and snow-giants. We are men, and where we come from, the existence of these creatures is not proven, so it would not be seemly to chat with them as though they were real.

Rosamund and the witch . . . I didn't like it. Anybody here can do what they like, but I do require them to tell the truth. Rosamund hadn't mentioned this rendezvous, and by omission had concealed it from me. I didn't like that.

I continued down to the Haunted Meadows. A zombie was standing at its edge. He was very tall and skinny, dressed in torn rags, his skin leaden, with that vague unfocused look zombies have.

I asked him, "Have you seen Rosamund?"

He stared at me with his dead eyes, trying to make me out. They can do it if they try. There's very little he could do about his interior blankness, but he managed to make sense of my words. I could almost feel his rotted brain working, and then a slow shaking of his head—no, he hadn't seen her—and then he shambled off in the direction of the swamp. I have it on good authority that zombies gather in the swamp and hunt for toads, and other unclean things. I do not try to control them.

I stood there on the sodden ground and I tried to think where to look next. My own knowledge of the village and its surrounds, usually my secure possession, suddenly became vague and blurry. I knew I was experiencing stress, and it was coming out as loss of memory. Where had I not looked? Was there a Demon Walk going up the mountain, and if so, should I examine it? Was there a sacrificial cave just beyond the mountain's peak? Or had I dreamed all that? Or made it up? I was unsure.

But there was one thing I knew: that I had to be at the train depot to greet the new arrivals.

I took the shortcut around the old Haunted House. The place was falling apart, and in the front yard I could see two ghosts, a man and a woman, and they were reclining in deck chairs, enjoying the sun. They were smiling at one another. I wondered if they were in a state of bliss, and how I might get there myself.

I turned past the Haunted House to the Train Depot at Town Square.

The train was just pulling in and the villagers had gathered. I put myself at the head of the welcoming delegation. The train halted in a paroxysm of black coal smoke. The conductors in their black uniforms and dark glasses let down the steps, and the new arrivals began coming off.

How forlorn and innocent they appeared. Women in ragged woolen shawls, men in old dark overcoats, all of them clutching suitcases. A child was carrying a bird cage almost as large as she was. A young man was holding a radio-tv set; he didn't know yet that we don't get any stations here.

When they were all on the platform, I addressed them.

"Welcome to the Village," I said. "After I have spoken, you will be permitted to walk through the town. There are several unoccupied houses and apartments. The available houses have small square green signs in front of them. You may live in any house that's not occupied. For those of you who can't find a house, we have apartments. That big building opposite the Depot is an apartment building. People will be waiting there to help you find a vacant apartment. After you have moved in, come down to the Community Kitchen, which is the large red building on the other side of the tracks. We will serve you a welcoming dinner. Food is not strictly necessary here, but it is always a pleasure to eat it. Tomorrow, any one will point you to the Bulletin Board. There are posted jobs, and you are invited to take one. That's all, and, again, welcome to the Village."

They clustered around me with many questions, but I told them they knew all they needed to know for the present.

It was then that I saw Amy. I didn't know her name then, of course. Only that there was something special about her, something beautiful, a quality that reminded me of Rosamund, though it was difficult to say how. She didn't look like Rosamund, who had been small and skinny with neat blonde hair, whereas Amy was on the ample side, with thick, curly dark hair. Nor were the features similar. But there was something . . .

"Miss," I called out to her. "May I speak to you for a moment?"

"Of course. You are the one called Zanthias, are you not?"

"Yes. But how did you know?"

"Oh, you are known, even quite famous. They say you keep this village in good order. I am Amy. Is there something I can do for you?"

"You can help me find my wife, Rosamund, and give me a chance to get to know you better."

"With pleasure." She fell into step beside me.

Like Rosamund, she exuded a sense of aliveness and goodness; it seemed to me she lit up the place where she stood.

As we walked along, the sky grew still lighter, until it was entirely blue. The sun came out and shone strongly, even fiercely. Snow disappeared from the ground and was replaced by grass. I could even see the ice cap on the mountain shrink a bit. And when we came to the river, it was no longer fed by melting snow, and was now safe to cross.

I had a feeling as we walked along that all the natural creatures in the village, that is, all the human beings, must have noticed the change, though not being of a communicative turn of mind, they no doubt failed to discuss it with each other. But that didn't matter, they all knew anyway.

And as for unnatural creatures, the ghouls and zombies, the chæimras, the calibans, the ghosts, the living dead in the swamp, well, I believe they were aware of it too. And no doubt they rejoiced in it to the extent their natures allowed.

We walked up the meadow covered with asphodel that led to Last Chance Mountain. Its peak, sheathed in ice, glittered high above us. We climbed steadily, but had to slow down once we reached the ice fields. Then we saw something colored a dirty white, striding purposefully across the field above us.

"What's that?" Amy asked.

"A snow demon," I said.

Something else moved, a dark brown shape higher on the mountain. "And that?"

"A yeti."

"Are they dangerous?" Amy asked.

"Not unless you tease them," I said.

"Are we going all the way to the top?" she asked.

I shook my head. "To a cave just below the top."

"What is in the cave?"

"Rosamund, I fear."

As we climbed to the cave I was thinking that if Rosamund was dead, as I now feared her to be, then this young Amy might make a good wife. I realized my thinking was doubtless premature, with Rosamund not yet proven dead. But I was not too shocked at my own thoughts. You get a bit cold and calculating when you've lived here long enough. You look out for what future you can have. I knew I was cold and calculating. Perhaps the village shaped me to that; but I suppose it's possible I brought in the quality with me.

I observed Amy as we climbed the icy rock face. She was agile and strong, and uncomplaining. I wondered why she had sought me out at the beginning. But I was pretty sure I knew the answer. I had been the person in charge, the man who knew what everyone should do. And, although I try not to claim too much for myself, I was obviously the only decent man among them all, the biggest, the strongest, the brightest. Why shouldn't she choose me?

We reached the entrance to the cave. This place had been used in the past for human sacrifices to the gods of this place. Torsos and hip bones were scattered on the ground of the cave. It was bitterly cold. Further in, long slender stalactites hung from the cave's room, and glittered in what light filtered through from the entrance.

As we moved into the cave, I felt a strange sense of exhilaration. Maybe it had something to do with the time of day. It was past sunset now, and the moon was coming up. Big and broad, it was the second night of the full moon. I glanced over my shoulder and saw it behind me just before I entered the cave. Amy seemed smaller as she scuttled in behind me. As we moved into the cave, crouched to pass beneath the stalactites, I felt the bones of my jaw shift, felt a lengthening movement in my forehead. My fingernails grew and narrowed and curled. I felt very good. But suddenly I remembered last night with Rosamund, and I was flooded with contrary emotions. Shame, for one, and sort of proud defiance for another. Shame at my own deeds, deeper shame at not remembering them now when the moon was full again; and also defiance at my own shame, And yet a part of me denied this knowledge and its implications, for I knew that most of the time I was a good man who helped others. What right, then, did the fates have to make me a werewolf?

I was starting to feel sorry for myself, and to feel a rage at that sorrow, and to feel a growing appetite rise in me. I looked around for Amy.

She had run ahead of me. She was standing now on the little altar. She was holding something in her hand—a piece of rope that went up to the cave's ceiling.

"Do you see Rosamund now?" she shrieked at me. "She's down in the pit there, where you tumbled her after killing her."

I was shocked at her words, but somehow I had also been expecting them.

"It was her own fault," I said. "She should never have left the house."

"And spend the rest of her life wondering when you would tear her apart at full moon? Rosamund had more spirit than that. She came here to make her preparations for you. But you found her before she had a chance to defend herself."

"Stop talking so wildly," I said. "We will go back to the village."

"Go back with you? Never!"

I lunged toward her. She pulled the rope and jumped back out of my way. Heavy sharp things pierced my body. I fell, and found I was pinned down by stalactites.

"Well, give us a hand, girl," I said. "It's not serious. I can't be killed, you know. Not like this, at any rate."

"There are some people here to see you," she said.

"What are you talking about? I do not choose to give an audience at this time!"

"They insist," she said.

And then they filed in front of me, the villagers, all of them, even the old witch, even the zombies, even the calibans, even the ghosts.

Tom carried the wooden stake, Amy positioned it above my chest. And each villager who came by, natural or supernatural, gave the top of the stake a tap.

It wasn't much force. But it was enough to drive the stake through my chest. I began to experience my dying. It was an uncanny feeling.

Amy began to address the villagers, to point out the moral of the story, no doubt. But I didn't hear that part. I was dead.

There is another version. This one was put together by the villagers, and doesn't have the important addition of Zanthias's point of view. In the interest of honesty, I present it now.

In this version, Zanthias never went to the sacrificial cave, and its very existence has been denied. In this version, Zanthias turned a corner and there in front of him was his own house.

"What are we doing here?" he asked.

"This is where Rosamund is," Amy said. "No sense wasting any more time."

They entered. And Amy said, "She is there, in the room you told her never to enter."

"Now wait a minute. This is wandering too far afield—"

"It will wander farther yet," Amy said. "Open the door and look at what you never thought to look at before."

Zanthias opened the door. There was a bed and a woman on it, Rosamund, bloodstained, dead.

"Now wait a minute," Zanthias said. "I never . . ."

"Spare me your lies," Amy said. "Over there is Rosamund's suitcase, which you might have examined, had you cared to."

Zanthias opened the chest. Inside he found bundles of

letters, tied together with lavender ribbon. He found a mirror, and when he looked at his own face in it, he saw written on it, the words—*Totally and unforgiving self-preoccupied.*

He was staring at the mirror when the wooden stake went into his back, through it and penetrated his chest, its point sticking out.

"I love you!" he cried, falling to the ground.

"I take my revenge. Rosamund didn't have time. I complete her work for her."

I am Tom, and I will have the last word.

The werewolf Zanthias was found dead the next day by foresters from the village. He was in a sacrificial cave high on Stark Mountain, with a wooden stake through his heart. The new arrival Amy was questioned about this, since she was the last to see Zanthias. She said Zanthias had invited her to his house, where she had spent the night. She had no idea where Zanthias went at night or what he did. We accepted this, since there was no evidence to the contrary.

We also learned that Amy was a sister to Zanthias's previous wife, Rosamund, also found dead in the cave, apparently killed by Zanthias the previous night. We don't often get people related to one another coming to our village.

Life goes on quietly in the absence of Zanthias, who was a good ruler, albeit a trifle absent-minded about his monthly forays at the full moon. We expect another werewolf to be sent to us in the next shipment of new people. It seems to be the custom.

Of Soil and Climate

Gene Wolfe

Gene Wolfe lives in Barrington, Illinois, and is widely considered the most accomplished writer in the fantasy and science fiction genres. His four-volume Book of the New Sun *is an acknowledged masterpiece. He has published many fantasy, science fiction, and horror stories over the last thirty years and more, and has been given the World Fantasy Award for Life Achievement. Each year he publishes a few short stories, of which at least one is among the best of the year. Collections of his short fiction (all in print) include* The Island of Dr. Death and Other Stories and Other Stories, Storeys from the Old Hotel, Endangered Species, *and* Strange Travelers. *The big fantasy news for 2003 was the publication of* The Knight, *the first volume of a major fantasy work,* The Wizard Knight *(the final volume,* The Wizard, *will appear late in 2004).*

"Of Soil and Climate" appeared in Realms of Fantasy. *It is a dream fantasy that revives and reinvigorates the "life is a dream" idea. A psychiatrist in jail for a crime he cannot recall finds himself a hero in a fantasy world, saving damsels from monsters. This is Wolfe writing at least partly in the heroic mode of* The Wizard Knight, *though clearly in a different fantasy world. The complexities of the ending are somewhat clearer if you read the opening again immediately after finishing the story.*

I have been looking into the crystal and have seen myself. I am tempted to put quotation marks about that last word, but I shall not. Is the self I have seen in crystal NOT the self I feel myself to be? Very likely it is. Very likely this second dubious self is someone else, an accessory to nothing—or so I would like to believe. But really now? There is no evidence for that.

I wonder what Jung would say? How I would love to know! Might it be possible? Hmmm! Could I summon up his spirit and question him? I may well attempt the experiment, although it would be dangerous.

What my dear Estar says—what Her Royal Highness the Most Puissant Princess Plenipotentiary says—I know already. "That's not you."

And yet, the face. It's the face I shaved for years, in my prison hospital office.

I cannot hear through the crystal, yet I know what is being said. It is all so terribly, awfully familiar.

Me (motioning toward the couch): "We don't have to use that. To tell you the truth, they only let me have it in here because so many patients expect it. If you'd rather sit the way you are now and just tell me, that's fine."

He (squirming): "I'll stay here."

Me: "Good. It's actually very comfortable, though. That leather's as soft as a glove, and it's nicely upholstered. To confess, I have napped there sometimes. Now let's begin. What's troubling you, Jim?"

Jim: "When I was a kid . . . think you ought to know this to start with, Doc. I always felt like everybody was, you know, shutting me out. . . ."

Me: "Yes?"

Jim: "I wasn't, you know, very good at anything. Baseball or anything."

Me: "Neither was I."

Jim: "I—I watched a lot of TV."

Me: "You feel that led you to your present difficulties?"

Jim: "Uh . . . No. Maybe it really would be better if I could lie down."

And so on. It will not do to be contemptuous of these men, and now that I find myself as I am, a head taller than anyone, with a sword at my side, I find myself less tempted to contempt.

Which is good. If I watch the crystal long enough will I not see myself in the office of some other psychiatrist? Perhaps my patients—but no. I am here. A stroke, perhaps?

Later. The bird has returned. The Armies of Night are mobilizing. We were fools not to attack while the sun was up—but we were such fools, and there is no point in denial. I could have ridden. With what? Half the Palace Guard, 20 or 30 other men-at-arms, and a few boys. Or a dozen men-at-arms. Half a dozen. We would have been wiped out in the Pass of Tears if not before. Perhaps after this . . .

If there is any "after this."

The light had awakened him. He had yawned and stretched, blinked in the sunshine, and wondered where he was. Wondered with the comforting certainty that he would soon remember.

A certainty that had proved entirely unfounded. There were no bars, and there was no cot. The horrors of imprisonment had vanished, and with them the certainty of regular meals, books, and the Net. He had slept in fern, in a cool and shadowy place where a beetling cliff held off the sun. The sun was setting. . . .

He squinted up at it: half down the sky. It might, he told himself, be midmorning instead; he knew that it was not. There was a warm, sleepy feel to the air that could not have come before late afternoon.

How did you tell time save by looking at the sun? He glanced at his wrist. Numbers? Why weren't there numbers there?

There were none, and he began to walk. Surely numbers were attached, somehow, to the gauging of time.

A tree of a species he did not know stood at the edge of the clearing, a graceful tree with light gray bark and leaves that turned copper when the wind blew. He paused to admire it.

"You'll need a sword."

Who had spoken? He saw no one until a slender girl in russet silk stepped from behind the tree. "You'll need a sword," she repeated. "I know of one. I'd better not leave my husband to show you where it is, but I can tell you."

"How do you know I'll need a sword?" The question amused him because he had never expected to say anything of the sort.

There was no slender girl, only the slender tree. I'm hallucinating, he thought. I've never done that in my life, always been less interested in patients' hallucinations than I should have been. This is fascinating.

He walked for miles, south as well as he could judge. His clothes, he discovered, had no pockets (like the orange jumpsuits) but the purse on his belt held two small coins, and there was a knife on his belt as well, a short, single-edged knife with a broad, thick blade.

A phallic symbol? He had never really given much credence to those.

It was a good, sharp phallic symbol in any event; he used it very carefully to open nuts he brought down by throwing sticks. The nutmeat was small but good; the nuts large and satanically hard. He nicked a finger in spite of all his care, and walked on.

The sun was almost down when he found the road, a faint dirt road such as men make for themselves where the county will not make a road for them, a single, narrow, dusty track. It revived his optimism, and he followed it with enthusiasm, up a low hill and into a deep valley where the declining sun was lost behind wilder, more ragged hills, so that his own steps brought evening.

For hours after that he followed the road still, by starlight and moonlight. The moon, a small and pearl-like moon as round as a button, set; another rose, larger and holding a leering face. Leering or not, it shed more light and he resolved to press on.

Animals that were not wolves howled and bellowed in the forest to either side. As he passed a lightning-blasted tree, he heard a roar he felt certain had come from the throat of a tiger.

At last there came a time when he could walk no longer. He sat down, careless of where he landed, and pulled off the soft boots and sodden woolen stockings. His feet had blistered. They hurt, and were infinitely tired. His legs ached and throbbed so that, exhausted though he was, whole minutes passed before he slept.

The light woke him, or nothing. Twilight—nearly night, he thought. Or dawn, perhaps. Dawn seemed more likely. The sun was out of sight behind the hills. He began to walk again, saw a lightning-blasted tree, and turned about. He had been that way, and there was nothing save big trees robed in moss.

Far away, a tiger roared.

The road wound deeper and deeper into the valley, and it was night. Very near, just around the next bend, a woman screamed.

He was running toward it even as he told himself that he must run away from it. She screamed again, stirring an instinct he had not known he possessed. A dark form bent above—what? A bundle of rags? A mossy trunk? He saw the flash of fangs, plunged the short blade into something that was not quite a boar, and was thrown backward. He kicked with both feet and somehow managed to regain those feet.

A half-clothed, frantic woman thrust a cudgel at him. He seized it and struck the beast, great blows with a four-foot stick as heavy as iron, blows each of which would have killed a man. It fled at last, but not before he had felt its claws.

It was twilight when he woke again, and a woman held his head in her lap and sang, the wordless crooning of wind in treetops. He sat up, weak, sore, and sick.

"I heal," she told him. "There is a spring whose waters give strength." With her help he got to his feet, steadying himself with the broken limb with which he had beaten the beast. She wept beside him; he longed to comfort her and tried to as clumsily as any other man.

The spring rose among rocks; it was deep, or at least the light of a small and pearl-like moon made it appear so. He drank and drank, and it was cold and pure and good, and it did indeed make him stronger, as she had promised. "I lost some blood, I think," he said.

She nodded without speaking. Her robe of green velvet left a shoulder bare.

"Did it hurt you?"

"She killed my husband." The woman in the green velvet robe shrugged, and he knew her sorrow was too deep for words.

"We'll bury him," he said.

She shook her head. "He would not have wanted that. What he would have wanted is what he now has, to lie in the forest until Nature returns him to the soil. In time, new growth may spring from his root. I hope so."

He stared at her for a moment, then recalled that David had sprung from the root of Jesse. "What will you do now?"

"Follow you." She glanced at the heavy limb with which he had routed the beast. "As long as you have that, and longer. If I try to go with you, will you drive me away? Throw things?"

"Of course not." He picked up the limb and examined the ragged breaks at its ends; he could scarcely see them, so deep was the twilight, and his fingers told him more than his eyes. "This could use trimming," he said. "I think I left my knife in that animal, whatever it was, but it may have fallen out. If you'd rather stay here while I go back to look for it . . . ?"

She shook her head, putting her arm through his. She smelled earthy and sweet, he thought, an odor he associated with Boy Scouts and camping out. It was a clean perfume he had not smelled in a long, long time and was happy to greet again.

He could not have found the place without her, a fact he admitted to himself long before they came upon it. "It might be better if we wait 'til sunup," he said. "I doubt that we can find my knife in the dark, even if it's here."

"If you want to lie down, I will lie with you gladly," she told him, "but the sun will not rise for many rains."

"Then I want to lie down," he said. "I'm so tired I've stopped being hungry."

"Rest. I will weep for my husband first."

He did not, but followed her to a fallen tree a few steps away.

She knelt beside it. "They strip away the bark to eat," she said, "and when the tree is ringed, he dies."

A tear fell on his hand, and he put his arm around her. She was—she has been, he told himself—a holy woman in some strange cult in which girls who had been taught to accept such things were married to trees. That seemed plain enough, but he found it hard to imagine a place where such things happened. Where was he, in California? And how had he gotten here?

"We will rest now," she said at last.

"And I'll comfort you," he told her, to which she only nodded and wept.

She spread her gown on the ground. They lay upon it together, and it was soft, furry, and warm. When they were cuddled as one, spoon-fashion his mother would have said, her gown folded itself over them; that covering, too, was warm, furry, and soft.

For a time she wept on, but he kissed her shoulders and the back of her neck and drew her to him, and her weeping ceased.

The beast woke him, looming above him, huge and dark, not with a sound (for it was terribly silent) or the brute, dull claws that caressed his torn face, but by the animal stink of it. It was, he decided later, half ape and half bear.

"I have your knife," the beast said, "and I've cleaned it for you. I thought you'd like to have it back."

He froze, certain that he was about to receive it in the

chest; half a minute, perhaps, passed until he realized that the beast was holding it out to him in darkness.

Too numb to speak, he accepted it, pulled it gingerly below the strange stuff covering him, and returned it to its sheath.

"I was starving," the beast said. "You have to understand that. Starving, and I attacked a tree. That was all."

He spoke without thinking. "If you attacked me now, there wouldn't be much I could do."

"No," the beast said, "but you don't have to worry. I killed farther down." It paused. "We kill only when we have to eat. We're not like the Night People. Not even like you Sun People."

He was about to say that it had attacked the woman, but it vanished into the shadows before he could speak.

He slept again until the woman awakened him. They made love, and washed afterward in a small, cold creek. "Is it always night here?" he asked her.

"No," she said.

She had brought the broken limb with which he had beaten the beast; he carried it as they walked deeper into the valley. He had lost the road in the night, and they went by almost invisible forest paths.

"I don't suppose you know where we could get some breakfast?" he asked her.

She only shook her head.

"What are Sun People?"

"You are," she told him.

"Then you must be a Sun Person too."

"I am a Tree Person," she said.

A long while after that, while they were looking for a place where they could ford the river, she asked where he had come from.

"I'm not even sure," he said, and then, as if a fact that explained nothing explained everything, he added, "I'm a psychiatrist."

She nodded encouragingly; the trees were beginning to drop their leaves. One blew past her face.

"I had an office in the Brighton Hills Mall," he said. "It

was very up-scale. Everything there was very up-scale. Orthodontists and furriers, and so on. Saks. Gucci. I charged—well, it doesn't matter."

Memories flooding back.

"I went to prison. I remember now. That's what happened."

"What is prison?" she asked.

They forded the river. It seemed darker than ever on the other side, but they were going toward the light, which cheered him. Three men attacked them; he fought with the desperate courage of a man who knows he must win or die, killing two with shattering blows of the severed limb. The third fled.

He picked up the sword one had drawn against him. "A woman was going to get me a sword like this a while ago," he said, "and I didn't want it. I want it now."

"I don't like it," the woman with him told him.

He searched the dead men, finding soft, thin cakes that were not quite tortillas, and dried meat. "I don't eat that," she said when he tried to give her half.

"For Sun People?"

"They were Night People."

He ate everything, learning in the process that he was ravenous. His meal finished (it had not taken long), he picked up the sword once more and examined it. "Yesterday . . ."

Had it really been yesterday? Two days before? Three? He had gone from a changeless afternoon to an unchanging twilight.

"You said you didn't like them," he told the woman. "I didn't either. To tell you the truth, I thought they were silly. When you've needed something and not had it, you don't think it's silly anymore, I suppose. If I had a gun, I don't think I'd know what to do with it. I have a pretty good idea of what to do with this."

"I am of trees," the woman said. "That wars on trees."

"I'm flesh," he told her. "Flesh is what this wars on, not wood. I want it just the same."

The blade was somewhat discolored save where it had

been whetted sharp, as long as his arm and three fingers wide. He tried to think what that would be in inches and failed.

He made cuts in air.

"Don't," she said. "Please."

"Then I won't," he promised her. The grip was bone, the guard and pommel iron. "Do you know," he said, "I don't think I've ever told you my name, or asked yours. I'm Tuck."

"Nerys." She hesitated. "I am called Nerys. Is that a good name?"

He smiled. "Of course." She seemed to expect something more, so he held out his hand. "Pleased to meet you."

She took it, clearly uncertain as to what she was to do with it. "May I see your sword, Tuck?"

"Certainly." When she released his hand, he held out the sword, hilt first.

She took it, holding it level between them. "Have I been a good friend to you, Tuck?"

"A very good friend," he said.

"I am going to ask a favor. It is a small thing, and only one favor—the only one I will ask. Will you promise, before you hear it, to do me this favor?"

He nodded. "You have my word, Nerys. If I can do it, I will."

"You can. That club you have borne was my dead husband's arm. I have loved you doubly because you bore it, even as he. Should the bone of this sword fail, you must replace it with wood from his arm."

He was about to say that it was not likely a bone hilt would fail when he noticed that fine dust was cascading from the hand that gripped the hilt. He said, "I will—trust me," instead.

She returned the sword to him, and he looked down at the grip. It had been smooth and polished, he felt sure; it was rough now, and hairy with splinters. He rubbed it, and bone dust fell. He drew his knife, and the bone split and crumbled under the edge, falling away until nothing remained save the steel spike that held the iron pommel.

When he looked up, she had gone. He called her name and searched for her in a hundred places, and at last he sat down with the club that had served him so well and cut away the smaller end. The pommel was screwed tightly to its steel spike; he had to carve a sort of wrench of the tough wood before he could unscrew it. But he did at last, and managed, with his knife, the end of the spike, and the sharp point of the sword itself, to bore a passage for the spike through the rough wooden grip he had carved.

When the work was done and the iron pommel back in place, he felt that a full day had passed—this though the twilight seemed neither deeper nor lighter than it had been. "I must go on for a few more miles today at least," he told himself. "If I don't reach civilization soon, I'll starve." He was about to throw aside his shortened club when he felt (a deep and somehow peaceful emotion he could never have put into words) that it wished to remain.

He picked it up and ran his hands over the smooth bark, seeing it for the first time as it saw itself: a mutilated tree. He dug a hole in the soft forest loam with the blade of a larger and coarser knife the other dead man had borne, and planted the big end of the club that was no longer his in it; then he dug shallow graves for the two men, one to either side of the thick cutting he had planted, and lay them in their graves and covered them with earth, and the earth with leaves and fallen branches. When all that was accomplished (and it seemed neither darker then nor lighter) he felt that he should pray. He had never been a religious man, but he did his best.

He had dusted off his hands as well as he could and was on the point of leaving when he caught sight of the larger, coarser knife and realized that he had neglected to inter it with its owner. Unwilling to undo much of what he had only just finished, he put it through his belt.

Which was well. The beast had said it had killed; he

found its kill by the odor of rotting flesh—a child, a girl, he decided, of perhaps fourteen. Save for her eyes, her head was largely intact. Little remained of the rest but scattered bones. He collected as many as he could and began to dig, muttering, "Poor kid," over and over.

"Are you going to bury those here?" The voice was a girl's.

He looked behind him and saw her half concealed by shrubs.

"I can show you a place," there was a long pause, "that she'd like better."

"You can?" He had not looked at her as he spoke, and there was no reply. When he looked around at last, she was gone.

A dress that had once, perhaps, been ankle length had been reduced to a blood-stained rag. He gathered the bones and the head into it as well as he could, though he had been unable to find one thighbone and the other protruded no matter what he did.

Then he was ready to leave, but the girl had not returned. He decided to press forward, carrying the bones and the head, not in the hope of finding her, but to bury them when he came upon a particularly suitable spot.

The land rose, and some light returned. At last he found a hut that was almost a small house, with three plots of vegetables on three bits of almost-level land. There were roots he did not know, and beans like no beans he had ever seen that most certainly could not be eaten raw. He tasted two of the roots, and decided that he could eat the second, which he did, scraping the dirt away with his coarse knife.

Behind him, the girl's voice said, "This is where."

She stood at the door of the hut, starved and insubstantial—"Like a bad hologram," was the way he put it to himself. "There?" he said. "Right where you are now?"

"At my feet."

He nodded, knelt at her feet, and began to dig. "Did you know her?"

"I thought I did."

A hole a foot by two feet would be sufficient, he decided.

He roughed it out with the knife blade and began to deepen it. "It's cold here."

"That's me," the girl said. She sounded sad.

"You're cold?" He looked up.

"Maybe you'd give me a little blood?"

She had sounded serious. "If you mean a transfusion . . . ?"

"You could just scratch a little line on your arm." She paused, and in a moment he realized that she was trying to take a deep breath but could not breathe. "A few drops? Please?" (Another deep breath that would not come.) "I'll be your friend forever. I swear it!"

He paused, sickened by the realization that he had lost utterly the life he had once known. This was a new life, in a new place; and no child—not even she—could have been more hapless and forlorn. "Friends answer questions for their friends," he said slowly. "Will you answer questions for me? Not just one question, or two, but a great many?"

"Yes!"

"I need help," he continued, "figuring out who I am and where I am. You'll help me? As much as you possibly can?"

"*Yes!*"

"OK." He stood up and took the short, broad-bladed knife from its sheath on his belt. "This isn't sterile, I'm sure." He wiped it on his sleeve. "I wish we had some way to sterilize it. But we don't, and clean steel will have to do." Carefully and slowly, he reopened the cut in his finger.

Seconds passed before the first drops of blood appeared. When they did, she bent over the cut eagerly, not licking or sucking it as he had expected but wetting a finger and smearing her nostrils again and again. "Deeper? Please? Just a little deeper? It won't hurt you."

It stung, but he ran the sharp blade down the cut again.

She drank now. Her lips were frigid when they pressed his hand, but grew warmer—as she herself grew more real, an actual and even ordinary girl, far too thin but very much alive, just entering womanhood.

At length she straightened up. "It's stopped," she said. "I'd ask you to do it again, but I know you wouldn't. Would you?"

He shook his head.

"But you'll bury me? Please?"

"Those are your bones?"

"Of course. I—we—it's hard to explain."

He knelt to dig again. "Try."

"It's like not being able to sleep. Well, it's really not like that. It's not being able to rest. If you could dig and walk around and talk to people, and maybe plow or hoe the garden. But you could never just sit in the shade and fan yourself, or shut your eyes."

He looked up. "You're her ghost? This was you?"

"Of course."

"You live here?"

"I lived here," the ghost said. "It got to be nearly night, and the Night People started. Night comes really soon to this valley. Everybody left when the sun did except me. I had to bury Mama and get the roots in before they rotted. I never did get them all in."

"You're a Sun Person," he said, still digging. "Like me."

"No," the ghost told him, "I'm a Dead Person."

He hesitated. "You look real."

"Because of your blood. If it was sunshine here like it used to be, you'd see. I think I'll fade pretty fast anyway. But I'm grateful. It feels really good, even if it won't last."

He judged the hole deep enough, picked up her head and bones and lowered them into it, then began to replace the earth, mostly by pushing it back into the hole with his hand and the broad blade of the coarse knife. "What's your name?" he asked.

"It was Mej."

"That's short. Maybe I could put up a marker."

The ghost shook her head. "That's just so somebody can find them and dig them up again. I was born here and I died here, and this is where I stay."

"Will you disappear when I finish filling the hole?" Within himself he added, "Will I?"

"Do you want me to?"

He shook his head.

"Then I'll stay a while, but pretty soon I'll want to go someplace warmer. I don't think you will either. Why should you?"

"I used to be a psychiatrist." He stopped shoving dirt into the hole to think. "Do you know what that is?"

"Someone like you."

"Yes," he said. "Yes, that's it exactly. May I tell you?"

She nodded.

"I treated people who had sick minds. I tried to make them well. Or if I couldn't make them well, I tried to get them better, help them just a little. It was hard, very hard, but I tried hard, too, and sometimes I could make a real difference. People who had hardly been able to function at all were able to function normally sometimes. Oh, they had quirks, moments of intense fear, and so on. But they functioned better than many others, and were happy now and then. That's the most any of us can hope for, to be happy now and then."

"I was happy here," the ghost said.

He had finished filling the hole. He piled the rest of the earth on it, forming a mound that he would later tamp down. "Before your mother died, you mean."

"No, after. While I was burying her and getting in the roots. I wasn't happy when she was so sick. I couldn't be. But afterward it was just me. I could do anything I wanted. I went to bed and listened to the owls; when I woke up I lay in bed and listened to the wren and the song sparrow." She laughed, a strange but almost living sound. "Once I put bread beside the bed, so I could eat before I got up. When I got it in the morning the mice had nibbled out a place." She laughed again.

"I went to prison," he told her, "because I helped a patient too much, and my records were very important to me. My notes. I had to know what my patients had told me, so I could review it. I couldn't remember everything, so I had to write it down. My patients had to know those records would never be made public." He tried to remember what those patients had called him, Doctor Something, and finished weakly by saying, "I'm Tuck, by the way." His mother had called him Tuck.

"I'm Mej. Are you going to step on that, Tuck?"

"No," he said, "I don't believe that would be right. I'm going to pat it down with my hands."

"Thank you. I think I'll get a little sleep."

When he looked around for her again, she was no longer there. He shrugged, selected a likely vegetable from the small garden, and walked on, eating as he walked. "There are no such things as ghosts," he told himself, "yet I'm nearly sure patients see ghosts frequently. From those two facts, two more emerge readily. The first is that things which do not exist are frequently visible. The second: I myself am a patient.

"If I am a patient, I must assist in my own cure; but how can I, if I do not understand the nature of my disease? Answer: By examining the symptoms, I can deduce the nature of my disease.

"First symptom: I frequently mutter to myself when my mouth is full." He chewed vigorously and swallowed, grinning.

"That symptom is disposed of. My disease remains, of course. Second symptom: I have lost all contact with reality. Presumably I am in the prison hospital in a vegetative state. To return to reality, I must comprehend the nature of my delusions. This darkness presumably represents the ethical desert of the penitentiary. It is less now than it was because I have been taken to the hospital where things are somewhat better. The vertical trees reflect the vertical bars on windows and doors. Take that one." He directed his own attention toward an inoffensive sapling. "It's even the right thickness."

Seizing it with both hands, he shook it until its dying leaves rattled. "Just so, Doctor Tuck. I cannot effect my escape by shaking the bars. I am still in prison. What if I take my sword to it?"

He drew his sword and slashed half-heartedly at the

sapling, scarring the bark. "No result. But what about a serious attack?" He cut, right and left and right again. Chips flew, and soon the sapling fell.

"Listen!" said a familiar voice at his elbow.

Tuck spun around. "Nerys?"

"Here I am." She stepped out of the shadows. "Did you believe I had left you?"

He nodded.

"I was with you. Where else should I be? Weeping among the living while I watched my husband's body rot?" She pointed to the sword he held. "There is my man."

"This?" He held the sword up.

"There." Her finger slipped between his to touch the wooden grip he had made. "Your hand warmed that. Thus you see me."

"When I carried the club . . ." He let the sentence trail away.

"Again! Listen!"

Screams, he thought.

Silence succeeded the screams; he visualized another Tree Woman like Nerys in the grip of a second beast, and dashed away.

Before he had run far he struck another road, the first real road he had seen, a road of pounded red clay wide enough for horsemen to ride four abreast. The man thundering toward him rode alone, and if he had ever had three companions it seemed likely they were dead—his clothing was bright with blood, which streamed from his head and shoulders.

Tuck stood aside panting and let him pass, receiving two drops of blood on his face for his trouble, and three on his shirt.

Jogging now, he topped a rise. Dead men lay in the road; not far from one lay a horse too badly wounded to rise, with blood pulsing from its nostrils. A second horse shied as soon as it caught sight of him, its reins dragging, its head up, and its eyes wide.

He stopped, careful not to meet its gaze. "You are mistaken," he said. "I don't hate horses or want to hurt them. I love horses." It was not true, and he felt obliged to amend it. "I like horses. Before Sally left me, we had three horses, two geldings and a beautiful little Arabian mare. You're a stallion, right? You would have loved her." He edged closer, careful not to look directly at the brown stallion with the trailing reins. "Sally loved her a lot more than she ever loved me, but I liked her anyway. She was as affectionate and gentle as any animal could ever be."

At the word, he had gotten a foot on the trailing reins. He picked them up, still careful not to look directly at the brown stallion. "You're a fighting horse," he said. "I'm not a fighting man, but I'm a man who'll fight when he has to. For the present that may be good enough. It may have to be."

Mounted, he wheeled the stallion and trotted up the slope.

They were nearer than he would have guessed, one covering the woman while six more watched. Those six turned at the drum-roll of the stallion's hooves, and one managed to raise a javelin before he was ridden down. The sword with the wooden grip split the skull of another. Frantic with victory, Tuck dropped the reins and threw the coarse knife at the man separating himself from the woman. The pommel struck his eye, and in a moment more he was ridden down as well.

The woman was naked and weeping, and for an hour or more unwilling to rise. Tuck found the ruin of a silk gown, covered her with it, and sat beside her stroking her hand. "It was terrible," he said. "I know how bad it was. Believe me, I know. Now it's over, and it won't happen anymore. For the rest of your life you'll know that nothing you face will be as terrible as what happened here today, and that you lived through this and came out of it better and stronger." He said this and much more again and again, perhaps a score of times.

At last she said, "Will they come back?"

He shrugged. "You would know better than I."

After that he lifted her onto the brown stallion's saddle and mounted behind her. "Where are we going?" she asked.

"Wherever you want to."

"It will be more dangerous if we go back," she told him, "but I would like to go back."

She had pointed as she spoke. He turned the brown stallion, holding it to a rapid walk. "Where are we?"

"This is the Valley of Coomb. You must be a stranger here. Are you from the west?"

"From a far country," he said, and to himself added, "I think."

"You are a brave man, if you are rushing to meet the night, O my husband. But I knew you for a brave man when you slew those who had slain my guards."

"I'm not your husband," he said.

"You have seen my nakedness. Do you not know the law?"

"More than I want to know," he told her, "but I don't think I've come across this one."

"If a man beholds the nakedness of a maid, he must restore her honor by wedding her, if he himself is unwed. That is the law for common women. But if a man beholds the nakedness of a royal maiden, he must put away his wife, if he has one, to wed the royal maiden and restore her honor, O my husband. Have you a wife?"

"Not anymore."

"Indeed. Indeed." She looked over her shoulder, smiling. "You that saved me are harmed the worse. Though I am most grateful for the hand that braces my waist in your saddle, might it not perhaps be some trifle higher?"

The light failed as they followed the road into the Valley of Coomb. "Here our poor folk left a hundred-eatings gone," she told him, "for this valley is the very Herald of Night."

"I'm surprised you wanted to come back here."

She wiggled closer, although they were already very close. "I have you to protect me. Besides, we met their group as we were about to leave the eastern side, thus they had only entered. Had there been others in deeper night, they would have attacked us sooner."

"I met bandits deeper in," he told her.

"Our own people?" She turned to look at him over her shoulder.

"Not my people," he said, "but Night People, which I suppose must be what you mean."

"My people are the Sun People," she said, "and because they are mine, yours as well, O my husband. Do you not know me?"

"No, but I should introduce myself first."

She nodded.

"I'm Tuck, at your service."

"You are Prince Tuck, my consort. My own name is Estar." She coughed apologetically. "Princess Estar. Please do not grovel."

"I'll avoid it if at all possible."

The smile she directed at him was almost a grin. "Thank you. I have met others, now and then, who did not know me. They groveled, and I hate that. That is a poor man's sword you wield so well. You are not rich?"

"I have nothing," Tuck said.

She dimpled. "Except me."

"No, you have me. You're the loveliest woman I've ever seen. I'm afraid that I'll wake up any minute and you'll be gone."

"You," she said, "are going to make a most satisfactory husband."

There was a farm at the western edge of the valley. He left her some distance from it and explained to the farm wife that she must sell a gown.

"Sacking," Estar said as she pulled it down, "at least you will no longer see that my hips and legs are fat."

"I've seen your hips, and your legs, and they are perfect. Both of them."

"Both legs you mean, and you are looking very far down. You have no money?"

"Nope. I paid the woman for your dress with what I had."

"You could have become rich by searching the bodies of those you killed back there. They took my jewels."

Tuck shrugged.

"You are right. Swords, not jewels, make a king. It was a saying of my father's."

"He's passed away? I'm sorry to hear it."

"Died?" Estar shook her head. "He seldom speaks. He is old, and . . . sometimes he will not eat."

"I see."

"If he were dead, I would be queen. You, my husband, would be our king until I bore an heir and he reached the age of maturity. But I do not want my father to die. Does that surprise you?"

"No. Certainly not."

"That is well. Look above those trees."

She pointed, and he discovered an unexpected pleasure in the slenderness and whiteness of her arm. His lips brushed the shoulder that held it in the lightest and swiftest of kisses.

"Do you see—" For an instant she seemed to choke, and coughed. "The flag? It is green and yellow, and so not easily seen above the trees."

"I think so."

"It flies from Strongdoor Tower. There is yellow stone beneath it. Perhaps you cannot see it."

"I'll take your word for it," he said.

"The baron's name is Blaan. He is my most loyal vassal, or says loudly that he is, and would wed me if you would step aside for him. Will you?"

"No." A woman—this woman—was much too precious.

She dimpled. "You have not seen how large and strong he is. You will shake with fear, O my husband."

He smiled back. "I doubt it."

"We must see. I cannot ride back to Cikili in this gown. Thus we must ask his aid. He has, I should think, three hundred men, if not more. Will you kill them all for me?"

"I doubt that it'll prove necessary."

The guard at the portcullis looked incredulous when Tuck said that the woman who shared his saddle was

Princess Estar, and gawked when he recognized her. Baron Blaan welcomed her, ignored Tuck, and turned her over to a housekeeper and a bevy of maids. He was, as she had said, a tall, beefy, and quite muscular man.

Tuck seated himself in the best chair in the Great Hall and stared at the fire, which was larger than any summer evening could have required.

He had refused to turn over someone's records. Who had she been? Records showing he had helped with what? Bit by bit he pictured a dozen patients and former patients. A woman accused of killing a child—accused on slender evidence, presumably, since they would not have wanted her psychiatrist's notes if they had a strong case. He himself had been psychoanalyzed 10 years ago, as all analysts were at the beginning of their careers. Could it have been those notes they wanted?

Could he have murdered a child?

He decided that he could not, but that he could certainly have been accused of having done it and worse. Anyone these days—any man, particularly—could be accused of anything by anyone.

"That's my chair you're sitting in," Blaan said.

"Sorry." Tuck rose and moved to another.

"That's my chair, too."

Tuck sighed. "No doubt it is. This is your castle and you own all its furniture. I thank you for allowing me, a mere prince and your guest, to use it. But if you want me to vacate it, you need stronger arguments."

"A prince? You don't look it. Of what nation?"

"Yours."

The word hung there for perhaps half a minute. At last Blaan said, "You're a dreamer. I can tell that—a dreamer with a torn cheek! What do you dream of as you peer into my fire, dreamer?"

He had been thinking of the prison wood shop to which he had initially been assigned, his practice in the prison hospital, and his fill-in work in the library. "Stevenson," he said. "Blinking embers, tell me true, where are those armies marching to, and what the burning city is that crumbles in your furnaces?"

Blaan blinked too; he was saved by Estar, who swept into the room, resplendent in cloth-of-gold, with two maids to carry her train.

Blaan rose, and Tuck with him.

"My husband is not obliged to bow save on the most ceremonial occasions." Estar's voice would have frozen sea water. "You, Baron, are not thus exempt."

"You have married this—this . . ." For a moment Blaan could only stare, at a loss for words. "This *vagabond!*"

Tuck laid a friendly hand on Blaan's shoulder. "Bow."

Blaan spun to face him. His sword was in his hand so quickly it seemed impossible that he had actually drawn it. *"Guards!"*

Estar screamed.

Tuck dodged behind the chair. "I think you need to consider what you're doing. Will you listen to reason? Just for a minute?"

"I will not only listen to it," Blaan told him, "I will voice it. The princess has wed a vagrant, a decision she must deeply regret. I will free her from her miscegenation. In gratitude, she will accept me and obey me as a good wife should. Or suffer the consequences."

The last word was nearly drowned in the pounding footfalls of the guards, a score of big men with helmets and spears.

"Wait!" Estar raised both her hands. "I am your Princess Plenipotentiary, the Regent of our King."

Tuck kept his eyes on Blaan. "Your lord's following a suicidal policy," Tuck said.

Estar's voice rose above the hubbub. "Hear the Prince Consort!"

"True loyalty lies in saving him from it."

Blaan lifted his sword for an overhand cut, edging to his right.

"That will preserve your own lives too. Obey him now or you'll die as traitors, and quickly."

"Die!"

Tuck got the chair up in time to block the swift sword cut, though the edge bit deep into its back. He grabbed one end of the wide sword-guard, and Blaan jerked to free it.

Estar spoke again. "Do none of you wish this barony? Not one?"

As if by magic, the blade of a spear emerged from Blaan's chest. His blood followed it, his eyes glazed, and he fell.

With all the poise she might have exhibited at her coronation, Estar approached the guardsman while her maids scurried behind her, trying to snatch up the cloth-of-gold train they had let fall. "Congratulations, My Lord." She smiled. "A good cast!"

The king lay in bed staring at the embroidered canopy eight feet above his snowy head. "He will speak at times," Estar whispered. "Let us hope this will be one." More loudly she said, "This is my husband, Father. The ceremony will be at sunset—we're hoping that will cheer the city as well as giving our warriors a new leader."

There was no response.

"Already he wears the seal, Father. Don't you see it?" She touched the heavy gold seal suspended from Tuck's neck. "The seal you wore for so many years?"

There was nothing to indicate that the old man in the huge bed had heard her.

"He is wise, and certainly much too wise not to listen to the advice of a man much older than he who has devoted his life to statecraft. A few words from you, now, might help him shape a better path for our whole nation."

"No," the old king said distinctly. "Go, Estar. Leave me."

"Better," Tuck muttered to her.

"Is it really?" She scarcely breathed the words. "I would have said worse."

"It's better," Tuck's tone was conversational, "because it doesn't point to Alzheimer's, which is what I was afraid of.

I can't treat that with what we've got here. This is senile depression, I would say, and I may be able to do something."

"Really?"

"Really. Will you trust me alone with him for half an hour or so? I won't hurt him, I promise, or demean him in any way. But this will be tricky and may not work."

When she had kissed him lightly and gone out, he took off the seal and pulled a chair up to the bed. Seated, he held the seal by its chain, letting it swing gently. "I wanted to give you a better look at this, Your Majesty. Do you see it? Look carefully, please. I know you wore it for years, but you were very busy during all those years. Did you notice how beautiful it is? See how it catches the light as it swings back and forth. See how it turns as it swings. It's bright gold, pure gold, and my valet polishes it every time I change clothes."

There was no response.

"I'm going to try something to take away the pain, or make it lighter if I can't take away entirely. The thing I'm going to do here this warm afternoon is called hypnotherapy. Hypnos is one of the names of sleep. Did you know that? That's why it's called hypnotherapy. It's sleep therapy, sleep healing. You're old now. You can no longer grasp a sword, and you hate that. It hurts you inside, I know. You can no longer walk like you used to, and that hurts too. I understand. But there's so much pain, so much pain like that. I'm sure you would like to get away from it for a while, even if it was only a little while. Haven't you noticed that it no longer hurts when you sleep? It doesn't. You're warm and comfortable then, and those things no longer matter, do they? It's so much better to sleep, and not hurt.

"To sleep and wake up better and stronger with no pain. Are you still watching the seal? That's fine, but I can see your eyelids are getting heavy. Close them if you want to. Rest your eyes. Get away from the pain while the seal swings back and forth."

When Tuck left the king's bedchamber, the king was

holding his arm. He did not grip it tightly, and with its slight help walked almost as well as Tuck himself. The crimson velvet retiring robe he wore was trimmed with ermine and was positively regal. He greeted half a dozen courtiers by name, while they bowed almost to the rich carpet of the corridor, or gaped open-mouthed.

"I am feeling better," he told Estar when they found her in the music room of the suite she now shared with Tuck. "It has been a great help to have you and this prince, a loving couple I can trust with everything, as my regents. I hope that you will consent to continue in your service to our nation."

"We will, Your Majesty," Tuck said.

Still too astonished to speak, Estar nodded agreement.

Later, in a curtained room, Tuck sat before the crystal watching the golden seal he had hung above it swing. "Wake," he murmured. "Wake up. This is a dream, a good dream, but only a dream. Awake. Awake. Awake . . ."

It took much longer than that. But a moment came when he realized he was no longer watching the seal—that he was sitting on a small, hard stool with his eyes shut.

He opened them and saw the stacks of the prison library. A cart showed that he had been reshelving books. He rose from the gray metal stool and went back to work.

That night a whistle shrilled in Cell Block Seven. "Lockdown!" a guard shouted. Two or three voices echoed him derisively: *Lockdown. Lockdown.*

Thirty seconds later, every door in the block that was not closed already slammed shut and every bolt in every door shot home.

"Wish it didn't make such a racket," the other man in the cell said, and sat up.

"We are the Night People." Tuck gripped the bars and looked out, wondering vaguely what the other man's name was, and whether he would ever recall it.

"What you mean by that, Doc?"

He turned and looked at the other man—at Clark. "You have to kill the Night People or lock them up. If you don't they will murder and rape and burn. It's the same everywhere, 'in spite of differences of soil and climate, of languages and manners, of laws and customs.' We are the Night People, and they are safe from us now."

"You're quotin' again, ain't you?"

Tuck nodded. "Wordsworth."

"My granny used to talk about them," Clark said, "them dime stores."

Murder, rape, and burn. And hide evidence.

There were patients next day, both alcoholics. When he had finished with them, he went to the library; secreted once more in the stacks, he tried by every method he knew to return to his dream.

Next morning he was in the library again. He ate lunch and endeavored to treat a man who fantasized—only fantasized, he insisted—about doing horrible things to women with long dark hair.

The next day there were no psychiatric patients and he filled in at the hospital, looking at sore throats and sprained ankles. In that fashion day followed day. And evening after evening he read while Clark watched TV. Had a book guided him to the dream? He hoped one had and searched his mind in spare moments, for if such a book existed it might be found again; found, it might guide him back. Might guide him home.

Once Clark asked him what he would do when he got out, and he said, "Lead those who'll follow me to blunt the next incursion." Clark asked him no more questions after that.

So one year passed, and another, until at last a patient explained that his sleep was haunted by a plaintive girl. "She's real skinny, Doc, and looks real poor. She keeps tellin' me and tellin' how I promised something, only I never done it."

Tuck nodded. "Something in your unconscious mind is trying to enter your consciousness. Have you any idea what it might be?"

The patient nodded. "Yeah, I do. That's why I acted crazy until they let me in to see you." He held out a scrap of wood. "A guy asked me to give you this, a long time ago. I promised I would, only I never did. You can just pitch it out if you want to."

Tuck examined it. It was a simple cylinder with a clumsily cut hole down its axis.

"Thing is, he got your old bench when they moved you up here out of the wood shop, and he found it in a drawer. He thought it might be a piece of somethin' you'd been workin' on, and you might like to have it."

"It's a wooden grip for a sword," Tuck told him.

When the patient had gone, he rubbed it between his palms, pressed it to his cheek, shut his eyes, and (feeling not at all foolish) kissed it.

There were hands upon his shoulders; he knew at once whose hands they were. "The Sun People have need of you," Nerys said, and somewhere a tiger roared.

He rose, wrapped in crystalline mist, and took three steps.

Escaped the crystal. He paused, brushing his lips with the end of the quill. *Half the city has burned. I have rallied the survivors. We must free Estar, and because was must, we shall. The Armies of Night are scattered, expecting no concerted attack. With luck and guts we'll teach them a lesson that will last a long, long time.*

Almost Home

~~~

Terry Bisson

Terry Bisson [www.terrybisson.com] lives in Oakland, California. He continues to write fantasy and science fiction full of detail and fascination with how things work, with deadpan humor, wit, and stylish precision. He has been publishing in the genre since the late 1970s. His latest novel is The Pickup Artist (2001), *which somehow combines the traditions of Ray Bradbury and Kurt Vonnegut, Jr. In the 1990s Bisson began to write short stories. One of his first was "Bears Discover Fire," which won the Hugo and Nebula Awards, among others. His stories are collected in* Bears Discover Fire (1993) *and in* In the Upper Room and Other Likely Stories (2000). *In 2003 he published several major novellas, including* Dear Abby *(published as a book),* "Greetings" at SCIFI.com, *and this one.*

"Almost Home" was published in Fantasy & Science Fiction. *Here Bisson does an extraordinary emulation of Philip K. Dick writing a Ray Bradbury story. It's a really likeable tale of a fantastic world of isolated rural communities that are nearly identical clones, duplicating every artifact and every individual. They are created alternate realities of some unexplained kind separated by geography. The characters are all kids. Sometimes one or another of them can perceive something fantastic, or some fantastic possibility underlying everyday reality. And this leads to a marvelous voyage.*

~ 1. The Old Race Track

Troy could hardly wait until supper was over. He wanted to tell Toute what he had discovered; he wanted to tell Bug; he wanted to tell somebody. Telling made things real, but you had to have the right person to tell. This was not the sort of thing you told your parents.

He fidgeted at the dinner table, ignoring his father's gloomy silence and his mother's chatter. She was trying to cheer him up and failing, as always.

Troy cleaned his plate, which was the rule. First the meat, then the beans, then the salad. Finally! "Excuse me, may I be excused?"

"You don't have to run!" his father said.

I know I don't *have* to run, Troy thought as he hit six on the speed dial. Toute's line was busy. He wasn't surprised. It had been busy a lot lately.

He dialed Bug's number. "Excuse me, Mrs. Pass, may I speak with Bug, please?"

"Clarence, it's for you!"

"Bug, it's me, listen. Guess what I found out. You know that white fence at the old race track? That broken down fence by the arcade?"

"The one with all the signs."

"That one. I just discovered something today. Something really weird. Something really strange. Something really amazing."

"Discovered what?"

"Well—" Suddenly Troy was reluctant to talk about it on the telephone. It seemed, somehow, dangerous. What if the grownups were to hear, and what if for some reason they weren't *supposed* to hear? It was always a possibility. Every kid knew that the world was filled with things that

439

grownups didn't know, weren't supposed to know. Things that were out of the ordinary worried them. Worrying turned them into shouters. Or whisperers.

"Well, what?" Bug asked again.

"I can't talk about it now," Troy said, lowering his voice, even though his parents in the next room obviously weren't listening; they were having one of their whisper-arguments. "I'll tell you tomorrow. Meet me at the usual tree tomorrow, the usual time."

"I have practice."

"Not till afternoon. We'll have time to do some fishing."

The usual tree was at the corner of Oak and Elm; the usual time was as soon after breakfast as possible, allowing for the handful of chores required by Life with Parents: in Troy's case, garbage take-out and sweeping (for some reason) the crab apples and leaves from the driveway.

The old race track was at the edge of town, where the houses gave way to fields. There was no new race track, only the old one, long abandoned. It was just a dirt oval around a shallow lake that was all grown over with lily pads and green scum. Troy and Bug called it Scum Lake. That is, Troy called it Scum Lake and Bug went along. Bug generally went along.

The race track could have been for horses, but there were no stables. It could have been for cars, but there were no pits. No one seemed to remember who had built it or what it was for.

As they rode their bikes toward the track, Troy tried again to tell Bug what he had discovered. "You know the white fence along the infield, the one with all the signs on it? Well, yesterday, after you left for baseball, I climbed up into the stands, and when I looked down. . . ."

"The stands! You climbed up there? They're so rickety, the whole thing could fall down!"

"Well, it didn't, and it won't if you watch your step. Anyway, here we are. I'll show you."

They parked their bikes by the chainlink fence. They

didn't have to lock them. Nobody came by the old race track, and nobody stole in their town anyway. Sometimes Troy wished they did.

"Come on, and you'll see!" Troy led the way through the hole *something* (not they) had dug under the fence, and then through the dark tunnel under the stands, lined with dead soda machines. Bug carried his backpack with his ball glove in it, and Pop-Tarts for lunch. Usually they just headed across the track for the infield and the lake; but today, after they emerged into the bright sunlight, Troy led the way up into the stands, using the board seats for steps.

Troy knew Bug didn't like high places, but he knew he would follow. The planks wobbled and rattled and boomed with every step.

"The cheap seats," Troy said, sitting down on the top plank. Bug sat beside him, with his backpack between his feet. From here, they could see the entire track, with the lake in the middle; and beyond the backstretch, fields of beans in long straight rows; and beyond them, the dunes.

"I stayed yesterday, after you left for baseball," Troy said. "I like to come up here sometimes and read, or just look around. You know, imagine what it was like when there were cars on the track, or horses, you know?"

"I guess," said Bug, who was a little short on imagining things.

"Anyway, look at the fence from here." A white fence followed the track halfway around the infield side. It was broken into two parts, which met at an old enclosed plywood food arcade near the starting/finish line. The fence opposite the grandstands was almost straight, but the part that led toward the lake wandered crazily, left and then right. Parts of it were fallen, and other parts were still upright.

"What's that fence for? It doesn't keep anything out or in. And see how both ends come together at the arcade. Don't they look like two wings of a bird, but broken?"

"I guess," said Bug. "But. . . ."

"Plus, have you ever noticed how they aren't really very

strong? They're made out of slats and wire and canvas, that white stuff."

"That's because they're just for signs." Bug read them aloud, like the answers on a test: *"Krazy Kandy, Drives You Wild. Buddy Cola—Get Together! Lectro with Powerful Electrolytes. Mystery Bread."*

"Maybe. But maybe not," Troy said. "Maybe they are wings."

"Huh?"

"You can only see it from up here. See? They look like the wings of an airplane—an old fashioned airplane, an *aero*plane, all wood and wire and canvas. The wings meet at the arcade, which would be the fuselage." Troy was proud of his knowledge of airplanes, which he had gotten entirely from books. "The front end of the arcade, there, by the track, would be the cockpit."

Bug was skeptical. "So where's the tail? An airplane has to have a tail."

"The outhouse," said Troy, pointing to an old wooden outhouse at the far end of the arcade that had turned over and split into two parts. "It makes a V-tail, which some planes have. Everything looks like something else, don't you see? If it was a crashed airplane, that crashed here a long time ago, and it was too big to move or get rid of, they would've just built a race track around it so that nobody would know what it was, because that would give away the secret."

"What secret?" Bug asked.

"The secret that it is an airplane," said Troy.

"I guess," said Bug, picking up his backpack and starting down. "But now it's time to go fishing."

With Bug, it was always time to go fishing. Fishing in Scum Lake was sort of like ice fishing, which neither of them had ever done, but Troy had read about in a magazine. You made a hole in the ice (or scum) that covered the lake, then dropped in your line and waited. But not for long. The little bluegill were so eager to get caught that they fought over the hook; they would take worms or cheese, but worms were better.

Troy and Bug climbed down from the stands, rattling the planks, and walked across the track to the infield. They slipped through a fallen section of fence, or wing, and followed the short path through the reeds to the lake. Their fishing poles were under the dock, where they had hidden them. Digging under an old tire, they found worms.

They sat on the end of the dock and caught bluegills, then threw them back. They were too little to eat, but that was okay; there were plenty of Pop-Tarts. Troy caught eleven and Bug caught twenty-six. Bug usually caught more. Troy was careful taking out the hooks. He wondered if it actually hurt the fish.

He was beginning to suspect that it did.

The bluegill weren't the only fish in Scum Lake. There was also a catfish as big as a rowboat. Troy had seen it once, from the end of the dock, when the light and shadow were just right. Bug had seen it, once, sort of; at least he said he had.

After he had caught his first "rerun," Troy quit fishing. He left the line in the water, just to make Bug happy, but left off the worm. It was fun just to sit in the Sun and talk about things. Troy did most of the talking, as usual; Bug was content to just listen. "Didn't you ever wonder how everybody got to our town?" Troy asked.

"In one little airplane?"

"It's pretty big. Then they multiplied. Didn't you ever wonder why they are all so much alike?"

"I guess. But I have to go to practice."

They hid their poles and started back toward the stands. On the way, Troy walked off the two ends of the infield fence. The two sections had different signs—*Buddy Cola, Krazy Kandy, Oldsmobile*—but were exactly the same length. Didn't that prove that they were, in fact, wings? And the arcade where they met definitely could have been the fuselage. It was about twenty feet long, with a flat roof; one side was open above waist-high counters.

"I'm going in," Troy said, climbing over a counter on the open side. Bug grumbled but passed in his backpack and followed. The roof and the floor were plywood. The roof was low enough to reach up and touch. They had to duck under a three-bladed ceiling fan. Troy reached up and spun it with his hand.

"It stinks in here," said Bug, wrinkling his nose.

"Mouse droppings," said Troy.

"What's that?"

"Mouse crap. Mouse shit," said Troy. "Let's look up front."

"All right but it's getting late."

The plywood floor creaked as they walked, bent over, toward the front of the arcade, where a dirty glass window overlooked the track. Under the window, there was an old-fashioned radio, filled with dusty vacuum tubes of all different sizes. It sat on a low shelf next to an ashtray filled with white sand.

"Here we have the cockpit," said Troy. "The control center. Why else would there be a radio?"

"Announcers," said Bug. "Anyway, I have to go to practice."

"Okay, okay," said Troy. He climbed out and helped Bug with his backpack. He stopped at the entrance to the tunnel and looked back. Even from the ground now it looked like an airplane. He didn't need to be up in the stands to see it. It just took a little imagination.

"What about a propeller?" said Bug. "An old airplane, made out of wood and canvas, would have a propeller."

True, thought Troy, as they descended into the tunnel. But not true in a way that opened up possibilities. True in a way that closed them down; not the kind of true he liked.

They rode together to the usual tree, before riding off in different directions. Bug lived in the old section of town, with all the trees. Troy lived in one of the new, big houses on the way to the mall.

"See you tomorrow," said Bug.

"I may not make it tomorrow," said Troy. "I have to go to the mall with my cousin."

"The bent girl? She's so bossy!"

"She's okay," said Troy.

∽ 2. The Bent Girl

Toute was Troy's cousin but more like his sister, especially since he didn't have a sister. When they were kids he and Toute had slept together and even bathed together, until they got old enough for the grownups to realize that, hey, one's a boy and one's a girl.

Toute was eleven, almost a year older than Troy. She got her name because when she was little, her mother had taken her to Quebec for treatments, and she had learned to say "Toute" for everything.

Toute means everything in French, which was funny, Troy thought, because Toute got hardly anything. First her mother died. Then she got more and more bent until she could hardly walk, and couldn't ride a bicycle at all. Once a week she went to a special doctor in the mall, and Troy went with her so they could pretend it was a trip for fun. But it wasn't much fun. Usually Toute was worn out from the treatments, and sometimes she looked like she had been crying.

The next morning Troy rode his bike to Toute's house, which was not far from the usual tree. There was an extra car in the driveway. The door was open. Toute's father and two strange men were in the living room, talking in whispers.

Toute was sitting on the stairs. She looked gloomy but she smiled when she saw Troy. "I had a dream about you last night," she said. "I dreamed you had your own airplane and you took me for a ride."

"No way!" said Troy. He sat down beside her and told her what he had discovered at the race track. Now he was more convinced than ever that it was real.

"Get my backpack," Toute said. "It's up in my room. Let's go."

"Don't you have to go to the mall for that treatment?"

"They're discontinuing it," Toute said emphatically, as if *discontinue* were something you actually did instead of stopped doing. "So I'm free all day. Get a bottle of Lectro out of the fridge. We can leave a note for my dad."

Toute sat on the crossbar of Troy's bike. She could sit okay, though she couldn't stand without holding onto something. They rode by the usual tree, just in case—and there was Bug.

"Where did she come from?" he asked Troy. "I thought you said you and her had to go to the mall."

"I want to see the airplane," said Toute.

"She wants to go fishing with us," Troy said.

"She doesn't have a fishing pole," Bug pointed out.

"She can use mine," said Troy.

They parked their bikes against the chainlink fence and crawled under. Toute was pretty good at that part; then she had to hold on between the two boys as they walked though the tunnel, past the dark abandoned drink machines.

Troy was wondering how he was going to get Toute up into the stands. It turned out not to be a problem. As soon as they emerged from the tunnel into the light, Toute blinked twice and said:

"Definitely an aeroplane."

"Huh?" said Bug.

"Aer-o-plane," she said, pronouncing each syllable. "More old-fashioned than an airplane. All wood and canvas. Let's look inside."

"It's just some old plywood," said Bug, but Troy and Toute were already heading across the track.

The boys helped Toute over the counter on the open side, and climbed in after her.

"Smells in here," said Toute, wrinkling her nose.

"Mouse droppings," said Bug.

"Here's the cockpit," said Troy. He tried to wipe the window clean but most of the dirt was on the outside.

"And here's the main power control," said Toute.

"That's the radio," Troy said.

"It's a receiver," said Toute. "It can draw power out of the air. There's a lot of radio waves flopping around out there that never get used. Turn it on."

Troy turned the biggest dial, in the center, to the right, then to the left. "Nothing."

"And here's why. This battery is bone dry," said Toute, stirring the white sand in the ashtray. "Hand me my Lectro, Bug. It's in my backpack."

She was too bent to reach into her own backpack. Bug grumbled but did it for her, handing her the plastic bottle. She poured a narrow stream of clear liquid into the white sand ashtray, making a damp spiral in the sand.

"What does that do?" asked Troy.

"Lectro has powerful electrolytes," Toute said, as she handed the bottle back to Bug. "You can put this back now."

"Thanks," Bug said sarcastically as he put it back. "Isn't it time to go fishing?"

Bug caught twenty-one bluegills, and Troy caught sixteen. Even Toute, a girl, caught eleven, on a handline.

Troy quit when he caught his first rerun, but Toute kept going. "I don't know why everybody feels sorry for the fish," she said. "I feel sorry for the worms."

"You get over feeling sorry for the worms," said Bug.

Toute was so bent that she had to sit sideways on the dock. "What I really want is to see this giant catfish you are always talking about."

"It's best on a cloudy day," said Troy. "Then the light doesn't reflect off the surface of the water, and you can see all the way to the bottom."

Just then a cloud passed over the Sun. They all three crawled to the edge of the dock; Troy made a hole in the scum with his hands. They could see all the way to the bottom, the little waving weeds and a few small fish, examining an old tire. But there was no giant catfish.

"It may be an urban myth," Toute said.

"What's that?" asked Bug.

"You're forgetting one thing," said Troy. "I saw it myself."

"Bug, did you see it?"

"I think I did," Bug said.

"I want to see it myself," said Toute. "Troy makes things up sometimes."

Troy felt betrayed. It was Toute who had showed him the Teeny-Weenies who lived in the roots of a tree in her yard. He tried to remember if he had really seen them or just wanted to see them. He couldn't remember.

Bug had two Pop-Tarts in his backpack, which they shared three ways. They had to take their lines out of the water to eat, because the fish were so eager to get caught.

They were just finishing the Pop-Tarts and putting their poles back into the water when Troy heard something strange. "What was that?"

"What?" said Bug.

"Sounds like groaning," Toute said.

"The wind," said Bug.

"I don't think so," said Toute. "Better go see."

Troy left his pole in the water and went to investigate. The infield section of fence was tipped over until it was almost flat on the ground. The other side, along the track, had fallen, too. Lying down, the fence looked more like a wing than ever.

"The wind probably blew it over," said Bug, when Troy returned.

"There isn't any wind," Troy said.

"There may be at the other end," Bug suggested. "The fence is all connected. And anyway—"

"There it is again," said Troy.

They all three heard it this time: a groan, a rattle, a splintering sound like a branch breaking.

"Sounds like the mating call of a tyrannosaur," said Toute.

They put away the poles and went to investigate, all three this time. Toute walked between the two boys, an arm around each shoulder. Her feet barely touched the ground.

Both fences were now completely flat. The front of the arcade was now sticking out onto the track; it had dragged the ends of the fences with it.

"The wings are swept back, like a jet," said Troy.

The outhouse on the back had tipped so that now it looked more like a V-shaped tail than ever. They could enter the arcade through it without climbing over the counter.

"Ugh, it stinks," said Toute. "It's like the butt."

The tubes in the radio were glowing. Toute held her hand over them, palm down. "It's warming up," she said. "Bug, the Lectro. In my backpack."

"You don't have to be so bossy," he said, even as he was opening it.

"Sorry," she said (though she didn't sound sorry). "You'd be bossy too if you were so bent you couldn't reach into your own backpack."

"No, I wouldn't," said Bug. He handed her the Lectro, and she poured half the bottle into the sand.

"What happened to the fan?" asked Troy, looking up. The ceiling fan was gone.

"I have practice," said Bug.

Toute gave Bug the Lectro to put back in her pack. They helped her out over the counter on the open side, because she didn't like the smell in the "butt." None of them did.

They walked around to the front. "Whoa, there's the fan!" said Bug. "Now it does look like an airplane."

"Aeroplane," said Troy. The ceiling fan was on the front of the fuselage, just under the front window. It was turning slowly, even though there was no breeze.

Troy stopped it with his hand. When he let go, it started up again.

"This is getting weird," he said.

"We're going to get blamed for this," said Bug. "Let's get out of here."

"Blamed for what? Blamed by who?" asked Toute.

"For making things different."

"Don't be silly," she said. But even she seemed uncomfortable. She got between the two boys and they started through the tunnel.

Troy stopped for one last look. Was it his imagination, or

had the aeroplane turned, just a little, so that it was starting to point down the track?

"It's growing, like a plant," Toute said. "Can we come back tomorrow and see what it's grown into?"

"I guess," said Troy.

"I have practice every day this week," said Bug.

"What did you kids do today?" Troy's father asked that night at the table.

"Nothing much," said Troy. "I took Toute for a ride on my bike."

"That's nice," said Troy's mother. "You should take her again tomorrow. Her father has discontinued her treatments, and she...."

"Claire!" said Troy's father sharply. Then they started one of their whisper arguments.

"Can I be excused?" asked Troy. He wanted to go to his room and think about the aeroplane. He was wondering if it would still be there the next day; wondering if it would fly.

⌒ 3. Into The Air

The next morning Toute was waiting on her front steps, with her backpack on.

"Don't go in," she said. "It's chaos in there." Chaos was one of her favorite words.

She perched on Troy's crossbar and they rode to the usual tree and picked up Bug. "I brought three Pop-Tarts today," he said.

They left the bikes in the weeds and crawled under the fence and hurried through the tunnel.

They emerged into the light—and there it was. Bug was the first to speak.

"It moved."

The aeroplane—for there was no longer any doubt what it was—was halfway on the track. The front of the arcade, the fuselage, was angled across the start-finish line, pointing up the track. The outhouse was split into a V-tail. The right wing was still in the infield, but the end of the left one drooped onto the hard clay of the track.

The ceiling fan on the front, under the windshield, was turning, very slowly. There were two spoked wheels under the front of the fuselage, though the back still dragged in the dirt.

"It even has wheels," said Troy. He noticed that two wheels were missing off a tipped-over hot dog cart nearby.

"Of course," said Toute. "It wants to be what we want it to be. An aeroplane."

"Maybe it's some kind of car," said Bug.

"With wings? Give me a boost," said Toute. They lifted her through the side window into the plane, and then followed after her. The plywood creaked under their feet.

The tubes in the radio were barely glowing. Toute stirred the white sand with her fingertips. "Needs more Lectro."

"Turn around, I'll get it out of your pack," said Troy.

"I forgot to bring it," said Toute.

"I thought you always carried Lectro," Bug said.

"I forgot it," said Toute. "Just because I don't have practice doesn't mean I don't have a lot of things to worry about."

"There's a Lectro machine in the tunnel," said Troy. "But it's dead."

"Not exactly," said Bug.

"What do you mean?" Toute asked.

"If I get you your Lectro, can we go fishing?"

"Deal," said Toute.

Toute and Troy watched from inside the aeroplane while Bug climbed out and crossed the track, and descended into the tunnel. "Aren't you curious?" Toute asked.

"I guess." Troy climbed out and followed, at a distance, like a spy.

At the bottom of the tunnel, where it was darkest, the

drink machines sat against one wall. There were three of them. Troy had always thought they looked like lurking monsters.

Bug walked up to the center machine and, after looking both ways, kicked it at the bottom.

A light inside came on, illuminating the logo on the front of the machine. *Lectro! With Powerful Electrolytes!*

Bug looked both ways again, then hit the machine once with the heel of his right hand, right under the big L.

A coin dropped into the coin return slot with a loud *clink*.

Cool, thought Troy. Bug had hidden talents.

Bug dropped the coin into the slot at the top of the machine and hit a square button.

A plastic bottle rumbled into the bin at the bottom.

Troy stepped out of the shadows, clapping.

Bug jumped—then grinned when he saw who it was. "I didn't know you were there."

"You have hidden talents!"

"Just because you never notice them doesn't mean they're hidden," Bug said, starting up the tunnel, toward the daylight.

"It's warm," said Bug, as he handed the bottle through the big side window into the plane.

"That's okay," said Toute. She poured half the bottle into the sand. "It's not for drinking. Look."

Troy could see the radio under the front windshield. The tubes were starting to glow, just a little.

He reached for the fan. It started to turn on its own, before he could touch it. He pulled his hand back. Weird!

"I thought we were supposed to go fishing," Bug said.

"Deal," said Toute. "Just give me a hand out of here."

Bug caught twelve and Troy caught nine and even Toute, the girl, caught six. Then they ate their Pop-Tarts. Bug had brought one for each of them this time.

"What's that noise?" said Bug.

They all heard it: a low groaning sound, from the race track.

"I'll go see," said Troy.

"I'm going too," said Toute, grabbing his shoulder.

The plane was all the way on the track. The wings were straight, no longer swept back; they drooped at the ends, so that the tips touched the clay. The fan, in the front of the fuselage, was turning so fast that Troy couldn't make out the individual blades.

"This is too weird," he said.

"Or just weird enough," said Toute. "Give me a boost." He helped her inside and followed after her. The tubes in the radio were glowing. Troy put his hand over them; they were warm, like a fire.

"What are you doing?" he asked Toute.

"What do you think?" She was pouring more Lectro into the sand. The fan was turning faster. A weird creaking came from under the floor. Troy knew what it was without looking—the wire wheels turning.

The plane was moving slowly down the straightaway toward the first turn. The fan turned faster and faster, but never as fast as a real propeller on a real airplane. Troy could still see the blades, like a shadow, under the front window—or rather, windshield.

"That's enough!" he said. Toute put the cap back on the Lectro bottle. There was only about an inch left.

"Wait!" It was Bug. He was running alongside, trying to carry his backpack in one hand and grab the wing with the other. "Slow down!"

"No brakes!" Troy hadn't realized the plane was going so fast. And it was going faster all the time. The wingtips were off the ground. "Throw me your backpack," he said.

Bug threw his backpack in through the big side window, then scrambled in behind it. "Careful!" said Toute. "Don't kick a hole in the wing!"

"Ooooomph!" said Bug, landing with a loud thump on the plywood floor. "How do we stop this thing?"

"Why would we want to stop it?" Toute was in the front, by the radio, staring straight ahead, down the track. "Troy, come up here! You have to steer."

"Me?" Troy tried to walk. The plane was lurching from side to side. The wheels were squealing and the plywood was creaking and rattling.

"It's your plane," Toute said. "You discovered it."

"I just found it, that's all," said Troy, joining her at the windshield. "Uh oh!"

The plane was almost at the first turn. It was going to run off the track and into the grass. Maybe, Troy thought, that would be best. It would bounce to a stop and—

"Try the knobs," said Toute.

There were three knobs on the radio. The one in the center was the biggest. Troy turned it to the right, and the plane turned to the right, just a little.

He turned it more.

The plane lumbered on around the first turn, the left wing tip just brushing the weeds at the edge of the track. Troy turned the knob back so the notch was at the top. The plane started down the back straightaway, going faster and faster.

"Fasten your seat belts!" said Toute.

"I don't like this," said Bug.

Troy couldn't decide if he liked it or not. The trees and weeds seemed to speed past, as the plane bounced and rattled down the track. It seemed to Troy that it was the world that was sliding backward while the plane was standing still. Well, almost still; it was bouncing up and down and weaving from side to side.

The little fan was spinning soundlessly under the windshield. Troy had read enough about airplanes to know that it was not nearly big enough to make the plane move. But the plane was moving.

It was not nearly big enough to make the plane fly.

But—

"Whoa!" said Bug.

"We're flying," said Toute. "We're in the air."

It was true. The wheels were no longer squealing and the

plywood floor was no longer bouncing up and down. Troy looked down. The track was dropping away, like a rug being pulled out from under them. They were approaching the finish line, where they had started, but this time they were almost as high as the stands—and getting higher.

"Okay, now make it go down," said Bug, looking out the side window.

"Hold on!" said Toute. "Everybody hold on."

Bug made his way to the front and squeezed in between Troy and Toute. "Okay, now make it go down," he said again. "Seriously."

Troy turned the center knob to the right, and the plane banked, following the curve of the track. He started to straighten it for the back straightaway, but Toute pulled his hand away.

"Leave it," she said. "Circling is good."

The circles got wider and wider as the plane got higher and higher.

Below they could see the whole track, with Scum Lake in the center, bright green. There was the chainlink fence, with their bikes in the weeds beside it.

There were the streets, the houses, the trees: all in miniature, seen from above.

Troy checked the wings, to the right and to the left. They were straight, then bent upward slightly at the tip. The canvas was stretched tight, except for a few wrinkles that flapped in the wind.

"We're going to get in trouble," said Bug.

Troy and Toute said nothing. What was there to say? They stood on either side of Bug, looking out of the front of the plane as it circled wider, leaving the track behind. There was the usual oak, and Toute's house, with several strange cars in the driveway.

"Doctors," she said scornfully. "Big meeting today."

There was the school, shut down for the summer. The baseball diamond in the back was empty. "At least you're not late for practice," said Troy.

"Not yet," said Bug. "Can't you make it go back to the track?"

"It seems to know where it wants to go," said Troy. "Like a horse or a dog."

"I never had a horse," Toute said wistfully. "Or a dog." Then she clapped her hands. "But this is better!"

The circles got wider and wider and higher and higher. They flew over the center of town. The clock on the courthouse tower said 12:17. A few cars scooted through the streets, under the trees. It was so quiet below that they could hear a screen door slam. They heard a dog bark.

A few people walked on the sidewalks, but they never looked up. *People in our town never look up,* Troy thought. And it was a good thing, too. What would they see? A plywood plane with long, square-tipped, white canvas wings, soaring higher and higher.

At the edge of town, Troy could see the bean fields and a couple of rundown farmhouses; and then the green fields gave way to yellow dunes, some of them as high as a house.

It was just as Troy had always suspected. The town was surrounded by a wilderness of sand. There wasn't a road or even a path leading in or out, as far as he could see.

Troy turned the knob back to the left, so that the notch pointed straight up.

The right wing creaked and came up, the left wing dropped, just a little, and the plane flew straight toward the edge of town.

"Whoa," said Bug, looking alarmed. "What are you doing?"

"Leveling off," Troy said, "Straightening up. Don't you want to see what's out there?"

"No way."

"Out where?" Toute asked.

"Past the town. Past the fields. On the other side of the dunes."

⌒ 4. *Across a Sea of Sand*

The plane flew straight, soundlessly.

It flew straight past the courthouse, between the water tower and the church steeple.

The trees gave way to fields, edged with fences. The last street became a dirt road. Someone was riding a bicycle; someone who didn't look up. The road ended in a field of grass, and the grass gave way to sand.

"I don't think we're supposed to fly out here," said Bug.

"We're not supposed to fly, period," Toute pointed out.

The dunes lapped like waves at the edge of the grass. At first there were patches of grass in the hollows between them; then that green, too, was gone, and all was sand, yellow sand.

"Nothing but sand," said Toute. She looked almost scared.

"Just as I always suspected," said Troy. "Though nobody talks about it, ever." The dunes went on and on as far as he could see. He leaned out the side window and looked back. The town was an island of trees in a sea of sand. It looked too impossibly tiny to be the town where they had all lived, until this very moment.

And it was getting smaller and smaller.

"Time to turn around," said Bug.

"Not yet," said Troy. "Don't you want to know what's out here?"

"No."

"Nothing but sand," said Toute. "A sea of sand."

The plane flew on. Troy stood at the front, at the controls, with his hand on the knob. There was nothing but yellow desert in every direction as far as he could see.

He looked back. The town was just a dark smudge against the horizon. Maybe it was time to turn back.

He turned the knob to the right.

Nothing happened. He turned it back to the left, but the plane flew on, straight. He wiggled the knob from side to side.

Nothing.

"What's the matter?" Toute asked.

"Nothing."

Troy turned the knob each way again, then straightened it with the notch at the top. No need to tell the others; not yet, anyway. It would just worry them.

He stood at the front with his hand on the knob. The sand looked the same in every direction. There were a few smudges of grass, an occasional dark spot where a dead tree poked up through the drifts. But no roads, no houses, no fences.

The plane flew on, tirelessly, soundlessly. Troy stuck his face out the left side, into the wind. The air was hot. It felt like they were going a little faster than a bicycle; a little faster than a boy could run.

"We don't have any food or water," said Bug.

"I have food," said Toute. "Look in my backpack."

Bug pulled out a Pop-Tart. He handed it to Toute, and she sat down beside him and broke it into three pieces.

Troy put his piece on the shelf beside the radio. He was too nervous to eat. He was afraid that if he let go of the knob, the plane would spin to the ground, or fall, or lose its way. He took his hand off the knob, as an experiment; nothing happened. But he felt better at the controls.

"What about water?" said Bug.

Toute passed him the Lectro. "Just a sip," she said. "We may need the electrolytes for power."

"None for me," said Troy.

He looked back toward the town and saw that even the smudge was gone.

He didn't tell Toute and Bug. He didn't want to alarm them. They were sitting on the floor, finishing their Pop-Tarts. The next time he looked Bug was asleep, with his head on Toute's bent, bony little shoulder.

Troy wanted to tell Toute not to worry—or was it himself he wanted to reassure? No matter: when he started to speak she smiled and put her finger to her lips. The next time Troy looked back, she was asleep too.

The dusty vacuum tubes still glowed hot. The fan was

turning steadily, a circular shadow pulling them silently through the air.

Troy studied the dunes, looking for landmarks, anything that would mark their way back. Airplanes don't leave tracks. The dunes were like waves, featureless. He searched to the left and the right, but he couldn't even find their shadow passing over the sand.

There were a few shapes in the distance, dark moving specks that might have been rabbits, or horses, or antelopes. It was hard to tell their size or shape.

Then they, too, were gone.

And it was just sand, a sea of yellow sand.

⁓ *5. Another Town*

"Look!"

Troy opened his eyes, wider. Had they been closed? Had he been sleeping?

Toute was standing at his side, holding onto his shoulder. Her grip was so strong it almost hurt.

"There's something up ahead."

Bug scrambled to his feet and joined them. Below the windshield, the fan was spinning away. The plane was flying smoothly, silently.

Ahead there was a dark smudge against the horizon.

"Did you turn around?" Toute asked.

"No, why?"

"Because!" Because the smudge ahead looked familiar. The dark was trees. Streets, houses. As they grew closer they saw the water tower, the steeple, the courthouse.

"We're back," said Toute. She sounded disappointed. "You must have turned the plane around."

"I didn't turn anything," said Troy. "Maybe it's like Columbus. You know, all the way around the world."

"Columbus didn't go all the way around the world," said Toute. "And besides, the world is a lot bigger around than that. I hope."

"There's the courthouse," said Bug. "Fly past it so I can see what time it is. Maybe I won't be late for baseball."

"I'll try," said Troy.

As the sand gave way to fields, and then tree-lined streets, the plane responded to the turning of the knob. Troy turned it to the right, and the plane banked right; left, and it banked left. Very gently. Troy was careful to keep it headed for the race track, now barely visible on the other side of town.

"Where's the clock?" Bug asked.

There was no clock on the courthouse tower.

"That's weird plus," said Toute, as they flew past.

Everything else was the same. There was the downtown, with a few people walking around. The same people? They were so small, it was impossible to tell.

There was the school, shut down for summer. The baseball diamond was no longer empty though. There were a few ballplayers, hitting flies.

"Whoa, I'm late," said Bug.

"It looks like they're just starting," said Troy. "You can still make it."

"And there's my house!" said Toute. The driveway was empty, except for her father's Windstar.

"Looks like all the doctors have gone," said Troy.

"Good. You should hear them talk. They all talk in big whispers."

Bug was silent, grim, looking worried. Troy ignored him and concentrated on the old race track, still far ahead. It seemed that the plane was going slower. It was starting to descend, toward the treetops.

He put his hand over the tubes. "They're not as warm as they were."

"We're losing altitude!" said Bug, pointing at the treetops, getting closer.

Toute opened the Lectro bottle. There was an inch left. She poured it into the sand.

The tubes responded instantly, glowing brighter. The plane nosed up slightly, just clearing the last trees before the old race track. Troy turned the knob to the right and the plane started to circle over the track, going slower and slower.

"It knows how to land," Troy said. "It's like a horse; it knows where to go."

He hoped it was true. Toute and Bug didn't look convinced.

Lower and lower they went. The fan was turning so slowly that Troy could see the individual blades, flashing in the Sun. He kept his hand on the knob but the plane followed the track on its own, gliding down over the stands.

The fan was spinning slower and slower; the tubes were glowing dimmer and dimmer.

"Fasten your seat belts," said Troy.

"What seat belts!?"

"It was a joke, Bug." Troy held onto the edge of the shelf that held the radio; Bug held onto the edge of the side window; and Toute held onto both of them as the plane hit the clay track—

It hit, bounced, hit again, bounced. The left wingtip scraped the track, raising a little cloud of dust. The plane hit again, rocked from side to side, rolled—

And rolled to a stop.

Troy opened his eyes and saw Toute just opening hers. Her face was filled with a big grin, a grin that was bigger than she was. She started to clap her hands and Troy joined them, finally realizing that they were not applauding him but the aeroplane.

Bug opened his eyes and joined in.

"Hooray," said Troy.

"But we're on the wrong side of the track," said Bug.

It was true. They were on the back side of the lake, in the middle of the back straightaway.

"So what?" asked Toute.

"How will we explain how it got here?" said Bug. "On the wrong side of the track?"

"Who cares?" said Troy. "No one knows we did it."

"They'll know now," said Bug.

"Then we'll taxi," said Toute. She shook the last few drops of Lectro into the sand. The tubes glowed warm again.

The fan, still spinning, spun faster, and the aeroplane moved off at a walk, lumbering around the track with the wings dragging and the wheels creaking. The tubes died again and the plane stopped exactly where it had started, in front of the stands at the start/finish line.

"Later!" Bug tossed his backpack out the side window. "I have my glove in my backpack," he explained, climbing out after it. He stopped and looked back in. "Can you make it okay?"

"I'll help her," said Troy.

"I can make it," said Toute. "Go on ahead."

Bug waved and disappeared into the tunnel, running for his bike.

"So here we are," said Toute. "But. . . ."

"But what?"

"Doesn't it look a little different?"

"The stands," said Troy. They seemed smaller. And there was no wheelless, tipped-over hot dog cart.

"Maybe it's just my imagination," said Toute. She put her arm around Troy's shoulder and they climbed out the back, through the outhouse/tail. It didn't stink as badly as before.

The stands definitely seemed smaller, thought Troy. Some of the board seats were missing. He decided not to mention it; it seemed best not to notice.

With Toute hanging onto his side, they went through the tunnel. It was as dark as before, and there were the machines, lurking in the darkness like waiting monsters. Two of them; hadn't there been three? Troy wasn't sure, and again, it seemed best not to notice. They hurried on through, into the sunlight on the other side.

"Uh oh," said Toute.

The chainlink fence was gone—and worse.

Bug was kicking the weeds, his fists clenched. "My bicycle is gone," he said. "Somebody stole my bicycle!"

True. There was Troy's bike, in the weeds where he had left it—but all alone.

"Maybe somebody found it and took it home for you," said Troy. Even though he didn't believe it.

"Yeah," said Toute. "Everybody knows your bike." It was a Blizzard Trailmaster, with front and rear shocks.

"Let's go," said Troy. "You can still make it to practice."

They walked to Toute's house, pushing Troy's bike between them, with Toute on the handlebars; they dropped her off, and continued to the usual tree.

"Go ahead and take my bike to practice," said Troy.

"It's okay," said Bug, who clearly thought it wasn't. "It's too late anyway."

True: it was getting dark. Bug waved good-bye and started walking home dejectedly.

Troy felt bad. But not too bad. Missing practice seemed a small price to pay for such an adventure. *Bug will get over it,* Troy thought. *He'll remember this and thank me some-day.*

Troy rode on home, through the darkening streets. His house was lit up when he got there. And there was a visitor. A little red sportscar was parked in the drive. It was a Miata; or rather, almost a Miata. The rear end looked different, and the grill was painted instead of chromed. Maybe a custom?

Troy started around the side of the house, toward the back door—and then stopped.

There was his father in the kitchen, talking to his mother, who was standing at the sink in a yellow dress. But he was smoking a cigarette! And he had a little mustache.

Troy reached for the doorknob—then stopped again. The woman at the sink had turned around. It wasn't his mother at all. She was wearing his mother's yellow dress, but she was younger, with shorter hair and bright red lipstick.

Troy backed up, into the shadow of the trees, almost tripping on the crab apples that littered the ground—the same crab apples he had raked up just the day before. There was a smell of weeds and rot. He watched while his father lit a cigarette and passed it to the woman—not his mother!—who took a drag and then laughed.

A strange laugh, Troy thought, even though he couldn't hear it through the glass. His father gave her a pat on the bottom and they both left the room.

Troy was frozen. He couldn't move and couldn't think. He didn't know where to go or what to think. It was his house, and yet it wasn't. It was his father, but it wasn't; and it was not his mother at all. The kitchen, he noticed for the first time, was painted a different color, although it was the same kitchen.

He tried to remember what color it had been. Yellow, like the strange woman's dress. This kitchen was more the color of sand.

I'll knock on the door and demand to know what's happening, he thought. *No, I'll slip upstairs to my room and . . . No, I'll run away, back to the race track, and . . . .*

And what? He was just starting to get upset when he heard a sound from the trees across the street.

Who-hoot.

Who-hoot.

It was a hoot owl call. Troy stepped out of the shadows and looked toward the street.

There was Bug.

"I found my bike," he said in a loud whisper.

"Where was it? Where is it?" Bug was on foot.

"At home. But something is weird!"

"I know," said Troy. "Here, too. My parents are strange. And my mother is not my mother."

"Come on," said Bug. "Ride me on your bike, back to my house. I'll show you what I mean."

They rode silently through the empty streets to Bug's house, on the other side of town. They left the bike on the street and went around to the back of the house. Through the window, they could see Bug's parents sitting down to dinner. There at the table was—Bug.

"Uh oh," said Troy. "That's you."

"Not me," Bug whispered. "I'm right here."

"Who is it, then?" The boy at the table looked exactly

like Bug except that he was wearing a red shirt that said X-TREME. Bug's T-shirt said GO AHEAD, HAVE A COW.

"I think it's my brother," said Bug.

"But you don't have a brother."

"I did, though. I was supposed to," said Bug. "When I was born I had a twin, but he died. I never knew about it but my mom told me once."

"And that's him?"

"She even named him," said Bug. "His name was Travis, after my dad. That's why I wasn't named after my dad."

Bug's real name was Clarence. He had always hated it.

They crept around the side of the house, by the garage. "And there's my bike."

It was leaning against the garage door. A Blizzard Trailmaster with front and rear shocks.

"Well, get it and let's go," said Troy. "Let's get out of here. This is not our town. Something is wrong."

They rode through the dark, empty streets to Toute's house. They sneaked around to the back, but they couldn't see anything. Toute's house didn't have a kitchen window.

"Just go to the door," said Bug.

"I'm afraid to," said Troy.

"You started all this. Plus, you're her cousin. Nobody will think it's weird if you knock on the door."

Bug hid in the bushes while Troy rang the bell. Instead of the usual ring it played a little song, twice.

Toute came to the door. She was wiping her mouth with a napkin. "Fried chicken," she said.

"Something is wrong," Troy said, whispering.

"I know," said Toute. "I knew it was you. Here." She handed him something wrapped in a greasy paper napkin.

Bug came out of the bushes. "What's that?"

"Fried chicken!"

"We're in the wrong place," said Troy. "My parents are all strange. And Bug's too."

"I know," said Toute. "Mine, too."

"Who's at the door?" a voice called out from inside.

"Just some friends," said Toute. She dropped her voice.

"That was my mother. My mother is alive here. She cooked fried chicken! And look, I can walk." She walked in a little circle. "A little sideways, but I can walk."

"That's great, but we've got to get out of here," said Troy.

"We're in the middle of dinner," said Toute. "I'm coming, Mom!" she yelled. Then she whispered again: "You guys have to wait at the plane. I'll come in the morning."

"In the morning? We have to go home!"

"This is my only chance to see my mother," said Toute.

"Can we come in and use the bathroom?" Bug asked.

"No!" Toute whispered. "You'll ruin everything. Besides, boys can pee in the bushes."

She shut the door.

"What if I don't just have to pee?" Bug grumbled.

They rode back to the old race track, avoiding streets that might be busy, even though few streets in their town were busy after dark. *This isn't our town,* Troy kept reminding himself; *not really. What if we got stopped by a cop? How would we explain who we are?*

They left their bikes in the weeds and entered the track through the tunnel. It was easy without the chainlink fence. The tunnel was darker and scarier than ever at night, but they knew the way and hurried through, without a word.

Troy felt a moment's fear—what if the plane was gone? How would they ever get back home?

But there it was, right where they had left it, shining in the moonlight.

"What if it rains?" Bug asked. "Look at those clouds."

Troy looked up. He had only thought it was moonlight. There was no Moon, but the clouds high overhead were bright. It was as if they were lighted from the ground. *Even the clouds here are weird,* he thought.

"We'll sleep in the plane," he said. The plane was the only thing that seemed normal, unchanged. The fabric on the right wing was torn where the wingtip had hit the track. The fan in the front was still. Troy spun it with his hand; it spun, then stopped.

They entered the back, through the old outhouse. It still stank, a little. "You can't use this outhouse," Troy said.

"Huh?"

"Didn't you say you needed to—you know?"

"I didn't say I needed to. I said, what if I needed to."

The inside of the aeroplane was just as they had left it. Troy was relieved. The vacuum tubes were cold. The sand in the ashtray was dry.

Bug threw his backpack onto the floor. "I'm hungry," he said.

"Look." Troy unwrapped the greasy napkin Toute had given him. There were two drumsticks inside. They each had one and threw the bones outside, through the side window.

"I'm still hungry," said Bug. "Aren't there any Pop-Tarts left?"

"There's this one." Troy found the third of a Pop-Tart he had left on the shelf by the radio. They shared it sitting on the floor of the plane.

"I wish we had something to drink."

"Well, we don't."

"I'm cold," said Bug.

"It's not cold," said Troy.

They tried using Bug's backpack for a pillow but it was too small for both their heads. Bug took out his glove; it just fit the back of his head. Troy used the backpack. It was lumpy, even empty.

"Why is everything so weird?" Bug asked. They lay side by side, looking up at the plywood ceiling. "If that's my twin, does that mean I'm dead and he's alive?"

"Don't think about it," said Troy.

"What about your mother?"

"Don't think about it," said Troy. It was funny. It had always been his job to make things interesting, but now he felt it was his job to make things as normal as possible. "Just go to sleep. Let's don't talk about it. In the morning maybe it will all look different."

He didn't believe it, but he felt that he had to say it.

⌐ 6. *Good-bye! Good-bye!*

Morning. Troy woke up wondering where he was, but only for a moment. The plywood ceiling of the plane brought it all back.

He sat up. Where was Bug? Troy was all alone in the plane. But someone was outside, tapping on the windshield.

"Who's there?"

He stood up and saw Bug, outside, sitting on his bike.

"Bug?"

"Who's Bug? Is he the one who stole my bike?"

Troy got it. "Wait a minute," he said. He climbed out the side window. The boy on the bike—Bug's bike—looked exactly like Bug, but Troy knew it wasn't Bug. He was wearing an X-TREME T-shirt.

"He didn't steal it," Troy said. "He just borrowed it."

"I found it out in the weeds. You guys are in big trouble. My dad's a cop."

"So is Bug's."

"So what? Who is this Bug and who are you, anyway, and what is this, some kind of airplane?"

"Aeroplane," said Troy. He introduced himself. He held out his hand for a handshake, but Bug's twin acted like he didn't see it.

"I'm Travis Michael Biggs," he said, "and my father's a policeman, and you are in big trouble if you think you can just steal my bike."

"I told you, we just borrowed your bike," said Troy. "And I can explain."

But where to begin? He was wondering how much he should tell this different, more assertive, and slightly obnoxious Bug, when the real Bug came around the side of the plane, carrying a string of tiny fish.

"Bluegills!" Bug said "We can build a fire and. . . ."

Then he saw his twin.

"Whoa," he said. "It's me. I mean, you."

"Whoa," said the twin. "Who in the hell are you?"

"I'll find us some firewood," said Troy, "and let you two sort it out."

* * *

When Troy got back with enough wood to build a fire, the two were cleaning fish, as if they had known each other all their lives.

"My Dad's a cop, too," said Bug. "His name is Travis."

"That's my dad, too," said Travis. "I'm named after him. This is just too weird. You mean there's another town just like this one?"

"Almost," Bug said. "Do you play baseball? What position?"

"First base."

"I'm a pitcher," said Bug. "Sometimes. Sometimes a catcher, too. What's your coach's name?"

"Blaine," said Travis. "He's a jerk."

"Same guy," said Bug. "I'm afraid he won't let me pitch next week because I missed practice."

"No-excuses Blaine," said Travis. "Same guy. But maybe flying in an airplane is a good excuse."

"*Aero*plane," said Troy. "And no grownups must know about this. They would go nuts. We have to get back before they find out about any of this."

"So, it actually flies?"

"It does. Do you have a match?"

Once the fire was going, they cooked the tiny filets on sticks. Each boy got half a fish. Cooked down, they were no bigger than candy bars.

"They need salt," said Bug.

"You're not supposed to eat them anyway," said Travis. "I just catch them and throw them back."

"So do we," said Bug. "But I was starving. Still am."

"Have some Pop-Tarts then."

They all looked around. It was Toute. She was reaching into her backpack. "I only brought three, but I already ate breakfast."

"Me too," said Travis, unwrapping the Pop-Tart she gave him. "But I'll have some more."

Toute seemed to notice him for the first time. "And who in the world are you?" She frowned. "Isn't one Bug enough?"

Bug explained, and Troy told what he had seen at his parents' house. Toute nodded as if she understood. *And maybe she does,* Troy thought. Weird was beginning to seem normal.

"How did you get here anyway?" he asked.

Toute grinned and pointed to a bike lying on the track in front of the plane. It was a pink and white girl's bike Troy had never seen before.

"You can't ride a bike," Bug pointed out.

"I can here. Plus, I have a mother, plus—" Toute's grin was almost too wide for her narrow face. "I can walk! I'm not bent. Not so bent, anyway."

She walked in a little circle, just like the night before. She still limped, and dragged one foot, but it was true: she could walk.

"That's great," said Troy. "But we've got to get out of here." He climbed back into the airplane. Toute followed, limping in through the tail.

The tubes were cold. Toute dragged her fingers through the sand in the ashtray. "It's dry," she said. "Plus one of the wingtips is broken."

"The fabric ripped when we landed," said Troy. "Maybe it'll still fly, though."

"Better to fix it," said Toute.

Troy followed her out the back of the plane. She limped to the wingtip, reaching into her backpack as she walked. Troy watched, amazed. She had never been able to do either before.

She pulled out a tube of glue.

"Girls are always prepared," she said. Troy held the fabric tight while she glued it to the wood.

"Good going," he said. "But we still need Lectro. Do you have any left?"

"You saw me shake out the last drops," Toute said. She put the glue away and pointed toward the two brothers, who were sitting on the ground examining a ball glove. "I guess it's up to the Bugsy twins."

* * *

They followed Bug down into the tunnel. There were only two soda machines, not three, but nobody except Troy seemed to notice, and he didn't point it out. Things were weird enough as it was.

First Bug hit the bottom of the machine, which should have made the light come on. But it didn't. Then he slammed his fist into the center of the machine, which should have dropped a coin into the coin return. But it didn't.

"You're not doing it right, Clarence," said Travis.

"It's Bug."

"Bug, then. Watch."

Travis kicked the machine on the side and the light came on. Then he slapped the big L above the coin return, and a coin dropped down.

"Let me see that," said Troy.

Travis tossed him the coin.

"There's no hole in it!"

"Of course there's no hole in it," said Travis. "It's real money. Gimme."

Troy tossed it back, and Travis dropped it into the slot and pressed a square button.

A bottle fell with a *thump*.

"It's not Lectro!" said Bug.

"What's Lectro?" Travis opened the bottle and took a swig. "It's Collie Cola—gooder than good." He held out the bottle. "It's warm, though. Here, we can share."

Troy grabbed it. "No way. That's our ticket home. If it works."

"It'll work," said Toute, grabbing it from Troy. "It's like everything else here, the same only different."

Troy climbed into the plane and Toute handed him the bottle of Collie Cola through the side window. He poured a thin stream of brown liquid into the sand.

Nothing happened.

"More," said Toute.

He poured in half the bottle.

"Now stir it."

Troy stirred the damp sand with his fingertips. The tubes started to glow.

"See? It's working," Toute said. She touched the fan and it started to spin—slowly at first, then faster.

"Come on, get in, you guys!" Troy said.

"This thing actually flies?" asked Travis.

"That's the idea," said Troy. "Come on, Bug, Toute. Get in. Let's go."

Bug was standing beside his twin on the clay race track. Except for their T-shirts, they looked even more alike than ever.

They both looked confused. They both spoke at the same time:

"I wish you would come. It would be cool to have a twin brother."

"I wish you would stay. It would be cool to have a twin brother."

Troy and Toute both laughed. Bug and Travis didn't.

"What I mean is, you could come too," said Bug.

"No way!" said Troy. "We don't know if this thing will even fly again with this stuff. How do we know it will carry four?"

"You could stay here, then," said Travis.

"What about my mom and dad?"

"Same problem here," said Travis.

"Maybe we should switch for a day. But wait, I'm supposed to pitch on Sunday."

"Not if you miss practice," said Travis. "No excuses!"

"Forget switching," said Troy, pouring another inch of Collie Cola into the sand. The fan was turning faster and faster. "There's no way to know we could ever find this place again."

The wheels creaked; the floor lurched under Troy's feet— the plane was starting to move.

"Whoa!" Bug scrambled in through the side window, and Travis passed him his backpack.

Then Travis took off his X-TREME T-shirt and tossed it to Bug. "Swap," he said. Bug took off his GO AHEAD, HAVE A COW T-shirt and tossed it to Travis.

"What is this, a strip tease?" said Toute.

"If you ever want a brother, just look in the mirror," said Travis.

"Cool," said Bug. "I will."

"Come on, Toute!" said Troy. The plane was starting to roll slowly down the track. The wingtips were bobbing up and down.

Toute walked alongside, shaking her head. "I don't think so."

"What!?"

"I'm staying here," she said, picking up her bike.

"You can't stay here! You don't belong here. This is not our real town."

"Yes, it is. It's just as real. And here I can ride a bike."

As if to prove it, she got on and started pedaling alongside the plane.

"Toute, no!" Troy pleaded. The plane was going faster and faster. "If you stay here, what about me? I'll never see you again. I can't come back to get you. I'll get in trouble. They'll say I left you here."

"Left me where? Nobody knows where I am. They probably think I'm at the mall. Nobody knows I'm with you."

"What about your dad?"

"He'll get over it. Plus I have a mother here, remember? And my dad is here."

"Not the same dad."

"Pretty much the same."

"You can't do this!"

"Why not!"

"Because—" Troy could think of a hundred reasons: Because you are part of me. Because we are like brother and sister. Because I love you. But none he could say. "Because you just can't!"

"I have to," said Toute. "I can walk here and ride a bike. Back home, it's just getting worse and worse. I can hear them whispering all the time."

"Don't!" The plane was picking up speed, lumbering toward the first turn.

"Steer, Troy!" said Bug. "We'll hit the wall."

"I will miss you," Toute said, pedaling faster and faster. "You are my best friend. But hey, maybe there's a you here."

"There isn't! There's not!"

"If there is I'll find him. But you have to steer, Troy, look out!"

The left wingtip was scraping the weeds at the side of the track.

Troy turned the knob to the right, and the plane angled into the first turn, still picking up speed.

"Good luck!" said Travis, catching up on his bicycle. "Good luck in the game."

The floor stopped bouncing. The plane began to rise off the ground.

Toute was pedaling faster and faster. Troy was impressed. But she was falling behind—

"What do I tell your dad?"

"Nothing," said Toute, out of breath. "I've already told him. Good-bye, Troy. I'll never forget you, ever, even if I do find another you. And thanks."

"Thanks?"

"For discovering the aeroplane!"

"Bye, Travis!" Bug yelled. "Bye, Toute." They were rising off the track, leaving Travis and Toute behind. When they circled back around, higher and higher, they could see them, standing in the center of the track by their bicycles, looking up and waving.

Then the plane made a broad circle out over the town, and they were left behind, too small to see.

⌒ 7. Flying Home

Troy remembered that flying in he had followed a line from the courthouse to the race track. So he left the same way, flying between the steeple and the water tower, past the clock-less courthouse, straight over the town.

They left the streets and trees behind, then the fields. Soon they were flying over trackless dunes again.

"Are you sure this is the right way?" Bug asked.

"Sure," said Troy. He wasn't. And Bug knew he wasn't. They both just wanted to hear him say he was. So he said it again. "Sure I'm sure."

The desert was just sand with an occasional stretch of bare rock, scarred as if by huge claws. The tubes glowed, the fan whirred silently, and the plane flew along at a slow, steady pace, not much faster than a bicycle.

"We should have brought some Pop-Tarts," said Bug. "What if we crash? We'll starve."

"You don't starve when you crash," said Troy. "You just crash. It sort of ends everything."

Troy kept the notch straight up. He was pretty sure this was the way home. But what if the wind blew him off course?

There seemed to be a wind. Below, he could see little puffs of sand along the tops of the dunes. And the occasional bush, in a hollow between two dunes, was shaking as if angry.

And there was a yellow wall of clouds dead ahead.

"It's a storm," said Bug.

"Sandstorm," said Troy. As if calling it by its right name would make it any better.

"Can we go around it?"

Troy shook his head. "I'll lose my bearings."

He kept the notch straight up; they flew straight into the storm. It was all around them, blowing not water and rain but gritty yellow sand. The plane was rocking from side to side. Bug was holding onto the bottom of the window, trying to keep his balance.

He gave up and sat on the floor. "I think we're going to crash," he said. "I still wish we had some Pop-Tarts. What if we survive?"

"Shut up," said Troy. He could barely see out of the windshield. It seemed that the plane was going slower. The wingtips were shaking slowly, up and down. The fabric was rippling, though Toute's repair seemed to be holding.

Then he couldn't see the wingtips anymore. He couldn't see the fan. Everything was yellow, yellow sand. The tubes were looking dim, or was that his imagination? He looked at the Collie Cola bottle. There was less than half a bottle left. A lot less.

Suddenly there was a break in the yellow cloud, and Troy saw white rocks, dead ahead. Was it a mountain, or were they going down? He poured the rest of the brown liquid into the ashtray.

The tubes glowed more brightly, and the front of the plane picked up. The right wing dropped, and the rocks were gone.

"We're turning," said Bug.

Troy wished he would shut up. Bug was becoming the bearer of bad news. "I know."

There didn't seem to be any point in standing at the controls, since the plane did what it wanted to do anyway. And it was hard to breathe. Troy had sand in his eyes, and it gritted between his teeth.

Bug was on the floor, looking like a bandit, with the collar of Travis's X-TREME T-shirt pulled up over his nose. Troy sat on the floor beside him, and covered his nose with his own T-shirt, which didn't say anything. He could breathe but he could hardly see.

There was nothing to see anyway. He closed his eyes. The plane circled higher and higher, shaking, creaking and groaning, through the storm.

Then all was still.

Troy opened his eyes. Bug was asleep. The sand was gone, except for the grit in his eyes and on the floor and between his teeth.

He wiped his eyes and stood up.

They were still circling, in calm cold air. The stars shone high overhead like little chips of ice. "I'm cold," said Bug, waking up. He joined Troy at the controls.

The sandstorm was like a yellow smudge far below. It was still daylight down there. For some reason, Troy found this encouraging.

He tried the knob, left, then right. The plane dipped its

wings, left, then right. Troy centered the knob and it straightened out. They were flying straight again—but straight to where?

Then Bug, the bearer of bad news, brought some good news. "Look!"

Far off to the left, there was a dark spot on the horizon. *Our town?* Troy wondered.

There was only one way to find out. Turning the knob to the left, he headed the plane toward it.

"Think that's our town?" Bug asked.

"For sure," Troy lied.

The boys held their breath, waiting and watching.

Hoping.

The plane was descending.

The smudge on the horizon grew into a blur of trees and streets and houses, looking more and more familiar. There was the courthouse, and the water tower, and the church steeple.

Still descending, the plane flew past the courthouse. Both Troy and Bug were relieved to see that it had a clock.

It was 1:37.

"I can still make it to baseball," Bug said.

"A day late," Troy reminded him. As soon as he said it, he wished he hadn't.

"Maybe Blaine won't notice," he added lamely.

There were a few people on the street, but they didn't look up as the plane flew over. *If they did, what would they see?* Troy wondered. The wings, white, with ads for bread and candy, cars and cola. The fuselage, a long square plywood tube, open on one side. Wire wheels spinning slowly in the onrushing air. A V tail, slightly cockeyed, and the propeller, a ceiling fan, turning slower and slower as they descended.

"There's your house, Toute," said Troy. Then he remembered that she was no longer with them.

"Look at all those cars," said Bug.

Toute's driveway and the street in front of her house were packed with parked cars.

Troy saw what looked like his father's car—not the little sportscar, but the big white Olds. He looked down at the crowd of people at the door, trying to see if his parents were among them. It was hard to tell. They were all dressed alike, in suits and ties.

"Hey! Pay attention," said Bug.

Troy looked out the front. The plane was too low. It was not going to make it over the last row of trees before the old race track.

Troy turned the dial to the left, and then to the right, banking the plane between two trees. He leveled off with the stands dead ahead. With the last drop of Collie Cola, he brought the nose up, barely missing the top row of seats.

"We're going to hit the lake," Bug said. "And drown."

"It's not deep enough," said Troy. "Shut up and fasten your seat belt."

He spun the dial and dropped the left wing. The wingtip scraped the track and the plane landed sideways, skidding, teetering first on one wheel, and then on the other.

CRUNCH!

Everything was dark. *It's always dark like this down among the roots,* Troy thought, *where the Teeny-Weenies live. It's okay, though. Toute knows the way.* "Let's go back up," he said to her. "It's too dark."

"You go on," she said.

"I don't know the way."

"Sure you do."

"Come on!" said Bug.

Huh?

It was light. Bug was dragging him out of the back of the plane.

"Hey! You're getting splinters in my butt!"

"You crashed us!" Bug said. "It's going to burn!"

"Let go of me! It's not full of gas, it runs on water and sand. How can it burn?"

"I guess you know everything," said Bug, dropping him. "I was trying to save your life."

"Sorry. Thanks." Troy stood up, his feet slipping. The track was muddy. The ground felt funny, after the air.

The plane was a mess. One wing had come off and landed in the mud along the infield, where it looked like a fallen fence.

The other was still attached to the fuselage, which was half in and half out of the infield. The tail was tipped over, like a fallen outhouse.

"Looks like there's been a storm here, too," said Troy. "Are you okay?"

"I'm okay, but I'm late." Bug was already heading for the tunnel, his backpack over his shoulder.

Troy followed him across the track and into the tunnel. They splashed through water at the bottom. The drink machines were dark, like sentinels. There were three of them. Outside, the hole under the chainlink fence was filled with water from the storm.

They climbed over instead of under.

Their bikes gleamed in the weeds, looking like they had just been washed. Bug got on his Blizzard and bounced the wheels, as if making sure it was real. "I can still make practice if I hurry."

"Go, then."

"What are you going to tell them about Toute?"

"I don't know. I'll think of something."

But the fact was, it was hard to think of anything. The place where Toute had been was like a hole in Troy's thoughts as he rode toward home. Her memory was like a dark patch he couldn't look into—but couldn't look away from, either.

"Where have you been!" Troy's father demanded, when he opened the door. Troy couldn't look at him; he kept remembering the little mustache. He looked away.

"It's okay." His father squeezed his shoulder in that way that fathers do. "I know you are upset. Your mother is over at William's house now. I was there all day."

William was Troy's dad's brother, Toute's father.

"Toute—" Troy began.

"Toute died peacefully in her sleep," said Troy's father. "William was waiting for it. He was prepared. She was prepared, too. She knew for a week, he said. I'm surprised she hadn't said anything to you. You two are so close. Were so close. Anyway, get dressed. Your mother is already there, and we are expected for the memorial. She laid your suit and tie out on your bed. Get dressed and I'll help you tie your tie."

⌐ 8: Almost Home

Troy hardly recognized Toute at the funeral, she looked so still and so straightened out. He tried to cry because everyone else was crying, but he couldn't. So he just sat with his eyes almost closed. It was like getting through a sandstorm.

In the days that followed he missed her, but he knew where she was. He even knew what it was like there, and what she was doing: riding her bike. Eating fried chicken.

Troy was in far less trouble than he had expected. He was surprised to find that his parents thought he had spent the night with Bug. Nor was Bug in trouble, either. He told his parents he had spent the night with Troy after they had been caught in the storm. Luckily, the phone lines had been down all night.

It was several days before the two boys met at the usual tree and rode to the old race track on the outskirts of town. The drink machines still lurked like monsters in the tunnel, but when Bug kicked the center one, no light came on.

"The rain must have ruined it," Bug said. He was wearing the X-Treme T-shirt. No one had noticed, he said.

Troy wasn't surprised. "Grownups never really read T-shirts," he said.

The aeroplane was in pieces on the track and in the infield. The track was still muddy in spots.

One good effect of the storm: the scum was almost all gone from the lake. *We may have to change the name,* Troy thought. It wasn't Scum Lake anymore.

While Bug went to get worms, Troy lay face down on the end of the dock. He could see all the way to the bottom. There was a concrete block, and a tire. Then, as he watched, a great blunt shape swam out of the shadows and stopped, right under him.

He started to call Bug, but didn't. It was better to be silent and watch. He wished Toute were there to see it. She would have liked it. She had always liked it when weird things got real.

Story Copyrights

"King Dragon" copyright © 2003 by Michael Swanwick. First published in *The Dragon Quintet*, edited by Marvin Kaye, Science Fiction Book Club. Reprinted by permission of the author.

"The Big Green Grin" copyright © 2003 by Gahan Wilson.

"The Book of Martha" copyright © 2003 by Octavia E. Butler.

"Wild Thing" by Charles Coleman Finlay. Copyright © 2003 by Spilogale, Inc. First appeared in *The Magazine of Fantasy and Science Fiction*, July 2003.

"Closing Time" copyright © 2003 by Neil Gaiman. First published in *McSweeney's Thrilling Tales*, edited by Michael Chabon.

"Catskin" copyright © 2003 by Kelly Link.

"Dragon's Gate" by Pat Murphy. Copyright © 2003 by Spilogale, Inc. First appeared in *The Magazine of Fantasy and Science Fiction*, August 2003.

"One Thing about the Night" copyright © 2003 by Terry Dowling.

"Peace on Suburbia" copyright © 2003 by Mary Rickert.

"Moonblind" copyright © 2003 by Tanith Lee.

"Professor Berkowitz Stands on the Threshold" copyright © 2003 by Theodora Goss.

"Louder Echo" copyright © 2003 by Brendan Duffy.

"The Raptures of the Deep" copyright © 2003 by Rosaleen Love.

"Fable from a Cage" copyright © 2003 by Tim Pratt.

"A Quartet of Mini-Fantasies" copyright © 2003 by Arthur Porges. First appeared in *The Magazine of Fantasy and Science Fiction*.

"Señor Volto" copyright © 2003 by Lucius Shepard.

"Shen's Daughter" copyright © 2003 by Mary Soon Lee. First appeared in *Sword and Sorceress XX*.

"Basement Magic" copyright © 2003 by Ellen Klages.

"The Tales of Zanthias" copyright © 2003 by Robert Sheckley.

"Of Soil and Climate" copyright © 2003 by Gene Wolfe; first appeared in *Realms of Fantasy*; reprinted by permission of the author and the author's agents, the Virginia Kidd Agency, Inc.

"Almost Home" copyright © 2003 by Terry Bisson.